KISS OF VENGEANCE

A TRUE IMMORTALITY NOVEL

S. YOUNG

SAMANTHA YOUNG

KISS OF VENGEANCE

A True Immortality Novel

By S. Young
Copyright © 2020 Samantha Young

Edited by Jennifer Sommersby Young
Cover Design By Hang Le
Cover Image by Wander Aguiar Photography

OTHER TITLES

Other Titles By S. Young

War of Hearts (A True Immortality Novel)

Other Adult Contemporary Novels by Samantha Young

Play On

As Dust Dances

Hold On: A Play On Novella

Into the Deep

Out of the Shallows

Hero

Villain: A Hero Novella

One Day: A Valentine Novella

Fight or Flight

Outmatched (co-write with Kristen Callihan)

On Dublin Street Series:

On Dublin Street

Down London Road

Before Jamaica Lane

Fall From India Place

Echoes of Scotland Street

Moonlight on Nightingale Way

Until Fountain Bridge (a novella)

Castle Hill (a novella)

Valentine (a novella)

One King's Way (a novella)

Hart's Boardwalk Series:

The One Real Thing

Every Little Thing

Things We Never Said

Young Adult contemporary titles by Samantha Young

The Impossible Vastness of Us

The Fragile Ordinary

Young Adult Urban Fantasy titles by Samantha Young

The Tale of Lunarmorte Trilogy:

Moon Spell

River Cast

Blood Solstice

Warriors of Ankh Trilogy:

Blood Will Tell

Blood Past

Shades of Blood

Fire Spirits Series:

Smokeless Fire

Scorched Skies

Borrowed Ember

Darkness, Kindled

Slumber (The Fade #1)

Drip Drop Teardrop, a novella

PRONUNCIATIONS

Irish Gaelic (Connacht dialect)

Fionn – Fee-on

An Breitheamh – Un Bre-huv

An Caoimhnóir – Un Keev-neer

Mo Chroí – Muh Kree

Mo Ghrá – Muh Graw

Aoibhinn – Ay-veen

Niamh – Neev

Caoimhe – Kee-va

Diarmuid – Dear-mid

Aine – Awn-ya

Samhradh – Sow-ruh

Solas – Sol-as

Geimhreadh – Geev-ru

Réalta – Rail-tuh

Earrach – Err-ack

Fómhar – Foe-var

Éireann – Air-un

DEDICATION

For Mum,
Thank you for being my sounding board, my ride or die, and my
biggest fan.
I love you to the moon and back.

1

Beams of light—green, purple, blue, red—bounced in frantic rays above the heads of the dancing crowd. The music pumped so loudly, the building vibrated with it. Rose, used to the pounding bass, the explosions of color that broke up the dark, glancing off stone walls and vaulted ceilings, mixed the mojitos a young clubber had requested.

Sweat glistened on Rose's skin as Croatians and tourists filled the space with their body heat. A wild freedom tinged the air with sex and recklessness.

Having bartended in different bars across mainland Europe, Rose was indifferent to the heady abandon of late hours in thudding nightclubs. She mixed drinks, served, and moved on to the next customer to ensure agitated, drunk clubbers didn't cause problems at the bar.

The only bodies that drew her attention were those of her colleagues, and that was only because maneuvering around them in the tight circular bar was something akin to a dance.

Fewer than three hours into her shift had passed, and Rose was already longing for the small bed in the tiny room she was renting above a bakery. The mattress was lumpy, there was no A/C, and the bakery opened just as she was getting to bed, but at least the place smelled like warm bread. Which was a million times better than what most places she rented smelled like.

Focused on making four Cuba Libre cocktails, it took Rose a moment to realize the hair on her arms had risen as though there was static electricity in the air. She stilled, frowning as goose bumps shivered across her skin.

What the ...

The music cut, and a new track played.

A thudding, prolonged bass, followed by electronic pop filled the club. The ethereal voice of Ruelle echoed around the room. Rose knew the song. It was called "Live Like Legends."

She looked out into the crowd of dancers to see they were writhing together, their movements becoming more sexual as the music built to a crescendo. Wondering at the strange feeling that had descended over her, Rose searched the dancers for something—she didn't know what. Perhaps for something that was out of place in the sixteenth-century building turned nightclub.

"Hej, ti, naša pića!" A customer snapped his fingers in her face.

It successfully yanked her from her study of the dancers. "Don't snap your fingers at me." She didn't care if he couldn't understand her. Her tone was of the universal language of, "I don't take shit from anyone."

He sneered but thankfully shut up.

She'd just finished serving the rude guy when the music hit its peak, the bass and drums deep and booming, strings—most likely violins—frenzied, beautiful, and the electronic pop sound Ruelle was known for building to a climax in the same style of an epic movie trailer. Awareness scored her spine, turning the damp, warm skin of her nape cool. It felt like strong fingers clasping her neck.

The feeling was so ridiculously powerful, for a moment Rose thought there *was* someone touching her. She spun away from the cash register, nostrils flaring as she took in the space around her, finding not even her colleagues near. Both Petra and Josip were on the other side of the circle.

And that's when she felt it.

Like all the air had evacuated the room.

Chest tight, Rose gasped as her gaze shifted over the parting crowds. Her feet moved without her command, stumbling toward the bar counter—as though someone had tied a rope around her, lassoing her. Holding her captive.

Then she saw him.

Head and shoulders above everyone else, she saw a hulking figure, hair of indiscriminate color illuminated every few seconds by the dancing beams of light. The crowd parted for him as he glided through the sea of bodies. For such a big man, he moved gracefully, light as air, impossibly so ... almost otherworldly.

Longish hair framed his bold face, the ends tickling his angular jawline. His nose was a sharp blade to match the sharp angles of his cheekbones. Thick stubble covered the lower half of his face, surrounding a mouth pressed tight with concentration as his head swung from left to right, as though he were searching for something or someone.

Rose swallowed hard, her mouth dry. The man was mammoth. He had to be over six and a half feet tall. If his height wasn't enough to draw attention, the way he dressed was. The club was hot, yet he swept through the rabble wearing a dark three-piece suit and a long, black wool overcoat.

He paused, his heavy brows drawing together. His body language reminded her of an animal catching a scent, alert, rigid—a hunter beneath that civilized attire. Then his head snapped in her direction and their eyes locked.

An invisible weight slammed into Rose's chest, and she wheezed. Thankfully, the loss of breath lasted seconds, and she sucked in a huge gulp of air. "Fuck," she whispered, shaking as the stranger continued to stare at her.

The lasers of light bounced off his face, highlighting eyes so green they couldn't be human.

It's the lasers, Rose told herself. *No one's eyes are that color unless they're wearing contacts.*

Nothing, however, explained the intensity of feeling that held her still beneath the man's regard.

Abruptly, something caught his attention to his left, and he released her from his captive gaze. He waded through the parting dancers, slowly disappearing into the dark. Straining to see, Rose walked along the bar, wanting to stay with him, but Josip stepped in front of her.

He frowned.

"Where are you going?" he said, his accent thick. "Are you all right?"

The interruption seemed to untie the invisible rope around her body. Rose shuddered and her limbs were her own again.

What the fuck was that?

A bead of sweat slid down her temple and she wiped at it with a shaky hand. "I'm okay," she lied.

Josip was unconvinced. "Take your break. You look like you need it."

Confused, thirsty, and uneasy, Rose agreed and left the bar area, her attention drawn toward where she'd last seen the hulking, well-dressed stranger. But he was gone. Disappointment flickered through her, but since that was a familiar feeling, it barely marked her. Instead, she was grateful. His absence allowed her to think clearly about what had just happened to her body.

It had been attraction.

Nothing more. Nothing ... unexplainable.

Pushing through the dancers, needing distraction from the weirdness at the bar, Rose approached the Staff Only door and grinned at Ivan, one of the security guys. "Kako si?"

His lips curled with flirtation. "I'd be better if you'd let me walk you home tonight."

Rose smirked. This was a dance of theirs and had been for the past two months. Ivan had made it clear he wanted in there, but Rose had rules. She stayed in one city for a few months, hoping to find something that would make her want to stay permanently. So far, she hadn't found that elusive place.

She had rules to protect her emotions. If she found a guy she was attracted to, Rose waited until she'd decided to leave the city before she slept with him. Kind of a farewell treat for them both. Ivan was the chosen one this time. He had been for a while. He was Rose's type to a T. Not traditionally good-looking, but charismatic, sexy, and a big ol' flirt. Rose loved a flirt. She didn't have time to guess if a guy was into her. She wanted one who made it clear that he was.

Rose wanted Ivan, and there was a bonus to denying herself something she wanted until the very last second. It could lead to pretty great sex. Not always. But enough to make denying herself worth it.

"Not tonight." Rose slid by him, deliberately pressing her breasts against his side as she did.

His dark eyes hooded as he watched her. "You're killing me, Rose."

She bit her lip, walking backward through the staff door. "It'll be worth it."

Ivan lifted his chin in acknowledgement of her promise, satisfaction in his expression, and Rose was glad for the heat of it for it made her shiver with anticipation.

Just the distraction she'd needed.

The staff area was a dingy room with lockers, a table, some chairs, a small refrigerator, a counter with a sink, and a cheap coffee machine. It smelled of deodorant and cigarette smoke. Rose took a bottle of water out of the fridge and emptied its contents in less than a minute. She heaved for breath and then hauled open her locker to find her cell before slumping into a wooden chair with a wobbly leg.

The sight of a voicemail from her mom caused a flare of longing. Rose tapped the screen a few times and held the phone to her ear.

Soon her mom's warm voice filled her head. "Hey, petal. It's just Mam, checking in. I'm guessing you're still in Zagreb. So ... your da and I are thinking about getting a puppy and I need your opinion on that. You know us better than anyone. Can we handle a puppy? I think we can handle it, but your da is on the fence. Push him off the fence for me, petal, or I'll be waiting another five years to get a damn dog. Okay. Call your mother back. It's only polite."

Rose grinned, hanging up. She knew why her dad was on the fence about a damn dog. Because her mother was flaky, and her dad would end up doing all the practical stuff, like taking it for walks and feeding it.

She missed them.

Just not enough to stop wandering.

Her parents were six hours behind in the US, so it wasn't too late in the evening there to call them ... but the dog was a trap. Once her mom had her on the phone, she'd pester Rose about coming home. The first year, her parents hadn't said a word. They even understood and were excited (but terrified) for her as she traveled across Australia.

But when year two came around and she got a flight to Europe instead of heading home to Maryland, their patience dwindled. Now, it was year three of the nomadic life, and Rose's parents wanted her to grow up and settle down. Preferably in Columbia, Maryland.

"I'm not ready," she whispered to the room.

At twenty-five, she still hadn't found what she was looking for, and she knew it wasn't back in the US. Problem was she knew it could take people a lifetime to find that quintessential "something" that completed them. Sometimes they never found it. Rose was determined to keep looking until she did, which did not bode well for her loving parents.

The door to the staff room flew open, causing Rose to startle. She jumped to her feet as two strangers hurried into the room. "This is staff only," she said, looking between the young man and woman. "Samo osoblje."

"We don't speak Croatian," the young woman said in a lilting Irish accent.

"Okay, then you understood me when I said staff only." Rose crossed her arms over her chest and eyed the man warily. Although young, he was tall and well built. The two were remarkably attractive —he was dark while she was fair. They shared the same tip-tilted aquamarine eyes.

Not averse to the sight of a gorgeous guy, Rose would usually be drawn to the man, but she couldn't take her eyes off the woman. It was hard to explain the compulsion. It could be her appearance. She was a beautiful girl, perhaps around Rose's age, with blond, fairy-princess hair, and she wore a long dress with billowing sleeves that cuffed at the wrist. It was a paisley print in bold fuchsia and aqua. Silver-and-moonstone rings adorned her fingers, and she wore long, silver-and-feather chandelier earrings. Her features were small and perfect, and she had a slightly pointed chin. There was something elfin about her.

Something ethereal.

For some reason, she reminded Rose of the man from earlier, which was ridiculous considering he looked like a Viking someone had put a suit on, while this woman was small, delicate, and stunning.

And staring at Rose with intense confusion.

"Well, get on with it," the young man said to his companion. He, too, was Irish. "*He's* here. We don't have time for you to stare at each other. I wish you could see that bastard coming, Niamh, *before* he lands in the same city as us."

"Guys, you can't be in—hey!" Rose yelled as the young woman suddenly accosted her, clutching her head.

She'd moved fast.

Too fast.

No one moved that fast.

Energy tingled along Rose's head, like bugs crawling across her scalp. She clutched at the woman's wrists, trying to pry her off, shocked when she couldn't.

Rose was strong. Naturally so. She always had been. It had held her in good stead during her time as a competitive gymnast through high school.

But this waif of a woman was stronger.

Inexplicable fear flooded Rose.

The woman let her go, her eyes round with shock.

What does she have to be shocked about? She isn't the one who's just been attacked!

"What the hell!" Rose shoved her away, and the man took a menacing step forward.

The woman held up her hand, stopping him, her attention never leaving Rose. "You have a block on you. A spell. Someone has blocked your access to your powers."

Okay, then. Ignoring the woman's freakish, unexplainable speed, Rose backed away from a person high on something or who took pranking people to another level. Or she was just plain old nuts. "Look, I will let it slide that you put your hands on me without permission and just ask you to leave." She spoke slowly, calmly, so as not to cause agitation. "Now, please."

"Don't talk to my sister like she's a lunatic." The man glowered. "You need to listen to her, and fast. We don't have much time."

"You don't know who you are." The woman gawked at Rose. "Oh God, you need to know who you are."

"I know who I am, gorgeous, and who I am is a slightly freaked-out bartender two seconds from calling security on your ass."

"Niamh, we don't have time to deal with an ignorant human. We have to go."

"She's not an ignorant human. Okay, she's ignorant but she's important, Ronan Farren," Niamh snapped at him. She turned back to Rose, irritation changing to earnestness. "More important than anyone else in the world."

Taking a step back, Rose's earlier fear returned tenfold. Niamh was either a great actress or desperately believed Rose was the Second Coming. And how the hell did she know her name? Had she asked one of the other bartenders? Probably. Fear wasn't a usual emotion for Rose, and the fact that this extra from the *Lord of the Rings* movies was freaking her out pissed her off. "Yeah, you two need to leave. Like, now."

"There are two paths, Rose. I see them clearly. At the beginning of one, you die, and if you die, the world as we know it will be over. I don't know why or how, but I know it's true. The other path, the one where you don't die, we all live."

She was so sincere, so believable, a chill cut to Rose's core. Anger immediately followed the unsettling feeling. "You need to get your tiny ass out of this club right now." Rose charged toward her. "You think this is funny? Is this some shtick the two of you do to complete strangers? Well, not to me. Not tonight. Go fuck yourself and while you're at it, get the hell out of this club."

Ronan moved toward his sister, but she shook her head. "She's strong, but she has no power. Not with that spell on her." She bit her lip, studying Rose like she was a high school science experiment. "We have to remove the block."

"Nee, we need to go. Does she die tonight or not? Because if not, we can come back."

"Is that a threat?" Rose swallowed, trying to look unafraid as she searched the staff room for a potential weapon.

"No. I'm not here to hurt you and you'd know that if there wasn't a bloody spell on your mind." Niamh froze, eyes wide, her mouth open as if in a silent scream. Her head began to shake from side to side in small, frantic increments.

"What the hell ..."

"Niamh." Ronan grabbed his sister, pressing her close and turning his body toward Rose as if to shield Niamh from her.

Uneasiness held Rose in place. "What is happening? Is she seizing?"

He cut her a dark look. "She's having a vision."

An impatient Rose threw her hands up in the air. "Of course, she is. Why wouldn't she be?"

As abruptly as his sister had started seizing—for lack of a better word—she stopped. Her small, elegant fingers curled into her brother's biceps. She looked up at him, seemingly shocked. "He's close. We need to go."

"And her?" Ronan gestured to Rose as Niamh released Ronan and started backing toward the door.

"I understand now," she whispered, staring at Rose in awe. "Only she can deliver us from him."

Ronan glanced from his sister to Rose. "Are you sure, Niamh?"

Niamh nodded, a small, strange smile on her lips. "You have to trust him, Rose. Even when he makes it impossible. Don't let us down now."

At that, Ronan grabbed his sister's hand and the two of them raced out of the room.

"Okay, then!" Rose called after them, even though they were gone. "Thanks for the mind fuck, assholes—ah!" She jumped in fright at the sudden appearance of Ivan.

He braced his hands on the door frame, filling the entire space. "Who are you shouting at? Is everything all right?"

"Did you see them?" Rose asked. She pushed past Ivan to glance both ways down the dark corridor. The awful aluminum lighting blinked in the darkness, like it was on the fritz. There was no one in sight.

"See who?" Ivan peered over Rose's shoulder, deliberately pressing his chest into her back.

She half turned to face him. "The two lunatics who accosted me in the staff room. How did they get past you?"

He frowned, tucking a stray strand of hair behind her ear. "No one got past me, Rosie. You sure you are all right? You look ... *blijeda*."

"Huh?"

He brushed a thumb over her cheek. "No color, yes."

Deducing he meant she looked pale, Rose huffed inwardly. *Yeah. No surprise there.*

She glanced down the corridor again, wondering if she'd imagined the whole night, from her reaction at the bar to Mr. Armani Viking, to the strange siblings who'd pretty much told her she was going to die. *But not tonight, so yay me!*

"I feel like I'm in a very strange dream."

"What?"

She sighed heavily and strode by him to put her phone in her locker. "Nothing. I better get back to work."

She wouldn't say it, but she was glad Ivan walked her out into the club. Her disquiet was strong. Rose searched the vaulted room as she made her way back to the bar, looking for the siblings, for the man.

Was it all just an elaborate joke?

"Of course, it was," Rose griped to herself.

But joke or not, Niamh had gotten to her. She'd freaked her out, and Rose didn't want to be alone.

When the club closed in the early hours, Rose broke her own rule and let Ivan walk her home.

2

Frustration seethed through Fionn as he let himself into his suite. The sitting room off the bedroom felt too small for his current mood. He needed somewhere to pace, to vent his irritation.

Shrugging out of his coat, Fionn had flashes of his previous visits to this hotel in Zagreb. He'd stayed several times in the past, always under a different name. His first visit was in 1926. The hotel was only a year old and the first stop for travelers on the Orient Express. He'd been there as an investor in a new radio station. The wealth he'd amassed over the last two centuries was convoluted. To stay out of the pages of history, he'd used false names, and traveled all over the world to make his investments in industries that were booming at the time.

His last visit to Zagreb had been twenty years ago, and he'd stayed in the presidential suite, a sprawling apartment that included a kitchen and staff quarters. Room to pace. To vent.

However, that visit hadn't required secrecy, and the presidential suite was too visible. Hotel staff more than paid attention to the occupant and Fionn didn't need that kind of scrutiny.

Speaking of which ...

Pulling his mobile out of his pocket, he swiped across the edge and hit the single icon with the letter *b* on it.

Brannigan picked up after two rings. "Fionn."

"Update?"

Bran chuckled. "And a good evening to you too," he teased in a thick Dublin accent time had never diluted.

"Update," Fionn repeated, in no mood for the boy's perpetually high fucking spirits.

"Right, right. There's no sign of the Blackwoods. If they've followed you to Zagreb, they're doing a good bloody job of covering their arses." Bran paused. "So ... was it the girl?"

For nearly three centuries, Fionn had waited for a prophecy to come true. Technically, he'd waited for over two thousand years, but he'd been asleep for most of that. Thank fuck.

As it was, it was hell to wait for the children of Aine's prophecy to be born.

Seven children born as fae in the human world, with the ability to reopen the gate to Faerie.

Seven children who had been hunted by several factions of the supernatural community, including Fionn himself. Fionn knew only of the existence of two of them. A young woman he called the psychic, and another called Thea Quinn, who was no longer fae, and as such, no longer of use to him.

But the girl, the psychic, she was the key to the ones who were left.

Using fae magic sent up a flare to anyone who knew what to look for and brought Fionn down on her every time. However, as soon as he got within the same city limits as her, she disappeared off his radar. Her signature had become familiar to him now, and he and Bran had studied the events surrounding her appearances.

The girl had been recorded in the same city as three of the seven fae children. Two of those three had been killed by his old acquaintance, Eirik, along with a third that the girl had no connections with as far as Fionn was aware. A woman the girl *had* met with was Thea Quinn. Fionn had no idea how they had connected, but he knew that days after their meeting in Prague, Thea Quinn had killed Eirik, the oldest vampire in the world.

Thea had then been turned into a werewolf by her mate, Conall MacLennan, Alpha of Pack MacLennan, the last werewolf pack in Scotland.

Fionn could be pissed off that he'd missed the opportunity to capture a woman as powerful as Thea to open the gates to Faerie, but she'd killed Eirik for him. Not that Fionn was incapable of killing Eirik. It was just that he owed the vampire for helping him escape Faerie in the first fucking place.

As the vampire gradually depleted the fae children, however, Fionn knew he'd have to take out his old ally.

Thea saved him from that.

Still, now there were only three fae left. Three keys to the gate of Faerie.

And the psychic woman was one of them. Moreover, he and Bran had concluded that she was searching for the others. To warn them? To connect with them? He had no idea. He didn't care.

All he cared about was that she'd lead him straight to the fae.

Except tonight.

Upon arriving in Zagreb, he'd felt the girl immediately and had followed her essence to a club fifteen minutes north of his hotel. He'd expected to feel another fae there. Yet, not only did the girl slip through his fingers, he hadn't found another fae energy.

But he'd felt something from that bartender.

Stretching his neck from side to side to work out the tension, Fionn took a beat before admitting, "I lost her. She sensed me coming and is masking her energy."

Bran sighed. "Ah, bollocks. What now?"

Fionn thought on the bartender. As he'd moved through the nightclub, he'd felt ... something. A magnetic pull toward the circular bar in the center of the old building.

That's when he saw her.

Staring at him in awe.

That was nothing new. Humans often reacted to Fionn that way.

At once terrified but drawn to him. The woman had strained against the bar, as if fighting the compulsion to come to him.

Fionn had sensed ... something. Not fae, but *something*. A whisper of energy around her. At first he'd dismissed it, but after searching that club, he'd found no other that could possibly be the reason for his psychic to be there.

His psychic could have been at the nightclub to dance, but Fionn didn't think so. Two days ago, Fionn had been on his way to Barcelona to retrieve an important artifact that was stolen from him. However, Bran had called to tell him a bank in Zagreb had reported someone had broken into their vault. No one had been hurt and the cameras showed what looked like a blur moving through the secure chamber.

Fionn would have suspected a vampire or even a wolf, except the safe in question was melted open. Bran had hacked the Croatian police's computer system and sent Fionn the photographs. There was a handprint melted into the safe.

A witch or warlock might be able to use a heat spell to do such a thing, but they were ultimately human and unable to move with the kind of speed recorded on camera.

Evidence pointed to fae.

Despite the urgency of taking back what had been stolen, Fionn couldn't turn down the opportunity to find one of the fae. Upon landing in Zagreb, he knew right away it was his elusive little psychic. And if she was willing to stick around the city after robbing a bank, then she was sticking around for something important.

Like another of her kind.

The bartender prodded at Fionn. Facts told him the answer was no, but his instincts said otherwise. "There was a woman ... there was something about her energy that suggests she's more than human. I discounted her at first, but after searching the club and the surrounding streets, I found nothing else that would warrant the psychic's interest."

"So, what's the plan?"

"I'll return to the club tomorrow evening for the bartender."

"The psychic can't mask her energy forever. It takes up too much magic. She'll exhaust herself."

"Then we can only hope she reveals herself while I'm still here."

"And *An Breitheamh*?"

Fionn cursed under his breath. "It will just have to wait."

"Or you could set someone else on the task of retrieving it."

He shook his head. "It's too important."

"Your control freakery might be the end of you, Fionn."

"Immortal," he reminded his only confidant.

"Ah, right, keep forgetting about that. Don't know how. Must be your modesty."

Ignoring Bran's sarcasm, Fionn exhaled heavily. "Anything else to report?"

"There was a murder in Zagreb two nights ago. It sounds like the work of a vampire."

Bloody brilliant. Just what he needed. Vampires, in general, fed for survival. But like any species, there were always those few who got off on killing for the sake of killing. "I hopefully won't be here that long to have to deal with it."

"I mention it because the murder took place outside the club near your hotel. I hacked into police records, and they think it's the work of a serial killer that's been killing women across Europe. Always near a nightclub the female victim was reported to have been seen at. Usually found in an alley near the club with neck wounds and drained of blood. They're working with Interpol on this one."

"Bloody hell," Fionn muttered. That probably meant undercover police at the clubs. "Right. I'll keep an eye out."

"No movement on An Breitheamh, FYI."

And that was one of the reasons Fionn put up with Bran. The vampire was young in the grand scheme of things. Only ninety-five years old. He was also brilliant. He managed Fionn's intelligence system and directed the many contacts Fionn had amassed all over the world.

Moreover, he was the only being that Fionn trusted.

"I want to know if the Blackwoods step a foot in Zagreb."

"On it. Speaking of the Blackwoods, you asked me to keep an eye on Thea and Conall MacLennan ..."

Alert, Fionn stiffened. The Blackwoods wouldn't dare meddle with the MacLennans after they promised not to.

If they had, their ruin would be their own damn fault. Arrogant swine. If it were a perfect world, he'd have nothing to do with that magical family.

Unfortunately, he owed the Blackwood Coven even more than he had ever owed Eirik.

It was that debt that stayed his hand against the witches and warlocks who desperately sought to open the gate to Faerie. Not to take down the bitch who had ruined Fionn's existence but to forge an alliance with her. To live among the faeries, to imbue their magic with pure power at the source.

The Blackwoods were an old, very large North American coven. They were also naive, sycophantic arseholes, and there was no telling them that the fae would destroy the humans. He had to keep one step ahead of them at all times.

Fionn had slipped up with Thea Quinn. The Blackwoods knew of her existence before he did, and they'd arrived in Scotland before he could. Layton Blackwood had met with him in Inverness, a city an hour and a half east of the werewolves' home in Torridon.

The obnoxious warlock, son of the coven leader, had lounged across from him in the hotel bar. "Thea Quinn is a werewolf and mated to Conall MacLennan."

It had taken a moment for Fionn to process this. After all, the information he'd gathered suggested the woman in question had survived numerous attacks over the years, many of them in just the past few weeks.

One of them by Eirik Mortensen, the oldest living vampire in the world. Fionn knew that for a fact, for he had known Eirik for over two thousand years.

Of course, that was until Thea had wiped out Eirik and fourteen of his vampire brethren for attacking Conall MacLennan.

Who was obviously Thea's mate, Fionn had mused.

Only a mate could turn fae into a werewolf without the bite killing her. A little-known secret he'd learned while enslaved to the Fae Queen.

Matings were not supposed to happen between the fae and the supernaturals born from their magic and interference with the humans. Yet, somehow, vampires and werewolves found themselves mated to fae. It had been rare. It had been forbidden.

But it happened.

And when the Fae Queen, Aine, learned that a werewolf bite could turn fae from immortal into a powerful but very mortal werewolf so long as the pair were mated, she decided that connection between the once-human supernaturals and the fae-borne was too dangerous to allow to continue. She'd banished the supernaturals from Faerie, sending them back to the human world.

All except Fionn.

Instead, she'd defied her own laws to turn him into the thing he hated most so she could keep him.

But he'd outwitted her and used Eirik to return.

To go home ... to Aoibhinn.

The pain that had once been so intense it was crippling was now just a flicker in his gut.

"We're considering killing her anyway," Layton had said, pulling Fionn from his memories.

He had flicked a glance at Liza and Lori, Layton's sisters. They'd shared a displeased look.

Clearly Layton was being a little too liberal with the contraction "we're."

"Killing her for what?" Fionn had asked blandly. "You were mistaken. She's a wolf. A mated one at that."

"But was she always a wolf? The pack says so. They say Conall sensed his mate in Europe and went off to find her and bring her into their fold," he'd sneered. "But evidence suggests otherwise. A wolf couldn't kill Eirik Mortensen." Layton had leaned toward him. "If you'd just confirm whether Jerrik's writings were true, we'd know if she was lying."

Layton referred to Eirik's brother, Jerrik. Where Eirik left Faerie over two thousand years ago, as enraged by their behavior and interference in the human world as Fionn had been, Jerrik was mated to a fae. Not just any fae—the equivalent of a fucking princess. He wanted back into Faerie for his mate. Eirik wanted to make sure that gate never opened again.

That's where his and Fionn's path had diverged.

But considering Eirik had killed Jerrik to protect the human world, Fionn had been very cautious about starting anything but a cold war with the vampire.

It was thanks to Jerrik's tales of Faerie that the Blackwoods started investigating the druid legends surrounding Fionn's curse. From there, they'd worked tirelessly to free Fionn. That resented gratitude was the only thing that had stayed his hand against the coven for almost three centuries. But Layton Blackwood could push an immortal's patience to its limits. That was quite a feat.

Fionn had stared dispassionately at the Blackwood son. Layton was young. Hotheaded. Unlike his father, Nate, who was intelligent and patient. Nate Blackwood had declared Thea MacLennan off-limits now that she was mated to the alpha and no longer viable as a key to Faerie.

"If you kill Thea, you start a war with Conall MacLennan," Fionn had told the boy. This should've been obvious.

"We're the most powerful coven in the world." Layton had shrugged arrogantly. "We can take out one alpha."

Jesus Christ, the boy was a moron. Fionn had flicked a look at his sisters who stared at their brother in open distaste. It was a pity they were younger than Layton. The hierarchy within the coven was age and power. Layton, unfortunately, was the eldest, and the most powerful among his siblings.

But he was a political ticking time bomb.

"If you kill Conall, you start a war with his pack. And did you not just tell me he's forged an alliance with Pack Silverton?" Pack Silverton was the largest North American pack, led by Alpha Peter Canid. An important ally for MacLennan. "MacLennan is one of the most powerful alphas in the world. Wolves came from all over to take control of his pack upon his father's death." Every supernatural who knew anything about the politics of their world knew of Conall. Pack MacLennan was small, but they owned several businesses, including a lucrative whisky distillery, and were wealthy. Conall had famously taken down every wolf that had challenged him. "Packs around the world practically revere the wolf. You take him out with no acceptable reason, you'll find yourselves at war with nearly every pack in the fucking world, boy."

Layton stiffened. "I'm not a boy."

"Then stop acting like one. You lost, Blackwood. Accept it and move on." Fionn had stood. "As I will."

"You refuse to help us at every turn. I don't know why my father allows you to live."

Uncaring of the humans who sat at the bar with their backs to them, Fionn had used a source of magic only fae could. *Travel.* One moment he stood on the other side of the table, the next he had Layton by the throat, pinned to the adjacent wall.

Magic had sparked at his back as his sisters prepared to fight.

Fionn had snarled in Layton's horrified face. "Your father does not *allow* me to live." He had leaned in as Layton gasped for breath. "*I* allow your coven to exist because I owe that debt. But do not think you can push me, *boy.*"

The magic at his back amplified and without even looking at the sisters, he concentrated on a pressure point on their necks. The carotid sinus. He sent out strong fingers of energy that hit both sisters there; it caused them to pass out instantly.

Layton had wheezed in outrage.

"They're still alive," Fionn had assured him, lowering him to the ground. "That was merely a warning ... that you need a lesson in diplomacy."

Fionn still felt agitated every time he thought on the encounter. It bothered him not just a little that the dangerous fucker would one day be head of the coven.

"The Blackwoods wouldn't dare interfere with Thea MacLennan after our encounter in Inverness," Fionn said to Bran.

"No, it's not the Blackwoods. But you asked me to let you know if there was any unusual activity there. Thea and Conall have left on a honeymoon."

A honeymoon.

Wolves didn't celebrate honeymoons.

"Where did they go?"

"They got on a flight to Paris yesterday."

"Connect the dots for me, Bran. It's what I pay you for."

"Already done it. Eirik was killed in Norway at the home of Vik Balstad. It took me a while but I hacked Balstad's computer. The man is a fucking genius and I want to meet him because only the best, i.e., myself, could get past the security measures on his system. I mean, he had this—"

"Point, Bran. Get there."

"Right. Okay, well, I found a few of his aliases. One of them popped up in Paris. He's renting an apartment there."

Fionn suspected Vik Balstad, a vampire with known affiliations with Eirik's movement to stop the gate opening, had led Eirik to Thea and Conall. "Could be a coincidence. Or ... revenge."

Fuck. Why couldn't the woman and her mate settle down in Scotland like normal wolves and stay out of this damn business?

"It's not our problem," Fionn huffed. "If they want to fuck up their lives with this shit, let them, as long as they stay out of my way. Anything else?"

"Nothing for now. Whichmeansyou'regoingtohanguponmebeforeIcansaygood—"

Fionn hung up on him.

He slumped back against the sofa. Wide awake but weary.

Not physically weary.

Although he grew tired after days of no sleep, he was never weary in his muscles and bones like he had been centuries ago after days of battle.

He missed that sensation.

He almost forgot what it felt like to lie his exhausted body down in furs after the physical exertion of war.

Yet Fionn *was* weary in the mind. He'd been planning for this moment for almost three centuries.

Now he was more than ready for it to be done.

3

As the bass thudded through the club like a heartbeat, Rose rubbed her fingers against her temple and ignored the clamor of calls from the club goers who wanted a drink from the bar.

She was done here.

Zagreb was a beautiful city. It had an interesting history, great architecture, a good vibe, and the people were friendly. But it was like a flip had switched inside her after the encounter with that strange girl and her brother the night before.

Suddenly the music in the club was too loud, the hundreds of bodies claustrophobic, and their never-ending desire for alcohol irritating. Rose just wanted peace and quiet. Somewhere to lay her head so she could think straight.

Where to go from here?

Someone nudged her hard, and she looked up to see Josip frowning at her. He pointed to the waiting customers without saying a word. Rose sighed. There wasn't much time left on her shift. The club was closing soon. She could finish up.

And then she'd finish up for good.

Mind whirring as she fixed a cocktail for a customer, it took a moment for the creeping sensation down her spine to take hold. She stiffened.

Someone was watching her.

Okay, she knew there was a crowd at the bar probably watching her, waiting their turn for drinks, but that wasn't what she felt.

Someone was *hunting* her.

An inexplicable ominous feeling settled over her. A sudden dread in her gut.

Rose lowered the bottle of gin in her hand back onto the shelf as her heart raced hard and fast.

A memory slammed into her of one of the worst things that had ever happened to her. College. Freshman year. Her roommate had invited her to a fraternity house party. Halfway through the night, after downing shots that had no effect on her since she had an almost inhuman ability to hold her alcohol, Rose had felt it.

The sudden dread.

The creeping feeling of crawling flesh, as if someone wasn't just watching her but hunting her. She'd thrown off the feeling as absurd. Until she'd climbed the stairs to the second floor of the frat house to find an empty bathroom and someone had attacked her from behind.

He'd covered her mouth with his hand as he'd hauled her into a dark bedroom.

Unfortunately, her attacker had thought she was drunk. He'd also underestimated her strength because of her slight build.

Rose was strong.

Exceptionally strong.

As he'd pinned her arms to the bed with one hand while he shoved his hand up her skirt with the other, Rose had unleashed that strength upon him. She'd yanked her arms free of his hold and shoved her hands against his body.

He'd flown across the room, crashing against the wall.

A still figure lying on the floor.

Fear had propelled her out of that room without even checking his identity.

Not that it mattered.

It was all over campus the next day that Judd Grant, a sophomore in the fraternity house, was dead. He'd died of a heart attack. Unusual for someone so young, yes. Not impossible.

The mystery had been the hole in his bedroom wall.

Rose's hands shook at the memory. She'd told herself over and over for years that his death was not at her hands. Adrenaline had bolstered her strength that night. The heart attack was, however, just nature. A defect lying in wait.

And she wouldn't feel guilty about it.

The boy was a would-be rapist.

What if he'd already raped other girls?

The trauma he'd possibly inflicted or intended to inflict was surely a factor in negating her guilt. All Rose had done was protect herself.

Now that feeling ... that feeling of being hunted was back.

Turning, Rose searched the crowd around the bar. Faces blurred into faces, none of them standing out.

You're being ridiculous.

Her eyes locked with a stranger's, and her disquiet intensified.

The dark-haired stranger's gaze sharpened on her. A smirk curled the upper corner of his mouth.

And then he just slipped away from the bar.

Disappearing into the crowd.

The crawling sensation abated but not the awful feeling in her gut.

Yes, it was definitely time to leave Zagreb.

Rose shook herself, willing her heart to calm, as she returned to mixing the cocktail. There wasn't much of her savings left. Enough to get her to the next place and then she was out of funds unless she got a great-paying job. Maybe she should put that degree in marketing to good use and find a job that would allow her to save cash for the next time she wanted to move on.

The problem was any employer would look at her résumé and see someone who couldn't settle down in one place for too long, and that was not an attractive quality in an employee.

Finally, the deejay announced the last track of the night and once it was over, Rose saw Ivan and two other security guards ushering the clubbers out. Ivan didn't look her way at all.

He hadn't all night.

When she'd passed him to take her break in the staff room, he'd given her a nod but invited no more interaction. Rose didn't care. It was just an awkward reminder of why she slept with guys the night before she left town so she wouldn't have to deal with them trying to ghost her.

Or vice versa.

And Rose was definitely ghosting Ivan.

Having slept with all kinds of men—short, tall, stocky, lean, athletic, nonathletic, plain, good-looking, and something in between —Rose had drawn some conclusions. The better-looking the guy in a traditional sense, the more selfish the lover. She imagined these guys thought they didn't have to work for it. She'd even gotten the sense from one or two that they thought she should be grateful for their attention.

More and more, Rose had found herself drawn to guys who were attractive in a nontraditional way. Masculine, rugged, charming.

Ivan was all three.

She'd expected the comfort she'd been looking for last night. To be taken care of in bed before taking care of him in return.

Unfortunately, Ivan had slam-bam-thank-you-ma'am'ed her and didn't seem to care if she reached satisfaction or not.

She hadn't.

It was probably time to take a sabbatical from men. What had been fun, casual sex was becoming depressing. The encounters were growing increasingly disappointing and empty.

Rose looked up from the glasses she was cleaning to see Josip and Kali, her two colleagues for the evening, disappearing behind the Staff Only door.

Seeing the dirty glasses they'd left, she cursed them under her breath and set to cleaning up. Twenty minutes later, Rose was alone in the cavernous club, the bar cleaned and ready for use the next night.

Usually she'd be pissed at getting left to deal with the cleanup herself, but Rose was feeling relieved that it was her last night in the bar. She'd leave a note for her boss, Marko, whom she rarely saw anyway, to let him know she'd moved on.

Yet, where to go, where to go?

Wherever it was, the time was now. The empty club was feeling like a great place for someone to stage an attack.

Rose huffed, chastising herself for acting like a scaredy-cat, but it didn't stop her from moving quickly. Once she'd collected her stuff and left a note on an old envelope in Marko's office, Rose said good night to Noa, the security guard who was locking up.

"'Night, Rose." He gave her a knowing grin, leering at her.

Ivan had talked.

She threw Noa a glower and turned left down the nearly empty street. The club was in Old Town, as was her apartment above the bakery. It was only a ten-minute walk north in the upper area of Old Town, yet as Rose left the club behind, she felt a crawling sensation down the back of her neck and spine again.

Shit.

She flicked a wary look over her shoulder but saw no one.

Heart racing, stomach roiling, she picked up her pace.

As Rose passed the familiar stores in the eerie stillness of the early morning, relief began to build. She was closing in on her apartment. She was almost there. When she got back to her apartment, she would give herself a good talking-to for letting the weird interaction with those siblings get to her. They'd made her jumpy for sure.

And that's when it happened.

He came out of nowhere.

No footsteps at her back to warn her.

Strong arms, like metal vises, bound around her, and then the world blurred into dark. Burning pain scored down her shoulder from her neck, and she gasped. Confusion had slowed her but the pain sharpened her focus.

She was in an alley.

Pinned against the brick wall of a building. It smelled of trash and urine.

A man's head buried against her neck. Her arms caged against the wall by his hands.

Rose pushed against him as the gnawing sensation on her neck grew unbearable—

He lifted his head in a gasp and moonlight revealed him.

The man from the club tonight who had been staring at her.

Hunting her.

His eyes reflected pure, unnatural silver in the moonlight.

Blood smeared his chin and coated his fangs.

Fangs.

Disbelief and horror paralyzed Rose.

No ...

He couldn't be ...

There was no such fucking thing.

He stared at her in wonder. "What are you?" he hissed through blood-soaked, long incisors.

Rose felt the blood pumping out of her body and knew he'd hit an artery. She didn't have much time. If any.

She could stand there, disbelieving, refusing to accept the utter weirdness of the world and her eventual death ... or she could fight this motherfucking vampire!

Vampire.

Something inside her, something primal, took over.

The pain receded as Rose snapped against the vampire's hold with such force, he stumbled away from her. She used that momentum, lifting her right knee to slam her foot into his gut with all the strength inside her.

He flew and smacked against the opposite wall with a sickening thud of his skull.

Unlike Judd, however, he just shook his head and lifted it, preternatural silver eyes glowing in the dark as he bared his teeth and unleashed an animalistic growl. Then he was on her, a blur through the night that took her to the cold ground with so much force, her skull slammed into the concrete.

It was the kind of hit to the head that surely would've knocked out someone else, Rose thought vaguely as she blinked, stunned. Yet she had no time to think on this, and not because the vampire was on her again, his teeth piercing the flesh on the other side of her neck.

But because something else was happening to her.

A golden shimmer danced across her vision as this weight, this unbelievably heavy weight that she hadn't even been aware of, seemed to lift from her body.

"What the ..." The vampire sat up, staring at her in confusion, her blood dripping from his chin.

That's when Rose realized the golden shimmer was a light peeling away from her body. She sat up, lifting her hand, and watched the light mimic her movement. It was shaped like the outline of her, like a silhouette. The vampire scrambled off her to watch as the light moved as one toward the center of her chest until it amalgamated into one large, glowing ball.

"Oh my—"

It exploded, throwing Rose to the ground and the vampire into a nearby trash can.

Darkness fell over the alley again.

A tingling sensation brought Rose's hand to her neck.

"Holy fuck," she whimpered, feeling her flesh knit together.

Shaking, she touched the vampire's other wound.

Blood smeared her fingers ... but the wounds were gone.

And the alley was no longer pitch-black. It was gray, and she could see the trash cans clearly ... she could see the vampire clearly, his silver eyes as bright.

Night vision.

As Rose sat up, her limbs felt strange, like for years there had been a heaviness in them, and now, only lightness and strength.

The vampire stood, staring at her in disbelief. Rose laughed at the thought, the sound disconcerting in the dark.

A *vampire* stared at *her* in disbelief.

"What the hell are you?" he asked.

Touching her neck, finding the worst wound healed over, her earlier fear melted away. Confusion remained, but there was also power flowing through her body. Inexplicable, incredible power that crackled from her skin.

Power that made her feel less afraid of him.

The vampire.

A goddamn vampire.

She lifted her chin in defiance. "I think I might be hard to kill."

Rose spoke too soon.

She realized that milliseconds later as the blur of his body shot toward her and she felt his powerful hands grip hold of her nape.

The last thing she heard was the resounding crack of her neck breaking.

4

At first Fionn was dismayed when he encountered the vampire at the club. Watching the dark-haired bloodsucker as he moved through the crowds, Fionn had suspected right away that this man was the killer Bran had warned him about.

Vampires didn't stalk humans. They socialized with them, drank from them only what they needed, leaving behind questionable wounds that only perpetuated human fascination with vampire mythology.

This vampire, however, was hunting.

Fionn, unfortunately, was too preoccupied with the bartender to deal with the vampire and his would-be victim. His psychic wasn't at the club, which meant she probably knew he was and was staying away. Could the bartender be that important, then? Was she even the reason the psychic had been there in the first place, or was Fionn reaching?

Earlier that day, he'd broken into the club and logged onto the office computer. He'd found the employee records, which included helpful photographs of each of them.

He found Rose. The bartender.

Rose Kelly.

That was an Irish name if ever there was one, Fionn had mused. She was Irish American. Twenty-five years old and her résumé belonged to that of a vagabond. The girl had been wandering for the last three years. First Australia, then numerous cities around Europe. Why? What was she running from?

Retrieving her Social Security number, Fionn had sent the information to Bran. So far all they'd discovered was that Rose Kelly was the adopted daughter of Anna and Bill Kelly. They adopted her when she was a little over a year old. Anna and Bill lived in Maryland in the United States but were both originally from Cork in Ireland. Anna was an artist and Bill was a website developer. Rose had graduated from the University of Pennsylvania with a degree in marketing.

From there she'd become a nomad.

Why?

Bran was working on gathering more information while Fionn followed Rose. He'd become aware of the vampire's presence, stalking Rose, as soon as she'd taken two steps away from the club.

At first Fionn was pissed he'd have to deal with the vampire for interfering in his business, but then he'd realized a vampire attack might give him some insight into Rose's abilities, or lack thereof.

He'd watched from the rooftops as the vampire pulled Rose into the alleyway and tore into her neck. To Fionn's surprise, he'd had to stop himself from getting involved. Watching Rose's attack was unnerving. Disconcerting. A strange feeling of guilt pricked him for letting the vamp get within touching distance of her.

It made no sense.

Unless his instincts were telling him she *was* important.

That she did have something to do with the fae children after all.

Still, he held himself back and was glad for it as he watched her push off the vampire with unnatural strength.

"Bingo," he murmured, leaning over the roof to see what would happen next.

It wasn't at all what he'd been expecting.

After the vampire knocked Rose to the ground with a sickening thud of her head, Fionn was sure she was supernatural.

That kind of hit would've crushed a human's skull.

When the golden light began to peel away from her body, anticipation curled in Fionn's gut.

He knew what that light meant.

Someone had put a spell on Rose Kelly.

That light gathered into a ball above her chest and then exploded, throwing the vampire back against the wall and Rose to the ground. Her energy blasted out of her and rolled over Fionn in wave after glorious wave. With it came her scent.

Floral and earthy, like summer in Ireland, tinged with a heady sweetness like caramelized sugar.

The hair on his neck rose.

Fae.

She was goddamn fae.

He watched as she slowly stood to face the vampire.

Someone had put a blocking spell on Rose Kelly to suppress her fae powers.

Fionn needed Bran to find out who her birth parents were and how they knew she needed to be protected. Because that was the purpose for the spell.

A spell his clever little psychic had seen through.

Standing to his feet, Fionn decided it was time to end this interlude with the vampire. Rose had proven herself brave and strong, but her confusion was clear. Fionn needed to determine how much or how little she knew. He was hoping she knew little.

It would be so much easier to manipulate her if she was clueless.

"What the hell are you?" the vampire asked from below.

"I think I might be hard to kill," Rose answered.

Fionn smirked at that.

Oh, she had no idea.

Not even a second later, his smirk melted as the vampire broke Rose's neck. She crumpled, not dead, but out for the count.

Possessive fury roared through Fionn as he stepped off the rooftop. Rose Kelly was now his to kill at the right moment. No other fucker would dare touch her until then.

The vampire whirled around as Fionn dropped to the ground on light feet. The blood drinker bared his fangs, hackles raised.

Fionn lifted a finger and waggled it at the vampire. "We mustn't touch what isn't ours."

The vampire lunged and Fionn used the force against him, punching his fist through the vamp's chest, feeling the warm, wet muscle of his heart pulsing in his hands.

Then he tore it out.

The vampire's body burst into ash that floated in the still night air. The wet muscle in Fionn's hand disintegrated into dust too.

Fionn stepped around the cloud of dead vampire and kneeled in the alley to brush away Rose's dark hair from her face. She was beautiful in a subtle way. All Aine's fae were attractive. It was part of their weaponry.

He perused her body. She wasn't short, but she wasn't tall. She had a gentle feminine flare to her hips. Still, she was lean and strong, like an athlete because she had been. Bran discovered articles on her. She'd been a gymnast in high school, en route to the US Olympic team, until she'd mysteriously walked away from the sport.

Despite the spell, she'd been stronger than the average human.

Had she guessed that she was different?

So many questions, Fionn mused.

He pulled out his phone and called Bran. As soon as the vamp answered, Fionn informed him, "It was the bartender. Someone put a spell on her to repress her abilities and energy. I don't know how big that energy blasting off her was, but it would be enough to alert any nearby supernaturals. I need you to check for movement from the Blackwoods or anyone else of interest."

"Jesus Christ, only a bloody powerful and ruthless witch or warlock could do that."

"I'm aware. Any headway with the birth parents?"

"Well, I was just about to go to bed, but I'll get on it right away."

"You do that."

"What are you going to do?"

"Discover how much she knows. I'm hoping it's less than zero."

"And then?"

"I'll convince her she needs me. Once I have her trust, it should be easy enough to lure her to Ireland. Call me if you see movement and when you find something of use." He hung up and stared down at Rose again.

She was a pig to the slaughter, he thought dispassionately.

Unfair for her, true, but what was one small woman against a two-thousand-year-old vendetta?

Fionn reached beneath her and lifted her into his arms with ease. Even if he didn't have supernatural strength, she would have felt slight in his arms. A growl burrowed out of him as he heard bone slipping back into place.

She was healing from that neck break.

The vampire had deserved a drawn-out death because a broken neck couldn't kill fae, but it could hurt like fuck.

Rose would wake soon.

There was no time to dawdle. Curious supernaturals might already be on their way.

5

As Rose's mind swam up out of a bizarre dream, she grew aware of the mattress beneath her and realized she was in bed. Yet, as she tried to let go of images of bloodied fangs and glowing golden lights, it occurred to her that the mattress in her crappy apartment was lumpy and didn't feel like a cloud of softness. The one beneath her did.

Her eyes flew open. Confusion and panic instantly hit her.

She was in a room she'd never been in before.

Rose sat up, surprised her head didn't swim with the movement.

The room was warmly lit by table lamps with pale shades. The light bounced up latte-colored striped walls. Matching silk curtains covered the windows. And Rose was in a huge bed. The comfiest bed she'd been in, in a long time. Everything about the room said luxury hotel.

Throwing her legs off the side of the bed, she abruptly stopped.

Her limbs felt ... weird.

Flexing a hand, she stared at it, trying to figure out—

Visions of a vampire attacking her, followed by a light exploding from her body, filled her mind again.

No.

No way.

She stood, expecting her legs to tremble, but they didn't. Power coursed through her limbs but as she crossed to a doorway adjacent to the bed, her whole body felt lighter somehow.

Strangely lighter—but stronger.

The doorway led into a small sitting room that matched the décor of the bedroom.

Yup, she was definitely in a hotel suite.

It smelled strongly of orange blossom but there was a slight trace of fresh cologne.

How the hell could she smell that?

She turned back into the bedroom and hurried across the room to the adjoining bathroom. A large mirror hung on the wall behind the marble sink, and Rose leaned toward it, pushing her dark hair off her neck.

There were no wounds.

No vampires.

It was just ... just a dream, right? But then why was she here? In this strange room? Who had brought her here? And why did she feel like she was walking around in a new body?

As her panic built, so did her fear. She watched in disbelief as bright gold bled through the blue of her irises.

"Fuck!" She scrambled back from the mirror, slapping her hands over her eyes.

Her breasts heaved with choppy breaths as she tried to calm down. Unsuccessfully.

Rose lowered her hands and opened her eyes.

Yeah, they were still bright gold!

Unnatural.

Remembering the way her wounds from the vampire's fangs had healed over, Rose moved closer to the mirror again.

"Fuck, fuck, fuck."

The fight had been real. The vampire had been real. But what ...

what did that make her? Was she a vampire too? His eyes had been silver in the light. Why were hers gold?

Vampires.

Strange powers ...

A door opened beyond the bedroom and it sounded like it had opened right next to her. She grew aware of the sound of voices in the room next door. A couple were discussing whether they wanted to get room service or dine in the hotel restaurant for breakfast. The man didn't care. His priority was sex.

Okay, then. Suffice it to say Rose's hearing was way better than it was yesterday. As was her sense of smell.

Huh.

Rose flinched back from the mirror, heart pounding. Was she turning into a vampire too?

"Rose?" an unfamiliar voice called her name.

Who was that?

What had happened in that alleyway? She'd sensed this unimaginable power in her limbs and faced the vampire to fight, but then everything went dark. The next thing she remembered was waking up in this room.

Not one to hide in fear and confusion, despite how afraid she was, Rose threw back her shoulders and strode out of the bathroom only to come to an immediate halt.

Standing in the doorway between the bedroom and sitting room was the man from the club. Not the vampire. The other one. The mammoth, well-dressed one who had moved through the crowd with a preternatural grace. The one she'd felt inexplicably drawn to. This close to him, she could see she'd been wrong about his height. He was taller than the six and a half feet she'd guessed. Rose swallowed hard as he ambled toward her.

"No need for golden eyes, Rose Kelly," he said in a deep rumble of a voice. "I'm here to help, not to hurt."

Rose stared up at him in awe. The only guy taller she'd ever met in real life was Patrick King, a basketball player at UPenn who went on to play for the NBA.

"Who are you?"

Piercing eyes the color of spring green stared back at her, mesmerizing. She'd thought they were contacts in the club. Now she realized the lasers had made them look eerier than they were. In fact, she'd never seen eyes so stunning. Other than when hers bled gold in the bathroom mirror.

The stranger waited patiently before her. Like the previous night, he wore a three-piece suit. His stylish, well-tailored attire was a sharp contrast to his massive shoulders, his blunt, rugged features, unshaven face, and unkempt, longish, dark blond hair. He reminded her of a caged tiger—the suit was an illusion of safety between you and an animal that could tear you to shreds with a simple swipe of his paw.

"Who are you?" she repeated.

The man cocked his head, frowning. "I can hear your heart racing. That's unnecessary."

"Are you a vampire?"

"No." He retreated and gestured toward the doorway. "I brought some food up from the kitchen. Tea too." He turned his back on her and walked out of the room. Rose gawked not only at the breadth of his shoulders but at the way he had to duck under the door frame.

Holy shit.

Think, Rose, think.

Taking a slow, calming breath, she gave her body a chance to catch up with her mind. As insane as it was, she still felt that weird pull toward the stranger. What she didn't feel was fear toward him. Her fear stemmed from the unknown. From the bizarre new things happening to her body.

Exhaling, Rose strode after the stranger and found him shrugging out of his jacket. She watched as he draped it over an armchair. His waistcoat and shirt were a perfect fit, as were the tailored trousers that cupped an ass that was clearly rock hard with muscle.

Attraction zinged through her as she watched him turn to sit.

Yeah, really not the time, she chastised herself.

"Good, the gold is gone." His tone was as warm and fuzzy as a prison warden's.

Rose touched the corner of her eye. "What does it mean?"

"Sit." He gestured to the sofa. A tray sat on the coffee table before it.

"I'm not hungry."

"Then don't eat."

His response irritated her, but Rose lowered herself onto the sofa anyway. "Are you Irish?" It was hard to tell. His accent was a little muddled, but there was a definite lilt to his words that reminded her of her parents' accents.

"I am. My name is Fionn Mór. And you're Rose Kelly."

"How do you know that?" She leaned toward him. "I saw you the other night at the club. And then ... was I ...?" She raised a hand to her neck.

"Attacked an hour ago by a vampire."

"How is this real?" Rose whispered to herself.

Perhaps she was still dreaming.

He studied her intently. "How much do you know about supernaturals?"

"Supernaturals?"

"Vampires, werewolves, and the like."

Rose gaped at him. "Werewolves are real too?"

She thought she detected a slight curl at the corner of his lips. An almost smile. But then he glared at her so Rose must have imagined it. "You know nothing of the supernatural underworld?"

She swallowed hard. "If I hadn't just been attacked by a vampire and watched my eyes change to liquid gold ... I'd think you were a crazy man for even suggesting it a reality."

"But you know I'm not crazy, don't you, Rose? The sooner you come to terms with the fact that the supernatural world exists, the sooner you can come to terms with who you are."

His matter-of-fact tone pissed her off. "That simple, huh?"

"I'm not here to baby you through this. I'm here to help you discover who you are and to control the incredible power that runs through your body."

"Why?"

Fionn studied the carpet. His tone was almost melancholy when he replied, "You and I are the same. There's so few of us left." There was something fierce in those striking eyes that made her breath catch. "Less than a handful. It's a miracle I found you."

Hearing the sincerity in his words, and perhaps even a hint of longing, Rose whispered, "What am I?"

"You," he said, leaning forward, "are one of the fae."

Rose stared incredulously at him. "The what now?"

His expression darkened with obvious impatience. "This will go easier if you suspend your disbelief. Someone put a powerful spell on you to block your abilities. The vampire attack, knocking you to the ground, it broke the spell."

The light that flew out of her body ...

"But I think you've always been strong, Rose, haven't you? Stronger than normal."

Yeah, she had always been. Especially for her size. Friends had commented on it. Her coach had too. But it had just been something everyone accepted about Rose Kelly.

She was weirdly strong.

"Spell?" The words from the girl at the club ... *"You have a block on you. A spell. Someone has blocked your access to your powers."* The young woman and her brother hadn't been messing with her. "That's what the girl said last night."

Fionn tensed, alert. "What girl?"

"I don't know. She was around my age. She and her brother ambushed me at the club. She said someone had put a spell on me that blocked my powers."

Even though his tone was bland, Rose felt waves of energy from him. He was agitated. "Did she say anything else?"

"Stuff that made little sense. Oh, and they were Irish. Her name was Niamh and his was Ronan ..." Rose frowned trying to remember the full name the girl had given. "Uh ..." Then it hit her. "Ronan Farren. Niamh and Ronan Farren."

Fionn sat back in his chair. "Farren? Are you sure?"

"Do you know them?"

"What you are is a dangerous thing to be," he said instead of answering. "Whoever put the spell on you did so to protect you. Of that I have no doubt. Could it be your parents? Do they have magic?"

Magic? Her parents.

Rose shook her head, her mind whirling. "My ... I'm adopted. My adoptive mother is my aunt. Her sister was my mom."

"Does your aunt have magic?"

"What?"

"Is your aunt a witch?"

Rose guffawed, standing to her feet. "A witch. They're real too?"

Fionn sighed and steepled his hands together under his chin as he studied her thoughtfully. "Witches, warlocks, werewolves, and vampires are real. Our world is made up of energy. There are some who can wield it —witches and warlocks can tap into that energy and use it to do things humans consider magical. But the energy here has limitations for humans. Fae belong to a world that crackles with an abundance of energy that runs through not only the ground beneath their feet but is also inside them. They're not just born to wield that energy ... they *are* that energy.

"Centuries before I was born, a gate was opened between our two worlds, and the fae began to invade. They treated humans as amusements, causing torment and leaving havoc in their wake, stealing humans and bringing them back to Faerie. I was born human in what is now Ireland. The gate was near the coast, miles and miles from my homestead. I led my men against the fae"—his features hardened —"but we couldn't win. Not even the druids could fight them. So I made a bargain with their leader ... the Faerie Queen."

Rose placed her fingers to her temples and stared at him in horror. He was insane. This was insane. "The Faerie Queene. As in the epic poem by Edmund Spenser?"

Fionn visibly tensed. "Do I detect mockery in your tone?"

Her blood chilled at the warning in his voice. "No. Just suspended belief."

"Where do you think the legends and myths about faeries come from, Rose?" He curled his lip. "From truths that have been altered by rumor and by time. But the fae are quite real. They're not mischievous tiny little flying people ... they look as human as you or me. But they're not. They have powers beyond human imagination. And Faerie is a world of creatures dark and light."

Slumping back onto the couch, Rose decided to play along. "Okay, so you said they opened a gate between our worlds. Are we talking multiple dimensions here?"

"Yes."

A bulb burst in the light shade next to her.

Rose let out a small cry and jumped in fright just as another burst on the sideboard near Fionn.

"Calm down, Rose."

The remaining lights flickered frantically.

"Rose." He held up an appeasing hand.

"What?" She stared at him in disbelief. "You think I'm doing this? No. No way. This is nuts." Rose flew to her feet. "You're just a psycho feeding me bullshit fairy tales. Let me leave."

Just like that, he disappeared.

Poof.

Just gone.

A prickling sensation tickled down her spine.

"Calm down—"

She yelped, whirling around to find Fionn standing directly behind her. "How ..." She stumbled away from him.

One minute he'd been there and then he was over there.

No.

"Holy fuck! I'm losing my mind, aren't I?"

He threw her an impatient look. "You know you're not."

"What ... what do you want with me?"

Fionn shrugged, looking weary. "There's more to the story but for now, I'll tell you that the gate closed over two thousand years ago, and the queen did it to protect the human world from a war with the fae we'd never survive. But there are beings out there who want to reopen the gate, and you're the key. If they kill you on the exact spot the gate exists, it will reopen.

"I'm trying to protect you. I'm trying to show you who you are. Moreover, I have the means to find out who your mother and father were."

"I already know who they were. They lived in Cork in Ireland. They died in a car crash when I was one."

"But someone knew to put a spell on you to protect you, Rose." He gestured to her head. "Someone in your family knows what you are and have lied about it. I can help you find answers."

Rose blinked rapidly. The pull she felt toward him was muddling her because she wanted to believe his nonsense. Mostly, however, she just wanted to get the hell out of there. "If you are trying to help me, prove it. Let me walk out of here unharmed."

A muscle ticked in his jaw seconds before he disappeared again and then reappeared by his jacket.

"Would you stop doing that?"

He shot her a dark look as he rifled through his inner jacket pocket and pulled out a card. Slowly, he crossed the room toward her. "I'm just trying to get you used to it." He offered her the card. "I can teach you to move like me. I can teach you to control the power that's been locked inside you. Take it." He gestured with the business card. "Call me when you're ready to believe."

As the door closed behind Rose Kelly, Fionn fought the urge to chase after the girl. His patience strained. Before walking into the hotel room with the food she didn't touch, Bran had called to say there was movement from the Blackwood Coven. Bran kept tabs on all the coven hunters, and two of their hunter warlocks had just appeared on the American Airlines database for flights to Zagreb.

They had time. But not a lot. If the burst of powerful magic from the spell breaking had alerted the Blackwoods, other supernaturals would have felt it too.

Yet, Fionn knew if he wanted Rose to trust him, to follow him willingly to Ireland and to her death, she needed to believe that he meant no harm. It was a risk to let her go, but she was so freaked out, he was 99.9 percent certain he'd get a call within twenty-four hours.

Her power was in its infancy. She had no control.

She'd need him before the next sunrise.

6

It was still dark outside so Rose had the hotel call a cab for her. It wasn't like her to waste money on frivolous things like taxis, but she was giving herself a pass since she'd just been attacked by a vampire.

That was the truth.

As much as what Fionn had told her was insane, the vampire attack was real.

And something *was* happening to her.

Adrenaline coursed through Rose's body, making her jittery and anxious. The farther the car drove from Fionn, the worse it got. Despite all his crazy talk, despite his less than warm, fuzzy manner, there was something about him that drew her.

Something about him that made her feel weirdly safe.

"Šta jebote ..." The driver slammed his hand on his wheel, drawing Rose's regard forward.

His headlights cast a glow across the quiet street, but they flickered frantically while his radio whipped through the channels.

"Glupi auto!" the driver growled, hitting the wheel again. "Ne treba mi ovo sranje!"

From the little Croatian Rose had picked up over the last few months, he was cursing his stupid car.

Yet, she realized, it wasn't the car's fault it was malfunctioning.

It was hers.

"Calm down, Rose," she reassured herself, drawing in a deep breath. *Calm. Calm. You're okay. You're safe.*

Almost immediately, the driver's headlights stopped flickering and the radio stuck to one station. The driver grumbled something unintelligible, and Rose tried to relax against the back seat.

The driver stopped outside her apartment. Once she'd paid and bolted from the car, the calm she'd been holding on to started to slip again. Mostly because in her frantic desire to get into her apartment, she pushed at the building's front door as she fumbled for her keys and she burst it open. Lock and all.

Rose gaped at the heavy door as it swung back to her, splintered wood sticking out of it near the locking mechanism.

Holy shit.

Even though it was still the early hours of the morning, she glanced over her shoulder to make sure no one was around to have seen that. Relieved she was alone, she hurried upstairs to her apartment, wishing she was already inside, and suddenly, the world blurred past her.

She was speeding.

Like Supergirl.

The realization made her falter, bringing her out of warp speed and causing her to slam against her apartment door.

Rose stumbled and stared toward the staircase.

She'd just blasted up three flights of stairs in seconds.

"Okay, that was weird," she huffed, looking down at her legs. A small, slightly hysterical smile curled her lips. "And fucking cool."

∼

WHEN ROSE WANTED a cup of tea and the kettle flew across the room at her head, that was less cool.

Her neighbor pounded on the wall seconds after the kettle smashed into pieces against it, leaving cracks in the plaster.

When she decided she wanted a shower and found herself in her bathtub in the blink of an eye, just like how Fionn had moved in the hotel room, Rose started to freak a little.

If she couldn't control these powers, she'd give herself away.

What if Fionn hadn't been lying? What if there were people, beings, out there who wanted to use her? To kill her?

Shaking, Rose slumped down in the tub.

Her whole life she'd felt like there was something missing. As a kid, she'd had this unnatural drive to succeed at gymnastics because the competitive sport gave her focus away from this strange feeling that had followed her around since before she could remember.

When her parents sat her down at sixteen and revealed they'd adopted her, Rose thought that was why she'd felt lost her whole life. Like there was a piece of her out there and she'd never feel complete without it. But to discover her birth mom was the aunt she'd thought had died in a car crash before she was born, along with her birth father, Rose knew she'd never find that piece. It was gone. Her adoptive mom, Anna, had told her there was no family left in Ireland. Anna's parents died when she was young, and her sister was all she'd had.

Tragic for Anna.

Tragic for Rose.

It didn't take a psychologist to realize that the reason Rose wandered was because she was still searching. And she'd been happy to wander.

Yet, now, sitting in the bathtub, scared but exhilarated by the possibilities before her, that ache inside her, the feeling she'd attributed to her missing piece ... it was gone.

The ache was gone.

Rose pressed a hand over her heart.

It was the spell. All this time it was the spell that had made her feel incomplete.

Without access to her powers, she'd felt incomplete.

Did her mom know? Anna. Did she know? Or was this something her birth mother had done to her? So many questions ... but who could she really trust?

Fionn's face drifted into her mind and her pulse raced.

What was it about that guy?

She frowned. He wasn't just a guy ... and yet he'd told her he'd once been human. How had he become what he was? And was he— was she—really one of the fae?

It was something out of a fairy tale, right?

On the back of that thought, Rose decided she might as well shower and start the day because there was no way she could sleep after all this.

A squeak made her heart falter seconds before a stream of cold water hit her on the head.

"Argh! Fuck, fuck!" She dove out of the tub, shuddering as she glared at her showerhead. It had come on at the mere thought of taking a shower. Rose whipped off her shirt and grabbed a towel, wiping away the freezing-cold droplets on her skin and scrunching her wet hair.

"Okay." She snarled at the shower. "Maybe it's not a fairy tale after all."

ROSE DECIDED it was safer to stick to her apartment for the day until she'd figured out her next move. Unfortunately, privacy wasn't on the menu. About two hours after she'd gotten home, the building had come to life with people leaving their apartments for work. The smells from the bakery downstairs were even stronger to Rose's heightened senses than before. But unlike normal, Rose wasn't hungry.

She felt too distracted to be hungry.

Rose sat staring blankly at the television, wondering if she should call her mom or use the business card Fionn had slipped into her hand.

It should have been easy. She should have been able to trust her mother over a stranger.

And yet, if her mom had something to do with this spell, then she'd been lying to Rose her whole life.

Another lie.

It was on this distressing thought her apartment door juddered under a pounding knock.

She sighed heavily. The only person who knocked on her door like that was the landlord, Craig. He was a Scot. And not one of the nice ones.

What the hell did he want?

Every time he paid a visit, he swept over the place, stating he was just looking to make sure there was no damage. He liked to intimidate people. Rose wasn't easily intimidated, and she knew it bothered him so he was extra smarmy with her.

With the way her newfound abilities were making themselves known whenever she had a mere thought, Rose didn't want to open the door.

"Open up!" Craig yelled.

Taking a deep, calming breath, Rose crossed the small apartment and unlocked the door. Before she could fully open it, the bastard pushed inside. At around five foot eight, Craig wasn't a tall guy, but he was overmuscled by gym visits. *And probably steroids*, Rose thought uncharitably. But she wouldn't put it past him.

He cut her a dark look as he shoved into the apartment, his gaze going straight to the wall.

Oh shit.

She'd totally forgotten about the kettle and the plaster.

"I got a call from your neighbor that there was a disturbance." Craig gestured to the wall. He turned to glare at her. "What the fuck?"

"Your concern is touching. Really." She gave him a dry smirk because they both knew he couldn't give a crap about her. He just wanted to keep his damn deposit.

He scowled as he approached her. Rose braced.

"You"—he stuck his finger in her face—"are not getting your

deposit back, and if one more thing happens like this, I'm evicting your arse."

Feeling her anger simmer, Rose noticed her lights flickering.

No, no, no.

"I'd appreciate it," she said through gritted teeth, "if you got your finger out of my face. I'll pay the damages. But I'd like you to leave. Please." She stepped back, opening the door.

Craig crossed his arms over his chest, glee glimmering in his eyes.

He thought he'd broken through. He thought she was afraid of him.

If only he knew she was afraid *for* him.

"What happened?" he gestured to the wall.

Rose clambered for a lie. "A ... a guy I was seeing. We argued. He did that. I threw him out. He won't be back."

She'd barely finished the lie when her landlord started moving toward her again. Rose tensed against the opened door.

At five six, with a slender, athletic build, Rose was dainty compared to this guy, and he wanted to make her as aware of that as possible. He stood so close, she could feel his breath on her face.

"Say the word, Rose," he said, touching a finger to her cheek, "and I'll protect you from arseholes like that. I might even cover the repair work on the wall, depending how good you are."

Revulsion roiled in her gut.

Every time he paid a visit, the slug propositioned her, and every time he got a little more forceful about it. What was it about her that attracted this kind of attention? It wasn't as though she was some stunning, sexy bombshell. Was it the faerie thing? Were guys attracted to her because of magic?

Images of the frat party, of Judd Grant flying across the room, flooded her.

Oh my God. She sucked in a breath. Had she attracted his attention because she was fae? And ... maybe she had killed him after all.

Horror eclipsed all other emotions.

One by one, the lights in her apartment exploded.

"What the fuck!" Craig ducked as he spun to see the last, the ceiling light, burst into pieces.

The sun had already begun to rise, so the room was merely dull, not dark.

Her landlord turned to her, a terrified, vicious look on his face, and he grabbed her by the hair, pulling her toward him. "You're a fucking witch!"

Astonishment flooded her.

He knew about supernaturals?

His grip on her hair tightened as spittle flecked from his lips. He snarled, "How the hell did I miss it?"

"Step back," Rose warned.

"Oh no, no." Craig shook his head. "I haven't come across a witch in a long time. You'll be useful to me, Rose."

Wincing at the sharp tug on her head, Rose wrapped her hand around his wrist. "I said, step back."

All she'd meant to do was tug his hand out of her hair.

That was it.

Instead, she gave it a jerk. A loud crack, followed by his scream, filled the apartment. Agony pervaded his features as he fell to his knees, clutching his broken wrist in his other hand.

Holy. Shit.

Rose stared at her hands.

Her strength ... she didn't know how to control it.

"You bitch!" Craig screamed.

The whole building would have heard, including the staff at the bakery below.

In a whirl of panic, Rose blurred across the room to the drawer by her bed where she kept her passport. Shoving her feet into her comfiest boots, she then grabbed her wallet and her phone, along with her jacket. Turning toward the door, she saw Craig was gone.

She pricked her ears and heard him stumbling down the staircase.

Damn.

Okay. You can do this, Rose. Just focus.

Concentrating on the building door, Rose blinked and she was beside it.

"Holy...," she whispered. It worked. A strange giddiness flooded her before she remembered to worry about being seen using magic. Thankfully, none of her neighbors saw her pop out of thin air. Shaking with a mix of fear and excitement, she lunged out through the building's door.

Fionn.

Fionn knew what she was and he was here in Zagreb.

Trust him or not, someone had to help her control her abilities. And maybe he could tell her if she'd killed Judd. There was still a possibility he'd had a heart defect.

God, she hoped so.

Rose concentrated on Fionn's hotel room.

Just like that, she was in the middle of a street with a tram coming right toward her!

Sidewalk!

She stumbled as she popped onto the sidewalk, fearful as people startled at her sudden appearance, staring at her like she was a ghost.

Shaking with panic now, Rose whirled, trying to get her bearings. Why hadn't she ended up in Fionn's hotel suite? Was it too far? Were there limitations?

Nearest alleyway.

She fell against a trash can, landing on her ass in the smelly alley-way. Tears glittered in her eyes. What if she'd just broken some cardinal rule about using her abilities in front of humans?

Humans.

She wasn't human anymore.

In fact, according to Fionn, she never had been.

For the longest time, Rose had felt a distance between her and everyone else ... and now she knew why. Deep down, she'd always sensed she wasn't one of them.

Shit, shit, shit.

Pushing up to her feet, hands trembling, Rose pulled the business card out of her back pocket along with her cell. Sucking in a deep breath, she dialed.

He picked up after the second ring. "Where are you?"

"From what I can guess, about five blocks from the hotel ..." She glanced around and saw a sign on an exit door. "I'm in the alley behind Bar Zubec. I, uh, a lot of people just saw me pop out of thin air."

The words barely left her mouth and Fionn Mór was in front of her.

Rose cried out, tripping over her feet and falling against the downed trash can again.

"How did you do it? I tried to 'poof' to your hotel suite from my place and ended up nearly being crushed by a tram."

Fionn's lips twitched with a surprising show of amusement. "You have natural abilities and powers, but like any gift or talent, it needs practice to stretch to its absolute limits. And *traveling* has limitations."

"*Traveling?*"

He shrugged. "To shift from place to place. We're the only beings on earth who have this ability. But you cannot think of a person and *travel* to where they are. It doesn't work like that. You *can* think of a place within the city or town you're in and go there."

Rose frowned. "It's like putting a wheel boot on a car. What's the point in having the car?"

"It can prove very useful in a fight." Fionn took a tentative step toward her. "Don't worry about being seen using the ability. Humans always rationalize these things to make sense."

"Okay."

"Does this mean you're ready to accept my help?"

Rose felt her skin prickle at his nearness, her awareness of him almost supernatural in its intensity. She tried to retreat but had nowhere to go. Lifting her chin in stubborn defiance of this weird pull toward him, she shrugged. "It seems like the logical thing to do at this point."

More amusement flickered in his cold, stunning eyes. "How you stroke my ego, Rose."

"Somehow I think you'll live." She brushed past him, needing a little distance. "So, what now?"

Fionn turned toward her, all amusement dying. "Give me your phone."

Frowning at the request but deciding if she was going to trust him she couldn't half-ass it, Rose handed over her cell.

Seconds later, as he crushed it into dust in his big fucking paw, she wished she hadn't.

"What was that?" She lunged too late for the now-nonexistent phone.

"Your phone is the first thing enemies will use to track you."

She glared at him. "I'm loving this so far. What next, oh wise one? Cut my hair, plastic surgery on my face?"

He ignored her sarcasm. "Nothing quite so drastic as that."

"Then what?"

"Now ... we get the hell out of Croatia."

7

Although Fionn traveled light, he'd left his iPad and his other suit, which the hotel had just dry-cleaned, in his suite. Anticipation thrummed through his body as his long strides ate up the sidewalk. He threw Rose a quick glance as she hurried to keep up with him. She was staring straight ahead, expression alert, her delicate chin set with determination.

A thrill of possession eclipsed the anticipation.

Rose belonged to him now. The restless animal that was his fae told him so.

She was the final key in this long road to revenge.

Fionn turned away, feeling a flicker of unease that he attributed to the once-human man he'd been. It was a shame to kill the girl. So far, she'd impressed him with how easily the fae abilities were coming to her and how quickly she was adjusting to her new reality. The truth could derail weak minds, or send humans into histrionics that lasted an interminably long time.

Not Rose, though. She'd been skeptical, as anyone would be, but with insurmountable evidence piling up, she'd accepted the truth and moved on.

Moreover, she'd told him about the encounter with her landlord and how she'd had the good sense to grab her passport before fleeing the apartment after the man declared her a witch.

Which was why they would jump on the first flight to Barcelona as soon as he'd retrieved his things from the hotel.

"Why Barcelona?" Rose asked.

Fionn turned his head and looked down at her. She stared up at him with those striking light blue eyes. Most eyes had striations of several colors in them, but Rose's only had two. The dominant color was a pale blue; slightly darker blue striations bled out from the edges of the iris. Strangely, they reminded him of Cónán, the wolf he'd raised from cub when he'd been human. When he became king, they'd called him *Rí Mac Tíre*. The Wolf King, because of Cónán. He'd been loyal only to Fionn, and eventually Fionn's family. Everyone else kept a wary distance from the wolf, and for good reason.

A small splinter in his chest made itself known before Fionn adamantly ignored it. It had been years since he'd thought of Cónán and the fae captain, Lir, who had killed him.

Before Fionn had made his escape from Faerie, he'd used An Breitheamh to end Lir. Cónán had been one of the few beings in this life Rí Mac Tíre had truly loved. He deserved justice.

Rose's question and his thoughts of An Breitheamh brought Fionn back to the moment. "There's something I need in Barcelona," he responded. "And then we'll make our way to Ireland."

Before she could question him further, Fionn's mobile rang. The screen said it was Bran. Wanting her to trust him, she had to think he was an open book. "It's my associate, Brannigan. He's a ... researcher, for lack of a better word. He keeps me informed on anything of importance regarding the underworld we belong to."

She nodded, her expression thoughtful, as she watched him put the phone to his ear.

"Hello."

"Ah, you're not alone if I'm getting a polite hello." Bran's amused voiced filled his ear.

"That is correct."

Bran chuckled. "Is it the girl? Rose? Is she with you?"

"She is." And considering she was fae, she could probably hear every word spoken between them. "I promised her I'd help. So ... do you have any word about her birth parents?"

Catching on, Bran replied with a carefulness that was probably only obvious to Fionn. "For a start, William Kelly was born Cian Cosway, and Anna Kelly was born Rhiannon O'Connor."

The vampire stressed the name O'Connor, and Fionn stopped in the middle of the sidewalk. "As in the O'Connor Coven of Dublin?"

Rose tensed beside him.

"As in the O'Connor Coven of Dublin. Rhiannon *is* Rose's aunt. Her mother was Valerie, the eldest daughter of the coven leaders and heir to the coven. *I* remember when Valerie and her husband, Lorcan, died. It was a big deal in the supernatural community because they did in fact die in a car crash. A pretty horrific one. Folks surmised at the time that it had to have all happened too quickly for such a powerful witch and warlock to have not escaped it."

Fionn watched Rose's face and saw her expression fill with sadness as she eavesdropped on their conversation. If they hadn't been in public, Fionn would have just put the bloody phone on speaker. The fact that she could hear over the noise of the traffic told him her hearing was acute.

"They must have known," Fionn said, studying his captive's features. She had a slight sprinkling of freckles across the bridge of her nose, so light he hadn't noticed them until now. A tiny sparkling blue stud pierced the right side of her small nose. With her dark hair blowing back in the gentle breeze, he saw the cuff of her right ear was also pierced in several places.

"Aye," Bran agreed. "There's no way of knowing how they worked out Rose is one of the children. Perhaps even as a newborn she showed signs. A coven like the O'Connors would know of the legends and—"

"And they'd know her life was in grave danger," Fionn cut in. "They sought to protect her."

"Not just her. The O'Connors, unlike the Blackwoods, realize how dangerous it would be to open that gate." There was more than a hint of rebuke in Bran's tone. Fionn ignored it. It wasn't like he was planning on letting the fae into this world. He wanted into Faerie. Aine had worded her spell very carefully. It allowed people to cross from Earth into Faerie to stay permanently. Which meant that gate would close behind him.

"Is there more?"

"There is." Bran sounded grim now. "If you're planning on going to Barcelona, I wouldn't take the airport out of Zagreb."

Fionn marched toward the hotel with more urgency and felt Rose hurry to follow him. "Why not?"

"Because I've hacked into the security cameras and used face recognition tech. Not only did it alert me to several known lackeys of the Blackwood Coven walking through the airport like the guard dogs they are ..."

"Lone wolves." Fionn sneered. The Blackwoods were known for paying supes to do their dirty work.

"Yep. But they're not alone. There are members of the Garm waiting at the airport. So I hacked into the train stations' security cameras, and both the Blackwoods and the Garm have supes at every one of them."

"Fuck." Fionn grabbed Rose's arm and led her toward a coffee shop. "Get me a car, Bran. Untraceable."

"Got it." Bran hung up and Fionn shoved his mobile into his coat pocket.

"What's going on?" Rose jerked against his tight hold.

"When the spell broke, it was powerful enough to be felt by the supernatural community in Zagreb. Someone talked to the Blackwood Coven and the Garm."

"And they are?"

Fionn's patience was thin but he was determined to keep up this pretense of openness to secure her trust. "The Blackwoods are a North American coven, one of the most powerful in the world. They want to open the gate to Faerie."

Rose shook her head, amazed. "It's all true, isn't it?"

Fuck, he thought they were past that. "The faster you accept that, the easier this will be."

She swallowed hard and pressed her lips together before giving him a tight nod.

"The Garm is a group raised by an ancient vampire named Eirik. He was killed six months ago ... by one of the few fae left on this world. He hated the fae, even though they were responsible for creating what he'd become. Perhaps that's why, in fact. Like me, he knew the fae saw humans as mere playthings. And he knew how dangerous it would be if the gate to Faerie was opened again. I can't explain everything here, Rose. I promise I will once we're on our way out of the country. But what I can tell you is that his group, the Garm, go on without him. Do you know much about Norse mythology?"

She shook her head. "Valkyries and stuff, right?"

He tried not to sigh impatiently as he glanced from left to right, keeping his senses alert. "The Garm was a wolf described as the guardian of Hel's gate. Hel was a goddess who resided in the realm of the same name where portions of the dead were sent in the afterlife."

"That's relevant why?" she asked.

"The Garm believe themselves guardians of the gate to Faerie. They will destroy anyone who intends to open it, intentionally or unintentionally."

"You said I'm the key ... to the gate. So the Blackwoods want to kill me to open the gate and the Garm want to kill me to *stop* me being used to open the gate?"

Fionn nodded, ignoring that incessant niggle of uneasiness in his gut. "I want you to wait in the corner of this coffee shop. I'm going to *travel* to the hotel, get my things, and meet you back here. Bran is arranging a car for us. We'll have to drive to the airport in Venice."

"But wait." She grabbed his arm. "Are you a key? Are you in danger?"

He faltered, taken aback by her apparent concern for him. Most people would shit themselves at the news there were powerful people hunting them. He gave her a slightly discombobulated shake of his head. "I'll explain later." He pulled her into the coffee shop, led her to

a table in the corner, sat her forcefully down, and ignored her penetrating stare before he stalked toward the restrooms.

Once inside a stall in the men's restroom, he focused on his hotel
suite.

It took seconds to locate his belongings, along with the garment
bag draped across his bed with his other suit. With a flick of his hand,
he could send the garment bag to his apartment in Paris, but it was
quite a bit away from Zagreb and the suit might inadvertently get
ruined in all the conjuring. He'd have to take it with him.

Everything in hand, Fionn sent a quick text to Bran telling him to
check him out of the suite since it was no longer safe for Fionn to do
so himself. Then, in a blink of an eye, he was back in the coffee shop
restroom.

Rose was still at the table where he'd left her. To his satisfaction,
her expression softened with relief when she caught sight of him.

Good. She was starting to trust him.

That's what happened when you were desperate. You trusted
where you shouldn't.

There was that inconvenient niggle again.

Rose's gaze dropped to his garment bag and then lifted to meet
eyes. "Really? You needed to grab clothing?"

He scowled. "One, it's a $3,000 suit. Two, witches and warlocks
can use personal items in spells against you."

Rose startled in panic. "My apartment."

Fionn waved off her concern. He'd already texted Bran to take
care of it. "I have someone clearing your place as we speak."

"You are efficient, aren't you?"

"No time for chitchat, Rose. We need to leave. Now."

"Are we still going to Barcelona? Why?"

"You want to know who you are? Who you really are and where
you're from? Do you want me to teach you how to use and control
your abilities?"

"Yes to all the above."

"Then I'm taking you to Ireland. But first we need to make a stop in Barcelona. Someone took something from me. Something important. And I need it back."

His phone buzzed in his pocket and he switched the garment bag to his other arm as they strode out of the coffee shop.

It was from Bran.

Apartment is swept clean.

Another text came in.

There was a street address, along with the car model, color, and license plate.

Keys are beneath front passenger wheel.

Fionn almost grinned. The boy could chat for Ireland, but fuck, he was useful.

8

Fionn was what Rose called a "viber." She wondered if he even realized how much he manipulated the vibe of the surrounding space. The tension in the car was so thick as they drove through the city in the silver car Rose's chest was tight.

His guy, this Bran person, certainly was a resourceful dude if he could whip up a car within minutes.

Rose sat in the passenger seat stewing, her own worries magnified by the tension Fionn emitted. The thing was, he didn't look tense. He was relaxed in his seat, and he wasn't constantly checking his mirrors as though someone was pursuing them. Yet Rose's pulse was racing fast and hard and her palms felt clammy, and she instinctually felt he was the cause. Beneath his cool facade, he was worried. She was certain of it.

Ridiculous, right?

That's what she thought ... until they hit the E70 highway, leaving the city behind, and Rose felt an immediate lightening of pressure on her breast. Her pulse began to slow.

Shooting an incredulous look at Fionn, she noted no change in his outward appearance or body language. But why else would she be feeling emotions that, without a doubt, felt forced upon her?

As far as she was concerned, nothing seemed unlikely anymore.

"How long will it take to get to Venice airport?" She finally felt like it was a good time to ask.

"Around four hours. If you have questions, now is a good time to ask."

She smirked at the offer. "Something tells me you're not the chatty type."

"You would be correct. But you have questions and I have answers, so I'll deal with the discomfort of conversation."

Miraculously, Rose chuckled despite the madness that had descended upon her with incredible abruptness. Fionn flicked her a curious look.

"So ... what are your questions, Rose O'Connor?"

Her scowl was immediate.

Having overheard his entire conversation with the faceless Bran, it deeply hurt Rose to discover that her mom and dad had continued to lie about who she was. Who they all were. How had they hidden that they were from a magical family all this time? With her cell gone, it would worry them when she didn't check in, but that wasn't a priority for her now. Yesterday it would have been.

Despite Fionn's subtle prodding for her to ask about the O'Connors, the first question that came to mind was something else entirely. The O'Connors could wait too.

She exhaled and turned to watch the world go by. There was a lot of open space outside Zagreb. Fields of green dotted here and there with buildings passed by at high speed while she gathered her courage to speak.

"Freshman year of college, I was attacked at a party. He grabbed me from behind and pulled me into a bedroom. He tried to rape me." It was the first time Rose had said it out loud and although she'd convinced herself over the years she was okay, suddenly she didn't feel so okay.

She'd been a victim. That much was certain now, but that word had such negative connotations. People didn't like the word *victim*. Blame somehow always found its way to a victim.

What the fuck did that even mean? If someone made you a victim, that wasn't your fault. Being a victim didn't make you weak. Rationally, she knew that. But how she felt about the incident from her past was anything but rational.

Feeling her hands tremble, Rose pressed them between her thighs. She'd never been good with weakness. She didn't know if it was the athlete in her or if it was just who she was, but her mom was always trying to tell her it was okay to show vulnerability.

Rose had never felt like it was okay. She judged no one else for it. In fact, she empathized and understood when she saw someone have a weak moment.

But weakness in herself was not something she allowed.

Telling her story made her feel vulnerable.

Lost in her thoughts, it took a moment for her to realize the air in the car had begun to swell, until it was difficult to breathe. She glanced at Fionn.

His expression was as bland as his tone. "What happened?"

Despite his stoic demeanor, Rose felt his anger. She could taste the dark bitterness of it on her tongue.

Rose struggled to breathe.

"Hey, can you cool it?" she asked on a wheeze.

Fionn frowned at her. "What did I say? What's wrong?"

"It's ... not what you're saying." Rose felt unbearably hot. "Your emotions ... you're angry. It's making it hard to breathe. He didn't rape me. I got away."

Although the heaviness diminished from the air and no longer felt like pressure on her chest, Rose sensed his confusion.

"You sense ... my emotions?" he bit out.

"Yup."

Then, like a door had been closed on a vacuum, the air in the car returned to normal with a suddenness that shocked Rose. The energy she'd felt from Fionn ... it was gone. "What did you just do?"

He glowered out at the road. "Sensing another fae's emotion is rare. It's also a violation of privacy." He cut her a dark look. "I'm masking myself from you."

Rose tried not to feel hurt by this. Why should she be? They barely knew each other.

And yet she was stung by his actions.

"You can do that?"

"As can you. You can learn to mask your energy. It takes a lot of power and can be exhausting. Finish your story."

She blinked at the demand. "Uh ..."

"What happened to the fucker who attacked you?"

"Right." Rose glanced down at her hands. "I shoved him off and he flew across the room and smacked into the wall so hard, he took a chunk out of it. I called it adrenaline and got out of there. The next day, word was the guy died of a heart defect ..."

Fionn frowned. "Do you have a question to ask?"

"Could I have done something to his heart?" She lifted her shaking hands in front of her. "I pushed against his chest ..."

The radio blasted on and frantically flipped through stations.

Her companion coolly wrapped one of his large hands around her wrist. It seemed tiny in his hold. "Calm down," he ordered. "You didn't kill the boy. The spell that blocked your abilities was extremely powerful. Your power was locked down tight."

"I know I'm stronger now, but I was strong before the spell broke. I was on track to become an Olympian. Gymnastics. My coach used to comment on my remarkable strength ... I never thought anything of it ... until now."

"Your strength is different. The spell would have been concentrated here"—he let go of her wrist to gesture to her temple—"as your abilities come from the mind. It would make it hard for the spell to suppress your physical strength completely. Why didn't you make it to the Olympics?"

Rose was surprised by his curiosity. "At sixteen I qualified as a Senior Elite and made their National Team. From that moment on, I was an Olympian in training. But that summer, my mom and dad sat me down and told me they'd adopted me. That the aunt and uncle I'd been told had died in a car accident when I was a baby were actually my birth parents. I had questions. A lot of questions. But they didn't have a lot of answers.

"At the time, they said it was because nothing had changed. I was their kid." She glared out at the passing scenery. "Now I know they couldn't give me answers without telling me the truth. Anyway, my whole life I'd felt different, but they tell you that everyone feels that way, right? I just focused on gymnastics to distract me from ..." She trailed off, feeling weird about telling this stranger something she hadn't told anyone.

"To distract you from?" When she didn't reply, it was Fionn's turn to sigh. "Who am I going to tell, Rose? I'm over two thousand years old and don't exactly maintain friendships that involve gossiping on our coffee breaks."

Rose chuckled. "A bit of a loner, huh?"

"Pot, meet kettle."

"True. Maybe it's what we are. Because we're not supposed to be here in this world."

He grunted.

"If I finish my sentence, will you tell me how it's possible a man who was once human is now fae?"

Fionn seemed to hesitate but then nodded.

Satisfied, Rose continued, "I focused on gymnastics to distract me from the feeling I'd had my whole life. The feeling that some piece of me was missing. When I discovered I was adopted, I thought that was the reason. Confused, thrown off course, I quit gymnastics. But the feeling never went away. Not until last night."

Fionn frowned. "When the spell broke?"

"Exactly."

They were quiet a moment as they drove. Rose studied him surreptitiously but somehow knew even as she did it, he was aware of her study.

His head brushed the roof of the car. He'd pushed the driver's seat back as far as it could go, and he'd dumped his coat in the back seat along with his garment bag. White shirtsleeves had been rolled up to his elbows revealing thick, muscular forearms with veins and a dusting of fair hair across them.

His waistcoat was buttoned down a strong, flat stomach, and his long, big-knuckled fingers flexed around the steering wheel now and then. He wore a chunky, Celtic-looking silver ring on the middle finger of his left hand.

Rose felt an unwelcome flip of attraction low in her belly, and not for the first time.

Every second she stared at him, she found something new to like.

Like the hard, angular edge of his jawline beneath his stubble and the contrasting softness of his lower lip. He had an exaggerated curve in the middle of his bottom lip that made a woman want to trace it with her tongue.

Fuck.

Rose looked away and immediately felt him studying her in return.

She could not develop an attraction to her would-be mentor.

"Was that your only question?"

She turned back to him, saw the coolness in his startlingly beautiful eyes before he looked back at the road, and sighed at her own nonsense.

It wasn't arrogance when Rose said she was used to attention from guys. She'd never considered herself particularly stunning, but she'd always been comfortable with her body and with sex, and she'd often wondered if that was why she received so much attention. Now she wondered if it was her fae-ness giving off a "vibe."

Anyway, Rose knew when a guy was into her.

Fionn Mór ... was so not into her.

It was probably a good thing. Getting involved with a man who was over two thousand years old sounded complicated.

To say the least.

She bit back hysterical laughter at the thought and concentrated on finding out more about her mentor. "I want to know your story. If I'm to trust you, I need to know the background so I can work out why you're helping me."

He smirked. "You don't think I'm helping you out of the goodness of my heart?"

She decided if she wanted honesty, she needed to give it in return. "No, I don't. Your motives are as yet unclear."

Fionn flicked her a quick look. "You're astute, Rose."

"Well ...?"

His big hands flexed around the steering wheel. "How to condense such a tale into the length of a car ride ..."

"Just start at the beginning."

"At the beginning ... Well, in the beginning I was just a warrior, raised in the time of clan warfare and of the invading fae. They didn't come in legions; they appeared in our world as individuals and sought to make mischief at best and to torment and kill at worst. They stole our children, killed our livestock, and rape wasn't excluded to women."

Rose sucked in a breath, wondering at the legacy she belonged to and whether she wanted to know this stuff.

"They weren't *all* bad." It sounded like those words had been dragged out of him. "I know that now, after my time on Faerie, but it was the worst of the stories that met our ears when I was human. I was raised to fight.

"I'm going to tell you something that you must never tell anyone." The look he pinned her with was dark. A little scary.

"O ... kay."

"There are only two things that can kill a fae here on earth. The first is pure iron. And it has to pierce the heart to succeed."

The fairy tales of her youth came to mind. Stories about faeries and how they were allergic to iron.

It was all true.

"Few people know the truth of that," Fionn continued. "Then again, most of the supernatural community believe the origin story is a myth."

"Origin story?"

"That vamps and werewolves evolved from fae interference in the human world."

"They did?"

He nodded. "We learned that iron hurt fae, and we began to hunt them." Grim satisfaction crossed his features. "We were making progress in the war against them, and I led the way. My father-in-law was king of where Donegal is now, but when he died, I took the mantle. I destroyed so many fae, the entire upper half of Éireann—Ireland—fell under my kingship. It was the largest kingship on the island at the time, made up of five of the ten provinces making me *rí ruirech* — a king of overkings. They called me Rí Mac Tíre." If he'd been any other man, he would have sounded wistful, but Fionn was frustratingly unemotional.

"What does that mean?"

"It means 'The Wolf King.'"

She eyed him, a small smile curling her lips. It suited him. "Why?"

"Because I had a wolf as my loyal companion. Cónán."

"How very badass." She grinned. She could absolutely picture Fionn roaring into battle with a wolf at his side.

The image was also more than kind of hot.

"Together we killed many fae. Cónán would help me weaken them, then I'd stab them in the heart with an iron blade. One day we killed a royal prince. Of course, I didn't know who he was when I was killing him ... but for his death, Aine, the Faerie Queen, led an army into our world. She wiped out half my people."

Rose drew in a breath, knowing there was no way he could be as undisturbed by this memory as he seemed to be. "I'm sorry."

"One of her captains killed Cónán. My men had fallen. And the queen took me to my knees with her power, as if I were a mere babe."

Jesus, she couldn't imagine anyone powerful enough to take Fionn to his knees.

He hesitated a moment. "We made a bargain. Her army would go back to Faerie, my people would be spared, but in return I'd give myself to the fae as a slave."

"Oh my God." Rose reeled at the idea. Forty-eight hours ago, she'd never imagined she'd be sitting in a car beside a fae, talking casually about things that had until now been relegated to fantasy novels and movies in her mind. But now that she was, now that it was real, Fionn was real. And once upon a time, this huge, powerful being had been a human—an enslaved one. "Fionn."

He seemed to jerk slightly at his name but his expression never changed as he kept his attention on the road. "I was there for six years. I met all manner of fae. Some weren't all bad but all of them were superior. They don't see humans as equals because they aren't. The fae are higher up the food chain, and that is that. Think of how humans are with animals. How they raise them for slaughter or raise them as pets. In the latter case, no matter how much affection a human has for them, people consider themselves their *owners*. Masters over them. That is how the fae view humans."

Rose curled her lip in disgust. And this was what she was? "I'll never think like that."

"Because you were raised as human. Just as I was."

She nodded, feeling melancholy about her origins. Speaking of which ... "Vampires and werewolves, they're evolved from fae?"

"From fae and humans."

"What did that vampire do to me last night? One minute I was standing in front of him, the next waking up in your hotel room."

"He broke your neck."

Rose gulped, her hand automatically curling around her throat. "What?"

Fionn's expression was formidable. "Worry not. A broken neck will not kill you. Obviously. It also will not kill vamps and werewolves. Which leads me to the second thing that can kill us. A werewolf bite. Unless he or she is your mate, a werewolf bite will kill you. So take care around them."

Holy. Crap.

Iron and werewolves. Okay then. Just two things in the whole world that could kill her. Just two.

At her continued silence he asked, "Do you still want to hear the rest?"

It would take a lot longer than a few minutes to process that she was practically unkillable! But Rose nodded anyway, afraid if he didn't tell her now, he never would.

"For centuries, since the gate had opened, there was an unexpected evolution between fae and humans. It's complicated—I can break down the fae hierarchy now or we can leave that for later?"

"Just tell me everything."

She realized then that the car was slowing and turned from watching her companion to the road. They were approaching a large toll booth.

"To enter Slovenia," Fionn explained.

"Do you need my passport?"

He shook his head. "Not anymore. Now that we know you're on radar, we don't want anyone to track you."

"So how are we getting through without ID?"

Fionn didn't respond, but she had her answer when the car pulled up to the window and the guard asked them for ID. Fionn stared intently at the guard, no words passed between them, but the guard reached out as if taking hold of a passport, flipped through two invisible items, handed them back, and then gestured them ahead as the barrier lifted.

What the ever-loving fuck?

"What just happened?" she asked as they drove into Slovenia.

"One of your talents is the ability to make humans see whatever it is you want them to see." Fionn's stare was stony. "It's a dangerous talent, Rose, and you must utilize it sparingly. Only use it to ensure your survival."

Holy crap.

She swallowed, thinking of the way the guard's face had relaxed, going blank. Mindless. She shivered. "I don't think I want to use it at all. Have you done that to me?"

He cut her an even darker look. "Fae can't use it on fae. Now where was I?"

9

Before Fionn could continue his manipulation of Rose, a crawling sensation tickled down his spine. His pulse raced while a feeling not unlike dread filled his gut.

Danger.

Rose gasped. "Fionn ... I feel weird."

He looked in his mirrors and saw a black car traveling much too quickly toward them. He pressed his foot to the accelerator and weaved through traffic. "Do you know how they say animals have a sixth sense?"

"Yeah." She turned to look over her shoulder and her lips pressed together. "We're being followed?"

"We are. And the strange feelings you just had ... never ignore those, Rose." It crossed his mind in that second that maybe he shouldn't tell her this, but if she was going to sense danger in him, she would have already. "The prickle across your neck and spine—fuck," he bit out just as he missed clipping the front of someone's car. The other driver hit their horn, hard.

"The racing heart, the dread in the gut ... they're warning signs. Of coming danger. You feel those things, you get ready to fight or to flee."

She nodded frantically. "Who's following us?"

Fionn flipped up the armrest between them where he'd put his cell. Driving with one hand, he dialed with the other and set it on speaker.

"You do know I sometimes need to sleep," Bran complained as soon as he picked up.

"We've got a tail, Bran. Who the fuck is it?"

"Shit—"

The rest of his words were garbled as the black car caught up and slammed right into the back of them with such force, it sent them careening off the highway before Fionn could prevent it. Down the embankment the car went, juddering across a field.

Rose never made a peep, just sucked in her breath and held on.

Fionn watched in his mirrors as the black car pulled off just as theirs came to a stop.

He turned to tell her to unclip her belt but she was already doing it.

"Fionn!" Bran's voice called from somewhere in the car.

Ignoring Bran, Fionn tried to manage their next move. If Rose *traveled* too far, she could end up somewhere without him. There was nothing before them but a stretch of field. But in the distance, straight ahead were trees and a cluster of houses.

It would have to do.

He pointed. "You see those trees, those houses?"

She nodded, surprisingly calm.

"Focus on them. *Travel* there. That's where I'll meet you."

"Can't you just poof us both?"

The roof of the car began to squeal as metal crunched and pulled. The air crackled with magic. "The fuckers are pulling off the roof," he groused. "And no, Rose. I can't *poof* you with me. You must do this. Focus."

She gave him a tight nod, her lips pressed thin. Then she turned, stared out at the houses and trees in the distance, and then she was gone.

Fionn followed.

He appeared behind a tree and whirled around to find Rose. She was nowhere in sight. A cool breeze ruffled his hair as he strained to listen. Nothing.

Fuck.

"Rose?" he called softly.

Still nothing.

A feeling akin to panic filled Fionn, but that couldn't be right. He hadn't felt enough for anything or anyone in centuries to inspire emotions such as panic.

"Rose?" He walked toward the house that peeked out from between the trees. His heart raced. He was so close to finally having his revenge. The thought of losing Rose now was unthinkable.

Although that didn't explain the rage he'd felt when she relayed her story of the frat-boy prick who'd tried to rape her. Then again, rape was a touchy subject for Fionn.

It reminded him that Rose had sensed his emotions. He'd only known one fae on Faerie who could do that as an actual ability. The only other people able to sense emotions in one another had been mated fae.

What was Aine thinking bestowing such a powerful ability on one of the children?

"Rose?" he bit out, growing angrier as his anxiousness increased.

A groan met his ears and he hurried toward the sound. Her scent caught on the wind and he followed that summery, light natural perfume to her.

She was sprawled in the dirt beside a tree, slowly pushing herself up.

"What happened?" He reached for her biceps and hauled her to her feet. The feel of her under his hands sent relief through him.

Rose seemed unable to meet his eyes. "I *traveled* too far and ended up in one of the houses." She gestured behind them. "I popped right out of thin air in this woman's kitchen. She started screaming bloody murder. In my panic to get out of there, I popped into someone else's house and then popped out here and collided with this damn tree."

The thought of Rose bumbling around in people's houses with her newfound abilities was strangely amusing.

Her eyes narrowed on his mouth. "Are you trying not to laugh? You think this is funny?"

The incredulity in her voice was even funnier. His mouth twitched before he could stop it and he cleared the laughter from his throat. "Of course not. We're being hunted. Why would that be fun —" Pain blasted through his upper shoulder, threatening to take him to his knees.

"Fionn!" Rose cried, lunging toward him as he stumbled.

Growling, he glared at the thick tree branch impaled through his shoulder before pushing Rose behind him and turning to face his attacker, keeping her hidden at his back.

Two warlocks, flecks of blue magic sparking at their fingertips, walked toward them through the trees, an arrogant swagger in their steps that suggested they had no idea who he was. They couldn't be Blackwood warlocks. They would know who he was and wouldn't pick a fight with a two-thousand-year-old fucking fae who could annihilate them.

Fionn took hold of the branch and pulled it out, ignoring the burn and the little flecks of splinters that broke out inside him. His fae blood would disintegrate those. The wound healed instantly, the pain gone.

The warlocks ducked as he launched the branch at them.

Fionn found himself in a difficult position. He could deal with these two permanently and possibly scare off Rose, or he could just knock them unconscious and risk them continuing their hunt.

The warlocks exchanged a wary look after studying Fionn. They'd stopped several feet away, and Fionn felt Rose move behind him as if she were trying to peek. He stepped to the side, blocking her, and when she tried the other side, he did it again.

He heard her small growl of annoyance and bit back amusement. She was a strangely entertaining female.

"What are you?" one of the warlocks asked, his accent distinctly Dublin in origin.

Suspicion niggled at Fionn.

"You drive my car off the road and stick a branch in me and expect me to answer your questions? What business am I to you?"

"Perhaps he's like Rose," the other mused.

He felt Rose tense behind him and could have sworn he tasted her fear on his tongue.

Fury that these men would frighten a woman who had been strong enough to deal with a lot so far turned his blood hot.

The other warlock, the taller and older of the two, shook his head. "You're not our business. Rose is. The woman belongs to us. Step aside and you won't get hurt."

Fionn bit back a curse. They were O'Connor Coven members. They had to be. Whether they wanted to protect her or kill her was uncertain ... although Rose had felt danger from them.

He had to be sure. He needed to know if he was now bound to protect her from two bloody covens.

"What's your business with Rose?"

He felt her small hand settle on his lower back and a surge of possessiveness almost floored him.

"That's none of your business."

That's when he felt it. The escalated heart rate, the dread in the gut.

And when she whispered his name, fear in her voice, he knew for certain Rose felt it too.

These fuckers had come to kill her.

Her own bloody coven.

"I'm sorry," he said, not sorry at all. "You shouldn't have come."

Magic crackled in the air and several branches snapped off trees as if by invisible hands. They flew toward Fionn in a shower of lethal stakes.

Fionn swiped a hand over the air in front of him, easily overpowering their magic with his own, changing the message in the energy wrapped around the stakes. They did a sharp U-turn and flew back at their senders at high speed. There was nothing they could do to stop them.

The stakes hit the warlocks with such velocity, they yanked them off their feet. One found himself impaled into a tree trunk, the other collapsed at an awkward angle. Branches stuck out all over their bodies.

It was a gruesome sight and one he wasn't sure Rose needed to see. He tried to stop her looking, but she pushed past him and then stumbled to a halt.

"Oh my God."

"That was meant for us. I just turned it back on them."

Pale, trembling, she looked up at him with horror in her blue eyes. "Who were they? The Blackwoods?"

He shook his head. "The Blackwoods know who I am—they'd approach with more caution ... I can't say for sure but I think those were O'Connor warlocks."

"My family?" She looked like she might be sick.

"There's no evidence your adoptive parents know of this, Rose. I know it's a lot to take in but we can't stay here. I need to retrieve my things from the car. Stay here. Do not move. I'll be back in seconds." Hoping she'd obey, Fionn *traveled* and appeared by the car in the field, heard the sirens in the distance, and instinctively knew they were for his wreckage.

Fuck.

He quickly retrieved his mobile, iPad, and clothing from the car and returned to Rose.

She was right where he'd left her, staring at the impaled warlocks.

His jaw flexed as he took in her pale face. Those freckles he'd barely noticed before now stood out in sharp contrast to the whiteness of her cheeks. "Rose."

Slowly, she glanced up at him. After blinking a few times, she seemed to come out of her daze. "What do we do now?"

"They must have something of yours to trace you. I had the apartment wiped clean so they must have gotten the item from somewhere else." Like her adoptive parents.

Rose frowned. "What does that mean? That they went to my

parents' house and took something ... or are you insinuating my mom and dad betrayed me?"

At her defensive tone, Fionn trod carefully. "I'm not accusing anyone of anything. In all likelihood, your parents could do nothing to stop their coven from taking something of yours."

"So ... what does this mean?"

"It means we'll have a tail until we get to Ireland. There are faerie pools near my home that have special properties. One dunk in them and it'll wipe you clean. They won't be able to trace you then."

"How?"

"I'll explain later. For now, it means we need to watch our backs, and we need to get moving."

Fionn took her small hand in his and led her out of the woods. There was no car in the driveway of the first house they approached but there was a Volkswagen Golf at the next. Fionn touched the license plate on the back of the car and concentrated on switching out a letter with another. He kept a hold on Rose as he did the same to the front license plate.

Sending electrical impulses into the mechanism with just a press of his palm to the door, he unlocked the car and ushered Rose into the passenger seat. He dumped his stuff in the back seat but kept his phone in hand.

As he got into the driver's seat, he saw the front door to the house open. A stocky man flew toward them, face scrunched with fury, but Fionn was already speeding out of the driveway. Pulling out of the small neighborhood, he turned left, and then left again, following the signs that would lead them back onto the highway.

Fionn dialed Bran with his free hand and wasn't surprised when he picked up on the first ring.

"Fionn, are you okay?" He sounded frantic.

"Fine. Two warlocks found us. They're dead. But they weren't Blackwood. I'm sure of it. I think they might have been O'Connor, and they wanted Rose dead."

Again, he swore he could feel her tension rather than merely sense it.

What the—

"I'll look into it and get back to you on that. For now, change direction. An Breitheamh went up for auction last night."

Fionn bit back an expletive.

"The Blackwoods must suspect you're going after it because they've got people at Venice Marco Polo Airport and people at El Prat airport in Barcelona. More than that, they've put in an offer. Along with a bunch of other powerful supes."

Bloody hell, it would take them weeks to get back to Ireland at this rate. "When does the auction close?"

"Four nights from now."

"Pull up train schedules from Ljubljana to Barcelona."

"Just a second ..." Fionn could hear Bran's rapid typing. "Okay, there's a train leaving in three hours for Ljubljana. It'll get you to Milan. From there you'll take a couple more trains to get to Barcelona. It's about a day's journey."

Fionn sucked in a breath. Bloody brilliant. "Buy the tickets for me and Rose. First class if you can and then email them over."

"You got it. She okay?"

Fionn flicked a look at her. Her color was returning to her cheeks, but he could tell she was lost in her thoughts. He had to hope he hadn't damaged the tenuous trust between them by killing the warlocks. "Time will tell," he answered honestly.

"Remember to feed her." Bran hung up.

Fionn dropped his cell in the open armrest as they drove through Drnovo. Ljubljana was an hour away. "Are you hungry or can you wait until we get to Ljubljana?"

"What is An Breitheamh?" she turned to him. "And why are you really helping me?"

"I told you why."

"You've killed. A lot. I can tell by the way you just brushed off their deaths like it was nothing."

Hearing the judgment in her voice, Fionn ignored the pinch in his chest that felt remarkably like betrayal and pushed down the anger she inspired. "I was a warrior. Of course I've killed. And they were there to kill us. I turned their magic back on them, nothing more."

Rose blanched.

Then, she sagged. "I know," she whispered. "I know that. I'm sorry. But ... no one helps someone out of the pureness of their heart. No matter how much they identify with them."

That unwelcome but now familiar niggle of guilt reappeared, and Fionn stuffed it down inside himself too. He'd gotten good at controlling his emotions while living on Faerie but since meeting Rose, it was getting harder. "I'm trying to protect the world from the fae," he blurted out the lie. "To understand, you need to hear the rest of the story."

He flicked a look at her and watched as she squeezed her eyes closed, her features strained with stress. "It can wait," Fionn surprised himself by saying. "Take this time to process everything that's happened. We'll pick up the story later."

10

It had taken them an hour to drive to the capital city of Slovenia and in that time, no more words had been spoken between them. Fionn had meant it when he said he'd explain everything later.

Truthfully, despite the feeling Rose got that he'd insisted on waiting for her sake, she imagined he was kind of glad for the reprieve from conversation for a while too. He seemed more comfortable with silence.

Once in Ljubljana, Fionn abandoned the car near the train station, and Rose pondered when it became okay to her she was his accomplice in murder and theft. It seemed her survival took precedence over morality. What disturbed her most was how quickly—not easily—she defended Fionn's actions.

Those warlocks were sent to kill her, and Fionn had saved her.

She felt sick to her stomach every time she saw their deaths again in her mind, but it was either her or them. Right?

Thinking perhaps Fionn would find somewhere private at the station to tell her the rest of the story, Rose was bewildered when he settled them in a dark corner of a café and said nothing while they waited for their train. At the nightclub, people had stared at him. He was a huge guy—it wasn't a surprise.

But people weren't staring, and it made no sense. Fionn was someone you stared at.

"Why is no one looking at you?"

He quirked an eyebrow.

She shrugged. "You're kind of hard not to look at."

After a moment of studying her, expression typically blank, he relayed, "It's a trick. If I don't want to be noticed, I cast an illusion. I become nondescript, of no import, to the people around me."

Rose's pulse increased as she tallied up his list of talents. "Can I do that?"

"In time, you'll learn how."

"You didn't do that at the club. I noticed you right away."

"There was no reason. I wasn't being followed. I was following Niamh. And she knew I was coming, anyway."

Rose nodded, and they fell into companionable silence.

Now and then their gazes would meet and hold. Butterflies fluttered in her belly and a hot tingling sensation gathered between her legs as those green eyes wandered over her face. Her reaction to him was inexplicable considering how unreadable his cool expression was.

"Are we safe?" Rose eventually asked.

Fionn gave a slight shake of his head. "We're not being followed. You'll sense that like last time. But that doesn't mean you're safe, Rose. You'll understand soon."

Soon crawled toward Rose, her patience wearing. Without Fionn's storytelling, she was left to think about her parents and how they had lied to her about her very existence. Then there was the possibility they'd betrayed her to their coven. Fionn suggested they wouldn't have had a choice.

Still, she was furious.

If they loved her, they'd be worried sick unable to contact her. She hated that idea, but, unfortunately, even if she was ready to talk, it was now too dangerous.

To her relief, a few hours later, Fionn stood and gestured for her to follow him. They boarded one of the first-class carriages of a train bound for Milan with the e-tickets Bran had emailed. They sat opposite each other, a small table between them. First, Rose watched Fionn lay his coat and garment bag across the luggage rack above them, not having to stretch to reach the damn thing. Then she tried not to smirk at the way he attempted to fold his large body into the seat. His knees hit the table.

"You can sprawl your legs out toward me. I don't mind."

He stared at her a second and then did just that.

She felt his right leg brush her left one. She looked away so he wouldn't see her reaction and guess at how hyperaware of him she was.

More silence descended upon them as they waited for the train to leave. The first-class carriage wasn't full, but Rose wondered how Fionn could continue his story with so many ears listening in.

Just as she was about to ask, Fionn stood, his balance perfect against the slight rocking of the train, and reached into the pocket of his coat. The air tingled with magic a second before he pulled something out of the pocket and sat back down. His legs brushed hers again. He then placed folded-up black headphones on the table between them.

Rose felt a shiver of magic again as he covered the headphones with his hand, feeling that wave of hot energy envelop her. The noise of the train and of the other passengers quietened, dulling to a barely perceptible hum in the background. "What did you just do? Where did these come from?" she asked.

Fionn lifted his hand off the device and gestured to it. "I conjured them. They're noise-canceling headphones. I've just ... expanded their reach. We can't hear them." He gestured to the other passengers. "And they can't hear us."

Staring at the headphones, Rose felt a thrum of excitement. Despite the craziness of her new existence, of the horror she'd seen magic do, she couldn't help but find these abilities pretty damn cool. "That's brilliant."

"Are you ready for the rest of the story?"

If her own coven wanted her dead, then whatever she was, whatever she'd been born for, had to be ominous. Still, Rose had to know. "Tell me."

"I was about to explain the hierarchy before those warlocks tracked us down. It can get confusing, so tell me if you need me to repeat anything."

"I think I'm smart enough to follow."

"I meant no offense."

"And I take none. I just don't need anything mansplained to me."

He smirked, and Rose felt an answering flutter in her belly. She wondered what he looked like full-out smiling. She bet his handsomeness was blinding. Right then she wished for the ability to make him grin. "How about faesplained?"

Surprise brought amusement to the corners of her mouth. "Did you just crack a joke?"

"If you have to ask, then clearly I failed."

His dry tone made her laugh. "Faesplain away, Fionn."

The fae gave her a sardonic nod. "You have the queen, her name is Aine, and below that are her royal subjects, below them the aristocracy, below that a middle class, and below them, peasantry. Aine lives in Samhradh Palace among the fae courtiers of the Samhradh Royal House. Colloquially, they're referred to as the Day Lands because they live in a part of Faerie that never grows dark and is in constant summer. And among them live princes, princesses, lords and ladies, their servants, and, once upon a time, their human slaves.

"On the other side of Faerie is Geimhreadh Palace, ruled over by a Geimhreadh prince of the Geimhreadh Royal House. It is known as the Night Lands as they live in constant darkness.

"Between these two are the countries ruled by the Earrach and Fómhar Royal Houses, called the Dawn and Dusk Lands. The royals are powerful fae who rule over a slightly less powerful aristocracy, and even less powerful middle and peasant classes.

"When the fae first invited humans to Faerie, the royal houses began to play games with them. This led to supernaturals. A new species first came to be when a courtier of the Geimhreadh House was fighting over a human woman called Isis with a member of the Samhradh House. In their fight, the woman was killed, and the fae of Geimhreadh tried to heal her with his blood. This was forbidden."

Rose was so enthralled by his story, it took her a minute to realize he'd hesitated. "Why? Why was it forbidden to heal her with his blood?"

Fionn frowned. "They discovered when they started invading our world that their blood healed humans. In *our* world. However, on Faerie, like I said, magic is different. It's *more*. Humans reacted to it differently because there's a wildness to it there, an instability. So ... it *changed* the human instead. Isis was the first vampire. She would live forever, like the fae, as long as she drank blood and no one killed her. Side note: she was hunted by vampire hunter after vampire hunter in the twelfth century and one eventually killed her.

"But back to Faerie. Aine allowed it to stand, to let Isis live, despite the danger she posed. But the other houses were angry. Samhradh House," he said, curling his upper lip, "cast a spell over Isis so a wooden stake, a weapon of nature, could kill her. And the greatest weapon they spelled against her was the earth's sun. It was amusing to them to take a creature of the Night Lands and trap her in eternal night. They sought to make Isis the antithesis of nature.

"What they didn't see coming was her ability to bite and turn other humans into vampires. But as she did, the spell they'd cast over her transferred to those she'd turned. They're not dead like the myths would have people believe. They eat and drink things other than blood, but they need blood so they don't starve. Unlike wolves, vampires are immortal, yet they have their weaknesses. On Faerie, vampires were unaffected by the sun, but on Earth, they can only come out at night. And the earth's sunlight turns them to ash.

"That was the beginning of the worst of the games meted out on humans," he said, his bitterness finally betraying emotion. "They used humans to distract them from their pitiful, empty eternal lives.

"When a shapeshifting fae, a rare species among the Day Lands, bit a human while wolf and accidentally transferred her gift to the human man, the werewolf was made. The Night Lands remembered what Day did to Isis, and they spelled the wolf. While vampires were controlled by the earth's sun, they made sure the full moon would control the werewolves.

"Moreover, the fae wore jewelry as symbols of their houses. Geimhreadh House wore silver. Samhradh wore all precious metals and stones but usually fashioned to look like leaves and trees. Earrach wore gold, and Fómhar House, copper. Because Samhradh fashioned a weapon for the vampires from wood, Geimhreadh fashioned a weapon for the wolves out of silver. A werewolf can heal from almost any injury if he or she shifts. But if a wound is inflicted by silver, it'll leave a scar at best, kill at worst."

"Holy crap," Rose whispered, staring wide-eyed at him. "Do you have a *Guide to Faerie* I could borrow?" Momentarily, she forgot she'd asked him not to mansplain.

To her shock, Fionn almost smiled. "I told you it's a lot to take in."

She stared at this huge warrior fae, thinking of him stuck in another world as a human slave. "What happened to you there? How did you escape?"

The ghost of his smile died. "I was there for six years as the queen's slave. I learned much. Even befriended some fae."

"Really?"

"It was hard to trust them, but I watched. Always watching. Trying to figure out their natures. There was a princess of Samhradh house who was gentler than the others. She'd taken in a little human girl who'd been stolen into Faerie and was raising her. She loved her. I began to trust the princess a little, and she began to trust me.

"One day when she was summoned to the palace on royal business, I got word that a Samhradh courtier the princess had spurned was intent on taking from the child what he couldn't take from her."

Rose's stomach lurched. "Oh my God."

"I was still human. I knew there wasn't a lot I could do in a fight, so instead I took the child before he could get to her, and I hid her. The princess learned at court what was happening and returned to protect the child only to discover I'd already seen to her protection. From that point on, she felt she owed me a debt.

"Days before an annual festival was to be held in Solas, the capital city of Samhradh, the Queen's Seer had a vision. Humans had discovered fae blood healed them and, as you know, humans are obsessed with the idea of immortality. We were on the brink of a war that would decimate the humans. Aine was afraid. I could see it in her eyes, and I'd never seen her afraid before. She was afraid for Earth but more than that, she was afraid that during the war, she'd lose her own people to the humans. Not through death, but through allegiance."

"What do you mean?"

"Humans talk of soul mates," Fionn said, his green gaze blazing, "but it's just a romantic notion. On Faerie, it isn't. They are literally destined for one other fae. Not all meet their soul mate, but when they do, the bond that connects them is something ... cosmic. Something that cannot be broken. Something beyond any fae, even the queen. Once they meet and know each other, they love forever."

Rose frowned. She'd never met anyone she'd want to be with forever and as such, the idea was a foreign one. "That sounds ... nice?"

"It makes them fools," he muttered. "Anyway, something had happened that no one saw coming, not even Aine. Something that could not be explained. The mating bond began to forge between supernaturals and fae. Vampires and fae, werewolves and fae, druids, and fae ... soul mates. The problem with that was there were supernaturals who still clung to their human past. Like Eirik."

The name was familiar. Rose scanned the overwhelming information Fionn had provided over the last few hours. "The vampire who was the leader of the Garm? The group who are hunting the fae kids?"

"The very one. His brother Jerrik and he were made vampires, and Jerrik loved the fae. He had a mating bond with a fae princess. Eirik, on the other hand, despised the fae for what they were doing to humans. He also fancied me."

"Unsurprising," she answered honestly. There was no point hiding the fact she thought he was attractive. He had to know how hot he was. "But why is it relevant?"

"It's relevant because when Aine's seer told her about the coming war with the humans, Aine began to plan. Being the slave she was most ... fond of ... I was privy to those plans." He exhaled. "She would close the gate. Permanently. Before she did, she would send back all the humans and supernaturals to Earth, even those who'd mated to the fae. But she liked her games. She wasn't wicked enough to wish the decimation of an entire world, but she was just cruel enough to want to imagine them twisting themselves into knots, warring with one another over the centuries, for a shot at eternity.

"So she announced her plans at the festival. Without giving the supernaturals a chance to process it, she told them she was sending them back to Earth and she told them why. But she also told them she'd cast a spell. I remember every word: *'As I close the gates, I will cast a spell out into the human world. In time, that spell will come to fruition in the form of seven children, born to human parents, but faeborne. Seven children and with them the ability to open the gate.'*

"Whoever used the children's blood to open the gate would be welcomed into Faerie where they could live among them forever."

Rose let go of the breath she'd been holding. Strangely, tears burned her eyes. "That's what I am? Part of a spell?"

"Yes. That's what you are."

"And you ... how are you fae?"

"Because the queen was not above flexing the rules to suit herself. Aine is queen for a reason, Rose. There's another continent on Faerie where truly dark creatures are said to live. A millennium before we even knew of Faerie, they fought a war there and Aine rose to incredible power because she could wield magic like no other. There were no limits for her. And she used it to expel the dark creatures, to banish them to another part of their world. She became queen and has remained queen because of that power. Power she used to turn me fae."

Why? Why would she turn Fionn fae? Unless ... "My God, was she in love with you?"

He gave a huff of dark laughter, surprising the heck out of Rose. His laugh was a deep, delicious rumble of wickedness. "Aine doesn't know what love is. Not really. She is ... possessive. She turned me fae so she could keep me, yes, but also because I'd never shown her true subservience. To punish me for it, she made me the thing I despised the most."

Rose ached for him. "Fionn ..."

For the first time, Rose saw him smile, and although it was wicked, it made her breath catch. Attraction enveloped her completely. Rose knew she'd never felt this aware of anyone before ... and of course, it would have to be with the most unattainable being on the planet.

His smile disappeared, a muscle flexing in his strong jaw. "I was smarter than she thought. I'd made alliances where she did not know. I was too late to avoid the spell that made me fae, but I wasn't too late to get the hell out of there and back to my people. The Queen's Seer was second in line when it came to power. There was rivalry between her and the queen, although she technically worked for Aine. I used that against Aine. I became the seer's lover behind Aine's back."

Lucky faerie. Rose felt more than a flicker of envy toward the seer.

"I convinced the seer to tell me what I'd need to do to get the hell out of Faerie. She never imagined I'd be able to leave undetected, so she told me. All I needed was to attach myself to someone who had feelings for me and hated the fae. That level of emotion would be powerful enough to bind us when Aine sent that person back."

"Eirik?" Rose guessed.

"I don't fancy men, but that never stopped him from admiring me from afar. And I knew he hated the fae. So, I went to the princess who owed me a favor, and although she was frightened, she cast an illusion spell over me. It allowed Eirik to see through it while others didn't. When Aine cast her spell to send us back to Earth, he let me hold on to him."

"And that was it. You were home?"

"She sent them all where they'd come from. Eirik and Jerrik belonged to a Germanic tribe near what is now Denmark. As fae, however, it didn't take me long to get back to Éireann."

Rose considered the glimpses of bitterness that had slipped past his stoic demeanor. "I sense this story doesn't have a happy ending."

His tone was as bland as ever. "My people despised what I'd become, but out of loyalty for what I'd once been, they didn't kill me. Druids from all over Britannia had come to Éireann to fight the fae, and they gathered now to cast a powerful spell over me. They put me into a dreamless sleep and buried me in the earth."

Horror suffused Rose and the agitation she felt over this, over what they had done to him, a man who was practically a stranger, seemed out of proportion. "Death would have been kinder," she bit out.

Fionn shot her a curious look. "Are you angry for me, Rose?"

"Of course! Treacherous bastards."

"Aye. That they were."

"What happened? Obviously, you woke up."

"The Blackwood Coven. They found druid stones with my story carved into them in old Gaelic. Our language then was cruder, but they eventually worked out that the legends passed down through the centuries about an Irish warrior king turned fae were true.

"They knew about the gate from a journal written by Jerrik. They wanted to reopen it. So they spent decades trying to find me. Finally, in 1726, they unearthed me. Two years after that, they broke the spell and woke me up."

"You've been awake for nearly three centuries?"

"That I have." His expression was too deadpan for someone who had suffered through what he had. Rose had never met anyone with such control over their emotions, but it had to be bullshit. There had to be a well of simmering resentment and hurt and betrayal buried beneath his cool facade. Otherwise, he was the most well-adjusted being in history. Somehow, Rose doubted it.

"The first five years I spent learning all I could about the history of the world, from my burial to my awakening. That was the most unsettling part. Playing catch-up and seeing how far the world had progressed in my absence. Learning new languages, coming to terms with my powers, and honing them. The next three centuries of progress leapt ahead at an alarming rate."

Rose was quiet a moment. "If the Blackwood Coven saved you, why aren't you working with them?"

"Because they intend to open the gate, and I don't want that to happen."

"Then why aren't you trying to kill me?"

He frowned at her. "Because I know what it's like to be something that was forced upon you. Why should you die for that? And there's only two things that can kill you, Rose, and a bastard needs to get close enough to do either. So, I will teach you how to protect yourself because once you know what you're fully capable of, no one will get close enough to put iron through your heart."

11

As Fionn's vow echoed across the table between them, he almost wished it were true. He had a low tolerance for most people—a misanthropist made, not born—but Rose was surprisingly likable. She'd handled her new reality with amazing strength, with an open mind, and with humor. Moreover, she could sit with him in comfortable silence without feeling the need to fill it. Fionn liked this about her.

He liked too much about her.

In fact, it was a damn shame it had to be her.

"I don't know what's weirder ...," Rose said. "The fairy tale you just told me or the fact that I believe it. I might not have believed it if I hadn't discovered my powers ... or if I hadn't seen those warlocks die."

Fionn nodded, refusing to feel guilty for the O'Connors' deaths. Regret was no longer in his vocabulary.

"So ... that brother and sister from the club. Are they a witch and warlock?"

Niamh and Ronan Farren. For the last few years, Fionn had followed the psychic and never gotten close enough to know her name. "No, Rose. Niamh is one of the fae-borne."

Her stunned silence followed by her crestfallen expression made him frown. "What is it?"

"She's practically family, right? I wish I'd known."

"I don't know if she can be trusted," he lied. "I've been following her activities over the last few years, and several children have died after meeting with her."

"How many are dead?"

Fionn hesitated, wondering how much he should tell her. He'd already omitted pivotal facts in the story, but that was so she wouldn't draw the wrong conclusions. Or, the right ones.

Finally, he decided telling her the truth in this case wouldn't hurt. In fact, it might push her even further into his confidence, fully understanding the danger she was in. "There are only three of you left. A girl was killed almost a decade ago when she was sixteen. Two boys were killed a few years after that within the space of a year. All by Eirik. Another fae-borne wasn't killed—she was turned into a werewolf by her mate."

"Uh ... what?"

He'd done more talking in the last few hours than he had in his entire life. Fuck, it was exhausting. Still, for the good of his revenge ... "Her name is Thea. A werewolf with remarkable tracking abilities was engaged to hunt her, but when he found her, they discovered they shared the mating bond. Rumor has it she was stabbed in the heart by iron but as she was dying, her mate bit her, and she turned."

"I could get bit by a wolf and I'd no longer be fae? I thought you said a werewolf bite can kill us?"

It was difficult to know how much to tell this woman that would secure her trust but wouldn't make her knowledge a problem for him and others.

"Fionn?"

"She was being hunted by the Blackwoods. Her pack lied and said she'd always been wolf, but they suspected it was a lie. If I give you this knowledge and they find evidence of the truth, they'll start a war with Thea again."

"I wouldn't put someone who's the equivalent of my sister in danger."

He frowned. "You think of them as such? As siblings?"

"We're cast from the same spell, right?"

"Aye, but you're not related."

"We're bound in a way that's more powerful than mere DNA. Do you know where she is?"

"It's too dangerous to go to her." To distract her from that notion, he continued, "There are legends about the mating bond but now I'm the only one left who knows whether they're true. And I'm about to trust you with that truth. Don't betray my trust."

"I won't. I promise."

Only time would tell. Fionn wouldn't hold his breath.

It had been a long time since he'd trusted someone with information about the fae. He was only divulging it to Rose because he needed *her* to trust *him*. "The truth is a fae cannot turn from just any vampire or werewolf bite. That's not how vamps and wolves were made in the first place. Their fae mates made them. It can only be returned by their mate."

"Wait ... are you saying that if I found my mate and he was a vampire or werewolf, his bite could turn me into what he is?"

"Exactly." He cut her a dark look. "Be careful with this information, Rose. Not because it's likely you'll ever find your mate here on Earth but because of the danger it poses to Thea." Fionn might be a bastard who was luring Rose to her death, but there was no need for Thea to be dragged back into this war now that she was free of it. He'd never met the fae turned wolf, but if the stories about her were true, she was a rare breed, worthy of respect and deserving of peace.

"How is it not likely?"

"Mating bonds aren't something that occur here. It happened for Thea because she's fae."

"*I'm* fae."

"Yes." *But the likelihood of you being around long enough to find your mate is slim.* "It's a miracle she and Alpha MacLennan met. I don't want you getting your hopes up."

She snorted. "My hopes up? If you knew anything about me, Fionn, you'd know I'm more of the love 'em and leave 'em type, anyway."

An image of Rose naked and riding atop him filled his mind before he could stop it. Her eyes dark with lust and desire would be an extraordinary thing to see. Heat pooled in his loins, and he shoved the thought straight back out.

What the fuck was that?

"You said Niamh can't be trusted. Why?"

Niamh. Niamh Farren.

The thought of her cooled his hot blood.

Discombobulated by his wayward thoughts, he concentrated on Niamh.

When he was human, his clan name had been Ó Faracháin, the modern equivalent of which was Farren. As soon as Rose told him the name, his suspicions took root.

While they'd waited at the coffee shop at the station, Fionn had sent the names to Bran to see what he could find—his gut was telling him that the fucking Faerie Queen had made sure one of the fae children was Fionn's bloody descendant. It would make sense that Niamh was the one he'd been obsessed with following. Until he'd found Rose.

"Fionn?"

Rose's voice wrapped around his name like a gentle hand around his nape, drawing him out of his concerned thoughts.

"Why can't she be trusted?"

"There's no way of knowing if she's leading enemies to the fae-borne to have them taken out. She's psychic, Rose. It will be very hard to catch her because she sees her enemies coming. But if she doesn't want that gate to open, she could make sure those who want you all dead do indeed find you. She's the reason I found you."

A frown puckered between Rose's slim brows. The thought upset her.

Silence fell between them for a while, and Fionn found he

couldn't stop looking at her. There was something magnetic about Rose.

Fionn had a type. The woman he bedded all looked like Aoibhinn. Any sane man would do the opposite, yet nearly all his lovers had her red hair, full mouth, and full figure.

Rose was the opposite. Dark hair, pale skin, blue eyes, an athletic figure, small, perky tits, and her mouth wasn't full and lush. It was an intriguing mouth, nonetheless. Her upper lip was slightly fuller than the lower, giving her an upside-down pout.

Rose looked up from staring thoughtfully at the table, and he felt like he'd been caught doing something he shouldn't. She didn't seem to be aware of his perusal.

"Why are you helping me?" she repeated.

"I already told you why."

"And it was a very altruistic answer. I want the real answer."

Fionn felt a hot glow in his chest. Admiration, perhaps. Respect, even.

Guilt too.

The guilt he squashed.

Centuries he'd waited for this. No one, and certainly not a slip of a woman like Rose, would get in his way.

"I told you: I won't see you or the others killed for something that was *done* to you. I will help you, and the others when I find them, to control your powers so you can protect yourselves against those who would use you to open the gate. But make no mistake, Rose," he continued his lie, "if you or the other two try to open the gate, I'll be there to stop you."

It was a gamble to threaten her.

Yet it did the trick.

He watched her relax in her seat as if she understood him now.

"Fionn," she said, her voice soft. "I would never do that. I want to protect this world too. Tell me what to do."

Her sincerity pierced the hardness around his heart when sincerity in others usually elicited nothing but his disdain.

Fuck, he thought regretfully, *why did it have to be her?*

❧

FIRST CLASS CAME WITH A MEAL, and Rose descended upon the pasta dish with relish. She hadn't realized how hungry she was. Between bites, she watched Fionn eat, a little surprised to see that he needed to. She was beginning to think of Fionn as a godlike being who didn't need to deal with basic human needs such as eating and drinking.

And using the restroom.

But he did.

When he saw the guy coming to take their lunch order, Fionn had lowered the spell that blocked their conversation from other passengers and put the headphones away. The spell was still down as they settled into their seats. They'd only been on the train three hours. After he'd told his story, Fionn had fallen into silence. Rose had discerned correctly; he wasn't much of a talker beyond mandatory explanations.

The silence, however, was not awkward between them. It was comfortable.

"There's another four hours to go," he said, glancing out the train window. They traveled along the Adriatic coast, and the late afternoon sun glistened across the sea. "Perhaps get some rest. We have a two-hour wait in Milan."

Usually this would suit Rose. She was used to sleeping during the day because of her job, but now she was too wired. "I'll rest on the train to Barcelona."

He shrugged like it made no difference to him.

"So I'm immortal, right?" It sounded crazy saying that out loud.

"Yes."

"When do I stop aging and changing?"

"You already have. From what I gathered from my time on Faerie, the fae stop developing once they reach adulthood. Roughly twenty-one, twenty-two years old."

Huh. Rose let this sink in. No wrinkles for her, then. That was pretty cool.

Speaking of which ...

"When can we start training?" She was itching to learn to control her powers but also to see what she was capable of. The last thing she wanted was for Fionn to hide her behind him again like he'd done in the woods with those warlocks. Rose hated depending on anyone for anything, and that most definitely included her survival. "I need to take care of myself."

Fionn studied her a moment and then stood. "Wait here."

She frowned, watching as he disappeared out of their carriage. What the hell? She sat for several minutes wondering what he was doing and if he was coming back.

Of course, he was coming back, she scolded herself. The dude was trying to save her life and the world at the same time.

When Fionn reappeared, Rose breathed a sigh of relief. "Where did you go?"

Instead of answering, he gestured for her to follow him. "What about your stuff?"

"What stuff?" He waved a hand over his belongings and the air shimmered as shadows from the dark corners of the train crept over the items, camouflaging them.

A swift grin replaced Rose's concerned frown. "That is very cool." She looked to him from the items and found him watching her.

Something like amusement flashed across his expression.

But it was gone so quickly, Rose wondered if she'd imagined it.

Rose followed him out of the carriage and through several others. He halted when they entered an empty carriage. He turned to her. "Let's train."

The thought was both scary and exhilirating. "Here?"

"Where's better to train than on a train?"

She grinned. "Are you cracking jokes again?"

"Again, if you have to ask ..."

Glancing around at all the empty seats, Rose's smile slipped. Suspicion formed in her mind. "Why is this carriage empty?"

"I encouraged the occupants to move elsewhere. No one will disturb us here."

"By encourage, do you mean that mind-control crap?"

Fionn shrugged.

Shrugged.

Unease moved through Rose. "You said it was only to be used in a life-or-death situation."

"This whole situation is life or death, Rose."

She glared at him.

He sighed. Heavily. "You need to practice if you want to learn to defend yourself. I made it so you could. Unless you're happy to stand behind my back and let me protect you."

Anger suffused her at the taunt.

Fionn nodded. "I thought not."

"I don't like it," she told him. "The other abilities are exciting. But that mind thing—it seems wrong."

"Because it is. But you live in a new world now, and you must make decisions, choices, that won't sit well with you. That's your new reality. Or are you okay that I killed two warlocks to save your life today?"

As if on cue, Fionn's cell rang, thankfully saving her from answering his complicated question. The question was simple; its answer was complicated.

He pulled the phone out of his back trousers pocket. "Bran," he told her before hitting a button. "You're on speaker with me and Rose."

Bran's voice filled the empty carriage. "No humans listening in?"

"No."

"Sorry it took a few hours but my contact at the coven needed further incentive to divulge the info we need."

"Pay them whatever they want," Fionn acceded.

"Already suspected you'd say so and already did." He released an exhalation. "Rose, I'm sorry, but the two warlocks who came after you were in fact O'Connor warlocks. My contact relayed your story. Are you ready for it?"

She wasn't sure but she nodded mutely anyway.

Fionn replied, "She's ready."

"Each baby in the O'Connor Coven is put before a psychic. The

O'Connors have held a line of psychic witches in their coven dating back to the fourteenth century. Anyway, the psychic got a vision of what you were, so the coven gathered around you, felt your power, and brought your case before the equivalent of a high court to decide your fate. It should be noted they did this without informing the European High Council of your existence.

"Anyway, your parents pled for you to live. In the end, the majority decided to cast a spell that would suppress your powers. However, it was under the proviso that if the spell ever broke ... they'd sentence you to death, Rose."

Nausea welled inside her.

"They forbid your parents to leave Dublin with you, but when they died in a car accident and your aunt became your guardian, she had a different notion. You see, your mam was the eldest daughter of the coven leader and as such raised to be a leader, but her younger sister, Rihanna, whom you know as Anna, was a typical rebel. Apparently, she constantly disobeyed her family's wishes, including marrying Cian Cosway, whom you know as Bill. Cosway was coven-less and considered too common for the daughter of an O'Connor. Anna married him behind their backs.

"Once they became your guardians, Anna and Bill cast a spell that allowed them to flee Ireland. They took you to the States under a false identity, and they've been in hiding from the coven ever since.

"But when the spell on you broke, the entire coven felt it."

Her mom and dad hadn't betrayed her.

They'd been trying to protect her all this time. She looked over at Fionn, tears blurring her vision. "My mom and dad ... are they safe?"

Bran answered. "According to my warlock, they're still in hiding. The coven doesn't know where they are, but they're not a priority for them. The priority is finding you."

"Then how are they tracing Rose?" Fionn asked. "I assumed they were using personal items from her home back in the States."

"Apparently, you left a jacket behind at the Zagreb nightclub, Rose. That's what they're using. But the witch who has the jacket is relaying your position to others coming after you. They don't want to take the chance that the jacket will fall into your hands during a confrontation with the coven."

"How many are following us?"

"They've sent out a witch and warlock. They don't know where you're going, only where you are, so they're following by road. The problem occurs when you stop too long in one place."

Fionn stared impassively at Rose as she fought back tears of relief. "We need to destroy that jacket if we can."

"What do you want me to do?"

"Offer your informant double what you've paid them to take out the witch with the jacket and burn the damn thing."

Uneasiness swamped Rose. This was no longer defense playing. This was offense.

It felt like war.

"Because it is a war," Fionn said softly.

Had she spoken out loud?

"Aye," he replied. "I'm not a mind reader, Rose."

"Fionn," Bran said, his voice cutting through their staring contest. "Just a reminder—the Blackwoods are using Barcelona as a trap."

"I'm aware I have two covens on my arse, Bran," he said. "Anything else to report?"

"Not at the moment."

"Thank you, Bran," Rose said before Fionn could hang up.

"No problem. I'm sorry my news is so fucking dismal."

"It wasn't," she promised him. "It's good to know my parents have been trying to protect me and that they're safe."

Fionn hung up before Bran could reply.

"That was rude," she huffed.

He ignored her and took a few steps down the carriage in her direction. "We can leave training to later. Your mind might not be in the right place now."

Rose straightened. "No, I can do this. I want to ... but ..."

"But?"

"I need to let my parents know I'm okay. I don't want them traveling to Europe and getting caught up in this when they could be safe at home in the States."

Fionn let out another heavy sigh and then began typing on his phone.

"What are you doing?"

"Asking Bran to keep checking on your parents. If they make a move, we'll get a message to them."

Rose felt her whole body relax. Gratitude swamped her. "Thank you. I know you're helping me for reasons bigger than me, but thank you."

He frowned and strode to the other side of the carriage. He turned to face her again, his expression blank. "Don't thank me. Let's practice."

Bracing her legs to face him, Rose's body thrummed with anticipation. "Okay. How?"

"Sometimes, as much as it sticks in the craw, it's better to hide than to fight. The more supes you fight, the greater the likelihood of them discovering you're not a witch but fae. Witches can't *travel*, for a start." Fionn gestured beyond her. "What I did to my belongings, you're going to do now to yourself."

Confused, Rose blinked rapidly. "Uh ... say what, now?"

"It's a trick that works best at night; you can pull the shadows of the dark to you, to hide, to walk undetected. The shadows also cloak any noise you make."

"Seriously?"

Fionn nodded. "It's a fae talent that was passed onto vampires too. Concentrate on the shadows. Reach out to them with your mind and imagine pulling them over you like a hooded cloak."

Rose closed her eyes and saw the shadows in her mind's eye. She did as Fionn instructed and imagined tugging shadows toward her. Tingles prickled all over her skin at the telltale sign of magic.

"Concentrate, Rose."

She nodded and focused on the magic, turned that magic into hands and reached out into the carriage to gather the shadows. She pulled on them and felt something physically give way.

"What the ..." She stumbled back.

"Keep going," Fionn ordered.

Rose centered herself and repeated the process. This time when she felt the shadows peeling away from their natural positions in the carriage, she kept going. She kept going until she felt them surround her like a cloak.

They felt like dark ghosts on her skin; it wasn't the most pleasant feeling.

Opening her eyes, she saw Fionn through a veil of black.

"Well done."

With a tilt of her head, she let go of her hold on the shadows and they crawled away from her, back to where they'd come from.

Fionn nodded, something like satisfaction on his face. "You're a quick learner."

She smiled. "That was creepy, but cool."

His mouth twitched. "Everything is cool to you."

"False. There are many things, including modern slave labor, that are very uncool to me. Magic ... magic is fucking cool."

"Magic is dangerous. It isn't a gift. It's a burden."

She frowned in response to his clipped admonition and intimidating glower. "If you want to see it that way, go ahead. But I'm going to embrace 'the cool.'" She rubbed her hands together in gleeful anticipation. Discovering her abilities was just the distraction she needed from the scarier parts of her new life. "What's next?"

12

Telekinesis was next. Fionn first taught her a kind of self-meditation for her to begin to "become one" with her magic by fusing the magic with the wants and desires of her mind and body. If he wanted to pick up a knife that was too far from his reach, magic became his hands.

This took a little longer than the shadow business. But according to Fionn, Rose still grasped the ability with amazing speed. It had taken him weeks to master his abilities as fae, but by the end of two hours of training, Rose moved Fionn's cell phone up off a table and sent it to him without dropping it or throwing it against a window.

It was pretty bashed up by that point.

"Maybe we should've used something a little less expensive," she'd suggested as Fionn led her back to their carriage.

"Don't worry about it."

Rose decided not to. If the man could afford $3,000 suits, suites in five-star hotels, and first-class travel tickets, she assumed he could afford to replace his cell.

They'd gotten back to their seat just as a waitress came around with an evening snack. Rose took the sandwich with enthusiasm. She felt like she'd just spent hours practicing a floor routine.

Fionn watched her wolf down the food and pushed his sandwich toward her. "It takes a lot out of you at first."

She'd waved off his offer even though she could've eaten his too. "A big guy like you needs to eat."

He'd given her his hard-won lip quirk. "I'll survive. Eat, Rose."

Grinning at him in thanks, she took the sandwich and decimated it in seconds. Not long later, the train pulled into Milano Centrale. According to Fionn, their next train wasn't for another hour.

Despite her night-shift body clock, the lack of sleep and the miniature training session on the train had worn her out. Unfortunately, there was no time for napping until they were on the train to Barcelona.

As she followed Fionn to the main atrium of the grand railway station, she felt his impatience and his hyperawareness. He moved as he had done that night in the club, like an animal hunting prey. He took in everything around them.

An understanding had fallen between her and Fionn. She finally understood his mission. It was a noble one, and Rose found herself looking for approval beyond herself. Even as a gymnast, it had never been about making her parents or her coach proud. It was about striving to be the best because she desired to be the best.

Sure, she'd wanted her parents to be proud of her, to approve, but it had never stopped her going her own way.

Yet Fionn inspired this longing in her.

She wanted this warrior to respect her, admire her even, like she was growing to respect and admire him.

He'd protected her, and he'd done it with an incredible show of power.

He was teaching her said power with a patience that surprised and gratified her. And although the power was terrible and great, harnessing it excited the hell out of Rose.

"Bran said the O'Connors would become a problem when we stopped moving." Rose broke the silence. "Should it concern me we're stuck at this station for an hour?"

"Yes." Fionn glanced down at her. "I require all my strength in the event we meet an enemy here and to do that, I need to make a choice. I stop casting the spell of illusion on myself, thus making us more visible but freeing up more of my power, or I continue the illusion and take the chance that if an enemy finds us, you can help me best them."

A warm ache flared to life in Rose. "You'd trust me to help ... so soon?"

"Can I?"

She thought of how long it had taken her to control moving Fionn's cell with her powers. Putting her into battle might be premature, but what choice did she have? These people were coming for her and by the sounds of it, they wouldn't stop coming.

Whether she learned to fight today or tomorrow, it made no difference.

A kaleidoscope of butterflies awoke in her stomach at the thought of battling her new enemies. Despite her fears, Rose tilted her chin. "You can trust that I'll do whatever it takes to survive."

"Even so ..."

She felt a hum in the air and glanced around in time to catch a woman falter as she strode by them, her attention focused on Fionn. She frowned at her mentor, realizing he'd dropped the illusion on himself. "You don't trust me?"

"I do. But I also vowed to protect you and I'll need all my strength to do that." He walked toward a coffee cart. "Speaking of which."

She hurried to catch up with him, watching as humans took a wide berth around his massive presence. "You said I can do that, right?" Rose asked as she stopped beside him in line for coffee.

"Do what?"

"The illusion thing?"

Some emotion she couldn't identify worked behind his eyes. "Yes. You can learn."

"You call it a spell. Does that make you a warlock too?"

He grinned, quick, teasing, and over way too soon. "No. We're *made* of magic. We have natural powers. 'Casting a spell' is just a phrase for us. It doesn't mean what it does for witches and warlocks. Casting a spell for them means drawing from Earth's energy. We call it magic for want of a better word. And magic comes with a price for them. They need balance."

"How so?"

Fionn looked toward the line and Rose looked up to see the woman they were behind glancing over her shoulder at them with an expression that said she thought they might be crazy.

"Let me get coffee first. You need one too. You're lagging."

Rose frowned. "Do I look tired?"

"No. I can ..." He scowled, trailing off into silence.

"You can?"

"I can just ... sense it."

She nodded. "I haven't slept in twenty-four hours."

"You can sleep on the train. For now, coffee." His brief weirdness gone, they waited silently until it was their time to order.

As they wandered away from the cart, coffees in hand, their voices lost in the cacophony of the train station, Rose asked, "Do you *need* coffee?"

"Like any being, we need rest to reboot our energy. Caffeine can work as a quick fix for that. We don't need as much rest as werewolves and vamps, and certainly not as much as humans, but we do need it. Your powers are new within you, so *you'll* still tire quickly, but within a few days, you'll be at full strength and you'll need less rest."

She nodded. "So how does the whole magic thing work?"

"Our natural abilities are ours. They belong to us as magic belongs to us, for we're made of it. *Travel*, speed, strength, telekinesis, mind control, camouflaging ... all of that's ours. We do tire using those abilities, but it takes more prolonged use to tire us than it would for humans. It's different for witches and warlocks." Fionn paused to sip his Americano. "To use magic they harness the energy from the world itself, and that comes with a price."

"But how?"

"The warlocks who attacked us. Did you not see what happened to the trees they snapped the branches off?"

"No."

"They began to die, Rose." He paused in the middle of their wandering and Rose halted beside him. His expression was neutral, but Rose felt a welling of frustration and perhaps even sorrow inside her that did not originate from within her own emotions. "Their magic requires energy and they pull it from the natural world. A flower dies so a young witch can cast a glamour spell. Trees die so warlocks can turn the branches into weapons. Animals die so items can be used to trace the person it belongs to."

Something awful twisted inside Rose's gut, and she understood the frustration and sadness Fionn hid beneath his calm facade. "And what was required to die to put you into a deep sleep and then reawaken you? What needed to die to cast the spell that blocked my power?"

"The latter? Most likely animals. Usually lambs."

Rose winced. "The sacrificial lamb."

"Exactly. They represent purity and new beginnings. They offer a great amount of energy for a spell. A witch or warlock who intends the least harm will pull from plants, vegetation, and animals only when they must. A user of dark magic or a desperate practitioner of magic will use people."

"Surely not?"

Fionn nodded, grim faced, and then he began to walk again. Rose hurried to keep up with his long-legged pace. "There are councils," he continued, "that keep them in check. Bring dark-magic users to justice. But they can be corrupt. The Blackwoods are on the North American Council and although it cannot be proven, I know they use dark magic. They used it to bring me back just as the druids used it to send me into slumber for over a millennium. Nothing else would have sufficed."

"They sacrificed a human?"

He glared straight ahead as they stepped onto a moving walkway. "Five girls, representing north, south, east, west, and center, offered themselves up in sacrifice to the druids to put me to sleep."

Holy crap. "You're kidding."

"Five was a sacred number to the druids. The girls believed their spirits would be rewarded in death."

"They allowed girls to die for you even though they hated what you'd become?"

"The sacrifice was to honor the king I'd once been," he replied, and there was no hiding the bitterness in his tone this time.

Rose flinched inwardly. He'd sacrificed everything for his people, and they'd betrayed him for it. "And to wake you up?" Her question was almost a whisper.

"As I had unwillingly been put to sleep, they killed an unwilling warlock to bring me back."

She felt a muddle of strong emotion pouring out of him. "They bother you ... even more than the fae. Witches, warlocks."

He looked down at her, his countenance hard. "Make no mistake, Rose; the fae are infinitely more dangerous than a mere witch or warlock. And let's face it, witches and warlocks do not differ from ordinary humans who have sacrificed much in the pursuit of power."

Rose frowned as they stepped off the walkway. "If you disdain humans so much, why try to save them from the fae?" She walked fast to keep up with him. "Fionn?"

He halted below the departure and arrival screens. "Because," he said, his deep voice rumbling as he studied the screens, "the corrupt powers may influence this world, but they make up a percentile of a population of people, most of whom are good. The world has grown complicated." He turned toward Rose, his expression so fierce it made her temperature rise. "So complicated, it's hard for them to *feel* like they're good. I see it. I see how lost they are. And I don't know if they'll ever find their way or if corruption will bring them down as it once did civilizations before them. But I have hope. I have a purpose. Without either, we're nothing. Even if I'm wrong to hope, what choice do I have but to continue to do so?"

A sweeping, powerful feeling of admiration and longing that Rose had tried to keep minimized flooded her. How could she feel so much for someone she'd only met? It was ludicrous. And yet it was true.

Surprise flickered in the depths of Fionn's green eyes, and she realized he'd seen something of what she was feeling in her expression.

He looked away, a muscle ticking his jaw. "The train will be here soon." His tone was dismissive.

Deflated Rose turned from him.

It was unlike her to allow her emotions to overwhelm her. It was unlike her to attach feelings to strangers.

And Fionn *was* a stranger.

Even if he didn't feel like one.

Even if he felt like that elusive *something* she'd been searching for her whole life.

Inwardly she scoffed at the stupidly romantic and naive notion. Fionn wasn't here to sweep her off her feet like some moronic damsel in distress. He was here to teach her to protect herself.

Perhaps it was time she started taking that seriously because who she was meant she had to protect herself from everybody.

Even Fionn.

~

He wasn't lying. He did have hope. He did have purpose.

Just not the noble kind Rose assumed he meant.

Something niggled at him as he pretended to study the departure screens. An uneasiness.

Guilt.

Not guilt, he snapped at that annoying whisper. Fionn didn't feel guilt. It was just uncomfortable to sense Rose's emotions and find admiration in them, to see her look at him with something akin to fucking hero worship.

And attraction. He'd felt that too and seen it in her eyes as she stared up at him after his manipulative speech, and he'd caught her staring at his mouth several times over the last few hours.

Heat pooled in his groin. He stubbornly refused to acknowledge the reaction.

"Fionn." Her voice curled around him, tugging on him, and although he didn't want to look at her, he found he had to.

Then he tensed at her tight, worried expression.

He opened his mouth to ask her what was wrong, and that's when he became cognizant that his racing heart wasn't because Rose wanted him. A tingle down his spine and dread in his gut accompanied the fast heart rate. His mouth tightened. "They've found us," he gritted out, staring at the crowds.

She searched with him. "What am I looking for?"

"Don't just use your eyes, Rose. Use your senses. That racing heart, the dread ... it will intensify when you find the source of the danger."

"Would they attack here? In public?"

"Many a supernatural fight has been explained away as human in nature."

"So that would be a yes."

Her dry tone made him smile despite himself. "That would be a yes. Come, we don't want them to know where we're going. We'll lead them into the restroom to deal with them."

Rose followed him, keeping up despite her short stature. She was spry, fast, and a quick learner. All of this was good because he had no intention of seeing her dead before they arrived in Ireland. "I thought they could follow us anyway because they have my jacket?"

"Bran is taking care of that. For now, this is the last destination for these particular coven hunters."

"Are we going to kill them?"

He caught her anxious expression. "If we have to."

"Even so"—she looked up at him, determination blazing on her face—"let's try not to."

Impatience gnawed at him but his current strategy involved keeping her happy. "Fine."

"Do you feel that?" she asked a few seconds later as they followed the signs for the restroom.

His pulse had escalated; he assumed that's what she referred to. "They're following us." Fionn pushed Rose toward the men's restroom and she barged inside ahead of him as he cut a quick glance over his shoulder.

He saw them.

A male and female. They were looking right at him.

Fionn disappeared inside the restroom after Rose who stared up at two humans glowering at her from the urinals. He closed in behind her, his upper body brushing the back of her head, and bent down to whisper in her ear, "Your thoughts are theirs. Like the telekinesis, communicate with your magic. Send the order into their minds and demand what you want. Tell them to leave."

She'd stiffened against him, and he saw her flesh prickle with goose bumps where his breath fell upon it. Awareness shafted through him with hot suddenness and he stepped back.

"Do it. We don't have time."

"Then you do it."

"Rose—"

She whirled around to glare at him. "I'm not ready to do that shit to anyone. Capisce?"

Capisce? What were they, the bloody Italian Mafia?

He rounded her and glanced from one man to the other. Without saying a word, he ordered them to zip up and get out. As they fled, he kicked in all the stall doors to make sure no one else was inside the room.

"Get behind me," he ordered.

"Like hell." Rose widened her stance beside him, facing the door. "I want to fight."

The words were barely out of her mouth when the restroom door blew open and the witch and warlock strode inside. Energy crackled around them.

"There's nothing natural in here for them to use," Rose said, fisting her hands at her side.

"It need not be in here. If they use magic as a weapon, they draw that power from the nearest tree or animal outside."

"There's no use teaching her our ways, warlock," the witch said, throwing her red hair over her shoulder with an arrogant smirk as the restroom door banged shut behind her and her companion. "She won't be around long enough to use the information."

Good. They still didn't know what he was.

"What did you say?" Rose stepped toward the witch.

Fionn felt a stirring of pride inside him at her courage and forced himself to stand back to see what she could do. It wasn't easy for him.

The warlock stepped forward. "No time for conversation. Rose O'Connor, you've been tried and sentenced to death by the high court of the O'Connor Coven of Dublin. I, Ethan Mulhern, Dark Witch Hunter of the O'Connor Coven, will serve as your executioner. Do you have any last words before I carry your sentence through?"

Fionn almost rolled his eyes. You always got one who had to act to the letter of tradition.

Rose looked back at Fionn and gestured with her thumb at the warlock. "Is this guy for real?"

Amusement tickled his lips.

Rose grinned at him and he felt her lovely smile as a physical thing. "I guess I do have something to say, then." She turned to the hunters. "Want to help me practice?"

The chuckle escaped Fionn just as the tingling of magic intensified in the air.

"Uisce, uisce!" the redhead chanted. In answer, water blasted out of the tap of the nearest sink, flew at Rose, and encircled her head like a bubble.

"Anthea!" Ethan snapped at his companion.

She held up her hands, magic surging from them as she held the water in place over Rose, trying to suffocate her. "We don't have time for tradition. Do it."

Fionn's instincts were to kill the witch but if Rose was to survive, she needed to learn to fight back. It took every ounce of self-restraint not to intervene.

At first Rose clawed at the water, her fingers slipping through the liquid and making no purchase. The water couldn't kill her but it could distract her long enough—

He tasted the metallic tang of iron in the air and saw Ethan unleash a pure iron blade from a small scabbard. It glinted silvery gray in the light.

"Rose!" Fionn yelled, warning her. "The water can't kill you but that blade can!"

Immediately she stilled, panic receding as he watched her realize that human frailties were no longer hers. For twenty-four years, she'd been conditioned to understand that she could drown.

But fae couldn't drown. Their bodies healed from oxygen deprivation. That didn't mean it wasn't damn uncomfortable.

The blade whipped through the air toward her, and the bubble of water burst at the same time she held up a hand against the dagger.

Blood rushed in Fionn's ears.

A millisecond before it would have pierced Rose's palm, the dagger changed direction and sliced through the air and into the warlock's throat. He made a gurgling, choking noise as he fell to his knees, his hands hovering over the blade.

"Ethan!" Anthea cried, face reddening with grief and fury. Her dark eyes blazed at Rose.

Rose was transfixed by the sight of the dying warlock and unaware of Anthea's gathering vengeance sparking at her fingertips.

Fuck.

Fionn was a blur of movement across the room as he grabbed the witch's head between his hands and snapped her neck.

It took less than two seconds to kill her. She slumped lifelessly to the floor just as Ethan fell to his back, his eyes fluttering closed. Silence descended over the restroom.

Fionn stepped over the witch toward Rose, whose attention had moved to the female.

"What did you do?" her voice was hoarse.

"Broke her neck."

She managed a nod before she dove into the nearest stall and heaved over the toilet bowl.

He waited for impatience and disdain to flicker through him.

It didn't.

Instead, he fought the urge to go to Rose and press a comforting hand on her shoulder.

The first kill was the worst. He'd made his when he was thirteen, but he'd been born into a violent time. It was different for Rose, who belonged to a society that did all it could to preserve life. Sometime in the future, her mind would let go of the idea it was human, and thus her body would stop reacting as such. Throwing up would be a thing of the past.

For now, as she emptied the contents of her stomach, Fionn lowered to his haunches beside the dead witch and warlock. He laid a hand on each of their legs. Despite their deaths, their skin cells still carried oxygen, still lived. Unlike the warlocks he'd killed in the woods, whose bodies would be taken care of by the O'Connor Coven before the public could find them, these two would have to be disposed of.

Anything dead was devoid of energy, a mere husk. A husk could be broken down to dust.

It could take up to twenty-four hours for the human body to decompose.

They didn't have twenty-four hours.

"What are you doing?" Rose asked, her voice hoarse.

He glanced over his shoulder at her. She stood by the stall door, pale but alert.

"We can't leave them here."

"What will we do?"

Fionn turned back to the bodies. "Filleadh ar an talamh." He stood and watched as the bodies crumbled to dust.

Rose huffed. "What ..."

"A spell." He turned to her.

"Is that all it takes?" she whispered. "A few words?"

"We need not use words as commands for magic, but witches and warlocks do. For years, I've covered my tracks as fae by pretending to be a warlock. Using words to cast spells has become something of a habit." He studied her carefully. "Are you all right?"

Anger, defensiveness, guilt all blazed from her as she bristled at the question. "His blind condemnation got him killed."

"True. But that wasn't my question."

"I just killed a guy so no, I'm not all right. But I will be. Won't I?"

Fionn studied her carefully. "How do you feel about your powers now?"

She lifted her hands to stare at them with a mix of horror and awe. "They saved me." Her fierceness echoed through him. "*I* saved me."

Something like pride filled him. "Right answer. You'll be all right, Rose Kelly." He would never refer to her as Rose O'Connor again. The bastards didn't deserve her.

"*I* killed him, Fionn." She lowered her hands, devastation promptly obliterating the awe.

A feeling akin to sympathy flickered through him, taking him by surprise. He cleared his throat of the emotion and replied coldly, "It was self-defense. Say it."

She swallowed. Hard. "It ... it was self-defense."

"Again. Louder."

"It was self-defense." Rose glared at him.

"Good. It won't make it easier. Killing someone is never easy, Rose, and the first time you're able to walk away from it without feeling that death mark your soul means you're *losing* your soul." He nodded at her.

"Do you feel each death mark your soul? Even after all these centuries?"

Pain he kept locked down tight shuddered from within the emotional cage he'd created to contain it. "Every single one," he promised.

And Rose's death would be the last and deepest mark upon his soul. Aine's would come after Rose's, and Fionn knew that the Faerie Queen's murder would not make a mark upon him.

The day Aine died would be the day Fionn lost his soul.

Thus, the day Aine died would be the day Fionn followed her and Rose into the dark abyss of death.

13

There was blood on Rose's hands. No one could see it, not even her, but she could feel it. There was a tightness in her breast. The feeling reminded her of the time she'd been pulled out of class in sixth grade and sent to wait at the principal's office for her mom. Dread had filled her gut as she waited, her instincts telling her something awful had happened.

It had.

Her best friend, Sadie, the girl she'd grown up next to, had been diagnosed with cancer. She'd been in the hospital for months.

Rose's mom had come to tell her that Sadie had died.

The news brought not only grief but this horrible physical and emotional sensation—the knowledge that nothing would ever be the same again.

Nothing will ever be the same again.

Rose stared blindly out the train window as it rolled out of Milan's central station. Heaviness weighed on her eyelids but how could she sleep?

Logically she knew she'd acted to defend herself. And she knew that to survive what was happening to her, she'd need to move on from the warlock's death. But she kept seeing the pain and horror in Ethan Mulhern's face as he choked on his own iron dagger.

A dagger meant for your *heart*, Rose reminded herself.

"Sleep, Rose," Fionn said from across the small table between them. Bran had gotten them first-class tickets again. "Everything will seem easier to handle after a little sleep."

Hoping sleep would offer an escape, Rose nodded as she stared longingly at the young woman who slumbered across the aisle. Envy filled her.

Sleep.

Sleep would help.

She closed her eyes. A couple's murmured conversation, the whoosh of the train moving, the click of the wheels turning on the track, the hum of the engine, lulled Rose to sleep. She fell into unconsciousness with a surprising swiftness considering her current inner turmoil.

LIGHT FLOODED into the gargantuan hall from the impressive arched windows that lined either wall. There was a cathedral-like quality to the room.

Rose blinked against the light, her vision focusing as she took in her surroundings.

School desks sat in rows, students at them bent over papers, scribbling furiously. Several older people strolled up and down and in between the desks. A huge clock hung suspended from the ceiling at the north end of the hall.

It's ticktock was distracting.

"Para de hacer tic tac," a voice hissed.

Rose glanced down and realized she was standing over the desk of a young woman whose face was scrunched up with frustration. She looked vaguely familiar as she glared at the ticking clock.

So consumed with the girl's mounting panic, it took Rose a

minute to realize she had no fucking idea where she was. Her own anxiety began to mount.

"Where am I?" she whispered.

The clock fell from the ceiling and smashed into pieces.

"El tiempo ha terminado!" a female proctor shouted from the other end of the hall. "Entregue sus papeles, por favor!"

"No, no he terminado, no he terminado," the familiar girl murmured frantically as she stood, blank paper crumpled in her hand.

What the hell was going on? And why was everyone speaking Spanish? Rose glanced around, trying to piece this weirdness together. Hadn't she just been on the train to Barcelona with Fionn?

The stressed girl hurried toward the front of the room, and that's when Rose realized the girl had a glow of light around her that no one else did. It was like a full-body halo. Instincts told her to follow the girl. Perhaps she knew why Rose was here ... wherever here was.

However, as she took a step to follow the girl who was talking to the proctor, the room shifted.

It grew smaller, and Rose braced herself against the swift, strange change as it shrunk around her. Her heart pounded with fear; sweat coated her skin. What the hell was going on?

Attention fixed on the girl, Rose watched as the woman she was talking to disappeared and in her place was a handsome young man with dark hair and stubbled cheeks.

Rose spun around, taking in the dorm room they now stood in.

What the ever-loving fuck?

"Vas a estar bien," the young man said, patting the girl's shoulder.

"He's right." Another young woman appeared in the room, as if from thin air. She sat up from a sprawl. Her blond hair fell over her shoulders as she swung long, slender legs off a bed. "You'll be fine."

Rose frowned. The new addition was American.

The girl with the glow scowled, and Rose instinctually knew she hated the American. "I won't get into the program now," the girl said in accented English. "You don't understand. You have no *ambición*."

The American seemed affronted as she stood from the bed and

put her arm around the young man. "Are you going to let her speak to me like that?"

"No," he replied emotionlessly. "You should leave, Alejandra."

Hurt pierced Rose as the girl, Alejandra, stepped away from him and immediately collided into a guy who had appeared out of nowhere too.

What. The. Fuck.

Rose swayed as the room changed again and Alejandra turned to face the man. His features were slightly blurred. The room they were in was pitch-black, except for the three of them. The boy and his American had disappeared.

"¿Qué haces aquí?" Alejandra asked the man with the blurry face.

"Me necesitas," his deep voice rumbled into the dark.

"No."

"Sí." His hand slipped under Alejandra's dress and she moaned, swaying into him.

Arousal instantly flooded Rose. What the— "Okay, get me out of here."

Her discomfort grew as the sounds of sex filled the room, her pulse escalating as her body reacted to the desire pulsating between the two strangers. It was unsettling to say the very least. "Uh, someone get me out of here!" she yelled into the dark.

Then she heard a gasp and spun back toward the couple.

She froze when her eyes connected with Alejandra's as she clung to her blurry-faced man. "¿Quién es usted?"

Rose shook her head at the accusatory question. "What? I don't understand. Why am I here?"

"Who are you?" The blurry faced man vanished and Rose faced Alejandra alone in the dark. "Who are you?" she repeated in her accented English. "How did you get here?"

"I don't know."

Fear suffused Alejandra, and Rose felt that keenly too. "¿Cómo has llegado hasta aquí?" she demanded.

Rose shook her head, stumbling away from the girl.

"How did you get here? HOW DID YOU GET HERE!"

Rose jerked awake in her seat.

The low light from the train carriage stung her eyes as she tried to catch her breath. The sounds of the train moving through the dark reminded her where she was. On a train to Barcelona with Fionn. She'd fallen asleep.

What a weird dream.

She raised a hand to her forehead, finding it slick with sweat.

Where was Fionn? His seat was empty.

A gasp from across the aisle brought Rose's sleep-fogged gaze toward its owner, and shocked gripped her.

The girl who'd been asleep across the aisle from her was staring at her in abject disbelief.

The girl from her dream.

Alejandra.

Except when Rose saw the confusion and alarm on the girl's face, she realized it hadn't been her own dream.

She'd been inside this girl's head. Inside her dream.

How was that possible?

The girl scrambled to her feet, pulling a backpack down from the luggage rack. But the backpack wasn't closed and all the contents fell onto the aisle. Rose rushed from her seat to help.

"No, *por favor*, it's okay." She tried to brush Rose's hands away, fright clouding her expression.

Her fear left a bitter taste in Rose's mouth. She'd never been feared before.

She grabbed deodorant, perfume, and a bag of mints and handed them to the girl who snatched them out of Rose's hands.

With a sigh, Rose stood to leave her to it when a leather booklet caught her attention. A need to know the truth caused Rose to reach for the burgundy book. She flipped open the passport and a shiver skated down her spine.

The girl's name was Alejandra Amada Cruz.

Rose *had* infiltrated this girl's dreams. Trembling a little, she held the passport out to Alejandra who yanked it out of Rose's hands. She stared at Rose as if she were a monster before she hurried down the carriage and out of sight.

"Yeah, I'd run from me too," Rose whispered as she stumbled back to her seat, wondering if she'd ever stop being floored by what she was and what she could do.

Fionn. She wished he was here to explain. Where was he? His stuff was in the luggage rack above them so he was still on the train.

She didn't sense danger, so she assumed he was just stretching his legs.

When he got back, she'd ask him about the dream walking. Was it something he could do too? He hadn't mentioned it.

Fionn would explain and maybe even teach her how to control it. She didn't want to wander in and out of people's sex dreams for the rest of her goddamn life!

But wait ...

Her new companion, although forthcoming with some information, was still a mystery. Anyone else might think she was crazy considering Fionn had spent the last twenty-four hours telling her about his past. However, what he'd done was state a lot of facts, explain his agenda ... yet she knew nothing more of his life or his feelings. Not really.

Maybe Rose could walk into Fionn's dreams? Learn something about him. After all, she was trusting him implicitly. It would be nice to know her trust wasn't misplaced.

You dream-walk the guy, you're hardly trusting him implicitly, she argued with herself.

Truthfully, though, Rose was in no position to trust anyone implicitly. Not even Fionn Mór.

It was decided. She'd keep the dream walking to herself. At least for a little while.

FIONN FOUND a carriage that had only a few people in it. He sat near the back, conjured the headphones, and expanded their use so no one would hear his conversation with Bran, including a sleeping Rose if she awoke and came looking for him.

She'd appeared troubled even in sleep, a frown pinching the skin between her brows, her lips pursed tightly.

There was nothing Fionn could do for her. Unfortunately, she'd have to work through the warlock's death alone. All he could do was provide reassurance that it was a kill-or-be-killed situation.

However, even that didn't help if you had a soul.

Why the fuck do you care? he snarled at himself. He seemed to keep forgetting a pivotal fact where Rose was concerned. She'd be dead by the end of the week. Her feelings would no longer matter.

Rage churned in his gut as her face flashed through his mind. His whole being rebelled at the idea of killing her. It would seem, after all this time, after damning himself for what he'd become, Fionn still had enough humanity within him to regret hurting an innocent.

For centuries, he'd told himself that the fae were too dangerous to ever be considered innocent. Take himself, for example. He hadn't been a perfect human but for his time, he'd been a fair one. A just king. A good man.

That man died the moment he made the bargain with Aine.

All hope of resurrecting him faded when he became fae.

Yet watching Rose learn to use her fae powers was more entertaining than he'd anticipated. Fionn sighed, running a hand through his hair. She had a way of making him see what he was through fresh eyes. What he could be.

Well, until she killed the warlock.

He wondered how she'd feel about her abilities when she woke up. If she'd still want to train with him.

"Fuck," Fionn grizzled, pulling out his phone. He had too many thoughts and feelings about this woman. *Sacrificial lamb*, he reminded himself as he hit the button to call Brannigan.

He picked up on the second ring. "I know Rose's life is in danger, but you are aware that I sleep during the day? Because you've called me all day."

"It's nighttime now."

"Not my point. I should be wide a-fucking-wake right now, but all I want is a nap."

Fionn tried and failed to bite back an impatient growl.

"Fuck, you sound like an animal when you do that. You sure you're not part wolf or vampire?"

"Bran, if you don't shut up, I will rip your heart out when I see you. Capisce?" The word was out of his mouth before he could stop it.

He rolled his eyes.

That bloody woman was infecting him.

"Capisce? Are we now—"

"Bran," Fionn warned.

"Right, right. I take it you're calling for an update."

"I am. And you can be frank. No one is listening in, not even Rose."

"Where is she?"

"Asleep in another carriage." He sighed. "She killed a warlock today."

"Ah. Troubled, is she? The first kill is the worst."

"Aye, well, she's strong, she'll get through it. Any news on the jacket?"

"It's destroyed," Bran relayed.

Relief moved through Fionn. Not that he was afraid of taking on any more hunters. He just didn't want Rose to have to deal with it. Barcelona would prove challenging enough without more O'Connor hunters on their tails.

"You're not out of the woods yet. My informant tells me they'd already sent more hunters after you before we destroyed the jacket. They don't know what train you got on, but they know what direction you're taking. If they hear about An Breitheamh, then it's safe to say they'll be able to deduce you're on your way to Barcelona. They'll assume you want it to stop the Blackwoods from completing the gate ritual."

Just what they needed. Fionn sighed. "We'll deal with that if it happens. What about Rose's parents?"

"They've booked tickets to Zagreb. They leave in a few hours.

Look, I've been thinking, your phone is untraceable and their coven still doesn't know where they are, so as far as I'm concerned, it's safe for Rose to call them and tell them to stay put."

The last thing Fionn wanted was Rose getting sentimental with her parents. He needed her focused on him, staying with him, not hearing her parents' voices and longing to be with them.

"It would put her at ease."

Remembering the tight expression on her face even as she slept, Fionn cursed under his breath. It *would* ease her worries to know her parents were okay. "Fine, I'll let her call them."

There was a moment of silence between them and then, "You like her."

Fionn scowled. "What?"

Disbelief rang clear in Bran's voice. "You haven't complained about her once and you're doing her favors I thought I'd have to talk you into. You like the little fae. I mean, it's not surprising, I've seen her picture. She's definitely got that extra something."

"Bran," Fionn warned, sweat dampening his palms.

"And she's survived two attacks, even taking out a warlock, so she's an impressively fast learner, yes?"

"Bran ..."

"Maybe it's time to reconsider—"

"I'll kill you, Bran," Fionn threatened, voice devoid of emotion. "If you utter one more word about changing my mind regarding Rose and the gate, I will end your bloodsucking existence. Are we clear?"

Considering he'd never seriously threatened to kill his friend before, Fionn was guessing they were clear when Bran replied coldly, "Oh, we're clear."

Fuck.

"Do you think this is easy for me?" he hissed, the fae audible in his voice. "I have no other choice. You know that."

"You have a choice, Fionn."

"I don't, friend," he offered the word in apology. "I am nothing if I am not my revenge."

In answer, he heard fast typing down the end of the line.

"What are you doing?" he finally asked.

"Checking for the nearest underground fights."

"I don't have time for that." Although, it might do him some good. Underground fights between supernaturals had existed for centuries. It was a place for werewolves and vampires to unleash the aggression they tried to hide from humans. Now and then, a witch or warlock would fight, but they weren't allowed to use magic, so it was considered a death sentence for them.

At the fights, Fionn pretended to be a vampire. It explained his long life to those who were old enough to remember his face at other fights.

Only one being had ever questioned what Fionn was in the last three centuries, and that was an old werewolf acquaintance with secrets of his own. Although he wasn't sure what Fionn was, he knew Fionn was no vampire. He never spoke of his suspicions to anyone. He wouldn't. The lone wolf was that in the truest sense of the word.

A fight might work out Fionn's agitation, but he was on a tight schedule.

"Well, in case you change your mind, a three-night fight is being held in Orléans. The last night is the day after the auction."

"Rose and I will take a flight to Ireland once we retrieve An Breitheamh."

"That's not a given, Fionn. If anyone realizes you stole it back, the first thing they'll do is watch Barcelona Airport. If the Blackwoods find out, they'll watch Shannon Airport too."

"Then we'll fly to Dublin and drive to Galway."

"Fionn—"

"No one will stop this. No one. Not once I have both Rose and An Breitheamh."

"Aye, you've made that clear." Bran heaved a sigh. "Oh, and I'm still working on finding out if Niamh Farren is related to you. My genealogist is on it but there's a huge possibility we won't come to a definite conclusion on this. I've traced her and her brother to their birth certificates. He's two years older. They were born in County Kerry.

"From what I can tell, they were raised by their single mam until Niamh was seven. There was no one else to take them, so they were put in the foster system. After their foster parents died when Niamh was thirteen, the siblings fell off the map. I'd wager that's when they started running. My genealogist and I can work backward using their mam's info, but it's still a long shot."

"My gut tells me I'm not wrong about this."

"What does it matter? You're going to kill Rose and open that gate and never come back. What does it matter what happens to Niamh?"

Agitation itched beneath his skin; he flexed his fingers in reaction.

"Fionn?"

"If she's my blood, Bran, I need to know before I go. I'll make sure she's protected."

"Once you kill Rose—"

Fionn bit back a growl. He wished he'd stopped saying that.

"—the gate will close permanently. The fae children who are left will be useless to the Blackwoods."

"Not useless, Bran. They're still the most powerful beings in this world. Especially Niamh. They revere psychics among the covens. Can you imagine what they'd do to have a fae psychic working for them? No. If she's my family, I won't leave her unprotected."

"Your family betrayed you," Bran reminded him unnecessarily.

"And they would have betrayed Niamh too. I won't."

"Well, here's a question you might not like answering: If Rose is killed before you can use her to open the gate, will you kill Niamh instead?"

Damn him!

"This conversation is over."

"I predicted that answer." Bran sounded almost as pissed as Fionn felt. "Let Rose call her parents. I'll email over what I know about the players at this auction." He hung up.

Fionn stared blindly at his phone.

It was the first time Bran had ever hung up on him first.

With a sigh, Fionn released the spell on the headphones and slumped back in his seat, listening to the sounds of the train traveling through the night. The lights lowered in the carriage, and Fionn closed his eyes.

He hadn't slept in forty-eight hours but he could manage on little sleep for days. Still, he was weary in a way he hadn't felt in centuries.

"Fionn," Rose's soft voice whispered in his mind. "Fionn."

God, she couldn't even give him peace while he rested. She was haunting his thoughts.

He felt a hand on his shoulder and reacted instinctually. Fionn grabbed the hand as he tore out of his seat and thrust his attacker against the carriage door. The door cracked off its hinges.

It all happened so fast, it was too late for him to realize Rose was really there and had been attempting to wake him. He grappled for her as she stumbled against the broken door, his hands clamping down on her small shoulders to steady her.

She glared up at him in annoyance while he held her pinned in place.

In that moment, he noticed how truly small she was compared to him.

Aoibhinn had been statuesque for a woman. He'd never been aware of her fragility, and she'd been human.

And yet Rose, who would be as powerful as he was with training, felt feminine but breakable in his hands. The feminine part he liked. More than he should. The breakable part made him feel like a murdering bastard.

That familiar guilt niggled at him.

"Fuck," he gritted out as he released her slowly and retreated.

Feeling the tension in the carriage, he glanced over his shoulder and saw the two humans were awake and half standing out of their seats, trepidation and concern in their expressions. "Double fuck."

Rose pressed into him as she addressed the strangers. The skin on the back of Fionn's neck prickled as he inhaled her scent; at the same time, he felt the touch of her body in every molecule of his being.

Triple fuck.

He stared down at her, resentment flooding him, as she smiled apologetically at the other passengers. "It's all okay. My brother just got off a military tour. I startled him awake."

One passenger relaxed instantly, smiled in understanding, and then spoke in Spanish to the other passenger relaying what Rose had said.

"Your brother?" he queried.

Rose glowered. "They're more likely to think I'm safe with a sibling over a lover, and we couldn't have them calling the cops now, could we?" She pushed past him and shoved the broken carriage door aside.

She was pissed.

Great.

He caught her as she stepped into the next carriage, feeling the strength in her small biceps as he wrapped his hand around it. "You startled me, but I apologize."

Rose halted and heaved a sigh. "It's fine. I just had kind of a weird dream and then you attacking me ... I'm tired and cranky. It's all good." She tugged on her arm, making him realize he was gripping her too tight.

He released her as if she'd just bitten him.

She contemplated him with suspicion. "Is there a reason you jumped me? Is everything okay?"

No.

Far from it.

14

"Everything's fine. I just spoke with Bran." Fionn pulled his phone out of his pocket and handed it to Rose. "Call your parents. They've booked a flight to Zagreb. You need to dissuade them from getting on that plane."

The sudden announcement momentarily confused Rose. One minute, she was angry at Fionn for proving he could squish her in his big warrior fae hands if it amused him to do so, and the next she was wondering what those hands would feel like if they were caressing her rather than squishing her.

And now he was telling her to call her parents?

The truth was, Rose wasn't just pissed that Fionn had attacked her in his semiconscious state. She was pissed she'd found him sleeping in another carriage, as if he needed to get away from her.

"Is that what you were doing? Talking to Bran? You weren't sleeping?"

He frowned. "I didn't want to wake you so I called him from the quieter carriage." He nudged her gently. "Let's get back to our seats. I'll use the headphones so you can make your call in private."

Rose started down the carriage. People were trying to sleep, and they shouldn't have this conversation on a train at night, but still ... "Why were you sleeping?"

"I wasn't. I'd closed my eyes for a second."

"You need to sleep."

"Perhaps I will once we get back to our seats and you make that call."

The call.

To her parents.

Emotions rattled through her in a chaotic kerfuffle. She knew she had to speak to them but that didn't make it easy.

"Do you wish me to isolate your conversation so even I can't hear?" Fionn asked as they entered the first-class carriage.

As Rose slid into her seat, she felt a little dazed. Fionn could be unexpectedly perceptive when he wanted to be. More unexpected was the realization that she didn't mind if he witnessed this important call.

Where once she shied from anyone who perceived weakness in her, she found she didn't mind sharing that part of her with Fionn. Despite how vulnerable her position with him had been since they'd met, he'd never made her feel anything but empowered.

"It's okay." She tapped his phone screen. With a small, nervous smile, she held it out to him. "You need to unlock it."

He did so swiftly and returned the phone to her. Then he conjured the headphones; she felt magic prickle her skin as he used them to envelop them in privacy.

Stomach flipping, Rose dialed her parents' house phone in Maryland.

They rarely picked up the house phone, but the line clicked open on the third ring. "Hello?" her mother asked, sounding frantic.

Guilt pricked at Rose, despite all they'd kept from her. "It's me."

"Oh, thank goodness," her mom sobbed. "Oh, Rose—what, yes, it's her. Rose, I'm putting you on speaker so your da can talk to you too."

"Okay." Rose's gaze locked with Fionn's.

For once she could read his expression.

Are you all right?

She gave him a small nod.

"Rose, darling, it's your da." His warm, familiar voice caused a confusing mix of love and resentment to flood her.

"Hi." She found her voice to reply.

"Where are you?"

"I'm safe—that's all that matters."

"Rose, you have to know you're in danger. It's hard to explain—"

"You don't need to. I know everything. I know what I am. I know why I'm in danger."

There was a moment of silence until her father cleared his throat. "Then tell us where you are and we'll come get you."

"No. Cancel the flight to Zagreb."

Her parents murmured quietly between themselves. "How did you know we booked a flight?" her mom asked.

Rose felt her lips quirk in bitter amusement. "Because I've met a few friends who have divulged more to me than my own goddamn parents ever did. And these friends have eyes and ears everywhere."

Fionn scowled, and she swore she could sense he felt betrayed on her behalf.

Huh.

"... and we thought if you didn't know, it would never be an issue. We never thought the spell would break." Her parents had spoken while she studied Fionn.

"A vampire attacked me outside a club," Rose replied quietly. "He smacked my head against the ground and, poof, spell broken. But someone came to help—he's teaching me about my powers." She found she couldn't meet Fionn's gaze as she spoke of him because her feelings flooded to the surface. There wasn't much she didn't mind him knowing, but her stronger-than-usual feelings for an immortal man she barely knew was not one of those things.

"Who is this person? How do you know you can trust him?"

Irritated by her mother's interrogation, she bit out, "Well, he told me the truth and you didn't, so ..."

"Rose"—her dad sighed—"we did what we could. We couldn't

chance staying with the coven because if the spell broke while we were in Dublin, there would be no escaping them. You have to know they can use things that belong to you to trace you."

"I know that. My ... friend has already taken care of that?" Her glanced at Fionn, and he nodded.

"The jacket is destroyed," he informed her.

Relief flooded her. "Yeah, it's definitely taken care of. Everything in my apartment and at the club has been destroyed, so they can't trace me anymore. And they don't know about you. I'm pissed as all hell, but it would kill me if something happened to you, so stay put. If I find out they've discovered where you are, I'll give you a heads-up."

"How can you do that?" her mom demanded. "Rose, we need to come to you. Your father and I are not incapable. We are two of the coven's most powerful members."

She closed her eyes at the desperation and panic in her mother's voice. "Mom ... no matter how powerful you are"—she opened her eyes and they locked with Fionn's—"you'll never be as powerful as me. I've already ... I've already killed to defend myself," she admitted, the confession burning in her throat. "I'm not a powerless little girl anymore. I'm not afraid of your coven."

And she found that she wasn't. She had incredible abilities at her fingertips, and she had Fionn Mór on her side. "Your coven should be afraid of me."

At her statement, something wonderful happened.

Fionn's lips pressed together and curved into a small smile of respect.

A warm ache expanded in her chest. She felt about ten feet tall.

"You don't sound like yourself," her dad commented.

"No, Dad, I *finally* sound like myself. Stay put. If I think you're out there trying to find me, getting on the coven's radar, you'll distract me. I need to stay focused."

"They won't stop coming, Rose," her mother whispered. "Are you just going to run for the rest of your life?"

"Let them come." Determination blazed inside her. "I've done nothing wrong but be born different. If they try to take me out, I'll take them out instead. Until there's nothing left of them."

"You don't mean that."

"Would you have me stand still and let them kill me?" she bit out.

"What about your soul, Rose? It may be self-defense but it's still murder."

"And it'll mark my soul," she echoed Fionn's words and saw something dark flicker across his face. "Every single one. The day it doesn't is the day I'm lost for good."

"That day won't come," her father said. "You'll never lose your soul, my darling, but the weight of those marks will drag you down."

"Then I'll try to avoid it," she promised. "If I have to live my life constantly on the move, I will." And she realized the thought didn't fill her with panic. "I've always been a bit of a nomad."

"Is there nothing we can say?"

"What could you say?" She was exasperated now. "There's nothing you can do to change what is. I'm angry at you for lying to me my whole life. But I'm also grateful that you adopted me and sacrificed your life in Ireland to protect me. You did your job, and you did it well. But there's no answer to this. I'm a target. So, I have to learn to protect myself, and I've found someone who can help me do that. While I get stronger, you have to promise you'll stay where you are."

There was an annoyingly long moment of silence before her dad replied, "We'll stay, Rose."

Relieved, Rose gripped the phone tight to her ear as it occurred to her she may never see them again. It might be too dangerous.

Tears burned her eyes, and she swiftly looked out the window at the dark world passing by. Her throat grew constricted as she strained to hold back the tears, but a single drop escaped anyway, scoring hotly down her cheek. "I love you both," she choked out before she pulled the phone from her ear and hung up.

Without looking at Fionn, she slid the phone across the table toward him. He covered her hand with his, halting her retreat.

Surprised, she studied him as another tear let loose. He watched it trail down her cheek, and squeezed her hand beneath his before gently releasing her.

Missing his touch instantly, Rose let go of his phone and removed her hand from the table.

"We change trains at Dijon Ville in a few hours. Try to get more sleep if you can."

The dream-walking episode came flooding back to Rose. Part of her was afraid to fall asleep again. But maybe ... if Fionn slept ...

An ugly ache replaced the warmth created by Fionn's comfort. Was she so unable to allow someone completely into her affections, she'd invade his privacy rather than trust him? After the sweet moment between them, trespassing in his dreams felt like a horrible violation.

Or trespassing in anyone's, for that matter.

"I slept for a few hours. Why don't you try to get some sleep?"

Her companion studied her and then nodded. "I fear I must. Once we reach Barcelona, I'll need to be as alert as possible."

"Once we get there, will you tell me exactly what we're there to do? I know, I know, we're taking back something that was stolen from you, but details would be good."

"I'll explain everything when we get there." He stood and she couldn't help but watch as he removed his suit jacket and placed it on the luggage rack. Rose continued to ogle him as he unbuttoned the cuffs on his shirt and rolled them back to his elbows. The sight of his strong forearms caused an instant hot tingle between her thighs. She shifted uncomfortably in her chair as he quickly unbuttoned his waistcoat and settled back into his seat. His stomach was hard and flat beneath his white shirt. Rose would have given anything in that moment to see him shirtless.

But her imagination did a pretty good job filling in the blanks.

God, this fae's sexiness was a great distraction from the heavy crap plaguing her life.

She lifted her gaze from his hidden abs to meet his. He'd caught her checking him out.

"Nothing else is coming off. Show's over."

Despite his monotone, Rose knew from the quirk of his eyebrow he was teasing.

And although she knew she shouldn't, she smirked and flirted. "Well, that's a damn shame."

To her pleasure, his lips twitched as he studied her mouth for longer than appropriate. Then, just as excitement began to swell in all sorts of places, he slammed his eyes closed and commanded gruffly, "Sleep."

However, Rose found she couldn't sleep.

She'd just discovered the possibility that Fionn Mór returned her attraction after all.

Rose had never been one to fantasize about guys and romance ... but she couldn't help her thoughts as she watched her delicious mentor sleep, his handsome face appearing younger in rest. She couldn't help but imagine that her future on the run might not be so desolate if she had someone who excited her by her side.

15

November in Barcelona was warmer than Zagreb by a good eight to ten degrees, but as midevening struck, Rose shrugged into the jacket she'd removed when they first arrived in the city a few hours ago.

She'd been beyond relieved to get off the train in Barcelona. Once they'd arrived in Dijon Ville early in the morning, they had to hang around a train station for four hours before they boarded a smaller train to Montpellier. After another wait at that train station, they boarded the train to Barcelona. Nearly four hours from departure, they arrived in the city at around five in the afternoon.

Bran had apparently taken care of business because Fionn immediately hailed a cab that took them to a basic but clean hotel.

"We're near La Sagrada Familia," Rose noted as Fionn checked them in.

"You've been to Barcelona before?"

She nodded. "Last year. I stayed for a long weekend and did tourist stuff."

Bran had booked them adjoining rooms, and Rose prioritized taking a glorious shower over questioning Fionn further about their business in the Catalonian city. It was funny how a shower could make her feel human again, even though she wasn't one.

Hmm.

The whole nonhuman thing, despite her abilities, would take a while to process. She wasn't sure she ever would fully process it— until everyone she knew aged while she remained the same. According to Fionn, that was already happening. She'd stagnated somewhere around her twenty-second birthday.

Panic constricted Rose's breathing. Immortality sounded great and all, but it would be excruciating to watch her parents die. They would only be the beginning. Any connections she made in the human world, she'd eventually grieve. This whole fae shit was fucking with the natural order of things.

Putting morbid thoughts aside, Rose strolled out of the bathroom and halted upon finding a backpack and shopping bags on the bed.

Inside the bags, she discovered two new pairs of black skinny jeans that fit her to perfection, a slim-fit hooded sweater, two T-shirts, three sets of lacy underwear, socks, toiletries, and a hairbrush. Clearly the backpack was so she could carry all this stuff with her when they left.

Rose veered between being moved by Fionn's thoughtfulness and the discomfort that he'd paid for all of it. The clothes were designer, the fabric soft, and weirdly exact to her taste. However, since her clothes were in desperate need of a wash, she'd decided not to snub the gesture.

She pulled on the demure but still sexy underwear before she paired her new jeans with a black cotton T-shirt with a retro motel print on the chest. The word "Paco" caught her attention, and she checked the label before she pulled it on. It was a Paco Rabanne shirt.

The jeans were by Citizens of Humanity.

Holy shit. Fionn did not mess around with apparel.

After blow-drying her hair, Rose was pleased to find some makeup in the bag with all her new toiletries. Again, high-end makeup.

"Where did it all come from?" she asked Fionn as soon as they met in the hotel lobby.

He'd arriving dressed in something other than a suit—black trousers and a black, slim-cut sweater that did wonderful things for his shoulders and arms. Everyone in the lobby watched him approach her, and Rose had to force herself to close her mouth so she didn't look like a gaping groupie.

"I had Bran hire a personal shopper for our arrival."

"How did you know my measurements?"

He held the hotel entrance open for her. "I've been around a long time, Rose. I know women's bodies."

That matter-of-fact response should have been annoying.

Instead, it gave her all kinds of tingles. She'd bet her powers that Fionn Mór knew how to satisfy a woman in bed.

Throwing that dangerous thought away, Rose replied, "Well, aren't we a little obvious? We're staying in a three-star hotel dressed in designer gear. It doesn't add up."

"Are you complaining about the hotel?"

"Fionn, I've lived in crappy apartments for years. This hotel is a luxury in comparison. That wasn't my point and you know it."

"We can't stay in a five-star. We'd draw too much attention there. But I refuse to wear anything but the best." He cut her a look, something like self-deprecation in his eyes. "I've been used to the best for a long time, whether lying my head to rest on a bed of furs or wearing bespoke suits from Savile Row." He shrugged. "I won't apologize for enjoying fine things."

"I'm not asking you to. But I'm not sure I'm comfortable with you buying me $300 jeans."

"Well, it was that or leave you to stink."

She scowled. "I wasn't that bad. Hey, where are we going?"

"Dinner. I'm hungry. After that, we will train."

"And while we're eating, will you be explaining what it is we're here to steal back?"

He shook his head. "Too many ears. I'll explain while we train."

Dinner was a strangely comfortable affair at a nice restaurant less

than a block from La Sagrada Familia. They spoke little other than
for Fionn to ask how Rose was doing after the conversation with her
parents.

He'd slept on the train the rest of the way to Dijon, and then Rose
had fallen asleep on the train to Montpellier. A little more rested,
they'd chatted on the train to Barcelona about her life in Maryland
and she'd made a game out of how Fionn ably deflected personal
questions.

Apparently, his sharing time was over.

It was frustrating and challenging trying to get him to divulge
anything else about himself.

Now it was midevening in Barcelona and she followed Fionn for
two blocks before she realized he was walking them in circles back
toward La Sagrada Familia.

"What are you doing?" she asked as she shrugged into her jacket
against the evening breeze.

"Losing any possible tails."

"If we were being followed, wouldn't we sense it?"

"I'm just taking precautions."

"Well, while you're at it, tell me about Bran."

Fionn frowned down at her. "What about Bran?"

"How do you know him?"

He shrugged. "We met at an underground fight back in 1946. Bran
was turned overseas. Ireland may have remained neutral in the war
but thousands of Irish soldiers fought with the Allied forces against
the Nazis. The war was ending, Bran was readying to return home. A
vampire attacked him upon his arrival in France. He'd been out
drinking, celebrating. She seduced him and then she turned him. Her
name was Marielle.

"He was only twenty-one."

"Bran had a difficult time coming to terms with what he was. He
couldn't return to his family or the girl he'd left behind, and it didn't
help that Marielle, bored with her new vampire lover, abandoned
him in London. That's where Bran and I met. He was angry and

wanted an outlet, so he heard of the fights and came to take a beating. Which he did."

"Underground fights?"

"Places for vamps and werewolves to take that natural aggression they don't want pouring out around humans. They beat the living daylights out of each other with it instead."

Rose shook her head in disbelief. "I'll never understand men."

"Men?" He smirked. "You'll find all genders at an underground fight. It's nothing to do with gender. It's about a place to vent frustrations without hurting humans."

"You do this too?" She wondered if fighting helped Fionn vent the anger he must still carry toward the Faerie Queen and the people who'd betrayed him.

"I do. I pose as a vampire."

"How? You don't have fangs."

"I have magic." He shot her a dry look. "And the ability to make people think I have fangs. It doesn't always work. Vampires can sense each other, as can werewolves. The ones who looked closely enough at me could sense something was off. And then there are your more intuitive supes who can tell the difference between each kind of magic. The former and the latter have assumed in the past I'm a cheating warlock."

"Is that how Bran found out the truth?"

"Bran was in over his head at the fights. Too young. Too inexperienced and truthfully, not aggressive enough, even for a vampire." Rose thought she detected affection in his voice. "Bran's a lover, not a fighter. Despite being forced into war as a boy."

"He's your friend."

Fionn scowled, hesitated, and nodded. "He's my only friend."

Empathy ached through Rose. "I'm not very good at friendship."

He drew to a halt outside the closed entrance to La Sagrada Familia. "For friendship to grow, trust must develop. With Bran, I didn't tell him the truth until thirty years after we first met. The vampire is a genius, a curious one, a born researcher, and he'd developed an impressive network of contacts over the years. We met for lunch in Moscow in 1979 and he told me he knew what I was. It occurred to me that instead of killing him, perhaps I should trust him since it would have benefited him more to keep this knowledge to himself.

"Trust is hard for me. It didn't come naturally. However, Bran was determined to be an asset to me, to have purpose, and he was interested in my mission: waiting for the fae children to be born. It took years of loyalty, but he's now the only being in the world I fully trust.

"You can trust him too, Rose." Fionn's expression was deadly serious. "If anything should happen to me, go to Bran."

Her stomach flipped unpleasantly at the thought of anything happening to Fionn. "Nothing will happen to you. I won't let it." Her grin was flirtatious. "After all, I'd hate to be deprived of my daily dose of eye candy."

Fionn's shoulders relaxed a little and he rolled his eyes. "Stop flirting with me, Rose."

The eye rolling only made her want to flirt with him more.

As if he sensed this, he sighed in exasperation and strode past her to gesture up at the church. They stood in front of wrought iron gates that guarded the steps up to the entrance. Construction cranes towered between and above the unusual church spires. "It's time to train."

Rose stared up at the building. The basilica was incomplete, but that didn't mean it wasn't astounding. Gaudí's design of the Roman Catholic church was like something out of a sci-fi alien flick. Rose glanced from the astonishing architecture to Fionn. "Here?"

"We won't be interrupted by supernaturals here. They tend to avoid religious places."

"You mean vampires hating crosses is a real thing?"

Fionn shook his head. "No. Please do not think of fighting a vampire with a cross." He examined the building. "Many young supernaturals, including witches and warlocks, feel physically discombobulated on hallowed ground. There are a few theories as to why. Mine is that faith en masse creates energy—in a way, its own sort of magic. That energy is strongest in places like churches. I believe it's an antithesis to the energy supes are created from, the energy witches and warlocks tap into, and that's why it makes them feel physically discomfited."

Genuinely intrigued, Rose studied the building. "Why do you think it's an antithesis?"

"Because human belief in their deities comes from a spiritual plane. Our belief in our magic comes from the natural plane, from what we see with our eyes. The former is faith. The latter involves no faith, merely acceptance. Acceptance is important, but faith, I've learned, has its own unique power. At least that is what I've surmised over the centuries." He turned to Rose. "The only supernaturals I've seen enter a place of religion are those who have turned to gods to explain their existence."

"There are supes out there who believe God made them this way?"

He nodded. "They think the stories of the fae are fairy tales. Remember, very few people in the supernatural community believe the origin story is true."

Well, that made the prospect of going on the run seem a little more plausible if she wasn't constantly up against fae fanatics. She sighed and studied the basilica. "*I don't feel uncomfortable.*"

"You will. And that's why I brought you here. In a fight, you'll most likely be outnumbered and thus disoriented. You need to learn to focus through that."

Aghast at the realization he truly meant to train her inside La Sagrada Familia, Rose gaped. "You can't train me within the sanctity of a world-famous church."

"I can and I will."

"Uh ... I've been in there, Fionn. There are security scanners, cameras, and a lot of guards."

Her mentor tsked at her as he stared down in mock disappointment. Then he lifted a hand and waved it comically. "Faerie," he reminded her.

The whole thing was so un-Fionn-like, Rose couldn't help a bark of laughter. If anyone looked the opposite of the human depiction of a faerie, it was Fionn Mór.

The lights that lit up the basilica illuminated Fionn's face and the amusement glittering in his green gaze.

Grinning, she crossed her arms over her chest, waiting for two tourists to stroll out of earshot. "So, what are you going to do?"

"I'm doing it. Their cameras are, as we speak, on a constant loop. Once we get in there, I'll take out the guards—I'll just knock them unconscious," he assured her before she could protest.

"How are you going to do all that if you're disoriented?"

"My dear Rose." His tone was exasperated but the endearment still caused a flutter in her stomach. "I'm the oldest motherfucker on this planet. Very little can disorient me."

That flutter intensified. "I'm not gonna lie ... the 'oldest' part should put a girl off, but the whole badass immortal thing is pretty hot."

Fionn closed his eyes and pinched his lips together for a few seconds. When he opened his eyes, his expression was admonishing. "Stop flirting and concentrate."

She enjoyed irritating him way too much for it to be normal. "I'm a great multitasker. I can do both."

"If God exists," Fionn muttered up at the church, "give me patience."

Deciding to offer him a reprieve, she clapped her hands. "Okay, in all seriousness, if we're going to disrespect holy ground, let's get it over with. What's the plan?"

He studied her a moment and then, apparently assured of her earnestness, replied, "We will *travel* in. Be careful of anything that looks like iron. Most of it can't hurt you—only pure iron can, like the dagger Ethan carried. But better to be safe than sorry. You've—"

"I just had a thought," Rose cut him off and then gave an apologetic look. "How have I avoided pure iron my whole life?"

Fionn considered this. "It's not used as often as mixed iron materials because there's less carbon in it, meaning it's softer, more pliable. There's been a resurgence of its use commercially in the last few years, but it doesn't surprise me that you've had no contact with it."

"Does it hurt a lot?"

"I wouldn't know. I've avoided the stuff for three centuries, despite being attacked by supes in the know."

She smiled and couldn't help if it was somewhat coquettish. He brought it out of her. "You really are a badass."

Ignoring her, Fionn gestured to the building. "You've been here before, which will make it easier. But as soon as you're inside, you'll feel the effects of hallowed ground. Dizziness, nausea, a lack of concentration."

That did not sound fun.

"What about the guards?"

"I'm going in first to take them out. *Travel* in after me in five minutes." Then poof, he was gone.

Rose blinked, glancing around to make sure no one had seen him vanish, but the humans standing outside the church had their backs to where Rose stood. "Shit," she groused. "I will never get used to that. Also?" She threw up her hands. "I don't have a watch."

Waiting for an approximation of five minutes to pass felt like the longest moments of Rose's life. Despite knowing no human could hurt him unless they were in possession of pure iron, she worried for Fionn. He'd been in her life a mere two days, and yet that didn't *feel* correct. Despite all she didn't know about him, he felt familiar in a way so little in her life ever had. She had feelings for him.

If another woman came to Rose and told her she had strong feelings for some guy she'd only known forty-eight hours, she would've staged an intervention.

"Life is so weird," she mumbled, preparing herself to *travel*. Then she considered what she was about to do and mocked herself, "You think?"

Remembering the mammoth entrance to the church with its cathedral ceiling, marble floors, arched stained glass windows, and stone pillars, she visualized it as best she could. What she remembered most was the ceiling—how the columns split into branches to hold up the vaulting, like trees holding up the sky. How natural light poured in through spaces in the design. It was less alien inside than outside. Instead, it was like standing beneath the canopy of a great stone forest.

Rose focused, closed her eyes, felt the resultant tingle, and opened them again.

She stood inside the dark cathedral, near the chairs that faced the altar.

"You were seven minutes."

Startled at the sound of Fionn's voice, she turned toward him and felt the cathedral spin. "Whoa." She put out a hand to find balance, but a wave of a nausea flooded her. Clutching at the nearest chair, Rose leaned into it. A memory hit of when she was seven years old, at her first gymnastics lesson. The dizziness after each somersault. A dizziness that had dissipated quickly as her body got used to spinning and tumbling.

Fionn stepped into her path. "I told you it can be disorienting."

Rose frowned. She was an ex-gymnast.

No way was she going to let a little dizziness take her down.

She concentrated, focused, felt the room right itself, and stood. It still spun a little, but the nausea lessened. "The guards?"

Fionn eyed her a second and then nodded. "They're out. Come." He strode toward the center of the mammoth space.

Rose followed and felt the room spin again; she threw out her hands and imagined the floor was a balance beam, which helped her find her center. Following Fionn, she met him in the middle of the room.

"Very good," he said.

"We're not going to do any damage to the church, right? They've been working on construction for nearly 130 years."

"I can fix anything we damage." He shrugged, like damaging a Gaudí building, a religious one at that, was no big deal.

"You're insane."

"Keep insulting me. It'll inspire me to be more creative when I attack you."

Uncertainty made Rose retreat, and it was like doing it on a balance beam without concentrating. She stumbled. "Shit," she huffed as she straightened. Rose, belligerent now, crossed her arms over her chest. "How exactly are you planning to attack me, oh ancient one?"

"That would be telling. You're going to defend yourself using this." He punched a fist against his gut. "Instinct. You ready?"

Before Rose could answer, she felt a rumble beneath her feet and stumbled again, this time because the floor was moving as the marble began to crack, breaking apart. It tore out of the floor, only to float up in a collection of hefty pieces that hovered almost exactly halfway between her and Fionn. "I'm not going to lie, this feels very disre— ahh!" She ducked as the pieces flew at her and over her head. "—Spectful!"

The largest piece didn't fly over her head, though. It came straight for her face.

Son of a bitch!

Rose swiped a hand across the air in front of her, catching her finger on a sharp edge of marble. The piece immediately flew backward and once her surprise receded, she used her magic to slot it into its original spot in the floor.

Turning around, ignoring the way the room tilted at the edges of her vision, Rose concentrated on the broken marble that had landed behind her and commanded it back to where it belonged.

Wonder filled her as the pieces floated by and settled into the cracks. She watched the marble knit back together, good as new under her silent order.

Fionn heaved a sigh. "Are we going to fight, or are you going to spend this session cleaning up?"

She threw her hands up in disbelief. "It's La Sagrada Familia!"

His lips twitched. "I had no idea you had such respect for religion."

"I may not be religious but I respect that faith is important to billions of people around the world. Putting that aside, we're talking about a significant piece of architectural history." She gestured around. "Training here feels wrong."

"Which is why we're doing it." He deliberately misinterpreted her words.

Without preamble, Fionn swiped the air with his hands and three stained glass windows high above her shattered, the shards of broken glass flying in her direction.

Anger pulsating through her, Rose focused on the shards, mirrored Fionn's movements, and sent the individual pieces shooting toward him instead.

With a flick of his wrist, the glass halted in midair and then whizzed back toward her. Just as she focused her magic on returning the glass to the windows, a piece she'd missed from Fionn's initial attack sliced across her cheek.

Rose cried out at the sting, that split-second distraction causing the rest of the glass to fall to the marble floor and shatter into even smaller pieces.

Glaring at Fionn, she pressed two fingers to her cut cheek and felt it heal beneath her fingertips.

"Nice," she snapped at him.

"I'm teaching you focus. I'm not here to be nice." He strolled casually past, placed his hands above a section of the broken stained glass, and it rose from the floor.

Within seconds, every single piece was back in the windows, good as new.

Just like her cheek.

Rose touched it again, feeling the smooth, unbroken skin. The reminder that she was almost invincible dissolved the irritation she felt for Fionn. Her coaches had pushed her to her very limits, and that was just a sport. This was life or death, so she could forgive him for a little cut on her cheek.

Especially when she was practically unkillable.

Practically *unkillable*.

Feeling a buzz of excitement thrum through her, she stepped toward him. "Throw me across the room."

His step faltered. "What?"

"With your magic. Put all your strength behind it."

"Are you certain?"

She nodded.

With a glint in his eye, Fionn pushed his palm into the air in front of her and the next thing she knew, she was flying. The sensation so took her aback, she lost concentration.

Rose crashed into a pillar with such force, not only was the breath knocked out of her but she felt and heard a crack in her ribs. When she hit the floor with an almighty thud, pain paralyzed her.

She sucked in a ragged breath.

Then slowly, her ribs began to heal, and the pain receded. Rose lifted her head and stared across the room at her mentor. He was still as a statue, waiting for her to respond. She stood, turned, saw the crack in the pillar, and pressed a palm to the stone. Rose could feel the magic crawling up toward the crack, sewing the stone back together. No one would ever know her body had once broken a pillar in La Sagrada Familia.

So. Fucking. Cool.

Satisfied, she faced Fionn and strode toward him. Stopping several feet away, Rose braced her feet, anticipation, adrenaline, and excitement soaring through her. "Again."

16

Something like wonder caught Fionn off guard as he stared at Rose standing before him, demanding he throw her through the air for a second time.

Exhilaration blazed in her pretty blue gaze.

Wonder mixed with pride. Pride mixed with something more primal. Something that caused a heavy, hot need between his legs.

Fuck.

When he'd decided to keep Rose at his side by pretending to mentor her, he'd expected the woman who had been raised as a human to fear her fae side, to hate it, like he did. Instead, she found joy in it.

She was a natural with her abilities.

Watching her take him on, fearless and determined, on the back of dealing with her enjoyment in flirting with him, Fionn was stuck in the most unlikely of places.

He wanted to fuck the woman he planned to use in his vengeance.

It was inconvenient to say the least.

The fact that he needed to control these wants and thoughts about her was goddamn galling. Bothersome woman. First, he spent hours deflecting her personal questions only to end up telling her all about Bran, and then worst of all, sincerely suggesting she go to Bran for help if something happened to him.

It was petty to take his frustrations out on Rose ... but she did ask for it.

Concentrating a potent level of magic toward her, Fionn pummeled into her body with such an impact, he heard her gasp as she flipped backward through the air.

But something happened.

Instead of crashing into the nearest pillar or wall, Rose paused as she righted herself midflight. Then she dropped, landing like a cat, hand to the ground to balance against the disorientation caused by the church grounds.

A smile prodded at his mouth.

Damn, she was good.

With a cocky smirk, she pushed to her feet. "What's next?"

Obviously, the woman required a true challenge. "I want you to *travel* to the top of one of the two tallest spires. You're going to jump off, and you're going to land on the ground without breaking a bone. I'll be at the bottom waiting for you."

He noted more than a glimmer of concern flicker across her expression. "Are you kidding?"

"Even on a still evening, you can use the wind to control the fall. Tonight there's a breeze, so it should be easy."

"And if I break every bone in my body?"

Fionn shrugged, knowing it would annoy her and finding a little too much pleasure in the fact. "You'll heal within a few hours."

She scowled. "No worries, then, huh?"

"Sarcasm is beneath you." It was a hypocritical response since sarcasm was a second language to him, but, again, irritating her was fun.

However, this time, the last word had barely left his mouth before he found himself flying to the ground with a furious trainee fae on his hands.

Rose had been an impressive blur across the church.

Incredibly fast.

And strong.

He frowned. The little viper had smacked his head off the marble floor, and this annoyance had momentarily distracted him from the fact that Rose was sprawled atop him, *straddling* him, her forearm pushed against his throat. "Yeah, well, now *you're* beneath me, asshole."

This was not threatening.

This was disturbingly arousing.

Gripping her wrist in his hand, he easily pried her forearm from his throat. "What the hell was that for?" Fionn snapped, anger masking his desire.

"For not giving a shit if I shatter every bone in my body," she hissed.

Her eyes sparked fire. Her cheeks were flushed.

Fuck, fuck, fuck.

Fionn took hold of her narrow waist and pushed her off. Not gently.

She soared up off him but landed on her feet with remarkable grace.

He rolled up onto his and dusted off his sweater. "You're handling the disorientation well."

"You're an asshole."

"So you said," he replied dispassionately, and then caught sight of the cracks in the marble floor where he'd landed. She'd taken him down with some force. "Impressive." He gestured to the broken floor before using his magic to fix it.

"You know my coaches were tough on me, but they were at least concerned about my well-being."

Exasperated, he whirled on her. "I am trying to keep you alive," he bit out, losing his usual cool. Goddamn her. "Unless there is a graveyard of fucking pure iron spikes beneath you, I am not afraid for you if you fall from a building." His frustrations mounting, he marched toward her and watched her tilt her chin up at him in defiance, holding her ground despite her disadvantage in height and build. "I am afraid that falling will slow you down in a fight. If someone is chasing you through a city, that city needs to become your play-ground. You need to learn how to fall from great heights as if jumping over a fucking puddle. Capisce?"

Anger melted from her features. Her lips twitched. "Capisce."

"Good," he spat and strode past her toward the main entrance. "Spire. Now. And use the shadow trick to conceal yourself. The last thing we need are photos of you on top of the fucking La Sagrada Familia circulating the internet." He *traveled* outside before she could respond.

Seconds ticked by as he watched the tallest spires. The church was lit up, but the spires were less visible as they pierced the night sky. Fionn could still make out the tops of them with his fae eyes.

Impatience wriggled through him.

Uncertainty created waves of displeasure in his gut.

What if she fell?

Rose cannot die.

But she can break into a million pieces.

The reality of that caused something akin to panic. Fuck, she would fall. He prepared himself to *travel* to her, to stop her, but then he saw her atop one of the spires, pulling shadows toward her.

Before he could make a move, Rose kicked up off her feet onto one hand, suspended in a one-handed handstand for a moment before leaning her weight over and off the building.

His heart lurched into his throat as she fell too fast, too hard.

Even if he caught her, her neck would break on impact.

"Rose," he whispered, the word choking him as helplessness paralyzed his body.

But then the air changed and her shadowed body slowed just before she hit the ground.

Rose landed on the stone paving in front of him with the grace of a panther, stunning him.

The shadows melted from her body and the anxiety he felt melted with them.

Deciding the emotions he'd experienced as she'd fallen were far too complicated to contemplate, he focused on her cockiness.

The bloody woman just did a bloody handspring off La bloody Sagrada Familia.

He settled his face into a blank mask. "Show-off."

THE SENSATION of falling stayed with Rose as she followed Fionn, both *traveling* out of the church grounds to a shadowed corner behind the walls that protected it.

She was getting better at that too.

Still, Rose took a minute before hurrying to catch up with Fionn, already marching toward their hotel. He'd accused her of showing off but that wasn't what the handspring off the spire was. What Fionn had forgotten to mention was that *traveling* to the top of that spire was dangerous in itself. The precision required of a newbie was asking a lot.

She'd ended up on one of the construction cranes instead, and it had taken her a moment to gather the courage to *travel* to the spire.

The fearlessness she'd felt inside the church abandoned her.

It was all well and good to say to yourself, "Hey, I'm unkillable!" It was another to stand five hundred feet above the ground and jump. Fionn was asking too much. He must have known the possibility of her smashing her body to pieces was high.

She should have smacked him to the floor until she knocked some emotion into him.

The handspring off the spire was the only way she could convince herself to fall. Rose pretended the spire was merely an uneven bar in gymnastics. Then as she fell at amazing velocity, it had become a battle of survival versus panic. The world below was coming up to meet her way too fast, yet at the last second, she'd remembered Fionn telling her about using the wind to break her fall. Magic became imaginary wings on her back, flapping around her and slowing her descent.

The experience wasn't something Rose wanted to repeat, but it was nice to know she could do it.

Although she wouldn't admit that to Fionn.

He was lucky she didn't blindfold him, force him back up to the top of the damn church, and push him off. See how he liked it!

"You know, you take coaching to an illegal level of limit pushing," she commented as she caught up to him.

He grunted.

Rose sighed. "So, I guess training is over for the night?"

Fionn flicked a hand at her. "You're a natural."

Despite the pride his compliment made her feel, she frowned. "We won't be training anymore?"

"You still have much to learn so, yes, we will. But tonight, we rest. The auction is tomorrow evening and we need to steal back An Breitheamh before that."

Un Bre-huv. There was that foreign-sounding word again. Whatever it was. "This is the part you tell me all about that."

Fionn stopped in the middle of the sidewalk. He cast a look down an alley between two restaurants and then strode into the awaiting darkness. Frowning, Rose followed, trying to breathe through her mouth when they passed the most god-awful-smelling dumpster.

"What are we doing down here?"

"Last lesson of the night. Back in Zagreb, you tried to *travel* to my hotel and couldn't. I want you to try again. *Travel* to your hotel room."

"And if I end up *traveling* into an oncoming bus?"

He shrugged. "I'll clean up the mess."

She pulled her lip back in a growl. "I'm tired, I don't know why we're here, I just jumped off the La Sagrada Familia, and it would be nice if you could remember that smashing to the ground or being hit by a bus will still cause me emotional trauma, if not physical. I'm not over two thousand years old and used to piecing myself back together like a ninety-year-old plastic surgery junkie."

"I think I liked it better when you flirted," he griped.

"Just remember, in all your 'I don't care if you get squashed like a bug just as long as you learn' style of coaching, *you* need *me* to feed that hero complex of yours."

"I don't need you, Rose. You need me. Now get back to the hotel room."

Thankfully, Rose succeeded in hiding her hurt at his words. "I'm feeling the need for a little space, so I'm going to *walk* back. I'll meet you there." She turned around and let out a yelp to find Fionn blocking her path. Heart in her throat, she hissed, "Don't do that to me."

He stepped into her personal space, the top of her head just reaching his chin. Which meant she was faced with the impressive, hard breadth of his chest. Fionn bent his head toward her, and she inhaled the smell of his expensive cologne just as he spoke in a menacingly soft voice. "There is no time for space. If you want me to save your life, you'll do as I say, when I say it. Nod if you understand."

Blinding indignation rose inside her at his condescending attempt to master her. Perhaps his two-thousand year old mentality needed a reminder this was the twenty-first century.

"You know, I've been wondering something," she whispered, a careful glimmer in her eyes as she lifted a hand to trail a finger across abs.

She felt Fionn stiffen at her touch and fought very hard not to smirk.

Their eyes met and held, something undecipherable working behind his.

"How does it feel"—she cocked her head to the side as she gripped tight to his biceps—"when a fae gets kneed in the balls?"

Not giving him time to process that question, Rose launched her kneecap as hard as her fae strength would allow, right into his junk.

Pain strained Fionn's features as he dropped silently to one knee, his face turning red as he fought to hold back what she knew had to be sounds of major discomfort. He glared balefully up at her, his expression promising retribution.

Rose stepped back to enjoy the view and chuckled. "That would be 'painful,' then," she said.

As he pushed back to his feet, she spoke before he could. "Never try to bully me again. I'm here of my own free will. I am not your plaything to command." With a careful step back, she prepared to *travel*. "I'll meet you at the hotel."

The world turned black for just a second as she concentrated on her hotel room, and then a blur of color met her eyes before the unlit room settled into place.

Rose blew out a breath and smiled.

She'd done it.

She'd *traveled* back to her room—

"Ah!" A strong arm wrapped around her waist and she found herself airborne. She'd barely made the landing on the bed when she was pinned flat on her back by Fionn straddling her, her wrists held down at either side of her head in his brutal grasp.

It took her a second to catch her breath as he loomed over her in the dark room.

"Don't you ever do that again," he warned, his voice a terrifying low growl.

Or at least it should have been.

Now that Rose had asserted herself with him, she was feeling less annoyed and more turned on by their current position. "I made my point, didn't I?"

"I'd prefer it"—his mouth was inches from her as he spoke—"if you found other ways to communicate that didn't involve the abuse of my balls."

She tried not to grin and failed.

Fionn glared at her mouth.

Her blood, which had heated as soon as she found herself beneath his magnificent body, whooshed in her ears. Demanding need set in between her legs.

She shifted her hips beneath his and answered provocatively, "If you want, I could kiss them all better."

Desire flashed fiercely across Fionn's face seconds before he rolled off her and landed on his feet by the bed. "I'll see you in the morning," he bit out gruffly and marched toward the adjoining door.

Disappointment flooded her as she sat up. "What about An Breitheamh?"

His answer was to slam the door *hard* behind him.

Laughter trembled on Rose's lips. For whatever reason, Fionn was fighting his attraction to her. Pushing that button would be a much more entertaining way to keep him on his toes than a swift kick to the balls.

"If you want, I could kiss them all better."

Fionn flinched as Rose's husky offer played over and over in his mind, not doing anything to dispel the hot blood currently hardening his dick. He flicked a hand at the shower as he undressed in the en suite. Bracing himself as he stepped into the tub, Fionn sucked in a breath as the cold water hit his skin.

Determined to stay there for as long as it took to regain control of his body, Fionn withstood the icy spray.

She'd bested him twice.

First with a surprisingly impactful knee to his balls.

Then by trying to seduce him.

Fuck.

She was the devil.

Rose Kelly was the bloody devil.

He couldn't remember the last time anyone had gotten the better of him, let alone a little slip of a woman. Even Aoibhinn had not been able to lead him around by his dick.

Neither would Rose, he growled to himself.

In a mere few days, she'd be dead and out of his life.

Just like that, his arousal died.

Fionn turned off the shower, leaning back against the wet tile.

That woman next door, with her vital strength and complex soul, would be extinguished from this world and he'd be one step closer to his revenge.

The burn in his own soul reminded him that his was not yet lost. But that burn, a million times more painful than Rose's knee between his legs, would not change his mind. Tomorrow she'd help him retrieve An Breitheamh, the iron dagger that had belonged to him when he was human. The iron dagger that had killed the fae prince, his royal blood imbuing it with powers that made it legendary. An Breitheamh the only weapon purported to be able to kill Aine. The dagger that had taken him two centuries to find because the faerie bitch had hidden it so well.

Once he had that dagger, he'd use it to kill Rose to open the gate, and then, he'd plunge its fatal point into the heart of the Faerie Queen.

17

"Uh ... we're going to what?" Rose stared open-mouthed at Fionn from across the breakfast table.

Their hotel put on a breakfast buffet and Fionn had inadvertently supplied the morning's entertainment by eating his weight in food without breaking a sweat. That was until he'd told her they would steal an ancient iron dagger called An Breitheamh from a vault in a five-star hotel in Barcelona.

Fionn chewed the last of his toast, studying her with the blank expression he'd treated her to since joining him downstairs for breakfast. His empty expression was driving Rose nuts.

She surmised his current cold behavior was an effort to create walls between them after last night.

Usually, Rose would be good with that.

A guy didn't want to have sex with her? Fine. Plenty of other fish in the sea.

However, Rose wasn't a hundred percent sure Fionn didn't want to have sex with her, and there were *not* plenty of other men like Fionn in the sea.

He wasn't even a man.

He was a six-foot-seven behemoth of hotness. A fae warrior king who was frustrating, implacable, Powerful with a capital P, and fiercely noble in a way she'd never encountered.

Every time she looked into his spring-green eyes, her belly fluttered.

Actually fluttered.

Rose wanted him.

And for once, she didn't feel like giving up so easily.

"An Breitheamh is in a vault at Hotel Saber, a luxury hotel owned by a warlock," Fionn repeated patiently. "It will be removed from that vault tonight at midnight for the auction. For reasons I'm about to explain, I need your help to retrieve the dagger."

"How?"

"You'll *travel* into the vault. I'll be there to help you get out of the hotel with it."

"And how am I supposed to pick up an iron dagger?"

"An Breitheamh is kept in a solid silver case spelled to protect me from the iron inside."

"Protect you? You specifically?"

"The dagger is mine, so yes. But it'll protect any fae against the iron."

Rose leaned back in her chair, studying Fionn. She'd known that An Breitheamh had been stolen from him, but what wasn't clear was why he wanted it back so badly, it was worth risking their anonymity, and maybe even their lives. "Why is it important?"

"Because it was the dagger I used to kill the fae prince when I was human and thus, it's special. You're the lock to the gate to Faerie. Your blood, your heart. An Breitheamh is the key. Whoever stabs you in the heart with it opens the gate."

She sucked in a breath at this news.

Stealing the damn thing back was now pretty damn important.

"Now you understand my insistence on retrieving it."

He was trying to save her.

Again.

"Fionn," she whispered, "how do I pay you back for—"

"Don't," he cut her off impatiently. "*You'll* retrieve An Breitheamh. *You'll* save yourself."

His tone made her spine stiffen. He was right. Fionn may have led her to the dagger but Rose would be the one to steal it. It belonged to Fionn, but she trusted once it was in his hands, he'd keep it safe.

Except ...

"If this weapon can open a gate between worlds, how the hell did you let it get stolen in the first place? And by whom?"

Fionn reached for his coffee. As he raised the cup to his lips, he replied, "I'm feeling very judged right now."

Despite their grave discussion, Rose's lips trembled with the desire to laugh. She held it together, though.

"Ironic," he muttered after a sip.

"Ironic how?"

"That's what An Breitheamh means. It's roughly translated to 'the judge.'"

She snorted. "That's what you called your iron dagger back in your warrior king days? It's a little pretentious."

Unamused, he glowered. "I didn't name it," he finally said. "My people did. The Fae Queen spelled it to keep it hidden."

"How did you find it, then?"

"After searching for two centuries, I came across it by chance. I was swimming in the faerie pools by my estate and I'd dived deeper than normal. I felt it. Perhaps because it once belonged to me. It was buried beneath centuries of sediment. When I unearthed it, I returned with gloved hands to retrieve it and felt the electricity of magic humming from the blade. When I brought it home, my mistress couldn't see the blade. So, I tested it on my staff, leaving the blade out in the kitchen. Every single person passed over the dagger.

"That's when I realized it had been spelled to be hidden from the world."

"Except from you."

"Magic is strange. Although we have it at our command, we should never forget it has a will of its own. If it believes an object feels allegiance to someone, that object can never be spelled against them."

Rose was confused. "How can an object feel anything?"

Fionn leaned forward in his seat, his voice low. "Everything is energy, Rose. Everything."

She remained silent for several minutes. Minutes Fionn no doubt relished.

"Who stole it and how, if it's hidden?"

He looked up from the table. "The spell faded. It was only meant to last until An Breitheamh was reclaimed. Within a day, it could be seen by everyone. Which is why a treacherous mistress came across the vault it was hidden within. It was stolen six weeks ago."

There was that word again. Rose did not like the possibilities of its meaning. "By mistress, do you mean you're married and have a woman on the side?"

"Marriage is a human contraption. And you're putting the modern meaning to the word mistress. Mistress used to be just a common word for a woman you frequently bedded."

"Bedded?" Rose's lips twitched. "Fionn, if you want people to believe you're only in your thirties, not your third millennia, you need to update the vocab."

This time the blank expression slipped and he glared at her. "Fine. I frequently fucked her. Better?"

More than a gentle stab of jealousy unexpectedly pierced her. It was mixed with a not-so-surprising tingle at hearing Fionn use the word *fucked* in its most physical context. "Fine, she's your fuck buddy. So ..."

"Alice *was* my fuck buddy. When we met, she was human. Now she's a vampire."

"What happened?"

"There was a rumor a few months ago that a vampire had encountered a being of exceptional power. He was spreading it around that there was a species out there apparently no one had heard of. It all pointed toward fae, and I wanted to know if he'd been in contact with you or one of the others. This vamp has money. He holds parties for those interested in S and M."

Rose mouthed an *o* in reaction.

"He lures people to his fancy rented properties and while salacious but perfectly human debauchery happens upstairs, he picks his favorite for the night and takes them into a locked room in the basement where he drinks their blood while he fucks them."

There he went using that word again.

Rose shifted in her seat, squeezing her thighs together as she glanced from left to right to make sure no one was listening in.

Fionn considered her a moment, his eyes narrowing as they dipped down her body and back up again.

What was that?

Fionn frowned. "I angled for an invite with an acquaintance of his so I might speak with him. I was with Alice at the time and this acquaintance was taken with her. To get the invite, I had to bring her with me."

Uneasiness shifted through Rose. "Did you do it?"

He nodded, expression grim. "I regretted it, so you can remove that judgy little pinch between your brows."

"What happened?"

"I met the vampire and surmised he'd been lying about fighting an all-powerful being to cover up that he'd gotten his arse kicked by a fucking werewolf. Unbeknownst to me, Alice had caught his eye."

Rose considered this. This woman secured Fionn, attracted another guy, and then caught the eye of an indolent vampire. "She must be an intriguing lady."

"Alice is very attractive."

"Is that it?" Rose scowled. "A woman just has to be beautiful to warrant attention?"

He gave her an impatient look. "First, I said attractive, not beautiful. Many women are attractive. Beauty, being in the eye of the beholder, is harder to define. Second, Rose, I have no interest in relationships, which means a woman only has to be two things: physically appealing to *me* and sexually free. If that offends the feminist within, I could give a fuck."

"Charming." Did she really describe him as noble earlier?

"Anyway, this vampire was more than intrigued by Alice. He turned her. She came to me, said it was against her will, and I tried to help her come to terms with her new reality. But in truth, she was there as his spy. He'd heard I was a powerful warlock but beyond that, I was a mystery. He was a collector of information and he sent Alice to find out more."

Oh shit.

"I left her in an apartment I'd rented in London. I told her I was away on business, but really, I just needed some time away from her. I went home to Ireland. I've never left any personal item behind around a mistress—but she'd stolen a silk handkerchief from me. They used it to trace me and she followed me there. By the time I found her, she'd already relayed information about my vault."

"What happened to her?"

Seeing her fear, Fionn shook his head in disappointment. "My home is my sanctuary. It's spelled. It's almost impossible to find, but if a person stumbles upon it, they forget about it as soon as they leave. The only people the spell does not work on are Bran and the staff who worked there for generations. Bran has no spell on him but the staff were spelled to be unable to speak of me or my home.

"When I found Alice, I broke her neck. While she was unconscious, I had her removed. When she woke up, she had no memory of the place, but it was too late. She'd already sent the information on."

"Shit. So Alice came back and broke into the vault?"

"Alice is dead. Along with others who returned to my home."

Horrified at the casual way Fionn relayed this information, Rose couldn't hide her reaction. There was a ruthlessness to him that she couldn't pretend didn't exist. It was confusing. Worrying.

"It would never be a safe place again. Someone could find out what I was. What good would that do? And why should I explain myself against a woman who betrayed me for a chance at immortality? That was their deal. He didn't turn Alice against her will like she'd said." He curled his lip in anger. "He offered her immortality to get to me."

Betrayed again.

How could a person who had been continually betrayed through the centuries trust anyone? Let alone a woman he'd just met?

Rose didn't think the punishment fit the crime, but then again, this world had different rules from the human one. Conflicted, she looked away. "What happened next?"

"While I was chasing signs that pointed to Niamh Farren being in Budapest, Alice's vampire enlisted twenty lone vampires, killed my guards, my housekeeper, and my steward. They then used an industrial-sized steel laser to cut through the doors of my vault. Along with An Breitheamh, he stole valuable artifacts I'd collected over the years."

She thought of all the people who had died during that attack and didn't feel so much sympathy for Alice. "I'm sorry, Fionn."

His expression remained annoyingly blank. "Bran hacked the vamp's phone. Deleted Alice's original texts and searched his entire system to delete any information on my home. As soon as he and his vampires left my home, they had no idea where they'd gotten all the artifacts. That didn't stop me. I delivered retribution for the people they'd murdered, people I'd sworn to protect and failed to do so. I killed every bloodsucker that entered my home, and I'd do it again."

Fionn tensed, as if he'd said more than he'd meant to. Cursing under his breath, he looked away, seemed to gather himself, and turned back to Rose with a calmer expression.

"The vamp had sold most of the items by the time I tracked him down, including An Breitheamh. Bran has found pieces here and there that I've stolen back. An Breitheamh seemed lost to me until I received word of it being in Barcelona.

"Then Bran found out about the auction. It's being held by Oliver Schneider, a German businessman who also happens to be a powerful warlock. Schneider must know of An Breitheamh's historical importance and that some 'fanatics' believe enough in its power to pay a lot of money for it. Three times as much as he paid for it.

"But Schneider also knows it was stolen from me. The man he believes it was stolen from was the man Alice believed me to be—Edward Kent, an English warlock. Schneider may not know my real name, but he knows I'm a man."

"You, Rose, are not a man. So, you need to break into that vault."

Steal an ancient iron dagger from a highly secured vault in a five-star hotel in Barcelona? An ancient dagger that was the key to opening Faerie if plunged into her heart?

God, she missed bartending.

Heaving a sigh, Rose leaned across the table. "Explain that whole 'man' thing to me. Tell me what I need to do."

FIONN'S ROOM *is neat as a pin*, Rose thought as they strolled into it after breakfast. She'd left her bed unmade, her dirty clothes sprawled over a chair, and the bathroom was a mess of toiletries.

Fionn's didn't even look like it had been touched, let alone slept it.

Must be the soldier in him, she mused, glancing around as she followed him to the desk in the corner.

"What are we doing?"

"Bran hacked into the hotel's system. He sent over schematics of the hotel and vault." Fionn laid his iPad on the desk, the screen showing a partial of what looked like plans. Then, Rose watched in awe as he drew his hand over the iPad and across the desk. As his hand glided, it appeared as if the iPad was a printer, miraculously churning out paper with the schematics on them.

Despite the gravity of the situation, Rose couldn't help but smile.

Fionn glanced up in time to catch it. He frowned. "What is it?"

She shrugged, still grinning. "Dude, that is very cool. Don't you think that's cool?"

He blinked as if shocked. "Did you just 'dude' me?"

"Did you just make an iPad print out schematics of a vault with a wave of your hand?"

Fionn rolled his eyes and turned to the drawings. "Focus, please."

It occurred to her, for not the first time, that Fionn didn't seem to appreciate his talents. Now, she wasn't stupid. She realized as a human he'd hated the fae and being turned into one was probably a fate worse than death. However, he had not chosen to stick iron in his own heart and end his fae existence. He was still here. Which meant Mr. Mór had turned his bad fate into a purpose. If he could do that, couldn't he eventually grow to love being his own version of fae? Rose bumped his shoulder with hers. "You need to learn to find the joy in your abilities, Fionn."

He grunted. "Concentrate or die."

Assuming that wasn't a direct threat (she hoped), Rose leaned in to look at the plans, brushing her breasts against his arm. Although he did a good job of pretending not to notice, Rose caught the little tick of a muscle in his jaw. God, he was fun. Trying to suppress her smirk, she asked, "What am I looking at?"

He tapped a finger at the edge of the plans. "The vault is underground. Far underground. We must be inside the hotel to *travel* to that level. Once there, you'll *travel* into the vault."

"Why am I *traveling* in?"

"Because according to the information Bran has sent over, the vault is alarmed with a spell that will trigger if a man, other than Schneider, steps foot inside it."

"Again, why am—"

"Man, Rose. Not woman. Man."

Indignation flooded. "That sexist asshat. What? He thinks a woman can't steal from him?"

"The only person he's expecting to steal An Breitheamh is me. A male."

"Yeah, who could, and is, enlisting a female to help him. What is this guy's problem? He thinks a woman can't best him?"

"Yes." Fionn turned his head to meet her eyes. "From everything I've heard of the man, he thinks exactly that."

She was affronted. "Misogynistic dipshit. Chauvinist pig. Bigoted dickwad. Sounds like someone needs a good kick to the jewels, if you ask me."

Fionn studied her a second. They stood so close her breath caught. Then a definite glimmer of amusement crept over his face. "Let's leave the jewel-kicking out of it. At least physically. Metaphorically," he said, looking down at the drawings, "we're about to show the bastard that you never underestimate a woman."

18

The plan itself was simple.

What wasn't so simple were the people waiting to kill them at Hotel Saber.

Well, not exactly at the hotel.

Schneider had banned any supernatural from entering the hotel until after eleven thirty that evening. As a powerful warlock, he'd spelled the entire perimeter of the building with an alarm like the one inside the vault.

This meant that neither the Blackwood Coven nor the Garm would be inside the hotel, waiting to kill Rose. According to Bran, her parents' coven was unaware of the auction for the dagger and was still fumbling around in Europe trying to pick up her and Fionn's trail.

So that was something at least.

However, the Blackwoods and the Garm would be in the vicinity. They would see Rose and Fionn coming if they approached the hotel by foot. That's why they weren't going to. Fionn would create a gap in the perimeter spell so that he and Rose could *travel* inside via the delivery entrance at the back.

Once inside, they'd pretend to be a couple staying at the hotel to avoid suspicion, until they could get to the restrooms. With the memory of the plans in mind, Rose would *travel* into the vault, while Fionn *traveled* outside of it. She would then poof out next to him so he could double-check she'd collected the correct dagger, they'd *travel* back to the restrooms, then back to the hotel, and then poof several blocks away to the outer grounds of Camp Nou.

If they could do that and avoid everyone who wanted to kill them, great.

Butterflies, different from the kind induced by Fionn, swarmed in Rose's gut.

"You ready?" he asked.

They were outside Camp Nou, the soccer stadium, preparing to *travel* inside the delivery entrance at Hotel Saber. To be honest, Rose would have preferred if they could've departed somewhere a little closer to the hotel, but this was as close as Fionn was willing to get.

He insisted the Blackwoods and the Garm probably had the hotel surrounded for at least a block.

"I'm nervous," she admitted.

Nerves had always plagued her in competition when she was an athlete, but she'd never admitted it out loud. In her mind, that was admitting weakness.

Fionn was the most complicated man she'd ever met. She felt conflicted about the choices he'd made in the past yet ultimately decided she couldn't judge. Hadn't she killed a warlock in self-defense? Rose felt she understood her companion, and more than that, despite his often-grumpy demeanor, she felt safe to be herself with him.

He gave her a clipped nod. "It would be foolish of you not to be nervous. But you can do this. I'm right here with you."

"Okay."

"Ready? Visualize where that delivery entrance is."

Fionn had assured her that although she had no idea what the entrance looked like in real life, it was enough to know where it was situated in the building to *travel* to it.

"Ready."

The world blurred for a mere few seconds, darkening, then lightening as the surrounding space settled into place.

She glanced up at Fionn who gave her an encouraging nod.

He'd cast an illusion spell on himself so he'd blend, nondescript, as they moved through the hotel. Rose stayed glued to his side as he walked with confidence down the delivery corridor and out through double doors that led into the public areas of the hotel. As he stepped out into a corridor, signs on the opposite wall directed guests right toward the main reception and left toward the ballroom. Rose reached for his hand.

Fionn jerked away from her and glared.

Ignoring the little pinch of hurt, she glowered back at him. "We're supposed to be a couple. Couples hold hands."

He grunted in obvious annoyance and held his hand out to her like it was the last thing he wanted to do.

"What are you? Five?" She slipped her hand into his and ignored the tingles that shot up her arm. He had calluses on his palms, just below his fingers. She briefly wondered what caused them before the feel of him overwhelmed all other thoughts.

His grip on her tightened. "Concentrate," he reminded her under his breath.

Right.

Concentrate.

They stopped at the concierge and made a fake booking for tour tickets that included a guided tour of La Sagrada Familia—Rose had to stifle a snort. Then they casually walked, hand in hand, toward the signs for the restrooms. Milking the moment, she snuggled into Fionn, curling her free hand over the top of the hand that held hers.

He peered down at her, unamused.

Rose grinned.

His countenance hardened with more than just annoyance; she felt that look all over.

"Didn't you say you need to use the restroom?" he bit out.

She knew she should act with more solemnity considering the danger they were in, but teasing Fionn distracted her, calmed her, even. Raising their clasped hands to her mouth, she pressed a soft kiss to the top of his hand and then released it. "I'll be right back."

With a little swing in her hips, she left Fionn fighting back a scowl of outrage.

Fuddy-duddy, she laughed to herself as she entered the restroom.

Even though she'd checked to make sure there was no one there to see her *travel*, Fionn had told her to do it from inside a stall. Apparently, Schneider might not be above breaking the law by sticking cameras in the ladies' room.

Rose locked the stall and leaned her palms against the door, closing her eyes. Taking a deep breath, she visualized the plans for the vault. It wasn't a huge room, an entirely steel cube with very thick walls. Fionn seemed to have this unshakable belief that she could *travel* into it.

Called her a natural.

Exhaling long and slow, she chanted inwardly, *You can do this, you can do this*.

The vault enveloped her entire mind.

Go there. Be there.

Although her eyes were closed and she didn't move, she felt the door disappear beneath her palms and a chill blast across her skin.

Opening her eyes, Rose grinned.

She was inside the vault. There were four shelves that wrapped around the entire room except for the wall with the door. On the shelves were boxes and artifacts, some with gemstones that sparkled under the LED lights that she knew from the detailed plans didn't emit heat or UV.

The vault was also kept at a chilly temperature.

She shivered in her T-shirt, glad for her jeans and sneakers at least. Scanning the shelves, she searched for the silver box Fionn had described but stopped when she felt a tingle on the back of her neck.

Slowly turning, she faced the opposite wall and her attention zeroed in on a silver box on the second shelf.

Rose knew it was the one.

The solid silver case had engravings along the bottom half that wrapped around the entire box, depicting Fionn's story. Carefully taking it off the shelf, she ran her fingers over the etchings. A warrior on a rearing horse with a dagger in one hand, a sword in the other. The same warrior plunging the dagger into an elegant male. The warrior shackled before a beautiful woman. The warrior surrounded by cloaked figures. And finally, the warrior asleep in a tomb, his sword clasped between his hands.

Shivering for a different reason, Rose fought back overwhelming emotion. She felt Fionn's betrayal like that dagger through her heart. Anger and hurt burned inside her for him.

It made no sense.

How deeply she felt his pain made no sense to her.

Blinking back tears, she reached for the clasp on the box.

Fionn had said not to open it but Rose needed to see. She needed to see what the weapon, destined to kill her, looked like.

As soon as she lifted the lid, tremors affected her nerves, weakening her. Her knees gave way as if a huge weight was crushing down on her.

Rose slammed the box shut, closing the clasp, her strength returning.

"Fuck," she whispered, trembling.

She'd barely gotten a glimpse of the silvery-gray weapon.

When Fionn said pure iron hurt them, she assumed the metal would have to touch her skin to do it. Apparently not. Apparently, she just needed to be in its vicinity for it to affect her.

Then why hadn't she felt it when Ethan threw that blade at her?

Rose held the box firmly in her hand and focused on *traveling* outside the vault door. She was immediately faced with an irate Fionn.

"What took so long?" He took hold of the box before she could answer and unsnapped the clasp to lift the lid. She felt the strange weakening occur again just as Fionn flinched and shut the box.

Rose frowned. "Why does it do that? The blade Ethan threw didn't affect me, but this ..." She gestured to the box.

"Its effects are akin to being trapped in a room made entirely of iron. I told you. It's not just an ordinary iron blade. It's more powerful than that. Now, *travel* back to the restroom. From there to the stadium."

He vanished before she could answer.

Sighing at his bossy abruptness, Rose prepared to *travel*. There was a niggle of exhaustion working its way through her, and she didn't think it had to do with the iron. This felt more natural. As if *traveling* from place to place was draining her. With the vault so far underground, she couldn't just *travel* to the stadium from here. She needed to make the restroom pit stop as a precaution since she was still new at this.

Gathering her energy, Rose *traveled* into the hotel restroom stall and immediately felt her knees give away. Weakness flooded her.

What the hell?

A potent tingle filled the air.

Magic.

The stall door blew off and into the room.

Shocked, Rose lifted her weary head. Her limbs felt like lead.

What was going on?

Two witches and a warlock stepped into her line of sight.

How?

The taller of the two women, an attractive brunette, spoke. "You didn't think a little spell like Schneider's would keep us out, did you?" She was American. "We've been hanging out here all morning, waiting on you and Mór to show. Finally, you did but what do you know, we follow you in here and you'd vanished."

Rose cursed herself for using the stall.

She was trapped by its three walls and these three strangers and —she glanced down at the gap between the stall walls and the floor. No light came in under it because a band of iron filled the gap. In fact, the whole stall felt strangely dark. Straining to look up, Rose cursed under her breath. The stall had a ceiling now. A ceiling of iron.

"It envelops the entire stall. Like an iron cage," the woman informed her.

Fuck.

"Who are you?"

"Layton Blackwood." The warlock stepped forward and gave her an old-fashioned, gentlemanly bow. "At your service. These are my sisters, Liza and Lori."

He didn't look anything like his sisters, who were both brunettes with golden skin. Layton had shocking white-blond hair and pale skin. Rose licked her lips, thinking, thinking. *Dammit, think!*

Nausea made itself known and she groaned, desperately wishing she could flee the iron. The room began to spin.

"We're here to bring you into the safe arms of the Blackwood Coven, Rose."

No, no.

Kill her more like.

Her stomach roiled.

"Yeah," she whispered, "I feel real safe right now."

"We apologize for the iron, but we couldn't have you popping out of here without letting us explain." The warlock lowered to his haunches before her, his gaze crawling over her skin. "What is it about fae? I could look at you for hours and never tire of it, and I know Lori feels the same about Mór." Layton glanced over his shoulder. "What about you, Liza? Like what you see in Rose here?"

Liza was the shorter sister. She scowled at Layton. "We're not here to sexually harass her. Let's get on with things."

"It isn't sexual harassment. I just appreciate the finer things in life." He smiled at Rose.

Infuriated by his ogling, Rose bared her teeth at him. "If you're done objectifying me ..." Her words trailed off as the room spun horrifically.

"In a fight, you'll most likely be outnumbered and thus disoriented. You need to learn to focus through that." Fionn's voice filled her head, as did his lessons at the basilica.

Was that only last night?

Focus, Rose.

Layton Blackwood continued to speak but Rose didn't hear a word.

Instead, she strained against the strength of the iron, feeling her muscles burn as if she were pushing a mammoth weight off her body.

"Layton ..." She heard one of the sisters cut off her brother's droning voice.

Exultation pierced Rose's pain as she felt that weight shift. Every muscle in her body strained to its limit. *Almost there. Almost there.*

Then with one mighty shove, she screamed as if her whole body was being torn apart, abandoned the thought of agony and thought only of the stadium.

The world blurred and she collapsed on a sidewalk that was slightly warm beneath her palms from the November sun.

Panting, heaving, spitting up bile, she heard a surprised gasp behind her.

The weakness drained quickly from her body, but Rose was soaked with sweat as she pushed to her feet. She wiped at her mouth and searched her surroundings. There was no game on at the stadium, the grounds were quiet, but this female security guard had seen Rose appear out of nowhere.

If she questioned that appearance, she seemed to have buried it under her concern for the *state* Rose was in.

Rose waved off her concern, frantically looking for Fionn.

Where the hell was he?

HE WAITED five minutes for Rose to join him at the stadium.

Five minutes too long.

Something was wrong.

He could feel it in the racing of his panicked heart.

However, when Fionn had attempted to *travel* directly back to the ladies' restroom, he found himself in the corridor outside it instead.

A sheet of iron was placed over the entrance.

Fury roared through Fionn as he glanced left and right. There was no one else around, no approaching danger. Yet he could hear the murmurings of conversation within the restroom.

Focusing, he attempted to *travel* into the room, but his magic rebelled against the iron shield.

Sweat glistened on his temples as he gathered his strength and tried once more.

Nothing.

"Fuck," he bit out, clasping tightly to the silver box.

No guards or hotel staff had made an appearance, so whoever was in the restroom with Rose was powerful enough to get through Schneider's spells undetected.

The Blackwood Coven.

The Garm was mostly made up of vampires and werewolves.

It had to be the Blackwoods.

If it's the Blackwoods, she's safe, he reminded himself. Rose might believe the Blackwoods wanted to kill her, but Fionn knew the truth. The Blackwoods needed Rose alive to complete the spell that opened the gate to Faerie. That was the true spell Aine cast.

A fae-borne could open the gate and bring his or her companions into the world of Faerie to live there forever. All it would take was a drop of his or her blood.

But not with Fionn.

When he found the silver box with his dagger buried at the bottom of his faerie pool, Fionn discovered a piece of parchment inside. It held a note, from Aine, written in the dialect of Samhradh.

She warned that if he tried to use a fae child to return to Faerie with ill intentions, he'd have to kill that child, iron through the heart, to open the gate. She was always trying to best him, even from her perch on a throne on another fucking world.

Aine thought she knew him, thought he wouldn't sacrifice an innocent to take his revenge.

She underestimated the depth of his passion for vengeance.

His vengeance.

Fionn growled at the iron-shielded door. The Blackwoods wouldn't kill Rose but they'd bloody well tell her the truth. *Focus,* he demanded of himself. The rest of the room was not clad in iron. He could get past the door if he just bloody focused.

A scream tore through the walls of the restroom and shredded Fionn's soul.

Rose!

Terror and fury flooded him, all barricades insignificant in the face of reaching her in time. Just like that, Fionn stood inside the restroom ready to tear its occupants to pieces.

Layton, Lori, and Liza Blackwood whirled to face him, their expressions slack with bafflement. Fionn saw a stall covered in iron sheets to create a makeshift cage.

They'd trapped Rose like an animal.

The desire to rip Layton's head off was strong but the need to find Rose, who was nowhere in sight, was stronger.

She'd escaped the cage.

With one last look of promised retribution, Fionn sent out fingers of magic to the three siblings, hit their carotid sinus, and watched them slump to the floor in a tangle of unconscious limbs.

With one last snarl in their direction, he *traveled* to the hotel's side entrance, deliberately setting off the perimeter spell Schneider had alarmed the building with. *Let him find the Blackwoods and let them deal with each other.*

Job done, Fionn *traveled* to Camp Nou, hoping he'd find Rose.

Relief flooded him at the sight of his shaken companion searching the car park for him. He hurried toward Rose and she whirled around at the sound of his approaching footsteps. Without thinking, driven purely by instinct, he grabbed hold of her slim but strong biceps and hauled her against him.

She wrapped her arms around his waist, burrowing her face in his chest, and he hugged her with his free arm.

It was but seconds before her slim heat penetrated his anxiety and brought reality crashing down on him.

What the fuck was he doing?

Fionn pressed her away, bending his face to check her expression. She looked exhausted. "Are you okay?"

Rose nodded and he stepped out of her reach, putting much-needed distance between them. What was he doing *hugging* her?

He was losing his mind.

"Have you got enough left in you to *travel* back to the hotel?"

She shook her head, her voice hoarse. "I'm sorry."

"Don't be. They'd blocked the bathroom with iron. I couldn't get past it until I heard you scream." He flinched, knowing he'd remember the sound of Rose screaming for the rest of his life. "You were gone, but I saw what they'd done with the iron." Pride was an ache through him. The twisted fuck that he was. "You are very powerful, Rose."

She gave him a weary smile and shrugged. "My mom always said I have a will of steel."

"Your mam was right." And thank the gods for that. He nodded toward the street. "Come on. We'll grab a cab back to the hotel. I'm afraid from there, we need to keep going. We need to get out of the city before the Blackwoods catch up with us."

Rose walked toward the street and he hesitated to follow, wondering how much Layton had told her. "Moving on first and then sleep. Got it."

Fionn relaxed. If Layton had told her the truth, she didn't believe him or she wouldn't still be with Fionn. "What did Layton say?"

"He's creepy." Rose's voice was still hoarse as she threw the opinion over her shoulder at him. "I didn't hear much of anything he said. I was too busy concentrating on getting away from his licentious ass."

Licentious? "Did he touch you?"

"Nope."

Fionn relaxed.

"After we grab our stuff from the hotel, where to next?"

Fionn took in Rose's body as she walked slightly ahead of him. Her hips were gently rounded, not voluptuous like his past lovers', but they hypnotically swayed from side to side with her natural swagger.

He could smell fresh sweat on her skin blowing back on the breeze, and he zeroed in on her neck as she reached to lift her hair off her nape. Several strands stuck as a bead of sweat trickled down her spine.

It had taken some exertion but she'd retrieved An Breitheamh and then escaped an iron trap few fae could have.

Exhausted, she still didn't complain when he informed her they needed to keep moving. Just accepted it.

Strong.

A will of steel.

Beautiful.

As heat flooded low and thick inside Fionn, his frustration became a physical ache in his gums, in his very nerve endings. Curling his free hand into a fist, he fought against the overwhelming urge to surround Rose Kelly with his body and not let her up for air until they were both satisfied.

Fuck.

She'd want that from him. She'd made that plain and clear.

All thoughts of traveling directly to Ireland flew out of his head. There was no way he would touch Rose like that, make her take him deeper into her trust, only to betray her unto death. Which meant he needed another avenue to vent his frustrations, and soon.

"Eventually Ireland," he bit out as he caught up with her. "But first we're making a pit stop in Orléans."

"France?" She glanced up at him in surprise, those astoundingly blue eyes of hers making his stomach pitch. "What's in France?"

Deciding that staring at her was the problem, Fionn glared ahead, searching for a taxi stand. "Just something I need."

19

Bran arranged another car for them since the Blackwood Coven was now watching the train and bus stations and the airport. Fionn decided he would drive to Orléans. Despite it being an eight-hour drive.

"It's not an eight-hour journey in what we'll be driving," he'd replied when she'd questioned the length of the drive.

Rose understood what he meant when she saw the car. They'd collected their things from the hotel, he'd given her five minutes to freshen up, and then they were in a cab that took them across the city to its coast.

Their driver let them out at a luxury beachfront property. Outside it was a woman in a figure-hugging blue dress, leaning against a vehicle Rose was pretty sure belonged to Batman.

It hugged the road with elegant lines and curves; its nose and headlights created a hood that was somewhat feline. Dark matte-gray paint, black wheels, and wing mirrors gave it that Batmobile look.

It was the sexiest car Rose had ever seen.

The woman in the dress, with her impressive cleavage and tiny waist, pushed off the car at Fionn's approach, her gaze widening ever so slightly as she sashayed across the tarmac to meet them. She was wearing six-inch spiked stilettos and glided in them as easily as Rose could.

Rose wondered who the stranger was and tried not to feel agitated at the way the woman eyed Fionn like he was her next meal.

Sidling a little closer to him, the territorial action caused the stranger to offer Rose a genuine smile. They halted before each other and the stranger turned her attention to Fionn. She held up a key fob.

Fionn took it. "You got the money?" he asked.

The stranger nodded. "I hope you're not doing anything illegal in it?" she asked, her accent Spanish.

"We're not."

"Bran assured me as much, but I just needed to double-check. Her tank is full, but remember you can drain her in less than ten minutes if you go at her top speed."

"Noted." Fionn was staring almost avariciously at the car.

"Bran said you'll have someone trustworthy return her to me?"

"Absolutely. Thanks." Fionn moved around her, heading toward the car like he was under a spell.

The woman pouted. Actually pouted.

Rose could feel her pain. Right then she felt a little invisible to Fionn too. She stepped up beside the stranger. "Guess you're used to people admiring the car's curves."

"*Sí*, darling, but I'm used to having mine admired too." She eyed Rose. "Is he not attracted to women? Or just in love?"

With Rose?

She guffawed at the idea, grinning. "With your car, sure."

The woman chuckled. "She's easy to love."

"Apparently," Rose murmured. Fionn had opened the hood and surprised her by putting her backpack in a spot in there. Then he'd put his garment bag behind the passenger seat. He caressed the side of the car, and Rose felt a prick of envy.

Seriously, he'd forgotten she existed.

"What kind of car is it?"

"*Querida*, a Bugatti Chiron," the woman replied, as if Rose should know what that meant.

"Right."

"It's worth two million dollars, so if your boyfriend scratches it, he bought it."

Two million dollars?! Who would pay that for a car? "He's not my boyfriend," she murmured distractedly, staring at the car.

"*Right.*"

Before Rose could respond to the stranger's sarcastic drawl, Fionn looked up from his perusal and glowered at Rose. "Are you coming or what?"

"If I said 'or what,' would it matter?" she teased, gesturing to the vehicle. "Should I leave you two alone?"

His expression flattened. "Would you please get in the car?"

Truthfully, she was tired and looking forward to sleeping while he drove this thing through Europe. With a sigh, Rose held her hand out to the owner of the Bugatti. "Thanks for the loan. Nice to meet you."

The woman shook her hand, her fingers wrapping tightly around Rose's. "Jada García. If you're ever back in Barcelona, look me up."

A quick glance at Fionn warned her not to share her real name. "Emma," Rose supplied with a hopefully sincere smile as they shook hands.

"Well, *Emma*," Jada said, smirking, "it was a pleasure."

Rose nodded and strode toward Fionn, wondering who Jada was interested in. Fionn or Rose? A look over her shoulder at Jada's lingering gaze suggested it might both.

Laughing at the scowl Fionn threw Jada, Rose got into the passenger side and let her lips part in a gasp as she lowered herself into the sport seat of fine Italian leather in teal and dark gray. The center console was narrow and sported several knobs.

Fionn opened the driver's side door but seeing how close the seat was to the pedals, Rose called out for him to wait. She leaned over the console, felt for the buttons, and pressed the electric seat until it slid back as far as it could go.

"Done."

Fionn lowered his massive body inside. He still engulfed the space, his hair hitting the roof's leather lining. "Thank you," he said gruffly, as he felt for the buttons. Once he'd gotten his chair position as comfortable as he could, Rose pulled on her seat belt.

"Expensive car," she noted.

"Fast car. We'll get to Orléans in half the time."

"Isn't it a little conspicuous?"

Fionn started the engine; it purred in answer. As they pulled away, she waved to Jada. "The opposite. Only so many people own a Bugatti. It's registered under Jada's name." He swung them around a corner, faster than Rose would have dared, and she marveled at the way the car gripped the road.

She caressed the leather beneath her and relaxed into her seat. "Wow."

As they moved through city traffic, Rose fought the urge to close her eyes. She still had questions. "Who is Jada?"

"A friend of Bran's."

"She knows what he is?"

"People as wealthy as Jada often find themselves in our world. She and Bran are what you call fuck buddies. Not exclusive. She has a fiancé and Bran has many lovers, male and female. Jada, however, lets him drink from her."

Rose remembered the vampire tearing into her throat and scowled as she automatically reached for her neck. "Seriously?"

Fionn flicked her a look, saw where her hand was, and turned back to the road. "Rose, it shouldn't hurt. From what I've gathered, a vampire bite provides a human with much sexual pleasure. As they drink, the vampire releases pheromones that causes a chemical reaction. A sexual one. The bastard who bit you was all about the pain, so he didn't do that."

"I don't know what's worse," Rose grumbled. "Both are a violation of a different kind."

"Not when consent is involved." Fionn shot her a disapproving look. "Jada consents to the bite and to the sex. Don't judge what you don't understand."

"Says the man who hates what he is."

At his icy silence, Rose heaved a sigh. "Sorry. I'm just ... tired."

"Then sleep."

"I would but I don't know where we're going and ... I keep thinking about these powers of mine. Of ours."

"What about them?"

"You said witches and warlocks have limitations. That they have to pull from the world, exchange something for the magic."

"Yes."

"We don't. Except for exhaustion, werewolf bites and iron, we don't have limitations. Do we?"

He was quiet a moment as he seemed to consider her question. "Everyone has limitations. I can knock someone unconscious by visualizing my magic pinching their carotid sinus, which is what I did to the Blackwoods back at the hotel—"

"Seriously?" Rose stroked her throat again. "That's some trick."

"But I can't fly. I can fall with style but I can't fly."

She grinned. "Did you just quote *Toy Story*?"

He frowned at her. "What?"

That would be a no then. Rose chuckled to herself and shook her head. "Nothing. So no flying."

"Technically, no flying. Traveling has its limitations, as you've just experienced. And no cheating bodily functions. You have to eat, sleep, drink, piss, and—"

"Yeah, I got it."

Fionn frowned. "You have very few limitations, Rose. Once you fully let go of thinking of yourself as human, you'll discover how far your limits go."

She nodded, considering this. It was both a thrilling and terrifying concept. Something else occurred to her. "Why borrow this car? Why pay for a personal shopper to deliver clothes to our hotel? If you can just snap your fingers and make it all appear?"

His scowl this time was ferocious. "Because I can't just make it appear, Rose. If I snap my fingers and make this Bugatti appear, it's because I've stolen it out of Jada's secure lockup. When you're this powerful, you have to draw a line. It would be easy to use magic to amass wealth, just as Schneider has done. But what kind of man would that make me? I'm going to be here forever, and I will not spend eternity in lazy indolence, stealing from humans. What I have, I've earned. Unless necessary, I do not steal."

Her heart literally skipped a beat. She was in awe of him. "You have your own code. Your own sense of honor."

"I don't know if I'd call it that. But if I viewed the world and everything in it as my due, I'd lose myself. And if someone as powerful as me loses himself, I'd be putting the world in danger."

"Fionn."

"Yes?"

"I know you know that you're physically attractive."

He tensed. "Rose ..."

"You've never been more attractive to me than you are right now," she whispered.

In answer, Fionn flicked her an unreadable look. "Go to sleep, Rose. You've had a tough morning."

Disappointment at his avoidance sank deep in her gut. With a sigh, she replied, "I will when you tell me why we're going to Orléans."

The car sped up as Fionn drove them onto the highway that would take them out of Barcelona. "I'm going for a fight." The words sounded dragged out of him.

"A fight?"

"An underground one."

Their conversation from yesterday played over in her head. *"Places for vamps and werewolves to take that natural aggression they don't want pouring out around humans. They beat the living daylights out of each other with it instead."*

Rose considered Fionn. "Why do you need to fight?"

That telltale muscle ticked in his jaw. "I need a fight, that's all."

"You're frustrated?" Sexually or otherwise? Rose was hoping it was otherwise because Fionn deciding to take/or give a beating rather than throw her onto a bed somewhere and let their wild sides reign was a little insulting.

"Today the Blackwoods could've gotten you. That was my fault. I took too big a risk with you."

He felt guilty.

Rose relaxed a little. "Fionn, I'm a big girl and I decided to go after the dagger."

"Because I asked you to." He shot her a dark look. "Go to sleep, Rose, and give us both some peace."

She eyed him, in no way put off by his grumpiness. Instead, longing coursed through her as she watched his big hands change gears, pushing the Bugatti to 120 mph. It didn't even feel like it was doing sixty. Rose sighed, closed her eyes, and settled in to sleep. But before she let slumber come for her, she murmured throatily, "There are better ways to vent your frustration."

Even though Rose didn't open her eyes to see his reaction, she felt the air inside the car turn electric as a flood of desire gripped her belly low and deep.

It was foreign.

It was *his* desire.

Although pleased by the thought, his desire only inspired a natural response from Rose. She shifted in her seat, crossing one leg over the other, and willed her blood to cool. Thankfully, Rose was so goddamn weary from the encounter with the Blackwoods, exhaustion pulled her under.

The arousal never faded, though, pulling her deep into the dark where the only thing that existed was Fionn. Naked. Entwined with her.

THERE WERE few streetlights in this district of Orléans. Industrial buildings, sites, and warehouses occupied the street in Saint-Jean-de-la-Ruelle. Broken chain-link fences, old, tired concrete buildings, rusted corrugated iron, and faded red brick surrounded them.

Fionn had, with much regret, left the Bugatti with a contact at a luxury hotel near the Loire River. He had no idea who the man was, but Bran had trusted him to return the hypercar to Jada. Rose had chuckled sleepily as Fionn handed over the fob with obvious reluctance.

It was probably wrong that not buying a Bugatti before his final trek into Faerie now ranked on his list of top twenty regrets.

The woman at the top of that list, holding the number one spot with a painful, talon-like grip on his soul, watched the shadowed figures disappear into a large warehouse across the street, behind a secure chain link fence.

Fionn had assumed a sleeping Rose would be a reprieve from his unexpected and entirely unwanted attraction. Instead, it had proven the opposite. He didn't pretend to have the nose of a wolf, but fae had heightened senses. Rose's scent changed as she slept, becoming musky, feminine, and familiar.

Whatever she was dreaming about, she was enjoying it.

Too much.

Now and then, she'd emit little moans or groans that were driving him wild. At one point Fionn drove so fast down the highway hoping to run from his desires that he'd inadvertently taken the tank too low. Rose had slept through his pit stop at the gas station. He'd had to take a minute before getting out of the car or everyone in the fucking vicinity would know Rose had him primed like a prepubescent boy instead of the goddamn immortal warrior he was.

Fuck.

How is she doing this to me? he wondered as he studied her watching the warehouse.

By the time he'd handed over the Bugatti, Fionn was ready to unleash every molecule of pent-up frustration on someone. He just hoped there was a being up to the challenge in that warehouse. The plan had been to leave Rose at the apartment Bran booked for them in the center of Orléans. It was a beautiful space on the top floor of a seventeenth-century building in the heart of the city. Balconies led off nearly every room, looking down on the cobbled street with its shops and trams.

Rose had seemed energized by her sleep in the car and the new location, still seemingly unfazed by all the shit that had happened to her in less than a week.

She amazed him.

And that was the problem.

His plans for her had become a constant knife through his throat.

There was no relief from that knife. Not only did Rose insist on eating with him at a restaurant across the street, she'd then tried to insist, like a nagging wife, that he rest before the fight.

Fionn couldn't.

Too agitated.

Teetering on the edge of temptation.

Temptation he was destined not to outrun, apparently, because the bloody woman insisted on accompanying him.

"I want to see," Rose had said, her expression taut with stubbornness when he refused her request. "And I've got your back."

Just words. They irritated him almost as much as his desire for her. No one, except Bran, had ever had his back. "I hate to burst your bubble, Rose, but I don't need you to have my back."

Rose would not be shaken.

Damn her.

"So, this is an underground fight?" She gestured to the warehouse.

She'd showered and changed into the jeans and shirt the last hotel had dry-cleaned for her, but her singular summery scent overwhelmed the complimentary coconut shampoo she'd discovered in her en suite.

Fionn grunted in response and walked toward the fence. A man, almost as tall as Fionn, stood guard by the gate. He knew his face. The vampire was at least fifty years old, for this was the third fight in France Fionn had attended where this vamp acted as a doorman.

"I know you," the vampire said, opening the gate. "Here to do some damage?"

He gave another grunt as he made to walk by the doorman.

"I don't know her." The vamp grabbed Rose's arm.

Later Fionn would blame his response on his wasted nerves. As soon as the vampire touched Rose, Fionn whirled on him, gripped him by the throat, and lifted him off his feet. He bared the spell-cast fangs he wore to pretend to be a vamp at the fights and growled into the doorman's face, "We mustn't touch what isn't ours."

The vampire tried and failed to release himself from Fionn's grip, shock slackening his features when he realized he was the weaker of the two. Finally he nodded, and Fionn lowered the vamp to the ground.

He could sense Rose's tension at his back as he guarded her from the doorman's study.

The vampire rubbed his throat, gaping at Fionn. "No offense meant," he wheezed out. "I sensed magic, that's all."

"She's a witch," Fionn replied, "and she knows the rules."

Still holding his throat in bewilderment, the doorman waved them on.

Furious at himself for responding like a territorial animal, it took Fionn a moment to look down at Rose and ask after her welfare.

She nodded solemnly at him. "I'm okay. And just for the record, I can handle myself. But thanks."

Knowing Rose was right, that she could handle herself, only made him feel worse. He was born in the late European Iron Age, not long before the Romans would try to conquer his part of the world. Fionn believed differently from how modern humans might expect. Perhaps they assumed women were treated as they were for most of history, as the weaker sex, to be protected and owned by men.

As a human king, he had believed he owned Aoibhinn, but it was a mutual ownership. She owned him in return. As the man who loved her, he wanted to *protect* her, but as a king who was often away at war, he wanted Aoibhinn to be able to protect herself.

Just as he taught Rose to use her abilities, to defend herself, he'd taught Aoibhinn how to wield a sword as well as any man in his army.

This kind of belief in the fairer sex had been unconventional and only lent itself to expounding upon the uniqueness of his kingship.

That belief in Aoibhinn had been his undoing.

Three centuries above the dirt had allowed time to disintegrate some of those memories, to mute the pain.

But never his thirst for vengeance.

As Fionn strode into the warehouse, relief moved through him as he took in the two large circles that had formed. Two fights. Supernaturals circling each, fists above their heads, baying for blood. The coppery scent of it already filled the air, mingling with sweat, dirt, and some kind of chemical, most likely due to whatever had been stored in the warehouse before it had been converted into an underground fight club.

He searched the space, determined to find the supernatural that would prove the most challenging.

"Is this like a bare-knuckle boxing match?" Rose asked, raising her voice to be heard over the commotion. He heard the awe in her tone but refused to look at her. The bloody woman muddled everything up.

He opened his mouth to respond in the affirmative just as a huge figure strode between fights, observing the opponents, halting Fionn's answer.

The Fates were feeling sympathetic. A hard smile pushed at Fionn's mouth.

Kiyonari. Or Kiyo as the werewolf preferred.

Years ago, Kiyo had learned of Fionn's immortality. That did not worry Fionn, for Kiyo was an anomaly, the result of ancient Asian magic that even Fionn was ignorant to.

Kiyo was the world's only immortal werewolf.

Sensing him, Kiyo halted his progress around one of the circles and turned his head. The shadows beyond the overhead lights masked his face, but Kiyo had spotted him. Fionn knew.

They walked toward one another.

Rose followed at Fionn's side. "Who is that?" The awe in her voice penetrated this time. He shot her a quick glance and caught her ogling the shirtless Kiyo.

He bit back a growl of annoyance.

Kiyo drew to a stop before them, his expression the same as always—scowling and impatient.

Fionn had been accused of being a broody bastard but no one brooded like Kiyonari. The product of an illicit affair between an American doctor and a Japanese merchant's daughter sometime in the nineteenth century, Kiyo's life was difficult *before* he was bitten and spelled with immortality.

Although Fionn hadn't thought of it one way or another before Rose's reaction, Kiyo's mixed heritage (a curse during much of his human and immortal life) had favored him physically. Rose's expression said the werewolf wasn't hard to look at.

"I was just about to leave," Kiyo said, his accent distinctly American.

Kiyo had lived in New York until the 1960s. He'd been a nomad ever since, but he'd never lost his adopted accent.

"I assume you'll answer my challenge."

Kiyo nodded, his attention moving to Rose. His expression never changed. "She's like you."

There was no question in the comment, just an observation by the most perceptive son of a bitch in the werewolf world.

One of the things Fionn liked most about the werewolf, however —he wasn't a nosy arsehole.

"Hey." Rose held out her hand to Kiyo.

He stared at it and promptly ignored the gesture.

"Okay, then." She threw a "Who's this guy?" look at Fionn that would have amused him under other circumstances.

"Weapons?" the wolf asked.

Fionn rolled his shoulders, shrugging out of his coat. At the same time, he called on the weapons he stored in his Paris apartment. He had homes everywhere and weapons in every single one. Magic tinged the air around them as the swords appeared in his hands. The coat slipped to the ground.

The others were too caught up in the current fights to even notice.

Rose drew in a breath at the sight of the medieval claymores, steel glimmering in the dim light.

Kiyo quirked an eyebrow. "No katanas this time?"

"Last time you had the advantage." Fionn tossed one of the broadswords to the wolf; he caught it by the hilt with ease. "This time it's my turn."

"Like you need it." Kiyo brandished the sword with ease, feeling out the weight and balance of the steel.

"A sword fight?" Rose stepped between them to ask Fionn, her back to Kiyo.

"You're surprised? It's what I'm used to in a fight. And this way it's fair. No magic, just strength and skill."

She took a step closer to him. Too close, if you asked him. "Who is this guy?" she said under her breath.

Kiyo scowled at her back, having heard her easily with his wolf ears.

"This is Kiyo ... a friend. A werewolf."

Kiyo transferred the scowl to Fionn and this time, he failed in his attempt to suppress his smile.

"Your werewolf friend is hot," Rose said, causing his smile to wither in an instant. He glared down at her, and she grinned. "But not as hot as you when you smile." She smacked him playfully on the arm and stepped out of his way. "You should do it more often."

She really was the devil.

The werewolf offered him a commiserating look in return for Fionn's beleaguered one. A roar of animalistic growls rent the air, signaling a fight was over. Kiyo turned from watching a crowd disperse, calls for the next opponents circling the warehouse. "Now?"

Fionn nodded before handing his overcoat to Rose. "You watch. That is all. No interfering."

Her expression serious, she nodded, folding the coat in her arms. "What about..." she bared her teeth and gestured to Kiyo.

Amusement flickered through him. He guessed that was her way of asking if he was concerned Kiyo might bite him. "We're sword fighting, Rose. No teeth."

She didn't seem assured, but replied, "Got it. Go kick some ass."

Following Kiyo, they fell into step. The supes around them started to buzz with renewed energy. Those who knew of Kiyo and Fionn knew they were about to witness something different. They noted the swords in their hands, and the murmurs of anticipation grew.

"She's the reason you're here," Kiyo said. Again, not a question.

Fionn grunted in answer.

"Why not fuck her instead? I'd choose sex over a fight."

They stopped to face one another as the crowds encircled them, giving them enough room to battle. Kiyo offered the sword to Fionn to hold as he drew his shoulder-length black hair into a topknot.

"I have another, more important purpose for her." He held out the swords to Kiyo. The wolf waited patiently as Fionn drew his shirt over his head, threw the expensive material to the dirt, and then tied his own hair back out of his face. The shorter strands fell across his cheekbone, but there was nothing to be done about that.

Bloody hair would not get in his way.

"Can't you use her for both?" The wolf held out the hilt of Fionn's sword.

Images of Rose filled his mind: lying on her back beneath him; straddling him; on her knees, sweetly curved arse in his hands. His knuckles cut into the sword's pommel.

Kiyo raised an eyebrow. "Your eyes."

Fuck.

Rarely did Fionn allow his emotions to so overcome him that his eyes bled gold.

"That's new."

Fionn glowered. "You'll forget you ever saw that."

The wolf nodded. "Already forgotten."

"And in answer to your question, no, I cannot. Now, are we going to fight or sit down to fucking tea and gossip?"

Kiyo's answer was to attack.

The roar of the crowd filled Fionn's ears, mixing with the whoosh of blood as the fight cleared his mind, reducing him to a warrior facing a worthy opponent. There was nothing but the swing of blades, the clang of steel hitting steel, packed dirt beneath them, and quick feet following the orders of quicker minds.

THE CACOPHONY of supernatural crowds was something else. Rose held her breath as the men and women, vampires and werewolves jeered and rallied and shouted their support for whatever opponent they'd chosen to back.

She had never seen anything like the spectacle before her.

Kiyo was spectacular to look at, even without the mad sword skills. Although shorter than Fionn (who wasn't?), he was probably around six two. Rose had been a little preoccupied with his shirtless torso when he first approached because the guy had fantastic broad shoulders, a narrow waist, and pecs and abs to die for. His jeans hung low on his hips, showing off his incredible V-cut obliques. This masculine gorgeousness was all wrapped up in smooth, fawn skin, except for a long scar across his belly that Rose posited must have come from a silver weapon. It made him look even more badass than he already was.

Rose was not ashamed to say she was internally drooling even before she got to the beauty of his face. The werewolf was rude, intimidating as hell, and as warm as a swim in the Arctic, but there was no denying he was beautiful.

There was no other word for it.

Large eyes so dark they were a shiny black in the low-lit warehouse, a broad nose, high cheekbones, thick, black hair that was now pulled into a very attractive man bun, and a full-lipped mouth with a very defined, prominent cupid's bow. A person could stare at it for hours.

It was a wonder, then, that as swords slashed through the air, feet moved faster than a human's ever could, and muscles rippled under the aluminum lighting, Rose couldn't tear her attention from Fionn.

The wolf, Kiyo, held his own against her companion, considering Fionn towered over him by a good five inches and pounds of thick muscle, but the fae was a force to be reckoned with.

Her mouth was dry as she watched him, hugging his overcoat to her chin, his cologne tickling her senses. When he'd whipped off his shirt and tied back his hair before the fight, a vamp next to her made a crude, sexual comment that had her hissing like a jealous wife.

She never got jealous or territorial, but it was happening with alarming frequency around Fionn.

To her surprise and smugness, the guy who'd made the comment took one look at her and warily moved away through the crowds.

It occurred to Rose that she perhaps was giving off some badass supernatural vibes of her own. And she was okay with that.

Minutes ticked by as the well-matched opponents fought.

Rose didn't know how long the battle had been going when Fionn's blade caught Kiyo's forearm. The sight and smell of blood made the crowd surge.

Kiyo's lips parted in a growl, baring unnaturally long canines. Two hands gripped on the hilt of his sword, he spun into a jump, a blur of elegant movement, and brought his blade crashing down against Fionn's with such force, the fae stumbled.

Rose let out a little gasp, instinctually stepping toward him, and to her utter surprise, Fionn's concerned gaze flew to hers in the crowd.

He'd heard her gasp.

His expression pinched in pain as Kiyo took advantage of his distraction and cut a slice through Fionn's pants at the thigh.

With a growl of aggression, he returned his focus to the werewolf while Rose was thankful the cut was covered by his suit pants so the supes wouldn't see it heal unnaturally fast.

Kiyo's was no longer dripping blood, but it was healing at a slower rate than hers or Fionn's would.

How had Fionn escaped questions about this in his previous fights? Unless Kiyo was the first to make a mark on him?

So many questions. She always had so many questions, even she was exhausted by the continual onslaught.

A little while later, an awed female voice said, "They've been fighting for an hour."

Rose blinked. She'd been so lost watching the fight, she hadn't realized that much time had passed. She cast a look over her shoulder at the speaker and saw it was a short, curvy blond. Her hand was held in the tight grip of a stocky redheaded male. Just looking at them, at any of the supes in the crowd, Rose didn't know what they were. She wondered if there was a way to tell a vamp from a werewolf when they weren't flashing their fangs ...

Another question for Fionn.

If this fight ever ended.

It was then she heard what sounded like a sniff.

Sniff, sniff, sniff at her neck.

A prickling sensation followed; her heart began to race and a weird sense of dread filled her belly.

She knew that sensation.

"The racing heart, the dread in the gut ... they're warning signs. Of coming danger. You feel those things, you get ready to fight or to flee."

Holy crap.

Rose glanced over her shoulder and saw the blond and the redhead were now eyeing her with their silver gazes. Vampires.

The blond sniffed the air in front of Rose and hunger flashed in those strange eyes. "What are you?"

Uneasy but determined not to show it, Rose sneered. "None of your fucking business." Proud her voice had remained strong, she pushed through the crowd, away from the vampire couple, hoping they'd lose interest.

Unfortunately, the telltale feelings weren't easing up.

Worry filled Rose. She wasn't afraid she couldn't take on two vampires; she was afraid she didn't have enough control over her powers to hide what she was in a room filled with supernaturals.

A strong hand wrapped around her wrist and Rose spun, ready to fight.

Fionn stared down at her, anger etched in his expression.

His face shiny and his torso slick with sweat, he examined her body, clinically, like he was checking for harm. The crowds had melted away from her, murmuring quietly.

Then Fionn cocked his head, like he'd scented something. He whipped his head around, sword soaring up to just scrape the chin of the redheaded vamp.

His bloodsucking companion stood stiff and wide-eyed at his side.

"Take one more step and I'll cut off your fucking head," Fionn warned, his Irish accent pronounced.

The redhead raised his arms defensively. "We just wanted to know what she is. No harm meant."

"You were hunting her. I saw." He pressed the tip of the sword deeper, blood seeping out.

"Like I said, no harm meant." The vamp licked his lips nervously, his eyes no longer silver but still hungry as they moved to Rose. "She smells good. What is she?"

A shift moved through the crowd, and Rose's heart pounded faster, harder as she felt the change in the air. All focus was on her. They were curious. That, mixed with the bloodlust in the air, began a frenzy of murmurings.

They all wanted to know what she was.

Fionn turned toward them, putting Rose at his back. "She's mine!" His voice rang through the room.

Kiyo appeared at Fionn's side, sword at the ready. His statement was clear.

The smart supernaturals nodded at the warning and moved off, joining the crowds around the two supes that were fighting on the other side of the warehouse.

A small group stayed behind, their curious, avaricious, silver eyes on Rose.

Vampires.

Rose remembered the vampire who attacked her. The delirious, amazed hunger in his eyes after he'd tasted her. *What are you?* he'd asked. Apparently, a fae's blood smelled and tasted a little nicer than human blood.

Great.

Someone moved. Rose wasn't sure whom.

But she never even got a chance to join the fight.

Fionn and Kiyo sliced their swords through seven heads in seconds.

Actual seconds.

Ash danced in the air like dust, floating down to create seven piles on the packed dirt floor.

She couldn't breathe.

She'd never seen anything like it.

It had been like some violent, brutal dance watching the werewolf and fae deftly avoid fists and fangs and legs as they whipped, spun, and sliced through the group of vamps.

Holy shit.

"Rose." A touch on her chin stole her gaze from the piles of ash to Fionn's face. "You with me?"

"What just happened?" She gestured to the deceased.

"She *is* new, isn't she," Kiyo murmured at Fionn's side.

Rose touched her throat. "Can that happen to us?"

Fionn flicked a look at Kiyo before turning to her. His voice was low, so as not to be overheard. "No, we heal too fast. The sword would get pushed out by our healing abilities."

Holy shit. Looking beyond him, she noted none of the other supes seemed to care that seven vampires had just been killed.

As always, her companion seemed to read her mind. "There are rules, Rose. You don't feed on unwilling victims at an underground fight. I made a claim on you, they ignored it. No one cares if they're dead. Do you?"

Remembering how painful a vampire bite could be, she shook her head and then let out a slow exhale as she looked back at Fionn and Kiyo. "But you could've at least given me a chance to join in."

Fionn closed his eyes and gave a slow shake of his head, but she saw the slight tremble in his lips. He was trying not to laugh.

Good.

He'd been so serious all day.

Kiyo held out the sword to Fionn. "There's a big fight in Romania in two months. Bucharest. Only the very strongest are invited. Will I see you there?"

Ooh, Romania. It had been on Rose's European bucket list but she'd never made it.

The question caused Fionn's expression to flatten. "No." He waved off the sword. "Keep it."

Something like surprise flashed across Kiyo's face as he held on to the weapon. "Change your mind. I need the challenge." Then, without a backward glance at either of them, the beautiful Japanese werewolf strode out of the warehouse.

"We should go."

Rose nodded, handing Fionn his coat. Her mind was no longer on the amazing display of warriorship from her companion and his werewolf buddy. It was on the grimness of Fionn's expression. He'd gone somewhere hellish and dark in his mind, and she had no idea what had triggered the unsettling change.

20

The fight with Kiyo had burned energy.

Unfortunately, it had not burned his aggression, self-loathing, or frustration.

It might have, had he not felt his heart race mid fight, felt a tingle down his spine and that telling dread in his gut that warned him of danger. Fionn had known instantly that it wasn't his own danger, and he'd looked out to the crowds to see two fucking vampires hunting Rose as she tried to push swiftly through the baying supes around her.

Kiyo had known to withdraw without a word as Fionn was a blur across the room to put himself between Rose and her pursuers.

His protective instincts weren't anything noble. It was territorialism. Fionn could lie all he liked and tell himself he wanted nothing to happen to Rose before he got the chance to open the gate. That wasn't true. They'd already be in Ireland if it were.

This was a different territorialism.

This was something primal and ancient.

Something that terrified him.

Nothing had terrified Fionn in a long time. In centuries.

Until now.

Because even if what he was feeling was what he thought it was, it changed nothing. Rose still had to die for his revenge. If he chose her, she'd only betray him. The death of the Faerie Queen was too important. Fuck fate, if that was what this was.

Sensing his volatility, Rose had remained silent as they found a private place to *travel* back to the rented apartment. Fionn regretted not asking Bran to make sure they stayed at a hotel. Separate rooms.

They had separate bedrooms here, but it was still a shared space.

"Get some sleep," he practically snarled before turning to leave the open-plan living area.

Rose appeared in the doorway, blocking his path.

Two could play at that game.

He *traveled* into his bedroom.

She appeared at the foot of his bed.

Fuck. "Get out, Rose."

"No." Her expression was defiant as she crossed her arms over her chest.

Will of fucking steel.

"Rose," Fionn warned, the tenuous grip he had on his control slipping by the second.

"I'm not leaving until you tell me what's wrong."

He zeroed in on her luscious little upside-down mouth.

"Is it because I interrupted your fight? Drew attention to myself?"

"No," he grunted, catching a whiff of her musk in the air.

Fionn had smelled her during his fight.

Knew she was growing aroused watching him.

Don't do it.

"Is it because I noticed the hotness of Kiyo?"

Don't do it.

"Because that's nothing. Just appreciation—"

He sped across the room, lifted her up under her arms, her feet off the floor, and crushed her mouth beneath his.

She kissed him back.

Immediately.

Rose's lips were hot and searching, a little feminine moan vibrating from her throat.

Her scent enveloped him.

Fuck, he wanted to touch her everywhere—his hands didn't know which part of her to caress first.

With a gasp of unadulterated need, Rose broke the kiss but only to encircle his waist with her legs, to cling to his shoulders, and in doing so free his hands to move. This time *she* took *his* mouth.

Fionn's rational thinking malfunctioned.

Sliding inside Rose Kelly became the most important thing in the world.

They fell to the bed, Fionn of enough mind to brace one hand on the mattress to hold his weight off her. His other hand slipped under her shirt, fingers pushing beneath the lacy material of her bra so he could cup her sweet breast in his hand.

She was a perfect handful, her nipple hard against his thumb as he strummed it.

Rose arched beneath him, her soft hands caressing his skin, pushing down into the waistband of his trousers to feel his arse. She undulated beneath him, trying to push into his arousal as their tongues tangled in a wet, deep, uncontrolled kiss that was driving him mad with want.

As he squeezed her perfect breast in one hand, his other slid down her stomach and began unbuttoning her jeans. She arched into him, encouraging him, groaning into his mouth as his fingers slipped beneath her lacy knickers. At the feel of her hot wetness, her clit beneath his thumb, Fionn nearly lost his mind. His kisses ravaged as his thumb circled her while two thick fingers pushed into her tight, slick heat.

Fuck, she felt like heaven.

"Fionn," Rose moaned his name as she pulled her lips from his. Her hands were now on the buttons of his trousers, fumbling to release him. "Come inside me. I need you. I've never needed anyone like I need you."

The words penetrated the better half of him and with great reluctance, he opened his eyes.

Rose panted beneath him, her shirt askew, her long hair cascading over his pillows, her throbbing heat clutching his fingers.

Small, feminine, strong.

Silk and steel.

She stared up at him with affection ... and trust.

That, more than anything, tugged on the last bit of decency within him.

"Fionn?"

With a hard smile of regret, he reluctantly removed his hand from her sweet breast and placed his fingers gently over Rose's carotid.

Sleep.

Those stunning blue eyes of hers fluttered shut. Her dark lashes weren't long but there were lots of them. A thick frame around her eyes, now a curtain shielding her from light.

From him.

Her body relaxed into the bed and with a groan of unfulfilled need, Fionn fell to his back beside her. His hand rested at his side, touching Rose's. Her scent filled his nose, torturing him. Afraid to wake her, he didn't reach for her, but he felt a stab of something in his chest when he noted how small her hand was compared to his.

Pressing the heels of his palms to his eyes, Fionn willed his body to cool and his arousal to fade. It was difficult with her scent on his fingers.

He'd eventually done the right thing but he wouldn't pat himself on the fucking back for it.

Settling his hands on his stomach, he turned his head on the pillow to look at her again.

Rose.

Panic gripped him.

How could he hurt her now?

He visualized plunging An Breitheamh into her heart and made a low sound of agony.

Rose stirred in her sleep, her lashes fluttering, but she didn't wake.

Fionn shifted onto his side to watch her.

If he didn't take An Breitheamh to her, he'd have to find the last fae-borne. He couldn't kill Niamh if she was his descendant. If he couldn't kill Niamh, and he couldn't kill Rose ... Yet, that was taking a massive risk. What if he was too late to find the other fae-borne?

What good were these feelings, anyway? Fionn planned to take his revenge and die at the end of it. There was no future for him and Rose. Even if he didn't have a plan to die, he'd never learn to trust her fully.

And what of Rose's future? To constantly be on the run from fanatics who either wanted to kill her or use her to open a fucking gate?

Surely giving her a worthy death now was a blessing in disguise.

The mere thought nauseated Fionn.

"Rose," he whispered, reaching out to touch a silken strand of her hair, "what have you done?"

21

The streets had blurred together as Rose sped through them faster than light. She flew over rooftops, jumped from balcony to balcony on seventeenth-century buildings that changed as she soared midair onto La Sagrada Familia. One minute she'd been in Orléan, now Barcelona.

She gripped the side of one of the spires, feet secured in the gaps in the stonework. Laughing, exhilarated, Rose held on tight as she glanced over her shoulder and found Fionn floating midair with invisible wings. His brooding expression was firmly in place.

"Let go, Rose," he demanded.

Instead, she climbed.

"We mustn't touch what isn't ours," he called out.

She stopped, pulled her knees up toward her chest, her feet flat to the stone, and pushed, arching her back, lifting her chin as she did a backward flip off the spire. It felt like flying.

Landing on the ground was like landing on a cloud.

Her surroundings were vague now, like an incomplete sketch. However, when Fionn appeared before her, he was anything but. He was full-color 4K HD.

"Show-off," he said.

Rose felt excitement blossom low in her gut accompanying the flutter near her heart. "You like it. Admit it. You like me."

Just as his lips pushed toward a smile, a tornado—or something like it—pulled him up into its grasp, taking the vague world with it in a smear of colors.

Her heart raced, all joy gone, only confusion and fear left as she stood in an eternity of darkness.

"Hello!" she yelled, the word echoing and echoing and echoing.

Then she was on the move, like the blackness beneath her was a walkway in motion; one that rippled and wobbled and then propelled her out of the dark.

Rose landed in a large room. Struggling to even out her breathing, she spun in the spot, staring at the circular room with its conical roof. A whitish, cracked, claylike material created a circular wall that came to just above Rose's head. From there the ceiling, made of a wooden frame and hay, vaulted to a point in the center. In the middle of the room was a circle of stones, within which a fire was dying, the smoke filtering up to a small gap in the roof.

Edging the room was a table with pieces of pottery, a rough-hewn jug and cups ... There were wicker baskets and benches with furs thrown over them near an entrance.

Behind her, simple framework and fabric draped like curtains created a crude separation of living and sleeping quarters. Rose jerked in surprise at the sight of a beautiful gray wolf sprawled in front of it, his head resting between his paws as he dozed.

A groan drew Rose's attention from the wolf to the curtains as a large hand pushed the fabric aside, revealing more furs.

The wolf instantly woke up and stood, a large, majestic animal with piercing blue eyes. He began to pace impatiently until Fionn was there. There was a glow about him, and even though he sported a thick, long beard, Rose would recognize him anywhere. He stepped out of the furs, naked and magnificent.

Her breath caught.

He reached into the bed of furs, giving her an amazing view of that muscular ass of his, and pulled on rough trousers. With a yawn,

Fionn crossed the room and picked up something that looked like bread from a plate on the table. The wolf followed, and Fionn reached out to scratch behind his ears. "Maidin Mhaith, Cónán."

Chewing on the bread, Fionn strode toward the entrance, the wolf shadowing him.

Rose followed.

It had taken her slumberous mind to catch up, but as she dashed out of the roundhouse, her consciousness realized she was dream-walking again, this time in Fionn's dreamworld. And he seemed to be dreaming about the past.

Rose marveled at the view as she skidded to a stop outside the house. She was on a hill. Sprawled below her was a village, a collection of roundhouses of varying sizes, all with land that was being tended. A great stone wall surrounded the village border. A pale blue sky hung above them as Fionn took in the view of people working and talking in the small town below.

She followed his gaze to what looked like the entrance to the fortified town where men with weapons sat outside what might have been a guardhouse.

"Taispeánann mo rí an iomarca dó féin dá mhuintir."

The foreign words brought both Fionn, Cónán, and Rose's heads to the left, where a striking redhead appeared, walking up the slope toward the entrance to the roundhouse.

Fionn strode toward the woman, turning her in his arms, and shocking the shit out of Rose as he broke into a wide smile.

She'd never seen him smile like that.

"Éad, mo ghrá?" Fionn asked.

The redhead shook her head, laughing as Fionn pressed his lips to hers.

Jealousy seared through Rose as they held each other tight, their kisses passionate, their embrace loving.

Who was this?

"Aoibhinn," Fionn murmured as he broke the kiss. "D'airigh mé uaim mo bhanríon."

"Tá do chogadh tábhachtach."

Rose had no idea what they were saying, but the woman seemed to be reassuring him.

"Cá bhfuil na gasúir?"

The redhead grinned and turned her curvy body toward the entrance.

Fionn shook his head. "Níl siad istigh ansin."

The woman chuckled, tipped her head toward the entrance and yelled, "Caoimhe, Diarmuid!"

Two seconds later, a young girl, perhaps seven or eight, hurried out of the roundhouse followed by a tall, lanky young man who could have been anywhere between the ages of eleven and eighteen. His physique said he was older but his baby face said he was very young.

Rose frowned. Where had they come from?

Oh. Right. *Dream.*

But who were they? Taking a step closer, she peered at the kids as the girl wrapped her arms around Fionn's waist and he grinned down at her. He then turned to converse with the boy. Rose was stunned.

The boy had his smile. The girl had his hair.

Were these ... Fionn's children?

What?

Cónán moved toward the boy who curled his fist in the wolf's ruff as he grinned up at Fionn.

"Níor choir duit a bheith imithe chuici." The woman's words, whatever they meant, caused a massive shift in Fionn's dreamscape.

The children vanished and the village faded to a forest lit only with flame from a massive fire behind the woman. And Fionn ... he was now beardless and wore leather trousers.

A gold circlet rested low around his neck. His torso was bare.

Without his beard, he looked more like the Fionn she knew, except his green eyes blazed with the light of another world.

Cloaked figures appeared out of the trees behind him, advancing menacingly as the redheaded woman watched on, chin raised in defiance.

"Mo grá?" Fionn reached for the redhead.

Revulsion crossed her face, making her look hard and cold where only moments ago she'd been soft and loving. "Ní mise do ghrá!"

As the hooded figures reached Fionn, Rose wanted to yell in warning, the words almost spilling out when she reminded her panicked emotions that this was just a dream. Her reminder came just in time because as the hooded figures fell upon Fionn, the black of their cloaks whipped out at Rose, covering the world in the fabric, rippling and whooshing like banners in the wind.

Then there was light.

Greenery all around.

Rolling hills of grass.

A gentle brook bubbling somewhere in the distance.

Birds singing.

"Rose?"

Thinking he'd discovered her in his dreamscape, Rose whirled to face Fionn and instead saw herself with him.

A dream version of herself.

Light sparkled off her, her eyes impossibly blue.

She was ... beautiful.

Was this how Fionn saw her?

Rose ached at the thought.

She turned her attention to him. He was as he was now, dressed in one of his fine suits, his overcoat fluttering behind him in the soft breeze. Those startling green eyes gleamed in the daylight as he approached her with a tortured expression.

"Fionn, what is it?" her dream self asked.

He halted close to her, reaching to cup her face in his large palm. Rose touched her own cheek as if she might feel the tingle of his touch. Then he bowed his head toward hers and whispered across her lips, "I'm so sorry, *mo chroí.*"

So distracted by the fact that Fionn was dreaming of her like this, Rose noticed An Breitheamh too late. The dagger was fixed in his other hand, a dagger that he plunged into her dream self's heart.

Confused, horrified, Rose stumbled to her knees along with her dream self, watching miraculous tears roll down Fionn's cheeks as he held her dying in his arms.

"What have I done?" he rocked her, murmuring the question over and over.

What the fuck? Rose choked on silent screams as the air behind the dying Dream Rose shimmered and peeled open, like water receding from shore, revealing another world beneath.

Faerie.

The gate to Faerie.

Fionn laid Dream Rose on the ground and gently removed An Breitheamh from her heart. As soon as it was out, covered in her blood, he threw his head back and roared the most terrifying, anguished sound she'd ever heard.

Then he slumped over Dream Rose's dead body, the very image of defeat.

"Fionn."

His head jerked up to the right. The redhead was back.

"Aoibhinn?" he gaped, confused, his cheeks still wet with tears. He did not look like the Fionn Rose knew at all.

Aoibhinn gestured to Dream Rose's body. "This is worse than what I did to you. You shared the bond. How could you?"

"I can't take it back, can I?" he asked hoarsely.

She shook her head. "Do you want to? After all, it was the only way to open the gate."

Understanding and terror flooded Rose. She had to wake up, she had to wake up. She had to get away from him!

That bastard!

That lying, vicious, psychotic bastard!

Fionn's head snapped toward her, and he looked right at her.

Horror darkened his face. "Rose. No."

22

Her eyes flew open, blood whooshing in her ears from her pounding heart, and without even thinking about it, her body *traveled*.

One second Rose was lying in bed next to Fionn, the treacherous bastard, and the next on her feet by the bed, facing him.

He was awake. Already up on his feet by the opposite side.

His rugged features hard, his eyes glinted with determination and ... accusation?

"You can dream-walk," he growled. *Accusatory.*

Oh no. Rose was going to kill the motherfucker.

She flew at him, a blur across the bed, but he was fast, too fast, *traveling* from one side of the room to the other before she could thrust a fist through his chest. It wasn't something she'd ever done before but Rose reckoned he was the best son of a bitch to practice on!

"Don't." Fionn held up a hand against her, his expression implacable. "I don't want to hurt you."

The last few hours came flooding back, weakening her at the knees.

The fight.

His battling the vampires to protect her. Him being weird, her refusing to back down until he shared what was going on with him.

Him kissing her. Taking her to the bed, his hands on her body. The rightness of it. The desperate need for him.

And then ... she'd no longer been conscious, which was how she found herself in his dreamworld.

"What did you do to me? We were ..." she whispered, gesturing to the bed.

Fionn shrugged. "You fell asleep."

Oh, yeah, sure, she'd fallen asleep when the guy she wanted most in the world finally broke his damn control and put his mouth and hands on her.

"You *put* me to sleep."

The dream poked and prodded her, painfully reminding her of the truth. "You put me to sleep because ..." Misery unlike anything she'd ever felt clawed at her. The agony of his betrayal. Tears threatened, but she refused to give them to *him*. "You've been planning to kill me all along. That's why you'd look at me like you wanted me but then push me away. You're a sick bastard but not sick enough to fuck the woman you're planning to betray. To murder."

Her instincts were screaming for her to get out. To flee. Yet the naive woman who had begun to fall in love with a stranger needed answers. "Do you deny it?"

"It was just a dream," Fionn replied gruffly.

"Don't lie to me!" she shrieked.

Fionn looked away, running a hand through his hair. A slight tremble in the movement gave him away. If it hadn't, the wave of emotion hitting Rose—foreign, panicked, remorseful, and desperate —did. He'd forgotten to mask himself from her in all the confusion; she was feeling everything he felt.

Those were not the feelings of a man planning to kill her.

It would explain perhaps why she'd never felt danger from him.

And so she stupidly waited when every fiber of her being told her to escape.

Finally, he settled his flinty regard upon her. "The children who were born to open the gate need not die," he confessed. "Not for anyone but me."

"You?" she gritted out.

"I had a wife and children."

Rose remembered the shock she felt watching him interact with his wife. The jealousy, even. The disbelief at seeing his children. "I saw them."

"I had people and land that I vowed to protect when I became their king. When I agreed to go to Faerie to save them, I was agreeing to become Aine's whore, not just her slave."

Despite the betrayal of the dream still turning her stomach, it was not in Rose's power to halt the flash of anger and sympathy she felt at his confession.

"I tricked her as I said I did, and my people betrayed me upon my return. But what I left out was that I had a family. And my wife, Aoibhinn, had remarried. She was bound to the new king and together, they sentenced me to an eternal sleep. I was surrounded by druids as she stared in revulsion at me, at what I'd become, while the man who'd taken my place, a stranger, held back my son from coming to my aid. My daughter wailed her despair from the arms of one of my men."

"Your wife betrayed you?"

Fionn nodded, expression carefully blank. "The Faerie Queen took everything from me. Everything. Trapped me with powers I have no right to. Abandoned me to an eternity of emptiness. She may have closed the gates to protect both our people, but I will never forgive her for what I lost."

"Aoibhinn."

He curled his upper lip into a snarl. "Fuck that treacherous bitch. I'm talking about my mortality. My right to see my children grow, Rose. My Caoimhe and Diarmuid. Lost to me because of Aine and what she turned me into."

Rose glowered at him. She didn't want to be sucked into his sad tale of woe. "And how do I fit in to *your* story? Don't lie. I'll know."

"There's no point lying now, is there." Fionn studied her, his

iv   S. YOUNG

countenance dispassionate, completely at odds with how he'd behaved in his dream. At complete odds with the emotions she'd felt from him only moments ago before he got a handle on them.

"You need not die to open the gate. Just a drop of blood. In fact, someone can only go to Faerie as your companion. That's what the Blackwoods want from you. To convince you to take them to Faerie. But Aine made it so I can't enter Faerie with ill intentions without *sacrificing* one of the fae-borne using An Breitheamh. She assumed it would be a difficult decision for me since I'd been an honorable man."

Flashes of the dream pounded in Rose's head.

Fionn crying.

Roaring as if devastated by her death.

What was true?

What was the lie?

"You want to kill me to open the gate so you can take your revenge on the Faerie Queen?"

"She made me the thing I hated, and when I returned home, my wife and her new husband decreed I was a monster. My son, now a man, disagreed. Our people didn't disagree as such, but they were conflicted. This had been done against my will, to their king—their king who had offered his life to save them all.

"So Aoibhinn compromised. She asked the druids to put me to sleep, that if I was meant to ascend beyond my curse, the Fates would awaken me. Young women of the village sacrificed themselves in honor of the king I'd once been. Their blood is not on my hands but Aoibhinn's. She betrayed me and forced my children to watch. All because of that cruel bitch of a fae."

"So you'll kill me to get your vengeance?"

That goddamn muscle ticked in his jaw, his voice hoarse as he replied, "Do you really think I can kill you now, Rose?"

She scoffed. "I'm to believe you've reconsidered?"

"It seems the Fates have other plans for you and me."

"Fuck the Fates." Rose's fury and betrayal tore through her as she focused on the thought of Gare d'Orléans, the city's train station.

"You're dead to me, Fionn Mór. Come looking for me and I'll make it so."

Then he and the apartment vanished, and Rose was surrounded by people on their morning commute at the train station. No one even noticed her pop out of thin air. Tears and loneliness burned in her throat as she searched the station for schedules and stopped under a row of screens. She couldn't stop shaking, trembling from head to toe. Nothing made sense. She had no idea where she was going.

She couldn't go home to Maryland because that would put her parents in danger. God, Rose missed them more than ever. The only two people she could trust.

A face, a lovely one, framed by white-blond, fairy-princess hair floated across Rose's mind.

Maybe there was someone else she could trust.

Fionn had said Niamh Farren was *not* to be trusted, but he'd said that planning to kill—

Rose felt a strong wave of nausea and searched for the restrooms. Not caring who saw, she *traveled* there, making a woman at the sinks gasp in fright at her sudden appearance. Dashing into an open stall, Rose slammed the door behind her and fell to her knees.

She sobbed as she threw up, wondering how she could have allowed herself to grow attached to the fucking fae who was planning to stab her through the heart.

An Breitheamh.

Shit, she should have stolen An Breitheamh.

Exhausted, Rose slumped against the stall and stared unseeingly at the opposite wall.

If Fionn didn't want her to interact with Niamh, it was because he knew Niamh would reveal his deception. Niamh may or may not be trustworthy, but she was like Rose, and her only connection in this bizarre supernatural existence.

Other than Thea MacLennan. But Thea had changed to a wolf. What help would she be? Rose would only bring her back into a story she was lucky to escape from the first time.

Fuck.

Niamh Farren it was, then.

Rose pushed up to her feet and wiped a hand across her mouth, determination setting in. Fionn could trace her using the shit she'd left at the hotel. Although she wasn't worried about facing him, being followed was an inconvenience. And once she did what she did next, the Irish bastard would definitely hunt her down. That didn't scare her. Truthfully. There was so much rage inside her, Rose felt like she could obliterate him if she wanted to.

Bitter, furious, hurt, and dare she admit, heartbroken, Rose emitted so much ominous energy as she strode through the station that the humans gave her a wide berth.

Rose was no longer human.

It sunk in.

Despite the moral implications, she tried out the brain-muddle thing Fionn could do. Fueled by anger, she didn't allow herself to feel anything about doing it. Instead, she asked at customer service what trains she needed to take to get to Zagreb, booked the tickets, and then focused all her magic on penetrating the woman's mind.

She pictured herself handing over the correct change and demanded those thoughts transfer.

To her shock, the woman's expression slackened and she reached out to take the invisible money, typed something into her computer that caused a cash register to pop open below, and then put nothing into it.

She printed off Rose's tickets and handed them over. "Faites bon voyage."

"Thanks." Rose attempted not to feel guilty and failed miserably.

Focus on your rage.

So she did.

The first train would take her to Paris. From there she'd travel on to Stuttgart, Germany, then Munich, and then to Zagreb. Back to the beginning. The last place she'd encountered Niamh Farren.

But first, she needed something.

Now where would Fionn have hidden An Breitheamh?

DESPERATION.

It was a horrific feeling.

Fionn had always assumed he was *desperate* to open the gate to Faerie to fulfill his revenge.

However, he'd forgotten what true desperation was.

Desperation had been staring at his wife, standing next to the man she'd married while he'd been trapped on Faerie, ordering druids to curse Fionn with a fate worse than death. Desperation was wishing with every molecule of his being that her betrayal was a bad dream.

Desperation was seeing his children held back by others, grief suffusing their entire bodies as they watched their mother put down their beloved father. Desperation was knowing he might never hold his daughter in his arms again or talk with his boy as only father and son could, and frantically searching for a way to make sure all that wasn't lost to him.

Desperation was not being able to save those five girls from themselves as they laid their bodies before the druids, offering up their life energy so they could cast the spell that would put Fionn down.

And desperation was the emotion currently overwhelming him as he sat in the apartment, alone, while Rose was out there, *fleeing* him.

This couldn't be how it ended between them. Fionn wanted to find her, to convince her he no longer meant her harm, but he knew it was best he didn't.

From the moment he'd closed his eyes beside her on that bed, knowing deep in his soul from the stories he'd heard on Faerie that something greater inextricably linked him and Rose, Fionn's plans for revenge changed.

They no longer included Rose.

He'd find the other fae-borne.

Fionn remembered how it felt to kill Rose in the dream. It had felt so real. It had cut deeper than anything ever had in his long life, and Fionn had faced his share of tragedy and violation.

Rose would live.

He'd let her go. Even if it made him feel *desperate*.

A tingling sensation tickled down his spine seconds before Rose appeared in the doorway to the bedroom. "Ro—"

She disappeared and reappeared directly in front of him, his knees touching her thighs, her expression strangely blank.

"Rose?"

Too late. So distracted by his feelings for her, Fionn had no chance to react.

Rose's blue eyes gleamed coldly as she touched his neck.

Everything went dark.

BLINKING AWAKE, Fionn stared up at the cracked ceiling, momentarily confused.

What the fuck had happened?

Rose!

Fionn flew to his feet, letting his senses take over. She wasn't here.

But she'd come back for a reason.

Why?

It quickly dawned on him, and a guttural growl of disbelief and outrage ripped out of him. She wouldn't!

Of course, she would. It was the only damn thing that would open the gate for him!

She'd ransacked the bedroom. Drawers and cupboards were thrown open, the safe in the wardrobe broken into. Tearing out of the bedroom and down the hall, he found the living area the same. Some kitchen cupboards had been torn off their hinges. Blood pounded in his ears as he blurred across the space to the cupboard where he'd hidden the dagger.

The silver box was gone.

The little vixen had taken advantage of his emotions, caught him off guard, knocked him out, and stolen his fucking dagger!

And wait. "Her things?"

Fuck, fuck, fuck!

A tornado through the apartment, Fionn discovered Rose had also wiped the apartment clean of any personal items.

Standing in the bathroom, chest heaving with frantic, short breaths, he glared around at the space. Then he caught sight of the opened bottle of complimentary coconut shampoo in the shower.

Exultant, *relieved*, he reached out and snatched the shampoo bottle in his hand. Once opened and used, i.e., claimed, that shampoo was now a personal item.

Marching out of the shower room and into the bedroom, he picked his mobile off the bedside cabinet and dialed Bran.

Five long rings later, the vampire picked up. "Again, I sleep through the day. I just got into bed."

"Rose knows the truth," Fionn bit out.

Bran hesitated a second. "How?"

"She can dream-walk."

"She can what?"

Fionn suppressed a snarl of impatience but only just. "It was a rare ability among the fae. She hid it from me and then fucking dream-walked me."

"And I'm guessing you were dreaming bad things?"

He frowned. Before he'd fallen asleep, he'd started to understand all the things sparking between him and Rose—the way they could sense each other's emotions, how, despite his supposed dark intentions toward her, Rose never felt she was in danger of him.

While his conscious mind insisted it didn't change their circumstances, his subconscious felt differently and showed him so he'd know what killing Rose would mean to him.

It was bloody bad timing for his conscience to kick in.

"She found out about An Breitheamh and about her and the gate and my revenge."

Bran exhaled. "I take it she's gone?"

"She left and then she returned and used my own fucking carotid sinus attack against me."

Bran snorted. "You sound almost proud of her."

He kind of bloody was, beneath his outrage.

"She stole the dagger, Bran. I won't kill her but I can't kill one of the others without the damn thing."

"You're not going to kill Rose?"

The very thought made him sick to his stomach. "No, I'm not."

"I see."

"Once I get my dagger back, I'm letting her go."

"Well, tell me she wasn't smart enough to clear the place of all her shit."

"I can't."

"Double fuck."

Fionn stared at the shampoo bottle. "But she left behind a bottle of shampoo she'd opened and used."

"That's something, at least. What do you need from me?"

"I need to know if Niamh is my kin, and fast. If she is, then you need to search again for any signs of that other fae-borne."

Bran was silent so long, Fionn thought the bastard had hung up. Until, "Or you could let this go, my friend, and start living your life. Convince Rose to forgive you. Devote your bloody long life to protecting her, to making sure no one uses her. That is a worthy purpose, Fionn."

As if that hadn't fucking occurred to him. The notion of forever with Rose was at war with his revenge, tearing him in two.

The light bulbs in the room began to burst, one after the other, as Fionn lost mastery over himself for the first time in ... ever.

Bloody hell, get control of yourself, man!

Remember.

He did. He remembered Aine. Straddling him, beautiful and talented in bed, giving him pleasure despite his hatred for her, which only induced his self-hatred.

She'd made him a whore.

Him. Fionn Mór, high king of Éireann. The greatest warrior in his land.

Aine had violated him down to his very soul.

"I can't. I won't discuss it again. Just find out what I need to know."

He clutched the bottle tight in his hand and let his magic envelop it. It whispered to him. "Rose is heading north. Hack the train station security cameras here in Orléans. Let me know if you see Rose on them."

With a defeated sigh, Bran grumbled his assent. "Where do you think she's heading?"

"Paris is north of here, but I don't know what she'd want with Paris."

"Do you think she'd head home to her parents? Fly out from Paris?"

Fionn considered it but immediately abandoned the idea. "She wouldn't put them in danger."

"Perhaps she's just planning to keep running."

"Perhaps," he said.

But he'd seen the fury flash in Rose's eyes seconds before she'd touched her fingers to his neck. Was Rose planning to take her vengeance upon him?

Yes.

He couldn't trust her.

Oh, mo chroí, he thought sadly, feeling the sting of her coming betrayal, *revenge will always win.*

23

Without Bran, Rose was traveling blind.

To her relief, the train got her into Paris in just a little over an hour. Her train to Stuttgart was already leaving the platform when she arrived.

Rose *traveled* onto the train, focusing on one of the tiny restrooms. Although she banged her elbow on the small sink, she smirked. It was a hard smile. Melancholy.

Her abilities were still cool as hell. She wouldn't let that traitorous demon spawn take that away from her.

Stepping out of the restroom, Rose's backpack, carrying all her things and An Breitheamh, got caught on the door. She cursed, tugging it over her shoulder. The dagger needed to stay close. Inside the empty restroom at the train station back in Orléans, Rose had tried to destroy the damn thing. First she tried to melt it. Then turn it to cinder. Then break it. Ice it.

Nothing.

An Breitheamh was apparently immune to destruction.

Like she was.

Satisfied she'd successfully knocked out Fionn, Rose had hovered over him after she'd found the dagger. The box clutched in her hand, she seriously considered dealing with its weakening effects upon her, wrapping fabric around the handle so as not to scar her palm, and plunging the knife into his heart.

Will of steel, her mom always said.

Yet her will failed her as she stared at his rugged face in slumber. He'd once been a good man. Rose believed that. Circumstance had twisted him up inside.

She'd stepped back, slipping the box into her backpack. One day Rose would be ready for him if he came for her, but she didn't have the heart for revenge. Not on him.

Fionn wouldn't die by her hand while he was helpless, and she wouldn't seek his death in vengeance.

But when he came for An Breitheamh, Rose would not hesitate to defend herself.

Stirring beneath her fury was the hurt as she found a seat in one of the carriages. Rose had allowed Fionn beneath her skin. Into her blood.

Into her heart.

His betrayal was a fist punching that vulnerable little organ to pieces. It swiped away who she thought he was, who she thought he might become to her, a future together perhaps where she'd make him laugh and bring him light after so long without it.

Naive hopes and wishes shattered by the truth.

Gritting her teeth against the pain, Rose glared out at the passing world. Fionn was lost to her now, but that didn't mean she couldn't have purpose. She'd find Niamh and warn her about the warrior fae and An Breitheamh, and together they'd find the last fae-borne.

The three of them would protect each other.

However, without Bran, Rose knew she'd have to navigate the world always looking over her shoulder. The one thing she believed in was Fionn's desire to keep the fae out of the human world. No man hated a species so much, hated himself so much, unless the fae truly had done terrible things.

That she believed.

So even if the Blackwoods didn't want to harm her, Rose considered them her enemy.

The Blackwoods. The Garm. The O'Connors.

Fionn Mór.

Four powerful entities, all hunting her down.

As the train passed through a tunnel, she caught her reflection in the window, and any anxiety she felt was momentarily squashed.

The woman looking back with her eyes and nose and mouth was someone Rose didn't recognize.

Someone fierce.

Someone powerful.

Someone to be reckoned with.

ALTHOUGH IT ONLY TOOK A FEW hours for the train to arrive in Munich, Rose found herself stuck in one place.

That was the last thing she wanted.

It was early afternoon, light flooding into the enormous central station in the Bavarian capital. The screens that should have told her the platform number for the train to Zagreb informed her the train wasn't due to arrive for another five hours.

Five hours was a long time standing in one place, allowing for *someone* to find her.

Rose could only hope that her enemies were clueless about her whereabouts. Perhaps even three of them were right this second attempting to track down Fionn, thinking she was still stupid enough to be with him.

At the oddest times, she'd feel Fionn Mór's lips against her mouth, the bristle of his stubble against her skin. Of course, the devil could kiss. He'd had centuries to perfect his technique. She'd loved the disparity in their size, how big and masculine he felt braced over her body.

Rose had never considered herself particularly attracted to bigger guys, but Fionn's extraordinary warrior physique was a major turn-on.

Or maybe it was just everything about him.

Until she'd discovered the truth.

He wasn't on some noble mission to save the world.

Rose flinched at the ghost of his mouth and hands on her, thinking how cruel fate was. Since she was sixteen years old, Rose had kept boys, and then men, at arm's length. She was the one in control, always.

The first time in her life when she couldn't control her feelings for a man, and he turned out to be a traitorous, immortal asshole.

Ironic, really.

Furious with herself and pretty much everyone on earth, Rose was glad that humans continued to give her a wide berth as she wandered through the massive station. It would be easy to get lost. Low-level nausea had stayed with her since learning the truth, but Rose knew she needed to keep up her energy. She eyed the food court where there were plenty of kiosks to buy sandwiches and fruit.

Nothing there sounded appealing, so she kept walking, following signs for food that led her to the underground where the subway trains arrived and departed. Although hot, it was junk food, so she turned around in disappointment and caught an elevator back to the main train level.

Grabbing a sandwich, Rose sat at a table near the corner of a kiosk, her back to the wall, her attention on the crowds strolling by. No one would take her unawares.

The sandwich was like eating sawdust, but knowing anything would taste like crap to her at that moment, Rose forced the food down along with two bottles of water.

Afterward, she found a bench against a wall amongst the central hubbub of the station, clutched her backpack to her body, and sat vigilantly watching while she waited for her train to arrive.

The hours passed like days, slow, laborious, and irritating. Her nerve endings felt tweaked, her feet curling in agitation in her sneakers. Thankfully, no one seemed to want to approach the angry woman glaring at strangers, so she kept the bench all to herself.

Despite attempting not to, Rose couldn't help but replay the past few days in her head, disbelieving it had only been *days* since she'd met Fionn. How could she have been so sure of someone and yet been so wrong? Not once, after their initial meeting, did she believe he wanted to harm her. At no point had she felt danger from him, which was weird, right? If she caught up with Niamh, she hoped the young fae might have answers to her unanswered questions.

It was as if the thought conjured her.

One minute Rose had been looking a little unseeingly at the passing travelers, and the next her gaze met and locked with Niamh Farren's.

Rose's breath caught and she blinked hard, multiple times, making sure she wasn't seeing things.

Nope.

Niamh Farren stood beside the elevator doors, her brother, Ronan, at her side.

What were they doing here? Had Niamh discovered Rose's need to see her in one of her visions?

Follow me, Rose. Niamh's voice sounded in her head. Rose jolted with shock.

That didn't just happen.

No way.

Niamh nodded. *Yes, I can speak to you telepathically. Now follow me.*

Rose was flabbergasted. Could she do that? Or was this a gift only the psychic had? Fionn had never mentioned telepathy.

With a slight tip of her head, Niamh began to walk, Ronan following like a silent bodyguard. Rose launched to her feet and urged herself to stay calm and not hurry after the woman. She kept a casual distance and followed Niamh toward the restrooms. The ethereal blond disappeared inside the ladies' room while Ronan stood guard at the door.

Ronan's expression was tight with suspicion and warning as Rose approached him.

Trying to look reassuring, she passed him and entered the restroom.

Two of the stalls were occupied. A woman dried her hands at the automatic hand dryer, and Niamh stood at the farthest sink, running her fingers through her lovely hair, studying herself in the mirror with a casual interest.

Stomach fluttering, Rose approached, leaning against the wall by Niamh's left side. "Hey."

Niamh leaned a hand against the sink and turned to her.

The last time she'd seen the young woman, Niamh had been wearing a long, paisley-print dress with billowing sleeves. Today she wore low-slung, flared jeans and a turquoise turtleneck with long sleeves and a cropped hem that showed off Niamh's flat stomach and belly piercing. A purple jewel winked against her pale skin.

Her hair was a mass of waves and curls and thin plaits. As she flipped it over her left shoulder, she revealed peacock-feather earrings that were long enough to touch her collarbone.

Back in Zagreb, Niamh had reminded Rose of a bohemian fairy princess. Now she was a hippie fairy princess.

It occurred to Rose that beautiful Niamh Farren, who would not look out of place on a runway, was not an inconspicuous person. How was that not a problem when you were on the run?

"You can... you can talk to me in my..." Rose leaned forward. "Can I do that?"

No, I don't think so. We all are born with our own special... gifts. Niamh shrugged.

Oh. That disappointed her. Telepathy sounded like a handy talent to have in her arsenal. "How did you find me?"

"Two days ago, my brother and I were in Italy—Rome. Then suddenly, I just felt the need to be in Munich." Niamh smiled sweetly. "Didn't know why but I made him come here with me. And then last night, I got a vision of you at this train station and knew I had to be here. So, what's going on, Rose? Last I left you, things looked like they would work out how they were supposed to for you."

Rose didn't understand what that meant. "Niamh, the guy you've been running from, the guy who came to me ... he plans to kill one of us to open the gate to Faerie."

"I know." Niamh's frowned. "But meeting you was supposed to change that, and I haven't had a vision to say otherwise."

"How was it supposed to change it?"

"Because—" Niamh stiffened at the same time Rose felt the tingle down her neck.

Heart racing, dread in the gut, they stared at each other in tense silence.

"We need to go," Rose said, moving past Niamh.

They hurried out of the restroom and Niamh took hold of Ronan's arm. "Trouble," she warned, searching left and right as Rose did.

"What did *she* do?" Ronan accused as they began walking.

Rose scowled at him as she followed, hoping the siblings knew where they were going. "I didn't do anything."

"Well, who is after you?"

"The Blackwoods, the Garm, the O'Connors, and Fionn."

"I know who the Blackwoods and the Garm are, but who are the others?" Niamh asked.

"The O'Connors are the coven I was born into in Dublin."

"You're Irish?" Ronan asked as Niamh gasped, "A coven?"

"As for Fionn, he's the guy you thought I'd be safe with."

"So that's his real name," Niamh murmured. She then drew to a halt, clutching at her brother's arm, halting him too.

Ronan was tall, broad-shouldered, and strong-looking. Niamh was tall but willowy with feminine curves. She did not look like she could pull her brother to a stop with what amounted to a gentle tug. But, of course, neither did Rose.

There may be danger all around them, but Rose felt relieved to be with someone just like her. Deceptively, unnaturally strong and fast. And powerful.

"What is it?" Rose followed Niamh's gaze.

Two men stood out from the crowd, their legs braced, arms crossed over wide chests, as they blocked the exit the siblings had been hurrying toward.

The hair on her neck rising on end, Rose's instincts had her whipping her head to the right. A woman and a man were approaching them, determination etched on their faces. There was something about the way they moved that was familiar.

That was a little like ... Kiyo.

"Werewolves?"

"Yes. The Garm," Niamh told her.

But how had they found her? Rose's immediate thought was of her parents. What if someone had tracked them down?

Shit.

"I told you we shouldn't have come here for her." Ronan gripped Niamh's arms tightly, scowling as he gave her a hard shake. "Look what you've done."

"Hey!" Rose pushed him none-too-gently away from his sister. "Watch it, pal."

Fear flickered across his face before he cleared it. He looked past Rose to Niamh. "Well, what do we do now you've got us into this mess?"

Niamh flinched, guilt clear in her expression. "I'll distract them while you run. Rose, follow Ronan. I'll catch up."

"No way. Why can't we just *travel* outside the building?"

"*Travel?*"

"You know ... poof! One minute you're here, next minute you're there."

"You mean teleport?"

Rose made a face. *Traveling* sounding way less sci-fi. "Yeah, whatever, that."

"Because Ronan is human and I won't leave him here."

Personally, Rose thought he seemed like kind of a turd, but he was the girl's brother, so she understood. "Then you two run while I distract them."

"But you don't know where we're staying." Niamh shoved Rose toward Ronan. "Follow him."

Niamh took off running toward the werewolves approaching on their right.

"What—"

"This way." Ronan grabbed Rose's hand and tugged her in the opposite direction to the exit.

Thus began an exercise in running fast but not fast enough to overtake a very human Ronan who was the one who knew where he was going! A quick glance over her shoulder told her the two wolves who'd been guarding the exit were gaining on them.

"Ronan!"

He veered left and Rose followed. Up ahead was a stand that held newspapers and candy. Drawing up her magic, Rose thrust her arm behind her, making the stand fly. It collided with the wolves with such force, it propelled them across the station.

Cries and yells filled the atrium but Rose kept running.

They put distance between them and the wolves, but the tingling down her neck told her they weren't free yet. Ronan skidded as he changed direction, and Rose could only blindly trust him to lead their escape.

They burst out through an exit door into the gray, rainy November day. Rose glanced over her shoulder to see the werewolves run around the corner, just in time to catch sight of her.

She cursed and sped after Ronan who was tearing across the road toward a taxi stand. The cab driver of the first car in the stand was leaning against the window of the second car, chatting to the driver.

To Rose's mortification, Ronan threw open the driver's side door of that first cab and got in.

"Fuck, fuck, fuck," she chanted as she pulled open the front passenger door just as the cabbie noticed and yelled in German.

"Powers!" Ronan snapped as she slammed her door shut.

Seeing the cab driver reach for the door handle, Rose locked the car with her magic. "What do you mean?"

The cab driver pounded on the window.

"To start the car!"

Remembering Fionn doing that exact thing back in Slovenia, she placed a palm over the dash and willed the car to start.

The engine growled and Ronan slipped it into gear, skidding

across the road just as the werewolves spotted them from their position by the exit. Rose craned her neck to watch as one of them sprung over the hood of a car and ran after them at a speed no human was capable of.

"Ronan!" she yelled, just as the werewolf launched himself into the air, knees tucked to his chest, arms above his head, claws out.

The roof crunched beneath his weight as he landed on the car. Rose yelped.

"Hold on!" Ronan bellowed, swinging the car around a corner, tipping it onto two wheels, causing the werewolf to be thrown from the top. He rolled across the road in a fast tumble, forcing cars to slam and swerve to avoid him.

The cab fell back down onto all fours, and Ronan expertly changed gears and sped away.

They drove for ten minutes—ten minutes in which she barely breathed—before Ronan pulled over.

"What are you doing? Are we here?"

"No."

"Then why have we stopped?"

He scowled at her. "Fuck, you are new."

"Why does everyone keep saying that?"

Instead of answering, he threw open the car door and got out, leaving Rose no choice but to follow.

"We're about a fifteen-minute run from the apartment. But the police will have been called and they'll be looking for this cab, and us." He jogged away without another word.

Adrenaline coursing through Rose, she desperately tried to ignore the mounting felonies in her wake as she pulled her backpack over her shoulders and ran after Niamh's surly brother.

～

RONAN THREW himself down on a huge L-shaped leather couch, a bead of sweat trickling down the side of his temple. Rose took in their new surroundings. The residential area he'd jogged to was host to a spectacular penthouse apartment that he hadn't used a key to enter. The other buildings surrounding this one were nondescript. Nothing about them screamed luxury, but inside was a modern, loftlike home filled with contemporary design details.

"How did you—"

"There you are." Niamh wandered through a doorway in the middle of the left wall of the open-plan space.

Rose startled, her lips parting in surprise. Niamh had changed her clothes and was now wearing a yellow dress similar to the one she'd worn in Zagreb. "What—"

"I got here fifteen minutes ago." She flopped down beside Ronan and tapped his knee. "Are you okay?"

He cut her a dirty look. "Do I look okay?"

"Go take a shower," she suggested gently.

With a grunt of annoyance, Ronan stood, shot Rose a filthy look, and then vanished through the doorway Niamh had appeared in.

"I took the werewolves who stayed behind at the station on a little chase around the place until the security guards got involved. Then I teleported here."

Teleported.

Rose frowned. "It's called *traveling*."

"I do like the sound of that better."

"You can *travel* that far?"

"It took some practice and I'm always shattered after it, but yes. Can't you?"

Shrugging, Rose crossed the room and sat beside Niamh, dumping her backpack on the floor. "I'm getting there." She took in the glossy white kitchen and island, the doors beyond it that led out onto a balcony overlooking the tree-lined street. "How did you find this place?"

"We look up all the nicest places for rent in whatever city we're in. Found this one."

"What if someone turns up at the apartment?"

Niamh's blue eyes darted away from Rose's, almost guiltily, and Rose understood. "You mind-warp them."

"Is that what you call it?" she whispered, her remorse evident in her tone. "I guess it makes me an awful person, but when you're always running, sometimes there's no time to legally rent a place. It would also leave a trail people could follow."

Needing to reassure her, Rose reached across and placed a hand over hers. "I've done it once. To get my tickets to Zagreb. I was hoping I'd find you there."

Niamh stood and strode into the kitchen. "I've done it more than once. Coffee?"

Rose could only nod, understanding the desire to bury your head in the sand when life forced you to make shitty choices. "I have so many questions."

"I imagine you do."

"Will they find us here?"

"The Garm?" Niamh placed a pod in a small coffee maker and shook her head. "I don't think so. Unless they have something of yours. It's more likely they're watching the station. Since Eirik was killed, the new leader moved the Garm headquarters to Munich. That's why Ronan didn't want us to come here. The Garm consider the city theirs. They'll have full-time guards on the train station and airport, and one of those werewolves sensed us there."

Rose cursed inwardly. She'd unknowingly walked right into the danger zone, something that would never have happened if she'd had Bran. He and Fionn would've known that the Garm's headquarters was in Munich. "Shit." At least she could stop worrying that they'd somehow gotten to her parents.

"Eirik wanted us dead." Niamh moved across the room to hand Rose a hot cup. "But from what I've heard, he wasn't psychotic. He just believed in something. He got the job done and that was it. This new fella, his name is William. He's a Brit, but he's made his home here in Germany. And they say he's a bit of a psychopath."

"Vamp or wolf?"

"Vampire. Five hundred years old. He was Eirik's second-in-command, and they never went on hunts together, which is why he wasn't one of the fourteen vampires Thea killed. She's searching for me, you know."

Rose tensed, her spirits lifting at the news. "Thea? Are you kidding?"

"I'm afraid not." She shook her head, her hair shimmering with the movement. "I pushed her toward Conall."

"The werewolf she's mated to?"

"Yes. I started getting visions of the other children when I was fourteen. I tried to help the others and failed, but the visions of Thea were different. First, it was horrific," she said, her eyes glistening brightly. "It's her story to tell but, Rose, what Thea went through ... She was tortured."

What the hell. "By whom?"

"It's neither here nor there now, the bastard's dead. But when I started to get visions of Conall with Thea, I knew that fate wanted to make it up to her. I also knew that he'd been lied to and that he was hunting her, but if they could just trust each other, nothing would stop fate."

"What do you mean by fate?"

"They're mated."

"What exactly does that mean? Fionn mentioned it, how it was a fae thing, but that supernaturals started mating with fae, and how a mate has the power to change a fae into one of them."

Niamh nodded. "For years, I dreamed of Faerie. Hundreds of stories filling my head, providing me with the history. I knew much more than you and the others, and that's why I felt it was my duty to try to find you and put you on the path to keeping the gate closed. The mating bond is beyond the powers of even Aine, Rose. It's something more powerful. It's entirely in the hands of fate.

"From what I've seen, it's not like when two humans fall in love, even a powerful, long-lasting love. It's more. It's an *actual* linking of two souls. A completion. Neither one is whole without the other, which means, once a mated couple meet, they are forever fated to be together. To be separated from your mate is to live an eternity of grief.

"That's why Eirik's brother, Jerrik, was so determined to open the gate. His mate was on the other side."

For a moment, Rose couldn't speak. Finally, she said, "Wow."

"Even I didn't see Thea changing into a wolf, but I'm glad for her. She wasn't suited to an immortal life. She didn't want it, Rose. She didn't want the powers or eternity ... unlike you."

Rose stared wide-eyed. "You can sense that in me?"

Niamh smiled. "It is who you are. It's always who you were meant to be. But Thea was meant for a steadfast, peaceful life with a loving family in the highlands of Scotland. Unfortunately, despite her formative years, the now-alpha female is loyal and feels she owes it to me to find me. Which puts her right back in the mix."

"Why don't you go to her, like you came to me? Tell her to go home. Be safe."

"Because you needed me more."

Affection warmed Rose. "And who do you need, Niamh?"

"I need to make sure my pseudosiblings are safe or equipped to fight and win this battle. It's over for Thea—once she buggers off and gets on with her life like she's meant to—but it'll never be over for you and me. We'll always be running, Rose."

Ignoring what that meant, Rose asked, "And the other fae? Have you seen visions of her?"

"Him," Niamh corrected. "I've seen him but nothing that tells me what road I should help put him on. There's a pattern to my visions. An order. I can't move on to him until I know you will be okay."

"Will I be, if I'm always going to be running? I mean, I could stay with you and help you find the other fae." Rose opened her backpack and pulled out the silver box.

Niamh gawked at it. "Is that what I think it is?"

"An Breitheamh."

"I've seen it in my visions of Fionn."

"Yeah, that's because, unlike the others, he needs to use this dagger to kill one of us at the gate to Faerie to open it. He wants to take revenge against Aine for turning him fae, for all that came after. That's what he was doing with me." There was something about

Niamh, something that caused Rose's emotions to spill over. Tears burned in her eyes and throat. "He lied to me." She blinked up at her new companion, a salty, hot tear scoring down her cheek. "I thought his purpose was what your actual mission is—to protect the fae-borne and protect the gate."

Niamh reached out and peeled one of Rose's hands from the silver box to clasp it in hers. There was something sweet and soothing in her expression. "Rose, do you remember what I said to you at the club when you thought I was a crazy person?"

Rose shook her head. She couldn't remember. Too much had happened.

"I said, 'You have to trust him, Rose. Even when he makes it impossible. Don't let us down now.'"

It all came flooding back. How Niamh had seemed frantic at first until the vision she'd had in the staff room.

"Your vision. It was about me and Fionn?"

"They come at me like soundless images, yet somehow I hear words in the pictures," she said. "Never in order. A jumbled mess. But over the years, I've gotten the knack of sorting them out. Getting the gist of them. Trusting the emotion I feel in them. That night I knew— just as I knew Conall was Thea's mate and he would save her from the eternity she didn't want—that you would change Fionn. For weeks, I'd been getting visions of you with the Blackwoods. In them, you help them open the gate."

"What?" Rose stood. "I would never!"

"You don't know that. Not if they got to you first and lied to you."

Irritated by the notion, Rose began to pace. "So, what changed?"

"All I know was I had to get to you. But when I did, there was a bloody spell on you and you had no idea what you were. Then that vision came. He was there, the warrior fae who was stalking the life out of me," she huffed, exasperated. "I thought my visions of him opening the gate were about him finding me, that somehow, he'd best me. I know now I was meant to *lead* him to you. He was following me that night, but he found you—and it changed the future."

"But how?" Rose asked impatiently.

Niamh gave her a commiserating smile. "Because a fae would never hurt his mate."

Shock rooted Rose to the spot.

Mate.

"He might have thought his intentions were wicked, but the moment he met you, he could never hurt you." Niamh stood, her expression determined. "And I know he's broken your heart and you think you hate him, but the world kind of needs you to get over it ... because as his mate, only you can convince him to give up his revenge. For if you don't, he *will* succeed in opening that gate, and the world as we know it will be over."

As Niamh's words sank in, Rose learned something else in that moment.

An extremely stressed-out fae reacted as a human might.

Her blood pressure bottomed out and everything went black.

24

Fionn's rugged face hovered over hers. Agony, guilt, and remorse shone out of his beautiful eyes. "I'm so sorry, mo chroí.*"*

Rose's eyes flew open, and she threw herself onto her feet like a cat.

"Jesus Christ," Ronan said. "She's even more agile than you, Nee."

Gasping, Rose glanced around and saw Ronan at the kitchen island of the apartment in Munich and Niamh on the couch where Rose had been lying.

From having fainted.

Groaning, she covered her face with her hand. The last time she'd passed out was the day her parents had told her she was adopted.

"Are you okay, Rose? I'm sorry I told you like that. I would have been gentler if I thought—"

"You'd pass out like a wuss," Ronan finished.

"Ronan," Niamh snapped.

Embarrassed, Rose scowled at him. "Yeah, Ronan, keep in mind I could end your life in two seconds."

He glared but smartly kept his mouth shut.

Rose stumbled back to the couch. "This is not happening." She eyed Niamh plaintively. "Please tell me you have it wrong."

She grimaced sympathetically. "I'm sorry, Rose."

Burying her head in her hands, Rose contemplated what this meant. Going back to Fionn. Convincing him to give up his revenge. How could she do that when she still wanted to throttle him for planning to betray her?

"As his mate, only you can convince him to give up his revenge. For if you don't, he will succeed in opening that gate, and the world as we know it will be over."

"We barely know each other," Rose whispered.

"It would explain why you felt so connected to him so quickly."

Rose glared at Niamh. "How did you know that?"

She shrugged. "It's the way of mates. Two souls recognizing their missing piece."

"Oh, for God's sake, this can't be happening." Rose slammed back against the couch. "This is a guy who was planning to kill me! Maybe I could get over the insanity of that if he hadn't pretended to be my friend—and then almost had sex with me before the tiny bit of conscience he had left stopped him."

Niamh blushed. "Well ... you being his mate, I'd think it would be difficult for him to control his attraction to you."

"Don't make excuses for him."

"I'm so sorry, mo chroí."

Hearing his voice from her dreams, she glowered at the ceiling. "What ... what does '*muh kree*' mean?"

"Mo chroí? It means 'my heart,'" Ronan answered.

Jesus. A horrible ached flared inside her. "And '*muh graw*'?"

Niamh and Ronan shared a look and then Niamh replied, "*Mo grá* means 'my love.'"

He'd called Aoibhinn his love and Rose his heart. "Is there a difference? *He* called me the first and his wife the second."

Niamh shrugged. "It's the one answer I don't have."

"I'm sure it's interchangeable for a lot of people," Ronan said, strolling toward them. "But I've never been in love and I've called plenty of women the latter." He sat down on the coffee table in front of Rose. "I've never called a woman *mo chroí.*"

She eyed him suspiciously. "You're just saying what you think I need to hear so I'll go back to Fionn and convince him to give up his revenge plans."

"You're not wrong," he admitted. "But I'm also not lying."

Exhaling heavily, Rose thrust her hands into her hair and bowed her head, staring at the silver box that contained An Breitheamh. "Even if I found the strength to go back to the bastard, I'll never convince him. He told me before I left that he couldn't kill me. I didn't believe him at the time, but now I do. Problem is, I know in my gut that he hasn't given up. He'll come for you again, Niamh. Or the other fae-borne. Have you had a vision of your own future?"

"Magic is a strange thing ... I've never had a vision about myself. It's like magic has a sense of morality or rules or something. Knowing my own future would be cheating, I guess."

"Then how do you know your fate is to be immortal?"

"*That* I feel in my gut." Grief pinched her expression as she looked at Ronan. "I'm destined to outlive those I love."

Ronan's expression hardened and he looked away, staring out the window, apparently unwilling to discuss a life where they were no longer together. There was a tension between the siblings Rose didn't quite understand. It was clear Ronan was protective of Niamh, but something like resentment bubbled between them.

Getting back to the point, Rose said, "It's hopeless."

"You underestimate the mating bond." Niamh leaned toward her. "I know it's much to ask, but you need to put your current feelings aside and do what's right."

"And what about—" Rose cut off, her whole body electrified with warning signals as Niamh froze, eyes wide, her mouth open as if in a silent scream. Her head shook from side to side in small, frantic increments, just like it had done that night at the club. "Ronan!"

He hurried to his sister's side, grabbing on to her flailing hands, struggling to keep hold against her fae strength. "Nee, it's okay, it's okay," he murmured.

Then just as abruptly, she stopped.

And a wail burst out of her, a deep, agonizing, mourning cry that sent a shiver down Rose's spine. Tears filled Niamh's eyes as she clasped her brother's face in her hands. "No," she sobbed.

Ronan's face paled. "Nee?"

Before another word could be spoken, the world turned to chaos. The apartment windows blew open, screaming shards of glass flying everywhere. Pieces sliced at Rose's skin before she had time to register what was happening.

"Ronan, run!" Niamh yelled, her grief-stricken expression morphing into fierce determination as she threw herself to her feet.

Rose was on hers too as the front door blasted open and people poured into the room, over the balconies, and through the broken windows.

Encircling them.

Witches and warlocks.

There were many of them. Too many.

Twelve. Blocking every way out of the loft apartment.

Under normal circumstances, Rose would've *traveled* out of there, but she couldn't leave Niamh, and Niamh wouldn't leave Ronan behind. There was nowhere for Ronan to run.

That's when she caught sight of the weapon in each of their hands.

Silvery-gray daggers.

Pure iron.

"The O'Connors," Rose said for Niamh and Ronan's benefit.

A short, wiry witch wearing skinny jeans and a short leather jacket like the one Rose left in Zagreb stepped forward from her spot near the doorway. She twirled the dagger in her hand, her dark eyes focused on Rose. "This is no longer just duty, Rose O'Connor. This is justice. You killed Ethan, my brother." Without another word, she threw the dagger with accuracy and speed.

Rose blurred across the room, out of its path and into the path of two warlocks. She must've been a streak of color to them, not quick enough to get out of her way before she sent her magic out to their carotid sinuses.

Two down.

A flick over her shoulder informed her Ronan was throwing punches with a very tall warlock while Niamh dodged an iron knife and thrust her palms into the chest of the witch who'd slashed with it. That witch soared through the broken French doors near the kitchen, out over the balcony, and beyond.

Three down.

That's when the chanting began. Unintelligible words and sounds fell from the lips of all the magic-wielding humans as they positioned themselves at the room's edges, arms out toward one another, hands almost but not quite touching.

"Nee," Ronan wheezed.

His sister whirled around, blazing with fury and fear as Ronan's fingers dug into his chest. His legs gave way beneath him.

"What's happening?"

"They're using him!" Niamh cried. "Sacrificing him for the power to take us down!"

"He isn't enough!" Rose yelled at the witches and warlocks. "It won't work! You'll kill him for nothing!"

And that's when she realized she might be forced to end these people.

To protect Ronan and Niamh.

More marks on her soul.

Drawing on every molecule of anger within her, Rose spread her own hands wide. "Niamh, get down."

"Whatever she does," Ethan's sister yelled, "keep chanting! No matter the pain, you keep chanting!"

Focusing on the shards of glass that littered the apartment, Rose commanded them to rise. She saw the flicker of fear on her attackers' faces, but they kept going while Niamh bizarrely forced her bleeding wrist against Ronan's mouth.

Fionn's voice filled her head. *"They discovered when they started invading our world that their blood healed humans. In our world."*

She was trying to heal him while these barbaric assholes stole his life. Rose wasn't sure it was working, because as she called on the glass, she could feel a slight weakening in herself.

With a scream of outrage, she slammed the air with her fists, her arms outspread like a cross, and the glass flew at all those magical bastards. The sharp pieces made contact, the chanting faltering as glass struck legs and arms, and even a throat.

Four down.

Still, they kept going.

"Rose!" Niamh screamed in panic.

The girl braced over her brother protectively, desperation etched in her face.

Her blood wasn't healing him.

But she couldn't leave him unprotected.

It was up to Rose.

Turning to face Ethan's sister, the apparent leader of the wicked coven Rose had been born into, she knew she had to take *her* out. Focusing her magic toward the witch's carotid, she was surprised when she felt the magic bounce back.

The woman smirked.

A barrier spell?

Rose looked around at all of them, bleeding and wounded, their chanting louder, determined to get the job done.

I'm going to have to kill them.

"Don't do this," Rose begged Ethan's sister.

Still, they chanted.

Then he appeared. Out of nowhere.

Poof!

The last person Rose ever thought she'd want to see again, and yet her heart leapt gratefully at the sight of Fionn Mór popping into the apartment with a shampoo bottle—of all things—in his hand.

His head swung from side to side as he stood in the center of the chanting coven. Gaze swinging to Rose, those green eyes dipped down her body and back up again, as if checking for wounds. Satisfied she was all right, Fionn cut a look at Niamh and Ronan.

It took him seconds to figure out the situation, and Rose felt his magic tinge the air as the broadsword he'd used to fight Kiyo appeared in his free hand.

Stuffing the shampoo bottle into his overcoat pocket, Fionn gripped the sword with both hands and swung at the nearest warlock.

It broke the circle, the coven realizing Fionn could devastate them in seconds if they didn't use their magic defensively.

Rose blurred between witches and warlocks, punching and kicking, trying to knock them out, which was hard to do when she had four on her.

She glanced across the room to see Fionn had killed three coven members and was engaged in a fight with a witch who apparently had conjured her own sword.

Seven down.

Fionn struck the possible eighth, his sword impacting hers with so much force, she cried out in pain, dropping the weapon as she stumbled to her knees.

His back turned, sword raised to finish her, Fionn seemed unaware of Ethan's sister who ran across the apartment, jumping over the coffee table, iron dagger raised above her head in both hands, ready to bring it down on him.

Fionn.

A fist hit Rose in the face, but she barely registered it before she *traveled* across the room, appearing at Fionn's back, facing Ethan's sister as her dagger came down.

It plunged into Rose's chest before she could defend herself.

Agonizing pain blazed through her entire body, like fire licking at her insides.

"ROSE!" Fionn's voice bellowed in rage behind her as she slumped to her knees.

Her vision grew unfocused, her mind lost to everything but the pain. What looked like a bloodied human head fell next to her. Images of Fionn, a streak of vengeance across the room, sword in hand, slicing through the coven, came and went between moments of utter black.

"Rose ..." She heard his deep voice and the black retreated to the edges of her vision, revealing Fionn's face. "It didn't get you in the heart. I'm going to pull it out."

She wanted to tell him to hurry, to make the pain stop, but she couldn't. Agony stalled the words.

Something tugged in her chest, causing her torment to increase tenfold.

But then it was over.

The pain began to recede, and her vision came back into focus. Her breathing eased and feeling returned to her limbs.

A hand brushed the hair from her face, and Rose looked up to see Fionn kneeling beside her, his expression strained.

"You'll be okay."

She'd never heard his voice so soft.

"Why?" he growled, the soft crushed by his hard tone as he leaned his face so close to hers, their lips almost touched. "Why would risk your life for me?"

A broken sob cut through the air before Rose could come up with the answer to the most complicated question ever. The truth was, she hadn't thought. She saw the dagger that was meant for Fionn, and the thought of his death propelled her into action.

Turning toward the wretched sound, Rose's took in the apartment now littered with horror.

Fionn had killed the entire coven, except for the witch Niamh had expelled from the apartment.

The crying was coming from *Niamh*, who knelt over her brother's body, shuddering.

"No," Rose wheezed, stumbling to her feet to go to her friend.

Fionn reached for her, but Rose pushed his hands away, tripping over bodies that would haunt her nightmares. Falling at Niamh's side, Rose saw Ronan's slumped figure. His unseeing eyes stared up at the ceiling, his features resting stiffly in the fearful expression he'd worn before he'd ...

They were too late.

The coven had stolen his life. All for nothing. The spell wouldn't have taken Rose down, let alone both her and Niamh.

Fionn observed the siblings with a grim countenance, and Rose looked past him to the carnage he'd created. Fury filled her. Those hateful, narrow-minded, traitorous, murdering fools had brought this on themselves. Rose just wished Fionn had shown up sooner.

"Niamh." She rested a hand on the girl's shoulder. Niamh flinched when she looked at Rose. So lost, in far more pain than Rose had been when the iron entered her body.

"I tried." Niamh clutched at her own wrist. There were smears of blood on it but no wound. "It kept healing over. I tried."

Tears flooded Rose's eyes. "I know. I'm so sorry."

"I saw it coming. I saw it happen before—" Niamh retched, sagging sideways to vomit on the hardwood as far from her brother's body as she could get. Her back heaved as she tried to eject all the bile and grief inside her.

Fionn lowered to his haunches and surprised Rose by gently lifting Niamh's hair out of her face. When her body calmed, she sat back on her heels and looked at Fionn.

Whatever he saw in her made his usually granite expression soften. "You've nothing to fear from me, *ceann beag.*"

This surprised Rose. What did it mean?

"Not directly," Niamh's voice was hoarse, her words flat, dead. "I see that now. But you can still bring devastation to this world, Rí Mac Tíre."

Confusion crossed his face. Rose felt much the same. If Niamh had nothing to fear from Fionn, but he was still a threat, then the other fae-borne was still in danger of Fionn. At least according to the psychic.

Niamh pulled away and turned to Rose, who almost flinched at the deadness of her eyes. "Promise me, Rose."

Rose understood, and although she had no idea if she could ever forgive Fionn, she could trick him. She could make him think she had ... if it meant protecting this girl; if it meant protecting a world that could not withstand a war with hundreds of thousands of beings as powerful as Fionn.

"We'll do it together." She attempted to reach for Niamh, but the girl jerked away, turning to her brother.

Without another word, Niamh pressed an elegant, ring-bedecked hand to Ronan's shoulder and sobbed quietly as magic tingled in the air.

Rose gasped, falling back against the couch as Ronan's skin cracked and his body crumbled.

Just crumbled.

Into ash.

The ash moved around the edges, like wind was pushing it into a small tornado.

Until in its place was a dark blue vase with a silver eagle on its center.

Silently weeping, Niamh picked up the urn that Rose was sure now held Ronan's ashes, hugged it to her body, bowed over in pain ... and vanished.

Rose cried out, lunging at the space where she'd been.

Too late.

Silence filled the room. Rose's awareness moved beyond Fionn to the corpses, nausea rising in her gut.

Useless, meaningless death.

She watched as they crumbled, just as Ronan had, until they were nothing but piles of ash.

Fionn's doing.

Their eyes locked and she watched him as he stood, the silver box with An Breitheamh in his hands. He shifted it, cradling the box against his ribs, and held out his free hand to Rose. Uncertain of her next steps, she allowed him to pull her to her feet. His expression held her arrested for a moment. There was something working behind his eyes, something like disbelief. Maybe even awe.

"I can't leave you here now," Fionn finally said.

"Did you know?"

"Know what?"

Rose drew in a shuddering breath just as sirens sounded in the distance.

"We have to leave, Rose."

That the German police were on their way to the apartment

mattered little to her. She had a choice to make and no way of knowing which was the right one. "Did you know ... that we're ..." Her lips trembled before the word could choke its way out. With a huff of self-directed exasperation, Rose said, "Mates. That we're mated?"

Something darkened in Fionn's expression. Something that made her heart pound and her body shiver and sparkle with life, the kind of alive she'd never felt before. Despite everything. "I realized after the fight. How did you ...?"

"Niamh. She's known since Zagreb. That's why she disappeared. She knew ... at least she *thought* that I was safe with you."

"You are." Fionn glanced at the window as the sirens grew closer. "As is Niamh, which I'll explain later. But, Rose, we need to leave."

"Was I always safe?"

"Yes," he bit out. "I didn't even realize it myself, but yes. You've never been in danger of me. I could never hurt you."

He could never hurt her. This percolated in Rose's mind.

"Now let's go."

"You have An Breitheamh, which means you still plan to go after Aine."

He didn't answer verbally, but she saw she was right.

Apparently a mating bond wasn't everything.

Bitterness swelled inside her.

Niamh wanted Rose to convince Fionn not to take his revenge. She might be able to if she pretended not to feel betrayed anymore, if she seduced him and made him fall deeper into the mating bond.

However, that didn't mean he'd stop his plans. There was no certainty of that if their mating hadn't already changed his mind. This was an immortal who had been planning his vengeance for three centuries.

A twenty-five-year-old, Irish-American newbie fae would not alter that.

Then again, Rose could still hear him roaring her name after the iron knife pierced her body.

There was rage and grief in his voice.

"Did you come here just for An Breitheamh or for me too?"

"An Breitheamh. But then you saved my life." He wrapped a hand around her biceps and huffed impatiently, "Let's go. Meet me at Marienplatz."

Rose studied him thoughtfully. Fionn wouldn't exactly be able to search for the other fae-borne to use in his revenge plot if he was too busy chasing her around Europe. Not only would it keep him distracted, worrying about her fate and attempting to bring her to heel so he could get on with his stupid plans, but it also meant Rose wouldn't have to pretend she didn't want to knee him in the balls over and over again.

Softening her expression, she stepped into his space, a hand on his chest near the silver box. His green gaze locked on hers, desire in them he no longer hid. "You hurt me," she whispered, as she slipped a hand into his overcoat pocket.

"I know." The words seemed dragged out of him. "And I planned to let you go. But that was when I confused your actions for mine, or what mine would have been. I expected you to take revenge and instead ... You..." He hesitated, something like awe in his eyes. "Rose, I *need* to keep you safe."

The words caused an ache so deep in her, she almost faltered as she withdrew the shampoo bottle she knew he'd been using to trace her. Instead, she leaned into his hard body and pushed up onto her tiptoes, relieved when he bent his head toward hers.

Her lips brushed his, tingling with sensation, causing her hormones to beg her to kiss him again.

But she fought against the attraction she now blamed on the mating bond, let her hand slip to the silver box in his as she whispered against his mouth, "Too bad."

Rose blinked, and he was gone.

She stood beneath the steps at the Bavaria Statue, a towering bronze female that symbolized might.

In Rose's right hand was the shampoo bottle and in her left, the silver box.

Fionn knew where her parents lived. She had no doubt he'd go there, find a personal item of hers, and use it to trace her. However, that would take time. Time that allowed her to hide An Breitheamh so that when he came for her again, she'd keep him distracted, searching for it.

Hopefully long enough to work out her rage and betrayal.

Long enough to prevent the end of the world.

25

She'd done it again.

Rose had bloody well blindsided him.

As he drove his rental to Munich Airport, he shook his head in utter disbelief. At himself. Not at her. Fionn should have seen that maneuver coming.

Yet, somehow, he couldn't bring himself to be furious. He was pissed off, for certain, but once a woman takes an iron blade to save your life, it becomes damn hard to be anything beyond angry with her. Rose wasn't a vengeful person. She wasn't him. She was better than him.

No, the fury churning in his gut had nothing to with Rose taking the shampoo bottle and An Breitheamh. It was about the O'Connor Coven.

After *traveling* out of the apartment before the German authorities turned up, Fionn had called Bran to find out how in the hell the Irish coven had tracked down Rose. When he'd realized she was in Munich, it had aggravated him beyond belief because the city was now the heart of the Garm's territory under the leadership of William "The Bloody" Payne. Bran had called Fionn just as he was arriving in

Munich to tell him an incident was reported at Munich Central Station—word on the street it involved the Garm.

He'd expected when he'd used that shampoo to *travel* to where Rose was that he'd find her fighting off the Garm—not the O'Connors.

They'd come in force too.

When he thought Rose had taken that blade in the heart ...

Fionn gripped the steering wheel, the emotions too overwhelming to stand. For centuries, he'd tried to be numb to everything but vengeance, and mostly he'd succeeded. There had been women he'd felt a fleeting affection for, would even have been dismayed to discover they'd met an untimely death. Yet Fionn never thought he'd feel again the way he'd felt as a human man, never mind that he'd feel beyond his human capacity.

Seeing Rose crumble to her knees, iron dagger in her chest, was like watching a black hole swallow his entire fucking universe. His rage consumed him and in turn, he'd wiped out every single magic-wielding human in that goddamn room.

The relief that Rose would be okay was enough to make him tremble—literally shake as he reached to pull that dagger out of her. The urge to haul her against him, keep her there forever was strong, but first he had to know why she'd sacrificed herself for him.

Fionn still didn't have her answer ... although the mating bond seemed like the obvious culprit.

No one had ever sacrificed themselves for him and in doing so, Rose changed his plans.

He'd keep her with him, bring her to Ireland, to his secure home, have everything put in her name and so that when the time came to take his revenge, he'd know that his mate would be safe without him.

His mate.

Fionn couldn't think about what it meant to leave her. Not yet. He'd deal with that later, once he bloody well found her again.

As soon as he heard his mobile ring, Fionn hit the answer button and then the speaker. "What did you find?"

"We've been betrayed," Bran spat down the line. "The fucking contact at the coven didn't deal with the fucking jacket. He took the money and gave the jacket to Eva Mulhern. Ethan Mulhern's sister."

A growl vibrated in Fionn's throat. "Well, whichever one she was, she's dead. I slaughtered every one of them."

"Not everyone. Apparently a witch got away, but it wasn't Eva."

"I decimated their bodies. Clothes and all. They can't trace Rose now." That was something at least.

"You're booked to London and then to Baltimore. I'll have a car waiting for you at the Baltimore airport. You sure this is a good idea? You'll be on the other side of the world to her."

"It's this or wait for her to give herself away. This way seems more expedient."

"She's not stupid. She must know you'll do this. What's her thinking?"

Fionn wasn't sure. All he knew was that Rose was clearly determined to stop his plans of vengeance. To keep him with her or just to save the other fae-borne ... or both? He didn't know. But Fionn couldn't let her disappear. If something happened to her because he let her go ...

His plan was to fly to the States, break into Rose's childhood home, steal an item (or several for backup) that belonged to her, and use it to find her. "This is the plan. As for Niamh, just keep your ear to the ground."

"Who would have thought it? Fionn Mór: Protector of the Fae."

An ugly sting sliced through Fionn at Bran's teasing. "This changes nothing."

"Of course, it does. You're determined to protect Rose because she's your mate, and you're determined to protect Niamh because you think she's your descendant and the only living member of her family she has left was recently murdered."

It was true.

There was no way for Bran's genealogist to trace Niamh's family all the way back to Fionn's. But she had traced it back to the 1500s to an aristocratic clan called Ó Faracháin, a family rumored to have ties to the mythical Rí Mac Tíre.

The evidence wasn't one hundred percent there that Niamh was his descendant, but Fionn felt it in his gut. Moreover, it was just the sort of sneaky, cruel thing Aine would have done to him.

Except it didn't feel so cruel as he'd kneeled before his kin, an ethereal beauty who grieved for her brother with the passion of an Ó Faracháin. Fionn decided in that moment as she stared into his eyes, as if she could see into his very soul, he'd make sure Niamh Farren was safe too before he departed this world.

"That's all that has changed, Bran. The plan still goes ahead."

Bran emitted a rare animalistic snarl. "You're a bloody fool, Fionn Mór."

Then he hung up on him.

Bran hung up on *him*. Again.

It was like no one had any respect for him anymore.

THE SUN WAS SUPPOSED to make everything better.

It was supposed to assure her that there would be very few vamps in this part of the world. The sun was supposed to warm her skin, make her feel languorous and at peace. At least for a while.

However, as Rose laid on a lounger by the resort's cliff top pool, she felt nothing but worry and guilt.

Her felonies had racked up in the last day.

First, she'd experimented with her powers and placed a hand on an ATM in Munich and used her magic to dispense €5000. She'd intended to use that money to rent a car but discovered she needed ID for that. Rose would rather use the mind-control crap as little as possible, so she decided it was less immoral to pull a Fionn, mess with the license plates on a rundown car parked on a leafy residential street, and steal it. With the new phone she'd bought, she used GPS to get her back to Stuttgart—this time to the airport.

Upon a quick Google search, Rose discovered that Lanzarote, one of the Spanish Canary Islands, was the warmest place in Europe at this time of year. She didn't want to travel too far away because of Niamh.

Despite how wrong it felt, Rose knew she had to let Niamh go until her mission with Fionn reached a conclusion. It was what Niamh wanted.

Rose had booked a direct flight from Stuttgart to Lanzarote, remorsefully using the mind-warp shit since she didn't have a passport. Her powers, thankfully, weren't required at security because Rose had already rid herself of An Breitheamh. She'd taken an out-of-the-way route to Stuttgart Airport, and in a field outside a place called Buxheim, Bavaria, Rose had used her powers to dig a twelve-foot hole.

An Breitheamh was now at the bottom of it.

The airport afforded Rose a quick shop for weather-appropriate clothing, such as little shorts, tank tops, and bikinis, along with new underwear. She was ready to lead Fionn on this merry dance called distraction.

But if she had to do it, she wanted sun and relaxation—somewhere she could have a little peace and quiet for a few days before he arrived. Somewhere to forget that she'd never see her parents again, that she'd killed people, and that Niamh Farren was now out in the world all alone and grieving.

Oh, and that the fate of the entire world now rested upon her shoulders.

No biggie.

Rose opened her eyes, shaded by the sunglasses she'd bought at the resort store, and saw a couple floating in the pool, arms wrapped around one another. The hotel was adults only because Rose wanted that aforementioned peace and quiet. Yet she was surrounded by mostly couples who reminded her she'd never have a normal relationship.

It wasn't something she'd been looking for, but now that it was entirely out of her reach, it stung more than a little.

Fionn wasn't the *floating in a pool with his arms around you* type.

Of course, he'd have to give up his plans for revenge to even broach the idea of going on vacation with her.

Rose chuckled at the thought.

Never gonna happen.

However, he would find her there at the resort.

That was the plan.

To wait for him to come to her.

Butterflies fluttered in Rose's belly at the thought of seeing Fionn again.

Who knew it was possible to have such conflicting feelings for someone? Rose was still unbearably attracted to him, still felt protective toward him, and yet she was a furious, churning volcano of bitterness and resentment too.

Rose had sacrificed herself to save Fionn's life ... and he wouldn't even *consider* giving up his revenge for her.

26

It was day three at Misterios Resort on the southern coast of Lanzarote.

After the fast-paced, action-packed events of the last week, a week that felt more like a year, Rose was bored. She'd conjured a new e-reader from the nearest store, wherever that might have been, but not even the latest psychological thriller could cure her restlessness.

Rose liked to take one vacation a year—which sounded weird since she'd spent the last few years traveling around the world. But she was always working in whatever new city she'd temporarily settled down in. A cheap vacation to another European city for a few days or a beach resort on the coast was a break from the monotony of passionless employment.

However, when the fate of the world and her own future hung in the balance, vacation was torture. And her patience was about to be stretched to its limits.

The man had been watching Rose from across the pool for twenty minutes. In fact, she'd been an object of his fascination since last night at dinner, even though he was sitting across the restaurant with another woman in his company.

Clearly under some misapprehension that Rose would be interested in him, the man had attempted to catch her attention ever since. Rose felt his study the moment he'd come down to the pool.

Alone.

The lounger beside her creaked and Rose's skin prickled.

"You are English, yes?"

Oh crap.

With a barely concealed sigh, Rose lowered her e-reader and turned her head to the right.

Sure enough, there he was.

Through the brown lenses of her sunglasses, Rose took in the man. He was of middling height, stocky, with enough definition in his arms and muscles that he felt the need to oil them up. He glistened a little crisply in the morning sun, like a well-basted turkey. Sitting with his legs spread, junk haphazardly tucked into a red banana hammock, the man leaned his elbows on his knees and grinned at Rose, deep dimples popping in his cheeks. Although he wore dark shades, Rose could feel his scrutiny of her entire body. Her skin crawled.

"My name is Prince. Yours?"

Rose guessed from his accent he was from the Mediterranean, and she'd bet Prince was about to live up to the caricature of a Mediterranean sleazebag.

Getting straight to the point, she replied, "Where's your wife?"

He grinned, his teeth flashing bright white against his skin. "Girl-friend," he corrected. "She is having time at the spa, yes."

Rose promptly returned her attention to her e-reader.

She felt a tickle on her thigh and glanced down to see he was scoring his fingertip along her skin.

It was difficult to not let the trauma bubbling beneath the surface spew out all over this creep. Teeth gritted together, Rose ordered, "Remove your hand or lose it."

Prince chuckled but stopped touching her. "Oh, come. I just have fun, yes? I wonder to myself, what a sexy woman like you doing here alone. A tragedy, yes?"

"A tragedy?" Rose skewered him with a death look. "A tragedy is a woman spending her life with a man who hits on other women behind her back."

"Oh!" He nodded, grinning like he'd just figured something out. "You think I cheat, yes? No." He scooted closer to her. "Mia and I don't, how you say, do sex with just me and her."

"How nice for you." Rose brought the e-reader closer to her face hoping he'd take a hint.

"We could go back to your room, yes?"

Really?

She huffed and pushed her sunglasses up into her hair so he could see the growing annoyance in her expression. "How do I say this so you'll understand? I am not interested in anything you're selling."

He frowned. "No interested?"

"Nope. Go bother someone else."

"Oh, no, no." He reached out and pulled her hand from her device and placed it between his two palms. His voice lowered throatily. "I give you much pleasure, yes."

Feeling the tingle of her magic sparking beneath the surface, Rose fought for self-control. Taking a deep breath, she leaned toward him, watching his eyes flash with delight, and allowed a little of the supernatural purr to be heard in her words. "Unless you want me to neuter you permanently, let go of my hand."

His grip loosened, her tone making his smile fall. "Neuter?"

"Emasculate. Castrate. *Eviscerate*."

Prince dropped her hand like a hot stone, clearly understanding now.

Goose bumps prickled over Rose's skin, a shiver skating down her spine, and she knew without even having to turn and look that Fionn Mór was in the vicinity.

Her pulse took off.

Finally.

She heard his footsteps first, most likely the sound of expensive designer shoes slapping against the wet tile surrounding the pool.

Then he was there, a mammoth figure blocking out the sun, his features lost in shadows.

Something that had been hurting, like an infected wound, eased inside her. At the same time, all the anger she'd been holding on to burned in her throat.

Rose lowered her glasses back over her eyes and Fionn stepped between the two loungers, letting the sun shine on her again and consequently illuminating himself. Despite her turmoil, Rose inspected every inch of him, taking in the short-sleeved white shirt open at the collar, straining against his thick biceps. It was tucked into a pair of navy suit trousers. Expensive loafers, a stainless steel watch, and cool-as-fuck dark aviator shades completed his look.

Fionn's attention wasn't on her.

It was on the creep beside her.

"Fuck off," Fionn demanded.

Prince skittered out of the lounger and hurried toward the hotel as if the hounds of hell were nipping at his heels.

Rose turned from watching him. "Do you think if I had been that succinct, I'd have gotten rid of him as easily?"

Even though Fionn's eyes were hidden behind his shades, Rose could feel his gaze running over her body. Unlike how Prince made her feel, she shivered, a deep, wanting tug making itself known low in her belly.

"In that bikini?" Fionn grunted as he lowered himself to the end of her lounger. "Doubtful."

The flicker of pleasure she felt over this backhanded compliment enraged her. It took a lot not to launch herself at him and start a fight that would reveal their true natures to the surrounding humans.

His hand grazed the side of her foot as he aimed his body toward her. Rose shivered again, automatically pulling her feet away from him, folding her legs toward her chest.

"Interesting choice of hideout," Fionn commented, his tone bland.

"How did you find me?" She already suspected how but she wanted to know for certain.

"Your parents. I flew to Maryland."

The thought of her parents made her tense. "Are ... are they okay?"

"They're safe. And they'll remain safe under my protection."

Relief moved through her. They were safe. Thank God. "How did you ..."

"I broke in while they were out." He lifted a hand. A gold chain holding a gold *R* pendant and a little golden figure of a gymnast mid back handspring dangled from his fingers. Her parents bought it for her eighth birthday.

"What else did you steal?"

Fionn's lips twitched. "You know me that well, Rose?"

"I know that you wouldn't travel all the way to America to steal just a necklace. You'd need other items for insurance."

"I stole a few things. Don't want to lose you again."

Her heart literally skipped a beat at his words, and she hated that she wanted to read more into them than he meant.

"So, what now?"

"Tell me where An Breitheamh is."

Ah, straight to the point.

Feeling hurt, even though she'd known all along that's why he was there, Rose felt like inciting a little frustration in him. Setting aside her e-reader, she slid across the lounger, opening her legs so the point of the knee he had turned toward her contacted the inner thigh of her right leg. She felt him stiffen ever so slightly, and that was before she placed her hand on his knee, smoothed it down his inner thigh, feeling the hard, hot muscle beneath his suit pants.

"I've missed you." Unfortunately, it wasn't entirely a lie.

Just as Rose's fingertips neared the now-tented hardness between his legs, Fionn grabbed her wrist, stalling her movement. His grip was tight, bruising, as he hauled her against him, her chest pressed to his.

Warm lips tickled hers as Fionn growled against them. "Stop playing games, *mo chroí.*"

"Don't call me that," Rose snapped.

He surprised her by kissing her. Just a soft, tickling brush of his mouth across hers.

He might as well have flicked his tongue between her legs.

Rose sucked in a breath as Fionn retreated ever so slightly. "Where is An Breitheamh?"

In answer, she curled her free hand around his strong shoulder, nails digging in, and slammed her mouth over his, forcing her tongue past his lips. She kissed him with every ounce of passion, love, hatred, need, and resentment that filled her, until she felt his fingers tight in her hair as he held her by her nape.

His anger and desire battled hers in a hungry, dark, deep kiss that melted her to the core. Rose shifted so his knee pressed between her legs where she wanted him, needed him. Fionn made a guttural noise that vibrated through her.

His lips vanished, as did the delicious pressure of his knee.

Rose fell back on her hands, panting with exertion.

Holy shit.

She'd meant to punish him with her actions.

Seeing him stride away from her, tension radiating from every inch of his body, Rose was sure she'd succeeded.

But she'd also inflicted damage on herself.

Aware of the attention of the few people around the pool, Rose collected her things, slipped on her flip-flops and followed casually in Fionn's wake. He waited inside the doorway to the hotel, his back against the wall, his shades pushed up into his hair.

Those green eyes of his pierced her as she stepped inside, intensifying the fluttering in her belly.

"You done fucking around?" he snarled.

Her gaze dropped to his arousal and back up to his face. "Mission accomplished, I guess."

"Don't feel so smug, sweetheart. I can smell your musk. One slip of my hand beneath that tiny scrap of fabric you call a bikini and I'd feel your wet against my fingertips."

She inhaled a sharp breath as the visual escalated her arousal.

He looked at her breasts. "And despite the warm temperature, your nipples are hard, *mo chroí*."

Rose immediately crossed her arms over her chest. "I blame the mating bond. It's irrational and has a negative effect on my body. But my heart and mind are very much in control ... I still hate you."

"Negative effect? It may be bloody inconvenient but I'd hardly say the feeling was negative." Fionn took hold of her arm, his fingers tight around her biceps. "Show me to your room so we can discuss An Breitheamh. Among other things."

Deciding it was best they did this in private, Rose silently led him through the large hotel to her third-floor room. She had a balcony overlooking the pool and the ocean beyond.

"And how might I ask did you afford all this?" Fionn asked as he entered.

Rose forced herself not to stiffen at the underlying judgment in his question, her flip-flops flapping against the tile floor as she spun to face him. She shrugged. "I robbed an ATM."

He sighed heavily, staring around at the room, before returning his attention to hers. As if he couldn't help it, his gaze climbed her body. Rose felt the telltale tightening in her breasts as desire darkened his features. By the time they reached hers, it took everything not to throw something sharp at him in retaliation for causing her body to be so out of sync with her heart.

"Ah, Rose ... I don't want this life for you." Fionn gestured to the room.

"What life?"

"Niamh's life. Running and stealing."

Rose ignored the stifling prickle of guilt in her throat. "Then what would you have me do?"

"Come back to Galway with me."

Startled by the pronouncement, Rose's lips parted in surprise. Did he mean ...?

She took a tentative step toward him. "And do what?"

"Live there. No one can get to you there."

Could it be she'd been wrong? Was he here for her? Only her?

"You'll be safe for however long you want to be there. And it will always be your safe place, Rose. I will make sure you're taken care of when I'm gone."

Just like that, the hope that had been rising inside her crashed and shattered into a million jagged pieces, piercing her, gutting her. Every object in the room began to vibrate, floating several inches of the ground.

Fionn cursed under his breath and took slow steps toward her. "Calm, *mo chroí*."

Everything dropped, a fragile vase smashing on the sideboard. Rose glared at Fionn. "Don't. Call. Me. That."

He glowered back. "Why?"

"Because it doesn't mean anything to you. I am not your heart. I am the mate you are planning to leave behind."

To her astonishment, pain and remorse slackened his expression. "Rose ..."

"I won't let you. Not because I want to keep you. I have more self-respect than to hold on to someone who doesn't want me. And honestly, I still see you as my betrayer. Considering you can't give up your revenge, you'll understand the depths of my anger toward you."

His expression darkened.

"I won't let you do this because it means killing the last fae-borne." She'd already decided not to tell Fionn what Niamh had told her—that his entrance to Faerie would lead to something that would end the world as they knew it. She wouldn't tell him until it was necessary.

If Fionn was to change his mind ...

Rose held back tears as she realized why she was keeping it from him.

There was still a part of her that wanted him to choose her.

To end his plan of revenge not because it jeopardized the world, but because he couldn't leave Rose behind.

Furious at him for this too, Rose's expression set with determination. "So, if you came here to bully me into giving you An Breitheamh, it was a wasted trip."

Fionn vanished, making her gape in surprise.

Then she felt his heat at her back seconds before she felt his strong, calloused palm sliding around her throat, while his other caressed her ass before moving around to rest on her belly.

It was an embrace of primal claiming if ever there was one.

Rose held tense, hating that right then, she was imagining his hand dipping lower, sliding beneath her bikini bottoms.

Instead Fionn's palm flexed against her belly while his fingers stroked lightly across her neck. His breath tickled her ear as he bent his head toward it, his tone deep and seductive. "A mating is a gift, *mo chroí*. I never saw it as such until now ... and although ours cannot last, there is still time for us to revel in it, however short-lived it might be."

Closing her eyes against the temptation, Rose choked back the hurt and the tears and forced out, "I'm an all-or-nothing kind of woman."

Fionn's embrace tightened, his arm encircling her waist to pull her back against his hard body. "I'm not leaving here without you or that fucking dagger, Rose."

Her hackles rose at his warning.

"I've hidden it. Where no one will find it." She tried to yank herself out of his hold but as strong as she was, Fionn Mór had around a hundred and fifty pounds and over three centuries of experience on her. She hissed like a cat as she struggled to break away, spinning to face him, to claw his face off.

Eventually Fionn grappled hold of her wrists and yanked her into him.

He bent his head to hers as she squirmed to be free. "All this is doing is pissing me off and making me very, very fucking hard, so—"

"Asshole!" she yelled in his face. "Disgusting, primitive, Iron Age asshole!"

Fionn bared his teeth. "An Breitheamh, Rose."

"NEVER!" Every light bulb in the room shattered, halting her struggle.

Her captor's grip loosened ever so slightly and his expression softened. Fionn bent his head toward her, and she stiffened as he rested his forehead on hers. "Ah, *mo chroí*, I was afraid you'd say that." Then he cupped her face in his hands and pressed the softest, sweetest, most loving kiss against her mouth.

This time magic accompanied the tingle of attraction.

She tensed to fight, but it was too late.

Darkness descended.

27

A little tap of his magic against Rose's carotid would not do the trick this time. Instead, he cast a sleeping spell over her with the touch of his lips.

Fionn caught her as she slumped into unconsciousness and swung her into his arms with ease. Laying her down on the bed while he gathered himself, Fionn frowned at her almost-naked body.

When he'd seen her sitting on the lounger being hit on by that oily prick, wearing nothing but two scraps of cloth, it had taken everything within him not to act like a macho arsehole and throw a towel over her.

Rose was a modern woman. She wouldn't take kindly to being told what to wear. Honestly, it had never occurred to him to tell a woman what to wear.

Then again, he couldn't remember ever feeling such intense possessiveness over a woman as he felt toward Rose.

Her hair was wet from the pool, spilling across the white bedcovers, turning them damp. The little blue stud sparkled in her nose as sunlight cast a glow over her lightly tanned skin. The freckles people often described as fairy kisses scattered affectionately over the bridge of her nose were more prominent from exposure to the sun.

And he could still taste her on his tongue, still feel that perfect upside-down mouth pressed against his.

Rose's face was the loveliest thing he'd ever seen.

Right then, however, he wished it was all he could see.

Her small, rounded breasts might as well be bared for all the white bikini did to cover them, her hard nipples poking through the material. The sight of the small white scar on her chest, a reminder of the iron blade she'd took to save him, only intensified his desire. And so much more. The scar made him feel too much.

Forcing his study lower to her narrow waist, to the gentle curve of her hips and slender legs did nothing to ease his want of her. Although she was fairly short, her legs looked surprisingly long, thighs elongated and slim, calves perfectly toned, ankles delicate, feet small and feminine.

Fionn squeezed his eyes shut.

He could have done without knowing that Rose had gorgeous legs beneath her jeans.

Turning away, he gathered her belongings into her backpack. The thing was stuffed full. After a thorough search of the room, he'd discovered Rose *had* hidden An Breitheamh. There was nothing for it, then.

He needed to convince her to give up the location of the dagger, and there was only one safe place in the world where he could keep her.

"*Kidnap* her," Fionn muttered in exasperation.

For let's not pretend otherwise, you ruthless bastard.

He was kidnapping his mate.

With quick efficiency, mind determined to detach from the silky softness of her skin, Fionn dressed an unconscious Rose in jeans and a sweater. A little warm for where they were but not for a plane ride ... or Ireland.

She moaned as he buttoned up her jeans, and arousal rushed through him like a tsunami. Groaning, Fionn rested his head against the mattress by her hip and took a minute.

You are an ancient warrior. You've survived worse things than a bad case of blue balls.

With a grunt, he pushed himself off the bed and finished putting socks and sneakers on the object of his affection, and frustration.

Her things gathered, Fionn threw her rucksack over one shoulder and carefully laid Rose over the other. Casting an illusion spell so the humans would see only a man carrying luggage, Fionn left the room and cursed under his breath as Rose's limp hands gently swatted against his lower back with every stride.

This physical awareness of her was ridiculous.

Bloody mating bond.

With a huff, he shifted her more comfortably on his shoulder and set out of the resort.

Fionn had a private plane waiting on the island. He might be wealthy but private planes were an expense he liked to avoid. However, this one was worth it if it meant returning him expediently to the coast of Galway with Rose in his possession. The spell he cast over Rose would last until he awakened her, but Fionn didn't want her knocked out for long.

In fact, even though he knew she would be furious with him when she awoke, excitement and anticipation stirred in his gut.

Fionn was looking forward to the clash.

Sick, masochistic bastard that I am, he grumbled inwardly.

~

It was the wind she heard first.

Rose heard it whistling with force, a muted sound somewhere beyond her.

Her eyes fluttered open, her sleepy mind expecting to see sunlight pouring in through the French doors of her Lanzarote hotel room.

The sight of the roaring fire in a stone hearth within stone walls caused her to fly upward in panic. A velvet blanket imprisoned her legs, and Rose's heart rate escalated as she took in the luxuriously draped, four-poster bed she was in.

"Good, you're awake."

The familiar voice in the unfamiliar room relieved her, even when it shouldn't. Pushing off the blanket and the duvet under it, Rose lowered her legs to a stone-flagged floor and felt the cold rush up her legs. The room itself was warm because of the lively, crackling fire, the smell of burning wood not at all unwelcome.

The cold floor was.

A pair of women's velvet slippers popped out of thin air at her feet, and she knew it was Fionn's doing without even turning toward him. She slipped her feet inside and ignored the fact she was dressed in pajama shorts and camisole.

It was better to.

Otherwise an ancient warrior fae might just die. By her hand.

Crossing her arms over her chest, she walked around the bed, taking in the medium-sized room. It was sparsely furnished with two tall windows with deep, deep recesses on either side of the wall opposite the bed. Dull light poured in, and she forced herself to look at the chair beneath the farthest window.

Fionn lounged in it, dressed immaculately as always in a dark cashmere sweater and fine woolen suit pants. His dress shoes shone beneath the lights from the candelabras fixed around the walls. They were wrought iron and designed to look like old-fashioned candle-holders.

"Where the hell am I?" She took in the arched doorway with a wooden door. A huge tapestry hung on the wall, covering the stonework, and a large oak wardrobe was tucked into its corner.

"My home, in County Galway. The west coast, to be exact."

"Ireland?" Rose threw him an exasperated look and hurried toward one of the windows. The glass was thick, inserted into panes delineated by leadwork. Rose pushed the hefty old windows open easily and felt the strong gales blow into the room off the sea in the distance.

"Holy shit." She leaned over, glancing downward to see they were up very high.

In what appeared to be a turret.

Rose shut the window, pulse racing as she settled back on her feet. For a moment, she could only stare unseeingly at the recess.

Then she asked, "Are we in a castle?"

"Yes. Welcome to An Caomhnóir, Rose."

"Did you kidnap me, Fionn?" She turned to face him. "What the hell did you do to me?"

"A little spell." He said it so casually, like it was no big deal. Standing, he gave her a knowing look. "Would you have coming willingly?"

Was he serious? Searching the room, she caught sight of a wooden chair near the fireplace. That would do.

"Rose, don't—"

She gestured with her hands, making the chair soar through the room.

Fionn cursed, swiped his hands across the air in front of him, and sent the chair careening against the wall where it smashed into three pieces. He glared at the chair carnage and then her. "That chair was over two hundred years old."

"I couldn't care less if you whittled that chair with your bare fucking hands. How dare you kidnap me!"

He was a blur across the room, hauling her into his arms and then throwing her onto the bed. Rose huffed in aggravation as he towered over her. She pushed up off her back and promised him retribution with her eyes.

"Can we continue this discussion without yelling at each other?"

Disbelief coursed through her. "Oh, you want to be civilized? Now that you've knocked me out and carted me all the way from a Spanish island to the middle-of-nowhere Ireland!"

"Galway is hardly nowhere. But speaking of location and your obvious displeasure at being here, An Caomhnóir is, as I've said previously, spelled to be invisible from the outside world. No one can find you here. You're safe. You're as safe as I can make you until you do the right thing and return An Breitheamh to me."

The right thing? The right thing! Seething, Rose gritted out, "I couldn't even if I wanted to. It's not in this country."

"Use your magic." Fionn fisted his hands on the bed on either side of her hips, leaning toward her. Rose's body unfairly wanted to move into him, so she had to force it to lean back. "Just conjure it here and we won't have to fight anymore."

Her answer was to flick her hand, rip a candelabra off the wall, and throw it at his head. Fionn winced as it connected, his hand rubbing the spot where it hit before clattering to the floor by the bed. The vibe in the room grew considerably darker as he turned from the broken light fixture to her. "Very mature, *mo chroí*."

His tone was anything but loving.

"Don't—"

"Call you that." He pushed his face into hers, forcing her back against the headboard. "I'll call you what I like, Rose Kelly, because you're my *mate*. And as my mate, I expect you to return an item that means a great deal to me."

"Can you find a way to undo this mating bond between us?"

Fionn couldn't hide his astonishment. "What?"

"Can you find a way to undo this shit between us?"

His expression darkened. "There's no undoing this."

Rose sat up, pushing her face into his. "Then why should I return an item that means a great deal to you when you can't return something that means a great deal to me?"

Confusion flickered across his face. "Wha—"

"You have a piece of my soul, even though you don't want it." Hurt edged her words no matter how hard she tried to camouflage it. "So I'm keeping An Breitheamh, even though I don't want that. Fair's fair."

Understanding softened his features and he reached out to touch her. Rose flinched away. "Don't."

Sighing heavily, Fionn straightened, stepping back from the bed. His countenance and tone turned matter-of-fact. "The spell that keeps An Caomhnóir invisible from the rest of the world has its drawbacks. Neither of us can *travel* in and out of the castle grounds until we're beyond the spell barrier. You're stuck here, Rose. You're not going anywhere until you deliver An Breitheamh to me."

"Then I guess I'm stuck here forever."

"You *will* give me that dagger. Of that I have no doubt." He marched away from her, his long strides eating up the distance between the bed and the door. "Dinner is served downstairs in an hour. If I have to come get you, I won't be nice about it."

The urge to throw something else at him was real. "If I don't want to eat, I don't have to."

"You may be immortal, Rose, but starving yourself will lead to a very painful, uncomfortable existence, and since I've vowed to keep you safe until I'm no longer of this earth, it won't be happening on my watch." The door slammed hard behind him, making the tapestry on the wall flutter.

Ugh!

"What am I supposed to wear?" she yelled at the closed door.

In answer, the doors of the wardrobe in the far corner flew open, revealing a row of jeans and tops.

Rose huffed. "Show-off."

Answering masculine laughter, dulled by stone walls, met her ears.

She rolled her eyes at the sound, wishing it didn't cause that warm, painful ache to score across her chest.

28

The gale-force wind and wet weather had finally moved on. It was a crisp day, sunny and calm, with the ocean stretching out before the castle like a sheet of sparkling glass. There was a gentle breeze—it was unusual for there not to be on this part of the coast.

Fionn sighed and glanced over his shoulder to stare at the castle towering behind him. For two and a half days, Rose had coexisted with him at An Caomhnóir. She was uncharacteristically broody and to say her behavior frustrated him was an understatement. Not that Rose was stomping around like a sullen teenager; that wasn't who she was. If she was pissed, she let it hang out. Fionn preferred that to huffiness.

No, it was more that Rose was wounded and trying to figure out how to maneuver through the days with her new affliction.

He'd caused the wound.

Therein laid his guilt and frustration.

His current plan of just waiting for Rose to come to him was not working. He was no closer to mending their relationship or retrieving An Breitheamh. Pulling out his mobile, Fionn hit Bran's button.

The vampire picked up after a few rings. "You do this deliberately —I was just falling asleep."

"This will only take a second."

"Give me a minute, then."

Fionn waited and heard murmuring in the background. Suspecting he'd interrupted an interlude, he felt an unusual emotion: jealousy. He stared up to the castle. An interlude with Rose would not go unappreciated.

"I'm back," Bran said. Fionn could hear a beeping sound in the background followed by a door closing. A heavy one. Fionn knew what that meant. Bran owned a loft in Dublin near the docklands, and his office—or command center, as the vamp liked to call it—was only accessible by a digital security system that involved a code and retinal scan.

As soon as Fionn had walked into that apartment with its tall windows all the way down one side, he'd looked at his friend like he was nuts. Bran had merely shrugged, grabbed a remote control, and aimed it at the windows. Not only did fitted blinds cover the windows but heavy curtains moved from either side of the wall across a rail to meet in the middle.

The loft was in total darkness.

Fionn had never seen so much fabric in one room, but the curtains certainly did the job.

"They're on a timer too," Bran had said. "So I don't get cremated if I fall asleep before the sunrise."

Still, Fionn thought owning a loft was stupidly risky for a vampire. Bran was stubborn, though. The thing he missed most about his human life was the daylight, and he was determined not to live his life like a clichéd vampire with a basement habitat.

"Any word of Niamh?" Fionn asked.

"One day you're going to ask how I am."

Fionn had the ability to make even his silence impatient.

"Okay, I'll tell you, anyway. I just had the best sex of my long life with this vampire I met at Ruin."

Ruin was a basement club in the heart of Dublin and a hotspot for supernaturals.

"I'm happy for you. Niamh?"

Bran sighed. "Nothing. I'm sorry."

"Anything else I need to know?"

"There's been no more movement from the O'Connors. They're not a huge coven, Fionn. You wiped out their youngest and strongest in Munich. They might have decided this isn't a fight they can win."

"Let's hope so. The Blackwoods?"

"Still fumbling around Europe from what I can see."

"The Garm?"

"Same. Everyone's waiting for a sign from either Rose or Niamh."

"And nothing from the third fae-borne?"

The vamp was silent for a second.

"Bran?"

"What if there isn't a third? What if they're already dead? There's been no sign, Fionn."

Fionn shook his head, even though his friend couldn't see. "No, that fae is alive. Rose is still protecting this person, and I have to believe she'd only be doing that if Niamh gave her the impression that the fae-borne is out there."

"Speaking of Niamh ... you're determined to keep her safe, then?"

"She's my kin." Enough said.

"You don't know that for certain. There's no real evidence," he repeated unnecessarily.

Irritation burned in Fionn's gut. "I feel it. I *know* it."

"Or you're using it as an excuse to prevent you from killing an innocent to mete out your revenge. Maybe even an excuse to prevent you going after your revenge, full stop, now that Rose is in your life."

That irritation hotly converted to anger. "I'll have my revenge, Bran, make no mistake about that. Call me if you miraculously come up with something useful." He hung up, almost crushing the phone in his fist. Fionn didn't care if he'd been unfair to the vamp. The fucker kept pushing his buttons.

Striding from the cliff top toward the castle, determination pushed Fionn's strides. Today Rose would converse with him. Somehow, he would convince her to give him An Breitheamh, and it wouldn't be because he'd seduced it out of her. If Rose wanted him that way, *she'd* have to come to him. Fionn was burdened with enough guilt as it was; he wouldn't add sexual coercion to his list of crimes against his mate.

Fuck, he hoped she'd come to him.

ROSE WAS bored but no longer conflicted.

For the last two days, she'd wandered over every inch of the castle, peering into rooms that were filled with furniture but seemed to have no current use. She'd accidentally wandered into Fionn's bedroom, which was a bigger version of her room. Bigger space, bigger bed, and a lot of stuffed bookshelves.

She discovered this after coming across an actual freaking library. Her mate liked to read.

While she had to use a toilet across the hall from her room, Fionn's room had a small en suite and walk-in closet.

The man had more suits than Emporio Armani.

However, it was his bed that drew her attention.

It was the biggest sleigh bed Rose had ever seen, custom built to accommodate its very tall owner.

Something about the sight of that bed, on top of Fionn's scent lingering in the air, was arousing. Rose departed his bedroom quickly.

The main hall had massive fireplaces at either end that took up nearly the entire gable walls. Yet, the room was cozy, a dining table at one end and a spacious sitting area at the other. There was even a large flat-screen TV bolted to the stonework.

Tapestries hung on the walls to warm up the place and huge Aubusson rugs covered every inch of the flagstone flooring. There were two modern electric fires in the room—they looked like black wood-burning stoves—since the castle was darn cold. She found these fires all over the An Caomhnóir and wondered at the costs of running such a place.

But if the castle was off the grid, how did that work?

Rose was collecting questions for Fionn. Where was the vault he spoke of? She doubted he'd tell her. After his staff had been killed, had he not hired new staff? So far, Rose had met no other soul at An Caomhnóir. The kitchen was stocked with food, and when Fionn said dinner would be served that first night, he meant the dinner he'd cooked.

That's right.

Fionn Mór could cook.

Rose had witnessed it. The second night she'd found Fionn in the large kitchen searing steak before sticking it in a huge range oven at one end of the room. She'd then watched as he mashed potatoes.

By hand.

Dinner so far had been delicious.

And yet, Rose could not make conversation with Fionn. Yes, she was angry with him. But mostly she was nursing the heart he'd broken and trying to figure out where to go from there. Did she keep him distracted indefinitely? Resign her life to this castle and eventual mind-numbing boredom?

Or did she push wounded feelings aside and just seduce Fionn? Try to change his mind with sex and distraction?

Would that even work?

This had been Rose's turmoil for the last sixty-two hours. Longer, really, if she counted her time in Lanzarote.

Until the dream last night.

Since she'd only dream-walked two people—Alejandra and Fionn—and both were in the same room with her when she did it, Rose guessed that was the deal. She had to be in the same room as the person she dream-walked.

When she'd begun dreaming of Fionn and his children the night before, she assumed she was in Fionn's head. But the dream transitioned too smoothly to her running through a forest, free and fast, bounding over tree limbs and bracken. When Rose woke, she remembered that the images she'd dreamed were taken right out of Fionn's own memories.

Her very sore and shattered heart was reminding her subconscious that Fionn had his reasons. That maybe she shouldn't assume it was so easy for him to choose revenge over her.

Rose had a plan. She wouldn't force anything between them. Rose was going to talk, and Fionn, if he wanted An Breitheamh from her, would have to share himself with her.

The shitty weather had broken and Rose was determined to enjoy the crisp, sunny air. She dressed in jeans, a sweater, a jacket, and a scarf she'd found in her wardrobe, along with a pair of black leather ankle boots that fit perfectly. Seriously, the guy had an uncanny ability to pick a wardrobe.

After scoffing down some toast and coffee, Rose had searched the castle for Fionn. Her impatience (and worry) was growing by the second when she caught sight of a lone figure on a cliff top facing the sea.

At the sight of him, that overwhelming ache of want filled her.

She set out of the castle for the first time since her arrival. The main door was inconspicuous. One might expect mammoth arched double doors, drawbridge, and moat. But the single door was in a small vestibule off the main hall.

Well, not just a single door but a heavy, solid, wrought iron door.

Probably heavy to a human, Rose thought. She could push it open like it was made of cardboard.

Rugged stones acted as a stairway, leading her down to level ground. A garden that was probably spectacular in the spring surrounded her. Neat flagstone paths led off in all directions toward the high, defensive stone walls that encompassed the castle grounds. One huge wrought iron door seemed to be the exit. To her right, near the base of the castle, was an archway carved into the stone, leading out toward the cliff top where she'd seen Fionn. She was just about to walk that way when he appeared through it.

Rose shivered in the late November air.

The fae walked toward her, his expression unreadable. He wore only a black cashmere sweater with a shawl collar, dark blue jeans, and walking boots. Rose liked him like this. Sure, he was all kinds of hot in his suits and overcoat, but the more casual look worked well with the rugged unkemptness of his hair and stubbled cheeks.

Attraction awoke inside her. It was always there, ready to be prodded to consciousness with Fionn's arrival.

Jesus Christ, she realized she would never escape this mating bond.

Which was another thing she wanted to talk to him about.

As Fionn slowed to a halt before her, Rose gestured to the door leading out of the grounds. "Is it safe to go for a walk?"

"The spell reaches miles beyond the castle."

"So that would be a yes?" When he continued to watch her, Rose stuffed her hands into her jacket pockets. "Would you like to come with me?"

Fionn studied her, as if trying to work out her motivation. Finally, he nodded.

To her delight, Rose saw there *was* a little bridge outside the wrought iron gate. It was built over a small stream that ran past the castle and out into the ocean. "Where is it from?"

"Water finds its way throughout the hills here, moving over valleys, either funneling out toward the sea or downward to the faerie pools."

"Will you show me the faerie pools?"

She felt his perusal again before he answered in the affirmative.

Beyond the bridge was the coastline to their right and forestry to their left. Fionn pointed out dips in the cliff edge that led down to the dunes.

"There's not a lot of beach here, and it's pebbled, not golden sands. But, if you feel like dipping your toes in the water, that's where to go."

Rose nodded and then followed him as he led her to a worn path through the woods. The sun shone through the seminaked trees, the forest floor covered in a carpet of autumn leaves soggy from the last few days of rain.

"How did you come to own a castle?" She broke the silence, looking up at him, a towering figure walking beside her with the grace of an athlete.

"I bought it roughly a hundred years after the Blackwoods woke me up. It was built in the fourteenth century for a lord of Ireland. I'd discover upon awakening that Ireland had been invaded by England in the late twelfth century, and the reign of the high kings was over." There was a hint of grim melancholy in his voice. "Ireland would never be the same again." Fionn glanced down at her, his expression softening a little. "Almost two centuries before I'd awaken, the title of lord of Ireland would be abolished. By the late 1800s the castle had been added to over the centuries and was now under the ownership of an English lord whose coffers were rapidly dwindling. Such situations were commonplace among a dying aristocracy that refused to get their hands dirty by investing in the Industrial Revolution. I discovered this earl had financial troubles and offered a lot more than the castle was worth. He sold it to me."

"Why would you do that?"

"Because ..." He seemed to hesitate. "The gate to Faerie is on this land. I wanted to be able to protect it."

"Until you could use it." Her tone wasn't accusatory. Just matter-of-fact.

"Aye."

"You bought this place and spelled it. But you don't stay here all the time."

"No. But it is home."

"Is it near your old home? When you were human, when you were king?"

Fionn shook his head. "No, my homestead was in what is now Northern Ireland. Near Enniskillen."

Letting silence fall between them, Rose followed Fionn through the forest, wondering if he was taking a path buried under the leaves. When they reached a fallen tree, he held out a hand to aid her over it, even though they both knew she didn't require anyone's help.

Taking a deep breath, Rose accepted his hand, unable to meet his gaze as his fingers closed tightly around hers. She hopped over the fallen tree with Fionn's steadying touch and immediately let go of his hand as soon as he was over the obstacle.

He stepped over it like it was a puddle.

Tingles sparked all over Rose's hand and she stuffed it into her pocket, aware of Fionn flexing his before fisting it at his side.

He'd felt it too.

She gathered her courage to say what had been on her mind all morning. "I don't think I ever properly said how sorry I was about Caoimhe and Diarmuid."

His head whipped toward her so fast, she was sure he must have gotten whiplash. Green eyes blazed intimidatingly at her, searching her expression.

She allowed her sincere empathy to show. "I'm truly sorry for what happened to you. That you lost them."

Satisfied Rose was telling the truth, he gave her a clipped nod and focused his attention forward again.

Feeling brave, she continued, "I've had time to think about that. Kids weren't ever something I thought about. They were this possibility to consider way off in the distant future. However, they were a *possibility* ... and now they're not." Loss filled her. "It's not the same, I know that. But I feel like I've lost something, anyway."

Fionn cut her an unreadable look. She half expected him to commiserate, offer comfort, but that muscle ticked away in his jaw and he seemed to glance away guiltily. Why? It wasn't his fault she was fae.

"What age were you when you had Diarmuid?"

At first, Rose thought he wouldn't answer. Then ...

"Sixteen."

"What?" Her eyebrows must have hit her hairline.

Fionn smirked at her. "You're reacting as a modern woman. Back then, I was a man at thirteen, already warring. The fae invasion distracted the clans from their wars for territory. They hadn't come together as one just yet, but each were doing what they could to keep the fae from hurting their people. Aoibhinn and I grew up in the same village and as soon as she had her first bleed, she was considered a woman. She was fourteen when it happened. I was fifteen, almost sixteen. She was beautiful, her father was head of our clan, and she was much sought after. She could have been given to an older, more experienced clansman, but I'd proven myself in battle, her father viewed me as a son, and Aoibhinn wanted *me*."

"Jesus Christ," Rose croaked. "You got married when she was fourteen and you were sixteen."

"Again, Rose, times were very, very different."

"You were children."

"No," he snapped. "That was not a world you could be a child in for long. We're known as the Celts now. And we were a warring, violent people. You were lucky to hold on to even a modicum of childhood."

"Okay, okay," Rose soothed. "You're right. I don't know what I'm talking about. Twenty-first-century minds do not belong in the Iron Age."

Fionn relaxed marginally. "Aoibhinn fell pregnant quickly. Diarmuid was born just before I was about to enter my seventeenth year."

Rose couldn't even imagine being a parent at that age. "What was he like?"

His expression hardened but it was at odds with the softness of his voice. "He was my shadow. By the time he was seven, I'd taken over the clan and had started to bring the other clans together. He wanted to be like me, wielding the wooden sword I gave him with skill belying his young age. He even wanted his own wolf. Aoibhinn used to complain that she'd never met a child so focused on the duties of men. Diarmuid was a good boy." Fionn swallowed hard. "I was taken to Faerie days after his eleventh birthday. By that time, I was king, grooming my son to take my place when the time came. But I missed six years of his life. When I came back, he was already a man with his own wife and child on the way." His voice grew cold. "I'll never know what happened to him. Or to my gentle Caoimhe who cried when others cried and laughed when others laughed and felt more deeply than those around her. She was goodness and beauty in a violent, wicked world. She was the sky and the rolling hills and the wondrous sea—she was what made that life worth enduring."

Tears Rose couldn't control spilled down her cheeks at his beautiful but haunted words. "I'm sorry," Rose whispered.

Fionn looked down at her, following her tears. "She was loyal like you, Rose."

That ache inside her intensified. "No. She was loyal like you. The man you used to be."

Although she hadn't meant it as an insult, Fionn winced slightly and picked up his pace.

Rose hurried to follow. "I'm sure she and Diarmuid had a long, good life. They were no longer battling the fae, and they were royalty, right?"

"Which made them targets. A simple man often enjoys a more peaceful life than a chief or a king. Still, the village we built under my kingship was a hillfort. Highly defensible. It was called An Caomhnóir."

"Like the castle?"

"The castle is named after the village."

The trees began to clear, water sparkling in the distance, the sound of it rushing filling the silence.

"What about ... Aoibhinn?"

Fionn didn't reply. Instead, he kept walking until the trees fell behind them and they walked over massive, moss-covered rock. Hills that stretched for miles surrounded them. The stream of rushing water disappeared into the hills beyond and fell in a shallow waterfall into a pool separated by an arm of rock. The pool with the waterfall was large, the other small and enclosed.

The water was a startling Mediterranean turquoise.

Magic tingled in the air.

The faerie pools.

"I loved Aoibhinn," Fionn said, lifting his voice to be heard over the waterfall. "She was fierce and protective of our children. She wanted to able to protect them if I was ever gone so I trained her to fight, with her fists and with a sword. But ... not long after our marriage, a fae stole into the village and took Aoibhinn's mother. The fae used magic to fend us off. A powerful, powerful fae. We failed to protect her, and she was found a day later in the woods, naked and mutilated."

Rose covered her mouth, aghast at what her imagination conjured.

"Aoibhinn hated the fae, but that day something twisted inside her. I vowed to find the fae and kill him. And I did." He looked down at her. "I used An Breitheamh."

She pieced together what he wasn't saying. "He was the fae prince you killed."

Fionn nodded.

"You killed him for Aoibhinn and in turn started a war with Aine. Everything you did was for Aoibhinn, and she betrayed you for it."

"Her hate for the fae was stronger than her love for me."

"No," Rose said, her voice gentle, free of accusation. "Her thirst for vengeance was greater than her love for you."

She watched him process this, his nostrils flaring as their gazes held.

Satisfied she'd made her point, Rose took a step toward the faerie pools. "What exactly are these pools capable of?"

It took him a moment but Fionn eventually joined her on the edge of the rocks. "For us? They're warm and relaxing. Like a natural spa. The water can wash away the trace."

"How do you know?"

"Because it washes away all spells."

"Wow." She stared down into the water. "What's it like for humans and other supernaturals?"

"Cold." He smirked. "Uninviting. But it does wash away spells for them too." Fionn frowned. "I found An Breitheamh buried at the bottom of the largest pool. It was inside the silver box, with a parchment note from the Faerie Queen herself."

"Instructing that you needed to kill a fae-borne with the dagger to enter Faerie?" Rose guessed, hurting at the thought. "Knowing it wouldn't be easy for you."

She understood now, more than ever.

Fionn Mór was a betrayed husband, a grieving father, and a displaced king.

"Aye," Fionn answered quietly, so quietly she barely heard him over the falling water. "That dagger is the only thing that's come out of those pools with its spell still gripped tight to it."

More silence fell between them, the water rushing into the pool a soothing, peaceful sound at odds with the turmoil writhing inside her.

"I forgive you," Rose announced.

He stared down at her, arrested.

She nodded, a small, sad smile on her lips. "I forgive you for trying to use me to open the gate."

"Rose ..."

"And I get that you're on a mission that I might not be able to stop. But you have to promise me that you won't take me somewhere against my will again. Twice you've knocked me out. Promise me ... never again."

He nodded, turning toward her. Her breath caught as Fionn lifted one large hand toward her, his fingers tickling her cheekbone before he tucked her hair behind her ear. As he lowered his hand, his fingertips caressed her neck. Rose fought a shiver and Fionn lowered his arm back by his side. "I can promise that, Rose. However"—his expression hardened—"I can't promise to be something that I'm not. I made a vow long ago that I intend to keep. I'm sorrier than I can say that the vow conflicts with how I feel about you ... But I'm from a different time, *mo chroí*. I've lived too long. I will always have one foot on the wrong side of morality. I will never be the man who follows the rules or always does what's right."

Rose stepped closer to him, feeling the conflict emanating from his very being. She wished he could see that what they could be was worth giving up the vow he'd made centuries before. If he couldn't see it now, then Rose was determined to make him.

And she wouldn't play fair to do it.

She rested a hand on his strong chest, near his rapidly beating heart. "I don't know if you noticed, but I'm not exactly that woman either."

A small smile prodded his lips. "No, you're not. You follow your impulses, Rose. You embrace what you are with a freedom I admire."

"I can teach you." She grinned, only half teasing. "I can teach you to embrace being fae. To make it an existence you find joy in."

"I fear it's too late for that." He closed the distance between them, bowing his head toward her. "But I'd be happy to pass our hours here more pleasurably. I've never bedded a gymnast before."

Rose's lips parted in shock before she could stop herself. She snapped her mouth shut at his smug expression. "You didn't just say that."

Fionn's grin caused a riot of fluttering in her stomach. "Come on, Rose. Show an old man some new tricks."

Fighting a smile, she cocked her head. "How old are you, anyway? I mean ... how old were you before ..."

"Thirty-three."

"So you're almost a decade older than me."

This time, he chuckled. "Oh, if only that were true."

His laughter did more to knot her insides than his flirting. "I liked you better as Mr. Cold and Distant."

"I liked you better when you were flirting with me all the time. Ironic, that."

"I flirted because I liked you."

"And now you don't?"

Instead of answering, Rose retreated a few steps and crossed her arms over her chest. "How do you know we're mated? Niamh told me but how do I know she's right? How do you know?"

If Fionn was surprised by the turn of conversation, he didn't show it. "I didn't know at first. However, there were signs. To begin with, the way we were drawn to each other at the club in Zagreb. That sense of familiarity and attraction are symptoms of a mating bond."

Rose looked down into the faerie pools, considering this. When she first set eyes on Fionn, it was like someone had lassoed a rope around her, pulling her body toward him.

"When you told me you sensed what I was feeling, it surprised me. It's rare that a fae can do that. Yet it's not rare between mates. In fact, it's well known on Faerie that fae mates can sense each other's emotions. It's an ability that fades with time. Something that helps the mates find their footing with each other in the first flush of their relationship."

"But *you* never sensed *my* emotions."

"I did," he confessed, glancing away from her. "I sensed when you wanted me to. I sensed your admiration. I sensed your betrayal when you spoke with your parents. And I sensed your pain after you dream-walked me."

"Is that when you knew ... that we were mates?"

Fionn shook his head. "Like I said before, I knew after the fight with Kiyo. My feelings for you were taking over my common sense. I felt possessive, protective ... and"—his green eyes darkened with arousal—"I couldn't control my desire for you. Not even a little. It's beyond my control. I lived on Faerie long enough to recognize the signs."

Goose bumps prickled over Rose's skin and rubbed her upper arms, grateful for the jacket that concealed her body's reaction to his words.

"Once I'm inside you, the mating bond will snap into place permanently. You'll carry my scent as I will carry yours so everyone will know we belong to each other."

Rose exhaled at his provocative words, eyeing him incredulously as he stared at her mouth. "*Once?* You think that's going to happen between us when you're planning to leave me behind?"

"Nothing should last forever, *mo chroí*. Why should our connection be the same? Why don't we just enjoy it while we can?"

Hurt, aroused, and confused, Rose backed away from him toward the forest. "Because we've been given the gift of forever. We don't have to just enjoy it while we can. That's your choice. Not mine."

Fionn shook his head. "Eternity isn't a gift, Rose. You'll realize that soon enough."

"Eternity wasn't a gift for you because you've spent the last three centuries without me," Rose responded boldly.

His head jerked back, like she'd hit him.

"Forever for us might be a week, a few months, a year, or centuries ... But it should be up to fate to decide that, Fionn. Not you and your *thirst for vengeance.*"

Leaving him stone-faced on the edge of the faerie pools, Rose stalked back through the forest. She wanted some distance to collect her thoughts, but Fionn couldn't even give her that.

Within seconds he was striding by her side, lost in thoughts she hoped were now muddled by her honesty. Thoughts that may still be on a path to revenge, but hopefully that path was now blocked by the obstacle of their bond.

29

Fionn didn't ask her for An Breitheamh that day.

Or the next.

Instead, they fell into a companionable existence with Fionn offering to train her further in her abilities. This included using the castle as they had La Sagrada Familia. They didn't discuss much else, falling safely into a comfortable neutral zone.

However, the rain returned the following day in torrential sheets of blistering cold, pounding droplets. Rose woke late, tired from expending her energy on *traveling* all over the castle grounds yesterday. Fionn had been trying to teach her to fight using the ability.

It had been more than a little therapeutic to battle with him.

After finding breakfast muffins that Fionn had "popped" in, Rose meandered through the castle in search of him, a coffee cup in hand. Upon questioning him about his staff, Fionn told her he hadn't gotten around to hiring new staff. The conversation made him brood, so Rose didn't push the subject.

Rose wasn't happy to be cooped up at the castle indefinitely. She was slowly falling in love with An Caomhnóir. But it was becoming clear that Rose hadn't been on the move since college because she was searching for something.

Rose was a nomad.

It was just who she was.

Thankfully, that meant staying on the move for the rest of her life was less likely to affect her happiness.

Finding Fionn in the main hall, sitting on the large L-shaped couch reading a leather-bound book, Rose quietly made her way over to him. He glanced up from the page.

"Good morning."

"Hi." She settled on the adjacent two-seater sofa, curling her legs under her. They locked eyes as she brought her coffee cup to her lips, and Rose attempted to ignore the flutter in her stomach.

Her attraction to him was not going to dissipate soon.

The fires blazed at either side of the room, and yet Rose shivered.

A little smile quirked the corner of Fionn's mouth. A cocky expression told her he knew she wasn't shivering because she was cold.

Shooting him a glare, she huffed, "Stop it."

Fionn grinned. "I'm not doing anything."

"Yes, you are."

"I'm just sitting here, reading my book."

"You've lived for three centuries. Haven't you read *all* the books by now?"

He shook his head, still smiling.

Rose hated that she loved she could make him smile.

Looking from his face to his book before she did something impulsive, she studied the title. The illustrative wrap that had been covering the hardback was abandoned on the couch at Fionn's side.

"*A History of the Middle East*?"

Lowering the book, her companion shrugged.

"Fionn, you've been around for three centuries. Don't you know more about history than most people?"

"I missed over 1800 years of history while I was under that druid spell, Rose. And even living the last few centuries, I couldn't keep up with everything. You live that long, information battles for priority in your mind. Facts and memories are pushed out in favor of something your brain deems more important. This is the third time I've read this book."

Something occurred to Rose that hadn't before. "Does it bother you? I mean, apart from the obvious painful loss of personal connections ... does it bother you that you should have been around for 1800 years of history and you were denied it?"

The air around him grew colder. "How honest do you want me to be?"

"I always want you to be a hundred percent honest with me. No matter what."

"Then no. Apart from being denied the right to watch my children grow, I'm grateful I haven't *lived* for over two thousand years. The spell left me to my dreams but not once did I feel the passing of time while I slumbered. Three centuries is long enough to be alive, Rose. Time has a way of revealing man's inability to learn from his mistakes. It's frustrating to watch an entire species repeat its follies over and over. Time pummels the hopeful and strengthens the cynic. Immortality eventually isolates you. All the things that make you human are lost."

"Like what?"

"The beauty in fragility. The passion of inevitability. The gratitude for time."

Worry pierced Rose's soul. Would she, over time, lose everything that made her human? Wasn't she already? Already she was fearless in many ways. But in others, she wasn't. She eyed him thoughtfully. "You're still human, Fionn."

He glowered. "What makes you say that?"

She sighed, a little wearily. "Vengeance is a preoccupation of man."

"What do you think the spell that created you is, Rose?" Fionn asked casually, despite the telltale ticking of the muscle in his jaw. "Aine had her revenge on the human race for muddling up her perfect little world."

"That wasn't revenge. You said it yourself—it was wickedness. The boredom of immortality."

"And what about Niamh?"

"What about Niamh?"

Fionn rubbed a hand over his jaw, the bristle of his stubble sounding loud in the cavernous space. Rose fought the urge to go over and touch him.

"I have reason to believe Niamh is my descendant."

That announcement pulled Rose's focus. "What?"

"There's no evidence as Bran continues to remind me. Her name is Farren, which is the modern name for Ó Faracháin. That was my clan name. Her family dates back to a time when they were Ó Faracháin. They were also rumored to have connections to the mythical Rí Mac Tíre."

Wow.

Now she understood his interaction with Niamh back in Munich. And why he said she had nothing to fear from him. Fionn wouldn't kill someone of his own blood.

"I feel it in my gut, Rose. Niamh is my descendant. And it's something Aine would do to me." He curled his lip in bitterness. "Knowing I couldn't raise a hand to my own. So no, revenge is not just the purview of humans."

A subject Rose had been wary of pressing pushed at her, urging her to. Feeling brave, she said, "You said she made you her ..." She couldn't quite bring herself to say the word.

"Whore." Fionn's tone was brutally cold.

Rose nodded.

"Aye, she did."

As she observed the large, powerful figure lounging on the couch, her entire being ached for him. "It's difficult for anyone to feel powerless and used. To happen to someone who led armies ... I'm sorry, Fionn."

"Man, woman, child, poet, farmer, or king ... it doesn't matter who you are, Rose. It fucks with your mind all the same."

"Have you ever spoken to anyone about it?"

"A therapist?" A cynical smirk ghosted his lips.

"No. A friend."

He sighed. "There's nothing to say. I made peace with that a long time ago."

"Did you?" she pressed, dangerously. "You're still willing to ... I mean, you're still going after revenge."

"Not for that. Yes, the bitch violated me, and yes, it fucked with my mind that my body enjoyed it while my spirit fought not to crumble under self-hatred and fury. But why do you think she made me fae, Rose? Because she couldn't fucking break me. She couldn't twist me up inside and make me love her. Not romantic love. Not the love of mates. But the sycophantic love that she wanted from every one of her subjects.

"She pretended she liked the challenge of any being who stood up to her, but it wasn't that. She liked breaking people." His eyes were no longer dead. They blazed. "I wouldn't give that to her. So she made me the thing I hated most. And because of it, I lost the people I loved most. *That's* why I demand vengeance."

Considering this, Rose felt a complex mix of emotions take over, nothing new when it came to her feelings for Fionn. She admired him for his strength, for the beauty of his spirit that refused to be broken by what amounted to sexual slavery. Yet, it frustrated the hell out of her that someone who could stay so true to himself during such a horrific time couldn't see that he was now letting Aine win by giving up a second chance at happiness.

"You are not *them*. You are not *her*. You may be of the same species, but for Christ's sake, Fionn, Martin Luther King Jr. and Adolf Hitler were too. They hardly belong in the same sentence together, though, do they? It's not what you are that makes you 'good' or 'bad.' Your intentions and your actions define you, something someone as old as you should know by now.

"Do you think because I'm fae that I'm repulsive and wicked?"

"Rose." His tone was a warning.

"Do you? Because I don't think I am. I enjoy being powerful but not because I want to crush people beneath the might of it. I like the freedom in it. I like the magic. The possibilities. The world is so much different from what I expected. It's ancient and yet new, mystical and even more mysterious than I ever imagined. And I'm a part of that now. Just like you.

"Your intentions toward me were wicked." Tears glittered in her eyes as she watched his features harden with ... anger? Remorse? It was difficult to tell. "But what matters is your ability to change your mind and do the right thing. Before I knew the truth about you, I saw you as this otherworldly, noble being who made me feel exhilarated and safe at the same time.

"And despite your plans for vengeance, I still see you that way. It's who you are deep down. You're just too stubborn to see it."

As soon as the last word was out of her mouth, Fionn stood and strode out of the room. Without a backward glance.

The tears in Rose's eyes spilled over with her next blink.

AS MUCH AS Fionn craved Rose's company—and craved was the only word for it because his entire being lit up as soon as she ventured into his vicinity—he needed space.

She was prodding at old wounds and picking apart his reasons for going after Aine, muddling his brain as she forced ideas about who he was onto him.

Rose was confused. The mating bond was making her feel nonsense things about him.

If there was a corner of his icy soul that warmed under the glow of her impression of him, Fionn did his best to ignore it.

For all the rooms in the castle, Fionn's bedroom was his sanctuary. It had a spectacular view of the sea and was filled with his favorite books. Books were one of the best inventions of the modern world. He'd learned to read as quickly as he'd learned English. Then he'd learned French and German and Spanish and Latin, and he'd learned to read in all those languages too. There was much about the world he realized he'd miss when he returned to Faerie. And that astonished him.

Throwing a hand out toward the fireplace, the wood crackled to life with flame.

Slumping down on his large, custom-made bed, Fionn stared at the flames. He should push Rose harder for An Breitheamh. The days were passing them by. And her hold on him was growing more dangerous.

What had been at the start an offering of insight into his mind to manipulate her had morphed into something else.

Fionn told this woman things he'd never spoken to another soul.

Squeezing his eyes closed, Fionn flopped back on the bed and tried to settle his mind. To focus it. To regroup. Instead, slumber seductively whispered an offer of reprieve in his ear.

Fionn slid his legs off the bed, resting his elbows on his knees as he stared unseeingly at the wall. The queen's palace in Solas, the capital city of Samhradh, the Day Lands, was awe-inspiring. Upon his arrival on Faerie, Fionn did not know what repulsed him more: being brought here as a human slave, or finding beauty in the alien world.

Samhradh Palace was a towering building, with turrets and spires that stretched so far into the sky, they seemed to disappear into it. Moreover, it sparkled like a jewel. All over. The buildings here had window coverings they called gleamings, an opaque material that allowed you to see from the inside out. The palace appeared made entirely of shattered pieces of gleaming, winking and glittering in the sun. The interior walls sparkled beneath the balls of light that floated near the ceilings.

Fire was not required on Faerie as a source of light.

They had their terrible magic for such things.

"You're brooding."

Her voice was like the lash of a whip on his back.

"What do you have to brood about?"

Fionn glanced over his shoulder at the naked Fae Queen. Aine was strikingly beautiful. In fact, beautiful seemed too little a word for her. Lumines-

cent. Golden. Golden hair, golden eyes, golden skin, small waist, long, slender legs, rounded hips, and even rounder, lush breasts.

She laid casually sprawled, one knee bent, one leg stretched out in front of her, her upper body raised as she leaned back on her elbows. Her golden eyes stared intensely into his.

Fionn despised her.

With every fiber of his being, he despised Aine, Queen of the Fae.

"Is it because of the girl I killed today? She and her sister tried to escape the noblewoman they belong to. I spared her sister, though. I can be benevolent, Fionn. However, if I want to strike the right balance of fear and respect from my people, I must make difficult decisions."

Fionn was unable to understand the language on Faerie. It was unintelligible to humans. But the fae picked up human languages quickly and had adopted his people's language. He wished they hadn't. He wished he couldn't understand, so he didn't have to converse with the bitch. Rolling his eyes, he turned to stare at the wall again, preferring the view.

"Funny that you killed the sister with the red hair and spared the dark-haired sister. According to their own reports, the dark-haired girl was the instigator."

He felt her touch on his back, her finger trailing the pattern of an A on his skin. "You know why, sweet love. Must we verbalize it? It makes me seem so petty."

"You killed her because she looked like Aoibhinn."

Her touch disappeared and he heard her huff of annoyance. "Must you say that name?"

"I will never love you, Aine." Fionn stood, whirling to face her, cold hatred like ice in his veins. "So why don't you just kill me now?"

She smiled up him. A sweet, innocent smile that belied her wickedness. "Because I enjoy you. I enjoy the challenge of breaking you."

"It's been six years. If you haven't broken me yet … you never will."

Aine laughed, a delightful, airy, tinkling noise. Then she vanished before reappearing across the room where she kept a never-ending cup of pale golden liquid that bubbled on the tongue. As she took a sip, a golden dress, like liquid metal, covered her body. She eyed him with desire and malice. "Oh, Fionn, so naive. If it takes me centuries, so be it. But I will break you."

"Never."

She laughed again, throwing her head back so her hair shimmered like sunlit water down her back. Then she flicked out a hand and Lir, the captain of the guard, appeared.

Fionn tensed.

Lir was a sadistic fae who had a liking for rape. Man, woman, or child, the bastard didn't seem to have a preference. Not only had he killed Conall's wolf companion, he'd attempted to attack Fionn, only stopping because Aine appeared and brutally reprimanded him.

Had she changed her mind?

The Faerie Queen smirked, as if she could read his mind. "Not you, Fionn. I'd never hurt you that way. There are other ways to break you."

His heart beat incredibly fast, as though it knew something he did not. A glove appeared in Lir's hand, seconds before a pale silvery dagger rested in that glove.

An Breitheamh.

Fionn's pure iron dagger. The one he'd killed the fae prince with. Fionn tried to make sense of it. Somewhere, deep in his subconscious, he knew this moment had started as a memory ... But this, Lir being here with the dagger, that didn't happen.

What was going on?

Aine flicked her hand again and Rose was in the room, naked, on her knees before Lir. The captain yanked her hair back with his ungloved fist, and as she cried out, Fionn lunged toward her.

"Uh-uh," Lir taunted, resting the iron dagger at Rose's throat. It touched her skin and she hissed in pain, tears filling her eyes.

"You bastard!" Fionn rushed toward Rose but Aine blocked his way.

He tried to push her aside but with fae strength, she held him back, laughing at his growing panic.

Fionn pushed and shoved and swung punches that she easily avoided, all the while keeping him from Rose as Lir cut her body all over with the iron dagger. Then his hand fell to the buttons on his leather trews, his cruel *gaze fixed to Fionn. "I will rip her apart before I kill her and you will watch."*

Powerlessness burned like a hot brick in Fionn's throat as he watched Rose.

Tears streamed from her eyes and she whispered to him, "Look away, mo chroí. Look away."

Fionn panted, pushing himself up off the bed, and reality flooded in. Along with it came immediate relief.

Rose was okay. It was just a dream.

His hand trembled as he pushed his hair off his face and braced his elbows on his knees.

Fuck.

That dream had felt so real.

The need to find Rose, to feel her beneath his hands and know that she was alive and unhurt, was strong. Even more was the need to hold her, clinging to his need for vengeance at the same time wanting his mate in his arms.

Just a taste. Just a touch.

Something to take with him, hold to him, before the darkness welcomed him for good.

30

The castle library wasn't an epic, vaulted, multilevel archive of books worthy of a Disney movie. In fact, the only high-ceilinged room in the building was the main hall.

Although larger than many of the other rooms, the library wasn't huge. There was, however, a step ladder attached to a rail on the cases so the higher shelves could be easily reached.

Rose thought that was pretty cool, even though she could use her abilities to pull any book she wanted off the shelf.

Standing in the middle of the room, elbows bent, palms up, Rose did just that.

Romances.

An excited smile curled her lips as books floated out of their places on the shelves. Not for the first time, Rose wondered if she'd ever lose the thrill of almost childish glee she felt when her abilities allowed her to do something amazing.

She gently laid the books on the floor at her feet. Reading the titles, Rose realized most of the romances she'd pulled were medieval, tales of knights and chivalry and heroic deeds. A copy of *Le Morte d'Arthur* by Sir Thomas Malory; *The Canterbury Tales* by Geoffrey Chaucer.

Rose wrinkled her nose. She was looking for something a little less dark. Finally, she came across a first edition of *Jane Eyre*. Not exactly easy reading but at least Rose knew it had a happy ending for Jane.

She held on to the book and with a flick of her wrist, the others floated back up into their spots on the shelves.

A shiver skated down her spine, tickling around her ribs and across her breasts. Hugging *Jane Eyre* to her, Rose turned, knowing she'd find Fionn in the doorway.

There he stood, watching her.

Intense and focused.

Rose shivered again, as a low flip deep in her belly caused a welling of anticipation inside her.

What was going on?

"Fionn?"

He walked farther into the room, his pace casual, his expression anything but. Those green, intelligent eyes wandered all over her body before locking onto hers with a fierceness that made her breath catch.

"I need to say something," Fionn announced.

Tingles came to life all over. Rose nodded, her mouth dry.

"Whatever happens ... I need you to know that I haven't felt human in a long time. I even reveled in that fact, needing the simplicity of a purpose devoid of complex emotion. Purpose and revenge were all I needed. Everything else be damned." His face darkened with something more intense than mere desire. "Until you, Rose. You make me feel more human than I ever felt when I was one."

The ache that had lived inside Rose since she first realized she had deep, complicated feelings for Fionn bloomed inside her until there was no room for anything else. It pushed at her lungs until she was breathless. And only Fionn could breathe the air back into them.

"Fionn," she whispered.

"Your eyes," he said, his voice gruff. "They're gold."

Before Rose could respond, Fionn was a streak across the room.

She felt his hands on her waist and then she was slammed against a wall. The book in her hand slipped to the rug-covered flagstones just as several books fell off the wall at her side to join it.

Fionn's face bent close to hers, his fingers holding firm around her waist. His eyes were gold too.

"Tell me you want this," he whispered hotly against her lips. "I need to hear the words."

And understanding why turned the lust hot and thick inside her to something so much more.

She loved him.

Even knowing he would break her heart, Rose still clung to hope. And so she answered, every feeling she had for him blazing out from within, "I want you."

The words were barely out of her mouth when he captured her wrists in his hands and pinned them above her against the books, holding her captive. They both knew Rose could escape, and the melting of her body into the wall made the gold of his eyes brighten to an otherworldly glow. Breathing heavily, his face now but an inch from hers, Fionn stared into her eyes as if there was nothing else in the world he'd rather do.

Rose's skin flushed. Her whole body felt like it had been dipped into a hot liquid gold. She could feel her breasts swell against her tight T-shirt, and the tingling between her legs was now an insistent throb. The hitch in her breath caused Fionn's expression to darken. He looked at her mouth, and he leaned his body more heavily against hers until his arousal dug into her stomach.

Squeezing her legs tighter together, Rose lifted her chin, reaching her mouth toward his. "Fionn. *Mo chroí.*"

Awe flashed across his face and then Fionn's lips were hot against hers, his tongue licking at hers. The bristle of his stubble on her skin as he deepened the kiss caused Rose's nipples to harden swiftly.

No one had ever kissed her like Fionn.

Like she was air. Life. Food and water all in one.

Rose let out a little gasp of excitement as he released her lips to trail kisses down her throat. He squeezed her wrists as she arched against his mouth, wishing she wasn't wearing a T-shirt.

A chill skated over her skin as Fionn lifted his head, a pleased smirk playing with his mouth. Rose frowned and glanced down.

She'd literally wished her T-shirt off.

Poof.

Gone.

A bubble of giddy laughter left her lips as she locked eyes with him.

Amusement colored his words. "I hope you let me do the rest."

"No promises," she whispered.

"Then I best get on with it." Fionn released his hold on her hands, his gaze caressing her face.

Rose's lower belly did another flip at the hungry promise in his eyes.

Fionn slipped his fingers under the straps of her bra, and then stopped when his eyes caught on the scar on her chest. Rose wasn't bothered by the scar. She wore it as a badge of honor. The look on Fionn's face, the intensification of his desire, told her he liked what the scar symbolized too. Bending toward her, he pressed a sweet, warm kiss to the scar that brought tears to her eyes.

Raising his head they shared a look that made her lips part with need and she arched her back slightly with impatience. With a deliberate slowness that escalated her arousal beyond bearing, he lowered the straps of her bra, tugging on them until she was completely exposed. Her nipples drew even tighter into hard little points that begged for attention. Fionn made a guttural sound in his throat as he cupped her breasts in his large hands. He looked up at her, watching her as he gave them a gentle squeeze, his lips parting as she moaned and arched into him.

"Fuck, Rose." He kneaded her, thumbs strumming her nipples, as he flexed his hips against her.

The hard press of him, digging into her, almost made her eyes roll back in her head. She wanted the impressive arousal she could feel against her belly thrusting inside her instead.

However, Fionn seemed determined to savor her. His head descended, and she cried out at the provocative stimulation of his mouth sucking on her nipple. Rose reached for him, curling her arms around his neck, drawing him closer. She moaned, her head falling back against the books as he licked and sucked before moving on to her other breast.

Her senses were overwhelmed, the lights flickering in the room as the tension deep in her belly tightened and tightened with his attention. His scent, his heat, his power, and the promise of all that inside her ... Rose was surrounded by him. Already invaded.

Yet it wasn't enough.

She wanted to conquer and be conquered.

Rose writhed against him, and Fionn groaned against her breast, the sound reverberating through her deliciously. He didn't feel like an all-powerful being in that moment. He was flesh and blood and need and lust and want.

He was just a man who hungered for a woman.

For her.

Fionn ground his body deeper into hers and lifted his head to kiss her again. This kiss was hunger. Desperation. A mimic of what was to come. Her fingers curled in the hair at the back of his neck as she licked and sucked and flicked her tongue against his, her kiss as deep as she wanted him to be inside her, not just physically.

Rose slipped her hand under his sweater and traced his hard, ripped stomach before pushing her fingers down inside his jeans.

He broke the kiss on a hiss, thrusting into her hand as she tried to curl it around his erection straining against the confinement of his jeans.

Finding that difficult, Rose set to work on unzipping him, moving to slip her hands past the waistline of his black boxer briefs.

Fionn made a sexy growl as he took hold of her wrist and pinned it at her side. He gave her a slight shake of his head. "Me first."

He demonstrated his meaning by using his free hand to unzip her jeans, his fingertips tickling her belly as he slowly dipped his fingers beneath her underwear. "Keep your eyes open and on me," he demanded.

The gold in his eyes mingled with the green, but as his touch found her wet and she whimpered, lashes fluttering, Fionn's eyes glowed a solid gold.

He groaned as he pleasured her, his breathing escalating along with Rose's as he watched her thrust against his hand. Her fingers bit into his forearm and waist while she clung to him through the building tension. Her body was on fire, the pleasure causing her lashes to flutter closed with her mounting gasps for completion.

"Look at me," he demanded again, his lips almost brushing hers.

Rose's eyes flew open and locked with his as a climax rolled through her in obliterating pleasure.

She was still clinging to the orgasm when Fionn crushed his mouth over hers. Magic tingled the air, and she felt the telltale breeze between her legs and across her skin. Her jeans were gone.

His skin was naked beneath her touch.

Rose opened her eyes and saw he wasn't wearing a sweater. And she knew if she looked lower, she'd find him naked there too.

Rose chuckled into his mouth. In answer, Fionn grabbed hold of her naked hips and hauled her up the wall. Her stomach flipped, like on a roller coaster in a steep dip, and she gasped. She had presence of mind, however, to wrap her legs around him.

An explosion of sensation had her gripping his nape, pulling back from his deep kiss to pant against his mouth as she felt him hot and nudging at her center. She saw the final question in his eyes and loved him for it.

Rose nodded.

Fionn thrust into her, and too many sensations hit her all at once. The hard slam of her back against the bookshelves, his bruising grip on her hips, and ultimately the powerful, scorching thickness of him buried inside her slick heat.

He was perfect.

Heaven inside her.

The bliss was too much.

Lights blew out around the room, but nothing could diminish the heat between them.

"Oh, *mo chroí*." Fionn braced her against the wall, his hands holding tight to her hips as he drove in and out in smooth undulations. His expression was taut with need, his teeth bared as he seemed to strain to stop himself from fucking her savagely. This only made Rose hotter, her fingernails biting into his forearms as he took her against the wall.

The climax to end all climaxes captured Rose in its visceral, primal spell. She was barely aware of Fionn falling against her, burying his face in her throat until his drives inside her grew wild. She clung to him, palms flat to his lower back as he chased his pleasure through the hot pulses of Rose's own.

Fionn tensed, his hot mouth on her neck, and then his hips juddered hard against her as he swelled, his release throbbing and potent and causing another wave of reaction inside her.

"Rose ..." Her name was a deep groan against her skin as Fionn melted into her.

His hands caressed down her hips to her outer thighs, and he ground into her as if he needed more. "Fuck, Rose." He lifted his head, face slackened with awe and, if she was not mistaken, shock.

Rose fought to catch her breath. "Is it always like that?"

Fionn shook his head, a little dazed. "It ..." He glanced down at where their bodies joined and thrust again, hissing through his teeth. "Ah, fuck, Rose, it's the mating. It's heaven." He kissed her, hard, deep, still needful. When he came up for air again, his voice was hoarse. "It's heaven inside you."

Squeezing her arms and legs around him as tight as possible, Rose could only agree. Nothing had ever felt like this. It was an otherworldly bliss she could quickly become addicted to. She smiled, giddy. "Can we do it again?"

Fionn didn't smile. Instead, he bent his head toward her mouth and growled, "Fuck. Yes."

31

Sex had always been just a need for satisfaction. Even when Fionn loved Aoibhinn, their coupling had been a passionate, quick, albeit love-filled, encounter before sleep. There was no time in their world to savor each other through the night, for sleep was a more important fuel in times of constant war.

Aine savored him, yes, but Fionn was so emotionally detached from their interludes, it didn't count.

Other women had given themselves to Fionn over the last three centuries—human, werewolf, and even vampire. That was fucking. Quick, satisfying, to the point. Even with mistresses like Alice.

It was wonderfully strange and new, then, for Fionn to discover the euphoria of an entire day and night spent in bed with a woman. And not just any woman.

With Rose.

She slept in his arms, cheek pressed to his chest, her small, elegantly strong body sprawled across him. The woman was an addiction. Fionn suddenly understood the thrill of the mating bond. It wasn't just a deep abiding affection or the feeling that some piece he'd been missing his entire existence had finally slotted into place.

It was extraordinary sex.

The fae weren't just all about finding their mate because of the emotional connection—they wanted this drugging, blissful, other-worldly physical bond.

Fionn couldn't get enough of Rose. He'd conjured food from the kitchen in between sessions, but his woman was absolutely wrung out with multiple orgasms by the time she collapsed against his pillows and murmured she needed rest.

Unbelievably, blood pumped hotly in his groin as Fionn caressed her rounded, pert arse. Surely the lusting would fade a little over time.

He hoped.

There were things to be done.

Plans to be executed.

Eternity could not be spent rolling around in his big bed with his small, luscious fae mate.

"Fuck," he muttered, gazing at the stone ceiling above. Actually, that sounded pretty grand to him.

Aine. Revenge. Remember that?

Looking down at Rose's sleeping face, he felt a knifelike discomfort in his throat. It all meant leaving her to fend for herself, and although he knew Rose was quite capable of looking after herself, it hurt to think of her alone. Of something happening to her when he should have been by her side. Even before she fell asleep, she'd whispered her promise to try not to dream-walk him, and he'd heard the hint of anxiety in her tone.

It wasn't a talent Fionn was familiar with, but there had to be ways to help her control the ability—and he should be the one to help her do it.

His mobile phone buzzed from somewhere in the castle. Fionn uttered an inward curse hoping Rose wouldn't wake. It wasn't loud but with their fae ears, they could hear more than humans. He conjured the phone into his hand and answered. "Bran?"

"Aye, it's me. Why are you whispering?"

The gods, the vampire's voice sounded loud down the line. "Give me a second." Fionn gently slid Rose off him, his lips twitching as she flopped against the pillow, dead to the world. While eight hours of sex with a gymnast turned fae had only invigorated Fionn, his mate desperately needed rest.

Slipping out of bed, he strode out of the bedroom, heading toward the library where he'd left his clothes so he didn't wake her. He could conjure his jeans like he'd done to take them off, but Fionn tried not to get lazy with the magic.

Disappearing into the library, he immediately regretted choosing it as a destination. As he pulled on his jeans, memories of fucking Rose against the bookshelves were fresh and vivid.

Damn, he'd never look at his library the same way again.

Turning around, he headed downstairs toward the main hall.

"Are you there?" Bran asked impatiently.

"I'm here."

"Why are you being so quiet?"

"I don't want to wake Rose."

"She's asleep? It's only eight thirty in the evening." Bran sucked in a breath. "You slept together, didn't you?"

"None of your business." Fionn sat on the couch, flicking a hand at the nearest fire to light it. "Talk."

"Heavy Blackwood activity in Ireland," Bran informed him somberly. "They've met with the O'Connors ... the coven is gone, Fionn."

Fionn tensed. "Gone? The Blackwoods wiped them out?"

"Yes. Layton and his sisters came to Ireland as representatives of the North American Council, and they were supposedly accompanied by representatives of the European High Council. Their version of events is that they issued a suspension of all magical activities pending investigation into the disturbance in Munich. This was apparently met with aggression from the O'Connor Coven, who all just happened to be in the same house, wouldn't you know it, and a magical shoot-out ensued. The house was caught in an explosion started by one of the O'Connor witches. The Blackwoods and the reps from the European High Council were the lone survivors."

"Will anyone believe that shite?"

"There will be those who call for an investigation but do you care, Fionn? Blackwood getting rid of those who seek to hurt Rose means she's got one less thing to worry about."

He sighed, slumping back against the couch. "Somehow I get the feeling we're not off the hook yet."

"Well, you're right because I'm tracking the Blackwoods, hacked into Layton's cell. They're in Galway."

"Surprise, surprise," Fionn grouched, sounding calmer than he felt.

"I know they can't find An Caomhnóir but they can still find their way onto your land ... and they know where the gate is."

"How could they know I'm at home?"

"The only way to track you was through the private plane company you hired."

"I hired it under a pseudonym."

"Then I'm afraid it's time to retire that name. They must think the best way to track Rose is to track you. Plus, they saw you with An Breitheamh. They still think they need that dagger to open the gate. Killing Rose isn't on the agenda but her blood is still required in the spell."

The thought of Layton Blackwood anywhere near Rose caused a rumble of noise at the base of Fionn's throat.

"Guessing that terrifying noise means the mating bond is well and truly snapped into place, so I'll take this moment to remind you that the Blackwoods have kept their distance from you, Fionn. They haven't wanted to start a war with you ... but if you kill one of them, diplomacy will be over."

"Bran," Fionn replied as patiently as he could, which wasn't very, "if anyone touches a hair on Rose's head, I'll rip their fucking throat out with my teeth. I don't care if it starts World War III."

Bran released a heavy sigh. "So noted."

"I'll deal with this in the morning. Find some way to get the Blackwoods off my land. But as long as Rose is within the castle grounds, they can't touch her. Still no news of Niamh?"

"Sorry, no."

That was concerning. "Fine. Call me if anything important happens. But if it doesn't, leave me be, Bran. I go to Faerie soon. Let me enjoy my mate in peace while I can." He hung up, thinking how calm those words sounded coming out of his mouth, considering they now lingered in the frosty air like sharp-toothed monsters.

Fionn took long strides back upstairs to his bedroom. Rose had turned onto her side, one of her arms sprawled out across his pillow.

The thought of the Blackwoods out beyond his castle walls had pissed him off, but one look at Rose, warm and delicious in his bed, distracted him immediately. As he slid in beside her, lifting her arm out of the way, Rose rolled sleepily against him and then frowned with her eyes closed. The top of her foot slid up and down his now-naked calf. "Cold," she murmured.

Grinning, Fionn spilled her onto her back and caressed her belly, slipping his hand between her sweet thighs. "I can warm you, *mo chroí.*"

Rose's eyes fluttered open and stared up at him, already flushed from his touch. "Again?"

He chuckled at her disbelieving tone. "Unless you're too sore."

Challenge glittered in her sleepy gaze and then she lifted a hand to wave it. "Faerie," she said, reminding him of the night he'd said and done the same outside La Sagrada Familia.

His laughter was swallowed in her hungry kiss as she pushed against his shoulders, rolling him to his back, apparently not so tired after all.

As she moved on him, her slim hips cupped in his hands, her sultry blue eyes burning into his, Fionn felt the world as he knew it crumbling around him. He slid one hand up to cup one of her small but perfectly formed breasts in his hand, caressing and gently squeezing it as she rode him. He wanted this forever.

Fionn wanted to wake to Rose Kelly every morning, to make love to her, to fuck her, to drown in her. To protect her. Yet to do that, he'd have to give up his revenge against Aine. Hundreds of years of single-minded focus was obliterated by this slip of woman.

Bliss built and built inside him as Rose pressed her small hands to his chest for leverage as her rocking increased. Her features were harsh with passion, her beautiful upside down mouth parted as pants of pleasure escaped from it.

"Fionn, fionn," she whispered, her voice hoarse as she covered his hand over her breast, forcing him to squeeze harder. Rose took his hand from her hip and slipped it between her legs where they were joined. Understanding what she needed, Fionn pressed his thumb to her clit and began to circle it as her pace quickened.

Rose let out a cry, her face flushed with desire, and Fionn lost control at the sight. He flipped her to her back, gripped her slim thighs in his hands and positioned her legs up and over his shoulders. Her breathing stuttered at the new angle, her arms sprawled above her head on the pillows.

His.

She was his.

Thrusting into her, hard, deep, fast, Fionn's heart beat wildly as Rose came around him. The tugs on his cock almost threw him over the deep end, but Fionn was determined to shatter her. To give her so much pleasure Rose would never forget him.

Never want to leave him.

Muscles straining to stop himself from climaxing, Fionn tightened his grip on her thighs, spreading her wider, and pumped inside her, rough and true.

It didn't take long.

Eyes round with disbelief and awe and lust, Rose screamed as another orgasm ripped through her. Finally, Fionn let go, shuddering against her with a hoarse shout as he came long and hard inside her.

Falling against her, his forehead to her throat, he slid his hands up her waist and reveled in the feel of her pulsing and throbbing around his cock. She wrapped her legs around his back, letting out a breathy, stuttered sigh as she arched into him. It was as if she was desperate to milk every last drop from him.

Fionn groaned, his fingers biting in her ribs with need as he ground against her.

He never wanted to let go.

He was fucked.

Literally and figuratively.

Because Fionn realized now that he wanted Rose Kelly more than he wanted revenge. He wanted to lose himself inside her for eternity. Lifting his head from her throat, Fionn stared down at his mate's passion-flushed face. A dazed, sexy sleepiness filled her expression.

Gods but she was beautiful. Her voracious thirst for life poured out of her, shining, stunning and addictive.

She was his new obsession.

She was everything.

A vital, imperative piece of him, and Fionn Mór realized that if he gave her up, he'd not only destroy the one person that meant most to him, he'd destroy himself, too.

And in doing so, the Faerie Queen would win.

When Rose woke again, the last embers of the fire were dying and the purple sky outside Fionn's windows told her the sun was on the rise.

Turning her head on the pillow, her hair rustling in her ears with the movement, Rose found Fionn asleep by her side. She smiled as she took in his sleeping face, his eyelashes fluttering as he dreamed.

Although they'd slept by each other's side, Rose was glad to know she hadn't dream-walked him. At least she assumed she hadn't since she couldn't remember it. It was a worry, a concern. She wanted him to have as much privacy as possible despite their bond.

Control would have to be learned ... if it became an issue between them.

If.

Even with the bond between them before all the sex, Rose had never felt closeness with a person like she felt with Fionn. It was incredible. Like they really were two halves of one whole and all that cheesy romantic stuff just happened to be true.

So how could he still cling to his vengeance? When they could have this ... forever?

Rose was weary of the hurt. Not just that he would choose his revenge over her but that he would force her to grieve him. Ultimately, she knew she could tell him what Niamh had seen of the future if he opened that gate; however, Rose also knew she'd never be sure if he stayed because he loved her as much as she loved him, or because the world was at risk.

And Rose *was* in love with him.

Noble, wicked, selfish, loyal, stubborn, caring, protective, brutal, powerful, vengeful, loving, strong, fallible, vital Fionn Mór.

Rose loved him.

Impatient for her ending, happy or not, she decided in that moment there was no time like the morning after the greatest sex-a-thon EVER to force the subject.

Not wanting to wake him, Rose *traveled* to her bedroom and concentrated on An Breitheamh and where she'd buried it.

Though she could feel the tingle of it at the edge of her mind, it was like it was blocked from coming to her.

What?

Rose huffed, shivering and naked in her cold bedroom, and tried again.

Nothing.

Hadn't Fionn told her she could just conjure it?

Unless ... she couldn't *travel* beyond the castle grounds because of the boundary spell. Maybe Fionn didn't realize it blocked her from conjuring items from outside the castle too. Either that or she just wasn't practiced enough at it yet.

Or someone had found her hiding spot and she was trying to conjure it from the wrong location.

The thought caused Rose's breath to catch.

Oh God. That couldn't be true.

There was only one sure way to know. Rose would have to leave An Caomhnóir and try to conjure the dagger once she was past the boundary spell. She was sure she'd be able to tell where the boundary ended, being so hyperaware of magic as she was. Still, she'd have to move quickly. The last thing she wanted was Fionn waking up while she was gone and getting the wrong idea.

After all, she was bringing the dagger to him.

Rose would offer it to him.

And hope like hell Fionn made the right choice.

NOVEMBER WAS CREEPING TOWARD DECEMBER, evident in the cold morning air. Rose rubbed her hands together as she hurried across the bridge outside the castle walls and headed into the woods. Hoping she knew what she was doing, Rose used her magic to blow away the soggy leaves on the ground, grateful that her suspicions about a path underneath were true. The path led her to the fallen tree Fionn had helped her over and about ten minutes from there, it forked.

One fork pointed toward where Fionn had led her west to the faerie pools; the other continued north through the woods. Going with her gut, Rose moved north, picking up speed.

What should have been a thirty-minute walk, she completed in five minutes. The trees rustled lightly in the morning wind, waving her off as she stepped out into a field. A steep incline led to a low, old-fashioned stone wall, and beyond that rolling hills that eventually met the sky.

As soon as Rose climbed over the wall, she felt a shivery tingle of magic. The sensation disappeared completely as she lifted her hand off it.

The boundary wall of the spell was an actual wall.

Her lips parted as she looked back and faced a view of the ocean instead of the forest. From this side of the wall, it appeared as if it acted as a cliff-top barrier, the land falling away to the ocean below.

That was so Fionn.

She blamed her lovesick distraction and the boundary spell on the fact that she felt the warning signs too late.

That prickle down her neck.

The racing heart.

The dread in the gut.

Rose whipped around, ready to face danger, and stumbled back at the mammoth male who bared his canines at her.

His harsh-hewn face was the last thing she saw before he grabbed hold of her neck and gave it a brutal twist.

PAIN, excruciating, debilitating pain woke Rose out of unconsciousness almost immediately. Her eyes flew open as fire burned down her arms. She watched as the two witches and the warlock she'd encountered in Barcelona retreated to study her impassively.

A scream tried to burrow out of her throat but she stubbornly choked it down, tears of agony scoring her cheeks as she gazed up at her arms, suspended above her with thick chains attached to the ceiling, manacles clamped tightly around her wrists.

Manacles made of pure iron.

Her knees gave way, her wrists tugging excruciatingly against the manacles, and the scream burst out of her before she could stop it.

"You bastards!" a female voice yelled from somewhere in the room as Rose sagged and shuddered against the fire tearing at her limbs. "Is that necessary?"

The growl in the words, plus the American accent, brought Rose's head up. She took in her surroundings.

She was in a warehouse, or maybe a basement. No windows. Concrete floors.

And other than the Blackwoods, there was a woman manacled to the corner of the room. Rose tried to focus, her vision clearing. Her eyes connected with the stranger and the woman's brows puckered with worry and strain. That's when Rose scented the blood.

The stranger was wounded.

"Rose." Layton Blackwood, the sleazy warlock Fionn hated, lowered himself in front of her. "We'll release you as soon as you tell us where the dagger is. Does Fionn have it?"

Fionn.

She shook her head.

"Do you?"

Rose nodded.

"Good. Now all you have to do is tell us where it is, and we'll let you go."

Oh yeah, sure. It wasn't like they thought they needed both her and the dagger to complete the ritual to open the gate.

Not caring it would hurt even worse, Rose pulled against the shackles and used the chains to swing her closer to Layton. She snapped at his throat like an animal; he fell back on his ass.

Despite the pain, it was so fucking worth it.

The stranger laughed from the corner.

"Bitch," Layton huffed, getting to his feet. "I ought to teach you a lesson."

Rose let her head loll back. "Yeah? I wonder if you'd say that to me if I wasn't chained up right now."

"I'm not afraid of you."

She pictured herself wrapping the chain of her manacles around his neck and snapping it. "I'd be afraid of me if I were you."

"Yeah, it takes a big man to shoot off his mouth around a *trapped* fae," the stranger said dryly.

She knew what Rose was.

Huh.

"That's enough or I'll put another silver bullet in you," Layton warned casually.

"Rose." The shorter of the sisters stepped forward. Liza, if Rose remembered correctly. "We're sorry it has to be this way. But we will release you as soon as you give up An Breitheamh. I don't know what nonsense Fionn Mór has filled your he—"

"Let me stop you right there." Rose took a breath. Forcing words out past the agony was difficult. "I know who you are and what you really want. I will not be swayed. And I will *never* give you that dagger."

"She needs more time," Lori Blackwood offered quietly. "A day in those iron cuffs should be enough to convince her to change her mind."

"And if not?" Layton asked.

"Then two days. If not that, then three. But she won't be able to take it much longer than that."

"What if *he* comes for her?" Liza queried, sounding almost worried.

"He won't risk it." Layton shook his head. "The other two are still out there. He won't waste time on one who's lost to him."

Oh, how wrong you are, you stupid little prick.

"I still say it was moronic bringing the wolf," Liza snapped.

"She was once fae. None of us know how this spell works exactly, but the same blood runs through her veins as it did before that son of a bitch bit her. She's insurance."

"She's also a declaration of war with the packs."

"Liza, the packs won't go to war over one little bitch. Fionn was just trying to scare us into playing nice. The problem with playing nice is that you end up chasing what you want for fucking years—and getting nowhere." Layton strode toward a door to Rose's left. "We're not our father, sitting idly by. Our coven has been working on opening that gate for centuries. When we do it, we won't have to worry about the packs. We'll be living like gods."

Oh, great, so she was dealing with a totally sane person, then.

Rose whimpered as soon as the door closed behind the siblings.

"Hey, hang in there, okay?"

It took great effort, but she lifted her head to look at the corner of the room. The woman wore a sympathetic expression, despite the strain on her pretty features. No, not pretty. Beautiful. The brunette was stunning, even in pain.

And she was in pain.

Rose could see the bloody hole in her pale green sweater. "Are you okay?"

The woman stretched out her long jeans-clad legs and winced as the movement jarred her wounded shoulder. "The bastards shot me with a silver bullet." She wrenched at the short manacles that kept her from reaching above her waist. "If I don't get to it soon ..."

Shit.

"Who are you?"

"Thea MacLennan."

Holy double shit.

Rose groaned. "I know"—she panted—"I know who you are. God, what are you doing here?"

"My mate and I have been trying to track down a girl I met in Prague seven months ago. We lost her in Munich, but we got word the Blackwoods were hunting her too. They were easier to follow. When we followed them to the west coast of Galway, we had no clue what they were doing here." She rested her head against the concrete wall and squeezed her eyes closed. "We were trying to stay low key, which is hard to do in tiny coastal villages and even harder when your mate looks like mine. He's going to be so pissed."

"He's a pack alpha, right?"

Thea nodded. "Conall. Alpha of Pack MacLennan."

"He turned you. Saved your life when you got a dagger in the heart?"

Thea's nostrils flared. "How do you know this about me when I don't know a thing about you?"

"Niamh, the girl you were looking for, she knows you're searching. She's not happy about it. Wants you to live your life in peace now that you can." Talking was distracting her from the fire in her arms. "You should, Thea. As soon as you're out of here, go back to Scotland. This shit is over for you. It's not your fight anymore."

"Well, I don't see it that way. I'm trying to protect Niamh. And now you. If you want, once we're out of here, I can bite you. It's a risk, but it means you don't have to worry about causing an apocalypse or ... have to live forever."

Rose chuckled unhappily. "I hate to break it to you, gorgeous, but I like the idea of forever. Even if I didn't, that's not how it works. You survived the werewolf bite because your *mate* bit you. Only a mate can turn a fae into a vamp or a werewolf."

"What? How do you know that?"

"Because *my* mate was once trapped on Faerie before Aine turned him into a fae right before he escaped."

"Your mate ..." Thea huffed. "You're not talking about Fionn Mór?"

"You know him?" Fionn hadn't mentioned that.

"No, I have a journal. By Jerrik Mortensen, a vamp who spent time on Faerie. He mentions Fionn. I just assumed he was dead because no one's heard of him since."

The thought of him made her whimper. "No," she choked out. "He's very much alive."

"Shit," Thea whispered. "I can't believe this. The whole time I thought ... I thought I could help her."

"Niamh?"

"Yeah."

"No, you can't. The best thing you could do to help her is get out of here, take your mate, and go back to Scotland." Rose gritted her teeth as renewed flames ate at her arms. "Just ... keep your pack safe, yeah. That's your job now."

"I hate to break it to you, Rose, but I'm not going anywhere until I know you're safe from these wackos."

"I am. I'll never give them what they want."

"And what is that exactly?"

"An iron dagger. They th—" Rose cut off as it occurred to her the Blackwoods might be listening in. She didn't want them to know they might not need An Breitheamh to open the gate. "They need it to open the gate."

Silence fell between them. Rose did her best to ignore the excruciating agony of the iron.

"I went out to the store to get tea for our room," Thea said. "I left Conall sleeping in the little B&B we were staying in. We thought the Blackwoods were in the village two miles north. I had no idea they'd clocked us. Or that they'd take me." Her voice lowered, pain evident in her tone. "Conall will be going crazy right now."

Yeah, Rose groaned. She was sure her mate would be more than a little unhappy when he woke to discover Rose missing.

"Hey ... hey, Rose."

Rose's eyes flew open. Unconsciousness was blissfully coming for her. "What?" she snapped.

"I know that iron doesn't feel good. Believe me, do I know that, but I need you to stay with me. You're going to get us out of here."

Rose snorted. "By hanging tight?"

Thea ignored the bad joke. "Rose, have you ever been so scared or so angry, you emitted pure sunlight?"

"What?" Jesus Christ, she just wanted to pass out, not talk nonsense with a wounded werewolf. But somewhere in the recesses of her memories, the words started to connect with information buried in there.

Fourteen piles of ash.

"You killed Eirik." Rose forced herself to focus. "And his vampires."

"I did. I turned them all but one to ash. Conall had already killed one before I took out the rest. When the Blackwoods come back in here, you're going to kill one of them by doing the same thing I did, to force the other two to let us go."

"But how?"

"You'll picture everyone you love being put to the death by one of the Blackwoods. You have to make it feel real. Find that anger and grief and use it to obliterate them."

"What if it needs to be real?"

"I don't know ... but you have to at least try."

"Okay," Rose murmured, eyes falling closed. "Wake me up when they get here."

"Rose. Rose, I know it hurts, but you have to stay awake."

"Sleep is good." Darkness crept along the edges of Rose's mind, numbing the pain. "I choose Layton."

"Good choice." Thea sighed heavily. "It'll save Conall from ripping out his heart for putting a silver bullet in me."

"Aw, that's nice," Rose mumbled before she passed out.

32

Fionn had known from the moment he'd awakened to find Rose missing from his bed that she was gone.

It took him seconds to feel out the castle, discern its emptiness, and remember the Blackwoods were on the land beyond his borders.

Using magic to dress, Fionn bolted out of An Caomhnóir, shrugging on his overcoat as he hurried out the door. In his pocket was a hair tie belonging to Rose. He'd be able to use it to trace her once he was past the boundary spell.

Fionn was a blur, speeding through the forest as fast as his fae strength would allow. The almost-bare trees unwillingly saluted him with their branches as he sped out of the woods toward the stone wall that acted as the boundary marker for the spell.

Fionn halted at the sight of the extremely tall, extremely built werewolf sniffing the air around the wall. He took slow steps toward the wolf and although Fionn knew the wolf couldn't see him, he cocked his head as if he could hear him.

As he grew closer, the identity of the wolf hit him. He knew that face with the scar that scored down the left cheek. There was a scar on his neck too.

Scars from silver.

Scars Fionn had seen on surveillance shots Bran sent him.

The werewolf was no ordinary wolf. He was Conall MacLennan of Pack MacLennan—as in the mate of once-fae-borne Thea Quinn.

What the hell.

Fionn flew at the wall, bounding over it easily, the spell trickling off his skin as he did.

Conall tensed, not even flinching at Fionn's appearance. Instead, he scowled. "I knew there was magic here."

Exasperated, impatient, and fueled with worry, Fionn strode toward the wolf who stood his ground defiantly. "What the fuck are you doing here? Where's Rose?"

"Where's Thea?" he snapped back. "I followed my nose here for her and found this instead."

Fionn stilled, his worry escalating. "Did you encounter any Blackwoods?"

Conall grew visibly alert. "No."

"What are you doing here, Conall?"

His icy, pale gray eyes narrowed. "How do you know me?" He stiffened with realization. "You're fae."

"I'm Fionn."

"Mór?"

Fionn cursed inwardly. Did every fucker on the planet know who he was now? "Let's skip the part where I ask how you know me and vice versa. Why are you here and where is Thea?"

"We were following the Blackwoods. We were staying in the village ten miles north of here. When I woke this morning, Thea was gone. She should be here. Her scent is here."

"But does it end here?"

Conall took a breath, closing his eyes for a second as the breeze picked up around them. His eyes then flashed open, fury blazing within. "They've used magic to throw me off."

"Successfully?"

"A wee bit o' magic willnae stop me from tracking my mate. Or killing the fuckers who took her."

"Good. Because I'm coming with you. I have a feeling wherever we find Thea, we'll find Rose."

The wolf's nose caught in the air again, his expression hardening. "I scent another werewolf here. The Blackwoods didnae come alone."

Fionn considered this. "I imagine not. There's isn't much they'd be able to do to catch Rose unaware."

"And who is this Rose?"

Even knowing what he did of Conall MacLennan and his mate, Fionn still surprised himself by offering, "She's what Thea was. She's what the Blackwoods are after."

Conall processed this and then growled, "Fuck."

"You should know Layton Blackwood doesn't believe Thea was always wolf. That's probably why they've taken her."

Deep worry etched between the wolf's brows. "She's wounded. I found her blood where they took her."

Having learned a while ago that Conall was famous for his ability to track anyone, Fionn asked, "How does it work? The tracking thing?"

"Usually, once I have someone's scent, I just instinctively know where to go. But the spell they've cast over Thea is ... it's like my compass is haywire. I can sense her but something keeps leading me off track."

"Now that you know that, focus."

Conall snarled at him. Hands on hips, he gave his back to Fionn while he grappled against the spell.

"Anything?"

"Something's wrong." Conall glared at him over his shoulder. "I dinnae feel right."

Suspicions building, Fionn asked, "Do you have my scent now?"

"Aye."

"I'm going to hide, and you're going to try to find me."

"I dinnae have time for your games, fae."

"It's a test, *wolf*. Thea might not be the one they've spelled."

Conall turned fully toward him, understanding dawning.

Fionn nodded toward the wall. "Cross it."

The wolf eyed it. "The wall that drops right off a cliff and into the sea?"

"Does it?" Fionn sprung over it. Conall took a step back with surprise. Surprise that lasted but a second for he then threw himself over it. He studied the forest before him with a mere quirk of his lips.

Fionn *traveled* into the woods, hearing the wolf's startled curse at his disappearance.

He waited.

He waited as long as his patience would allow considering Rose was most likely in the hands of the Blackwoods. Conall traipsed through the woods, bristling with obvious fury, when Fionn *traveled* to his location. He spun on Fionn, canines bared. "What the hell have those bastards done to me?"

They'd put the spell on Conall. Not Thea.

Without giving the wolf a heads-up, Fionn gripped him by the collar and sped him through the woods, bursting out of the trees at the faerie pools. He threw the two-hundred-and-seventy pound wolf like he was nothing more than a small sack of flour.

He hoped MacLennan could swim.

The splash of his body landing in the larger pool was impressive. Under he went before popping back up, dark hair slicked back and icy glare threatening payback.

He moved unnaturally speedily through the water to the edge.

"Before you try to kill me, let me explain." Fionn gestured to the pools. "These are faerie pools."

Conall pulled himself out with ease, water falling off his now-soaked body as he faced Fionn with death in his eyes.

"They wash off spells. Try concentrating on Thea now."

Although the muscle in his jaw ticked, Conall took a breath and gave him a tight nod. Not even two seconds later, triumph lightened his countenance and relief moved through Fionn.

"I know where she is."

Fionn pulled the hair tie out. "This is Rose's. If you're wrong, we can trace her with this."

The wolf scowled. "Why the hell would you not just use this in the first place?"

"Because if Rose and Thea aren't together, you'll need your tracking ability to find your mate."

"And I'm to believe you helped me out of the goodness of your heart, fae?"

Irritation bubbled under Fionn's skin. "Rose is my mate. So, one, I understand what it would mean to you to lose Thea. And two, she and Thea need to be protected. The Blackwoods can't open that gate. If taking a few minutes out of my hunt for Rose so that my backup is working at his full capacity, so fucking be it. Now let's move."

Conall studied him a second and then gave him a nod. He gestured toward the woods. "This way."

Before he began to run at his wolf speed, he threw over his shoulder, "And I'm nobody's bloody backup, fae."

Fionn decided if he hadn't been worried out of his mind, he might like the Scot.

Rose, Fionn thought as he struggled to keep from speeding past Conall, *I'm coming for you*, mo chroí.

~

"ROSE. ROSE!"

The voice wouldn't stop. It tugged at Rose from a dark place of fiery hell.

"Rose, wake up!"

She groaned. It hurt in the darkness, but it was agony up where that voice was trying to haul her to.

"ROSE!"

Her eyes flew open, her blurred vision slowly coming into focus as the pain burst furiously across her nerve endings. "Argh!" She groaned, swinging against the chains and crying out with the movement.

"Rose, I'm so sorry, but I can hear them. They're coming."

It took Herculean effort to move her head toward the voice.

Thea.

The fae turned wolf was on her knees, begging Rose with her dark gaze. She looked paler than before.

Rose remembered the silver bullet.

Fuck.

"Remember what I told you," Thea said, her voice hoarse.

She's in pain.

"Imagine Layton hurting Fionn. Taking an iron blade to him."

Rose nodded weakly just as the door blew open and the warlock in question strode into the room.

He wasn't alone.

His sisters were with him, along with five warlocks and ... Rose eyed the mammoth male and remembered he was the one who'd snapped her neck. They had a werewolf as a bodyguard.

Oh, if Rose got out of this, the werewolf would be the first to get it. She did not enjoy having her neck snapped.

At all.

She glared at him and the wolf had the audacity to sneer. Then he signed his death warrant by turning to Layton. "You said I could play with the wolf bitch. When's that happening?" His greedy gaze sought Thea.

Thea snarled at him in warning and he grinned lasciviously at her.

Oh yeah, you're going to die, pal.

Layton cut the wolf a dark look. "I said the wolf was yours once we've opened the gate. You know you're not so much with the listening skills, are you?"

"Rose," Thea urged.

So, she tried. She really tried. She imagined Layton killing Fionn, emitting pure sunlight like the badass faerie she was.

Rose sagged, exhausted.

"Rose."

She cut a look at her pseudosibling. "I'm sorry."

"What's going on?" Layton asked, glancing between the two. He zeroed in on Thea, striding toward her. "What are you trying to get her to do?"

When neither of them answered, Layton grabbed Thea's hair and dug his thumb into her wound. Thea's gurgled scream tore through Rose. Watching the wolf grit her teeth, pain reddening her skin as she fought not to give Layton what he wanted, was unbearable.

"Stop it!" Rose yelled, forgetting her own pain as she yanked against the chains. Her right arm lowered and her breath caught.

Did the chain just pull from the ceiling a little?

"Oh, ladies and gentlemen, we have a winner." Layton straightened from his torture of Thea to smile at Rose. "I'm going to put another bullet in your little wolfy friend if you don't tell me where An Breitheamh is, Rose."

Thea launched herself at him, her jaw wide, canines out as she clamped onto his thigh and yanked her head back with such force, she took a huge chunk of Layton's leg with her.

The warlock's scream filled the basement as he fell to his knees. Rose watched in horror as Thea's body jerked seconds after a gunshot rang out.

Liza stood, her hands wrapped around the gun.

Thea slumped against the wall, unconscious, as Lori hovered over Layton.

"The fucking fae, you moron!" he yelled, spittle flying everywhere. "Her blood will heal me. I'm not turning into a fucking dog every full moon!"

No.

No, no, no!

Between the thought of Thea dying and Layton living, Rose was done.

Done being the victim.

What would Fionn do?

He'd use the pain, Rose thought. *He'd use the pain.*

With a scream of fury, Rose did just that, using the agony to fuel her strength. She forced her body to move, pushing herself onto her feet. She wrapped her hands around the chains above her manacles and with every bit of her fae strength, she yanked those fuckers from the ceiling like she was pulling a birthday candle out of a cake.

They were too shocked to react in time.

And Rose's rage was too great.

Using Fionn's training, Rose vanished, *traveling* to the spot behind Liza. She was a streak of movement as she used her full speed and strength, snapping the wrist holding the gun. Then she twisted Liza's neck, hearing the death crack. *Traveling* to the werewolf, Rose punched her fist through his back and tore out his heart.

One by one, fast as lightning, she broke the necks of all the warlocks.

Finally, she *traveled* to Lori.

Snuffed her out too.

Layton stared up at Rose in terror. "You're a monster," he whispered.

"Yes," Rose admitted as she lowered to her haunches, fire still blazing around her wrists, the weight of the chains pulling on them. "I can be. And this is what you wanted to unleash on the world. Hundreds of thousands of fae who would decimate the human race."

He shook his head. "Please ..."

"Do you know what the difference is between you and me?"

"Please."

Rose leaned into him. "I know what I am. I see the darkness inside me but it doesn't define me. But you ... you can't even see your own wickedness. How many people have you killed, Blackwood, in your pursuit of Faerie?"

"I tried to protect you," he pleaded, his hands raised to his chest in a defensive position.

"You tried to use me. You hunted me. You tortured me." As Rose pressed her hand against his chest, his pleading changed to anger.

"My coven will have their revenge."

"Good," she whispered inches from his face. "Let them come. I look forward to meting out justice for all the innocent people they've killed through the centuries." Pulling her elbow back, Rose thrust her fist into his chest and watched the maniacal light die in his eyes before she yanked his heart right out.

Dropping the muscle, Rose turned to her chains, breaking them off before concentrating on the iron. As soon as her fingertips touched it, pain had her yanking them back. It was like dipping her fingers in flame.

Cursing under her breath, she attempted to push the agony of the manacles to the back of her mind until she'd dealt with Thea. Rose crawled weakly over to her. Shuddering, she whispered the woman's name as she forced her arms up and her fingers into the bullet wound in Thea's shoulder.

The wolf jerked, eyelashes fluttering as Rose gritted her teeth and forced her fingers deep into the wound. Thea groaned, her eyes opening just as Rose connected with the flattened bullet.

With a heaving breath, she yanked it out and threw it across the room.

"Rose," Thea moaned, her focus hazy. "What—"

"Where's the other bullet?"

"G-gut."

Holy crap.

Rose's fingers fumbled to lift Thea's sweater as she grew weaker with the iron.

"H-hey. Can you break my cuffs?"

Sweat rolling down her back, Rose turned to the shackles around Thea's wrists. She concentrated and pulsed what little magic she could into the lock. They popped off.

Thea's hands immediately wrapped around one of Rose's iron-clad wrists. Gritting her teeth with a growl that sounded as if it came deep from her belly, Thea snapped the iron apart.

Immediate relief from the pain caused tears to burn in Rose's eyes. "Thank you."

Instead of answering, Thea did the same to her other wrist, and then slumped back against the wall, her eyes rolling back in her head.

"Thea!" Rose lunged toward her, ignoring the ugly scars around her wrists as she pulled the wolf's sweater up.

Silvery veins spread out from an inflamed bullet wound.

Shit.

The cry of pain Thea emitted as Rose dug for the bullet was beyond hard to hear, but Rose couldn't find the damn thing.

"Please, please," Thea moaned, her lashes fluttering, her face deathly pale. "Stop, stop. You need to go. You need to leave. Th-there might be others."

"I'm not leaving you!" With her strength returning by the second, Rose searched the room for anything that might work to pull out the bullet.

She didn't let her mind deal with the bodies.

The people she'd killed.

She looked at Layton and his voice rang in her head. *The fucking fae, you moron! Her blood will heal me!*

"Of course." Rose shook her head in disbelief. "I'm such an idiot." The iron manacles laid near her feet. Where Thea had cracked one open, there was a jagged edge.

This is going to be a whole lot of no fun.

Gritting her teeth, she yanked up the iron before she could think about it, fought through the pain, ripped the jagged edge across her already scarred wrist, dropped the iron, and thrust her bleeding wrist against Thea's mouth.

Thea automatically opened her lips and sucked at the wound. Rose pressed her wrist harder against her mouth. "More, Thea."

Watching Thea's exposed wound, Rose saw the skin move, the flattened silver bullet pushing out of Thea's body and landing on her thigh. *Whoa.* Rose threw it away, turning back to see Thea's skin healing over. The silvery veins disappeared.

Rose dropped her wrist as Thea stared at her, gaze clear and focused, her skin returning to its healthy olive tone. Rose's blood smeared her lips. "Thank you."

Rose slumped back against the wall, her wrist stinging as it failed to heal over with its usual speed. She clutched it to her chest and shrugged. "It was nothing."

Thea snorted. "Right, it—" She stilled, cocking her head. Something warm glittered in her dark eyes as she looked at Rose. "Backup just arrived."

33

A ninety-minute walk from Fionn's land, not far from the village of Costelloe, Conall led them to an industrial building that seemed to be some kind of medical warehouse.

It had taken them thirty minutes to run there at Conall's speed. That Fionn could've reached it in ten minutes and anything could've happened to Rose in those extra twenty minutes ate at him.

But he had to focus.

There were no humans in the building.

Two wolves guarded the door.

"I can smell Thea from here. She's bleeding," Conall snarled before he launched himself across the car park at the wolves. As one braced to meet Conall, Fionn *traveled*, coming up behind the other.

Almost in unison, Fionn tore out the wolf's heart as Conall ripped off the other's head.

They stared at each other, hearts hammering, knowing they could've easily just knocked out the wolves. But they'd helped take Thea and Rose and, Thea, at least, was wounded.

Without another word, they burst inside the warehouse, battle ready. Fionn followed Conall as he tracked Thea.

No one else came at them and as they approached a door at the back of the building, Conall looked at Fionn. "I hear Thea and another woman. I cannae hear anything else. No other heartbeats."

Fionn's hearing was good but nowhere near as acute as a wolf's, so he took Conall's word for it.

The wolf threw open the door, which led down a dank stairwell. They hurried down it, coming out onto a basement level. Conall turned right and jogged down the corridor, Fionn following him.

When Conall stopped at a heavy steel door and tried the handle, he found it locked. He turned to Fionn. "They're behind here."

Heart racing at what he might find in the room, Fionn lifted his palm to the door. "*Oscailte.*" The door swung open and back against the wall. He didn't want it blasting into the room and wounding one of their mates.

Conall rushed into the windowless room first.

The wolf came to a halt, and Fionn understood why as he strolled in. He was trying to remain as calm as possible while his whole body screamed with the need to release his pent-up worry and rage.

Bodies littered the concrete floor.

Warlocks with broken necks.

Liza Blackwood, dead, neck broken too.

A fucking huge bastard of a werewolf with a hole in his chest.

"Thea," Conall bit out, hurrying toward the far corner where a brunette was helping Rose to her feet.

A dead Lori and Layton Blackwood lay on the ground near them.

Fionn *traveled*, appearing in front of Rose, who gasped at his sudden appearance. His mate was pale and drained, and he knew why when he saw her wrists. She clutched them to her chest, shivering.

"Fionn," she whispered, expression slack with relief.

Fury boiled in his blood as he reached out and tentatively took hold of her fingers, pulling her wrists out, hands palm upward. Her right wrist was healing from a cut, but that wasn't what made him want to hunt down the Blackwoods and kill every last one of them.

Three-inch burn scars wrapped around each of Rose's wrists.

Fionn took in the chains and manacles scattered at their feet.

Two of the broken manacles were made of pure iron.

"I'm going to kill them all," he promised.

Rose tugged her hands from his, but only to rest them on his chest. Her blue eyes pleaded with him. "No more, Fionn."

"I'm sorry." The words were torn from his throat. "I failed you."

Rose pissed him off by giving him a tired grin. "Whose voice do you think was in my head when I needed to get myself out of this? Whose training?"

He shook his head. "It's not—"

"Fionn." Her fingers curled into his shirt. "You wanted me to be able to take care of myself ..." She swallowed hard, lowering her eyes. "For when you're gone. And I can."

Her words were like an iron blade in his gut.

"You saved my life," Thea interrupted, reminding Fionn he wasn't alone with his mate. Roaring at her that she was an idiot if she thought he was ever fucking leaving her again would have to wait.

Rose turned toward the wolf wrapped in Conall's arms. The alpha was holding Thea so tightly, it was a wonder she could breathe.

Fionn looked down at Rose. She should be in his arms like that. Why wasn't she? He scowled at her. *Come to me, mo chroí.*

She didn't.

So he hauled her against him and although she gave him a slightly startled look, she slid her arms around his waist and held on to him as she addressed Thea. "I have the feeling you would have done the same for me."

"Thank you," Conall said to Rose. "Sincerely. I owe you a debt."

"*We* owe you a debt," Thea corrected, caressing his chest.

Fionn glared down at Rose. *Do that to me, mo chroí. I need soothing.*

She didn't. Fionn gingerly lifted the wrist that wasn't healing from a cut and placed her palm over his heart. Rose curled her fingers into his sweater and buried deeper into him.

"I'm calling in that debt," she addressed the alpha wolves. "Go back to Scotland. Stay there. Keep your pack safe."

"We're past that." Conall glared at Layton Blackwood. "Once the coven discovers this, they'll come for retribution. It'll be war once I call upon my allies."

"No, they won't," Fionn said. "I know the Blackwoods. Nate Blackwood is not as ruthless as previous coven leaders. His son"—he gestured to Layton—"disagreed with his father's methods. This was a kamikaze mission. There's no way Nate Blackwood would have agreed to kidnapping Thea. He knew that would start a war with all the packs. I'd place a high bet that the rest of the coven have no clue about this. The Blackwoods know the gate is only miles from here, which offers an excuse for why the trail will lead to Ireland.

"There's no reason for them to think any of us were involved."

Conall frowned. "Do you know that for certain?"

"I know for certain that the Blackwoods have no idea of your involvement. I'm telling you, Nate would never sanction action against you."

The alpha couple shared a knowing look and Thea nodded, turning back to Rose and Fionn. "They came to us after I turned and I had to prove I was just a wolf, not fae. Obviously, they had their suspicions we were lying, but with no evidence, they were given orders to leave us alone once we proved I was a werewolf. So, you're right, we're safe ... but what about you two?"

"I doubt they know we're involved, but even if they do, they'll have a hard time catching us," Fionn promised, his hold on Rose tightening.

"And Niamh?" Thea asked Rose.

Rose tensed and Fionn tried to pull her closer into him, even though she was as close as she was going to get. "Thea, I'm guessing you're a pretty kick-ass wolf, but you're not fae anymore. You can't do what Niamh and I can."

Thea winced, contemplating the dead bodies littered around the room. "True."

"Go home to your pack. Be with your mate. Stay safe. I'll look out for Niamh."

Thea's lovely dark gaze filled with concern. "It feels wrong to abandon you to this."

Rose smiled. "Thea, you're not abandoning me to anything. This —being fae—it's what I am." Her smile dimmed a little as she looked down at Lori's body. "It comes with its consequences, and I'm not saying that's easy. At all." Her sad eyes returned to Thea. "But I'm not afraid of what I am. I'm not afraid of immortality."

Thea gave an embarrassed huff as she looked to her mate for reassurance. "It was arrogant of me to assume the others like me wouldn't want their abilities or the immortality."

Conall kissed her forehead. "Not arrogance, Thea love."

"I agree with your mate, Thea. But like I said earlier, even if I didn't want this, there is nothing you can do. Same goes for Niamh."

At Conall's questioning expression, Thea shook her head. "I can't change them to wolf. Only a mate can. That's why I survived your bite."

"What?"

"It's true," Fionn offered, his voice hoarse with the emotions churning inside him. "I heard it personally from within the queen's private court."

"Fuck," Conall cursed, giving his mate a commiserating squeeze. "I'm sorry."

She shrugged and then threw Rose a wry smile. "Doesn't seem to be a problem, anyway. Rose is powerful."

Fionn took in the room again, grimly. He was proud that Rose could defend herself, but he worried about her conscience. She wasn't born to be a warrior like he was, to compartmentalize death at her own hands.

"Enough chitchat. We need to leave," Conall said.

"Right." Fionn gestured to the room, sending his magic out to every single body. As one, they crumbled to ash.

"Holy shit," Thea whispered.

"Looks like you only touched the tip of the iceberg of your powers when you were fae, Thea," Conall muttered, looking a little awed himself.

"Uh ... yeah," she agreed.

"Why are we worrying about the Blackwoods?" MacLennan shot a look at Fionn. "If you can do this."

"Because the Blackwoods are powerful enough to trace their coven to here. Even if they don't find bodies, they can use spells to discern whether they're alive or not. This"—he gestured to the ash —"is to hide the evidence from the humans."

"It's like what I did to Eirik." Thea stared at the pile of ash that was Layton Blackwood. "But without the glowing-sunlight thing."

"No, what you did is different. It's easy to turn what is dead to ash. Harder to do it to a living thing." Fionn considered Thea. "You must have been very powerful as a fae, Thea."

"Yeah, still ... I prefer this version of me. Way less complicated."

"Right. Like I said, chitchat's over. Let's go."

At Conall's order, Rose pulled away from Fionn and followed the alpha couple out of the room. She held her head up and didn't look at the piles of ash.

Fionn followed behind her, dread filling him.

Why had she pulled away?

Fuck. Fionn growled inwardly, his hands tight fists at his sides. This was the downside to the mating bond—the overwhelming, complicated mix of emotions eating at his insides.

Forcing himself to stay alert, instead of gluing his attention to his mate, Fionn followed the small group upstairs and out of the empty warehouse. There was no one else here.

They'd killed every supernatural who'd been guarding the place.

Once outside, it was decided Fionn and Rose would escort the alpha couple back to the village so they could collect their rental car and get the hell out of Ireland. The couple's pride seemed a little pricked by Rose's stubborn refusal to leave them until she knew they were well on their way, but Thea gave in first. And then convinced Conall too.

Despite Rose's sudden distance with Fionn, there was no way in hell he was leaving her side, so he escorted the wolves as well.

An hour later, Rose and Thea hugged goodbye.

"You know where I am if you need me," Thea said.

"Yeah. And I'll find a way to make it so you can contact me if you need me too," Rose said.

The women hugged again as Fionn gave Conall a nod that issued the same overture. Conall nodded back, returning the offer.

Finally, they drove off in a rented Land Rover, leaving Fionn alone with his quiet mate.

He looked down at her wrists.

They'd be scarred forever, a constant reminder of what Layton Blackwood had done.

Fionn had never felt the burn of iron, but he'd heard it was excruciating. His fury began to build again at the thought of Rose enduring such torture.

She glanced up at him, tucking her tousled hair behind her ear, before placing her palms out and upward. His frown of confusion was forming when a familiar silver box appeared in her hands.

An Breitheamh.

A different kind of anger surged within him.

This kind directed at Rose.

"This is why I left this morning." She held the box out to him. "I couldn't conjure it from within the boundary spell. They caught me unawares as soon as I crossed the wall. But I wanted to give this to you."

He glowered silently at the box.

"I won't keep this from you. Not anymore. But you should know that even though I'm giving you this ..." The hoarseness in her voice brought his gaze to hers. Tears shone in her beautiful eyes. "I love you, Fionn. I love you more than I thought I could ever love anyone.

"But I can't let you kill the last fae-borne. I just can't. So, I'll be there to stop you if you try."

Furious with her, but mostly with himself, exultant at her confession of love, and still gripped with fear of what could've happened to her—what *had* happened to her—Fionn snatched the box out of her hands.

Without a word, he whipped it open and saw from her flinch that she felt the weakening effect of An Breitheamh too.

Then, in the middle of a small village in County Galway, Fionn placed a hand above the pure iron dagger and watched the fire of his magic melt it into nothing.

Rose stumbled toward him. "But ... but I tried that ..."

A weight Fionn hadn't even known he'd been carrying fell from his shoulders as the now-empty silver box clattered to the pebbled road.

He felt free.

For the first time in three hundred years, Fionn Mór was free.

"An Breitheamh was made by me and can only be undone by me."

Hope, bright and shining, glowed in Rose's eyes. "But what about your revenge?"

Fionn shook his head. "I'd already decided before those bastards took you that I wanted to stay with you. I can't leave you behind. Centuries of planning ... ah, Rose ... centuries of planning were blown to shit the moment we met. Finally there's something in this world I want more than vengeance."

Rose laughed softly. "You choose me?"

He stared at his love, his mate, his newfound purpose, and the future stretched wide open before them. Fionn stepped toward her, cupping her beautiful face in his hands. The gods, he loved Rose Kelly beyond anything he thought he was capable of. He loved every inch of her with every inch of himself.

Fionn bent his head to hers and whispered across her sweet lips, "No, *mo chroí*. I choose us."

EPILOGUE

DUBLIN

Bran, as it turned out, was a tall, somewhat lanky, good-looking vampire who appeared his mortal age of only twenty-one. His body was in that in-between place of youth and adulthood—strong, wiry, but not entirely filled out.

With his messy dark hair, brooding blue eyes, long lashes, sultry mouth, and angular jaw, he'd have been the exact kind of guy Rose would have had a crush on in college. There was a warmth to him that could change her mind about vampires, who, until this point, she'd only had bad experiences with.

He stared at her as she stared at him, in the well-lit loft apartment with its row of windows that seriously couldn't be good for a vamp once daylight arrived.

"Are you done staring at my mate or am I going to have to yank out your eyeballs?" Fionn asked from his place on the couch beside Rose. His body language said casually possessive, with his left arm spread along the back of the couch where Rose sat.

His tone was anything but casual.

Bran broke into a grin, dimples popping in each cheek.

Jesus, he was so cute. Rose bet he never had to worry about finding a woman to suck on.

"I'm loving this more than you'll ever know," he announced in his rich, Dublin accent.

Dublin was beautiful. At least the little of it Rose had seen. After the battle at the warehouse, Fionn had insisted on Rose getting some rest at An Caomhnóir before they traveled to Dublin to meet with Bran.

"What?" Rose grinned, finding the vampire's amusement infectious.

"Him." He gestured to Fionn. "Possessive. Territorial. Of a woman."

"Again—" Fionn began what she knew would be a renewed threat.

"Yes, yes," Rose interrupted. "It's a surprising development for us all. Let's move past that and tell us what we need to know."

Bran stared at her a second before turning to Fionn. "She's fucking perfect for you."

"Bran."

"Okay, okay." The vampire sat up, resting his elbows on his knees as he leaned toward her. "The Blackwoods have sent out a team to find Layton and his sisters. Word is, they think Niamh might have something to do with it since she was who Nate sent them out after."

"Shit." Rose threw Fionn an anxious look.

His expression softened on her and she felt his hand slip through her hair to rest on her nape. He gave it a reassuring squeeze.

"As for Niamh, there's a possibility I might have found her."

Rose tore her gaze from Fionn's handsome face to Bran's. "What?"

He nodded, his expression somber. "There was an early snowstorm in Vienna. A bus driver lost control of his vehicle. It was heading for a group of pedestrians, most of whom claim that a young woman with long, blond hair stepped in front of the bus and pushed it away. With her hands."

Fionn cursed under his breath. "She's being careless, acting like fucking Superwoman. It was that exact thing that nearly got Thea caught."

Melancholy swept through Rose. "Try to understand, Fionn. She couldn't save Ronan."

"So she's trying to save the world?" Bran huffed. "The Blackwoods will hear of this, Rose, and they'll come after her. If they think she's to blame for the deaths of Layton and his sisters, they won't make things pretty. They won't kill her but they could do other things."

She looked at her wrists, which her long sleeves thankfully covered. But she was scarred forever. "Believe me, I understand what they could do to her." She turned to Fionn. "We have to go to her."

To her shock, Fionn shook his head. "I want her safe too, Rose. I know you had these grand plans to tag along with Niamh and find the other fae-borne, but it's not safe. For any of you. I found you by following Niamh. If you were captured in each other's company, the gate would be in serious danger. It's safer for you all to be apart."

Indignation burned through her. "But what about Niamh? She's alone now. I know she probably protected Ronan more than he could ever protect her, but—"

Fionn squeezed her nape again, hushing her. "Do you think I'd leave her out there alone?"

"What will you do?"

"Yes, what will you do?" Bran asked.

Her mate let go of a slow exhalation. "I'll send someone I can trust to guard her. Someone almost as powerful as us."

Who could be almost as powerful as them? "Uh, and that would be?"

"Oh, you're not thinking what you're thinking," Bran said incredulously. "He's the coldest bastard I ever did meet."

Fionn scowled. "He's also the only immortal werewolf in existence. And his protection can be bought, for the right price."

"I suppose."

"Anyone want to fill me in? There's an immortal werewolf out there? How does that work?" Rose was stunned. There was still so much to learn!

"You've met him," Fionn told her.

When had she met an immortal—

"Oh my God." She gaped at Fionn. "You want to send *Kiyo* to guard Niamh?"

"He's the only one I trust to do it."

"But for how long? I mean, this gig is kind of an ongoing thing."

Fionn sighed. "I don't know, Rose. Until he discerns Niamh is stable and not going to lead the Blackwoods or the Garm straight to her. That also involves getting her to give up trying to find the other fae-borne. Which means entrusting the wolf with the truth."

Somehow, she didn't think even intimidating, brooding Kiyo would talk Niamh out of her personal mission.

IN THE WEE hours of the morning, Rose walked at Fionn's side, her small hand held tightly in his.

When they first met, Rose would never have pegged Fionn for the touchy-feely type. Yet, since her kidnapping days before, Fionn had stuck to her side like glue, touching her whenever the opportunity presented itself.

The cobbles of Fleet Street were almost empty of other people as they strolled through the Temple Bar district toward their hotel. They'd left An Caomhnóir because Rose preferred to be on the move, and Fionn wanted to give Rose whatever she needed.

Staying in one place gave her time to dwell on what had happened in that basement. She knew it would haunt her. It already was. But she also knew the one person who could help her find a way to deal with it was holding her hand. When she'd suggested they visit Bran, rather than get an update by phone, Fionn had seemed to understand.

Moreover, Rose wanted to see where it was her family came from.

From there, Fionn planned to show Rose the rest of the world. If they kept moving, stayed smart, they could avoid their enemies. Hopefully. But it also meant avoiding people she loved.

As if he'd read her mind, Fionn offered, "If you like, we can find a way to call your parents. Let them know you're still okay."

Rose considered this and nodded. "Do you think I'll ever see them again?"

"If I can make it safe for you and them both, then yes."

Love suffused her as she buried into him. Fionn let go of her hand, but only so he could wrap his arm around her shoulders. Words she'd been dreading saying because she feared his reaction bubbled out of her. There could be no secrets between them if they were to spend the rest of their very long lives together.

"I need to tell you something."

He squeezed her, a nonverbal go-ahead.

Rose cleared her throat. "Niamh told me something. A vague something, but ... Fionn, she had a vision or, I don't know, like a feeling or—"

"Rose." He kissed the top of her head. "Calm. Take your time."

She tried to relax but failed. Him being so adorable was not helping. "Okay. Okay." She pushed away, turning to face him on the moonlit street. "Okay. If you killed one of us to open the gate, it wouldn't have just ended with you killing Aine and then yourself."

He frowned. "What do you mean?"

"When I met Niamh in Zagreb, she said something I didn't get until she explained it on our second meeting. She knew we were mates. And she knew that if I didn't trust you to choose the mating bond over your revenge, the ... well, the world as we know it would end."

"Excuse me?" he crossed his arms over his chest, visibly confused.

"Read between the lines: Fionn kills Aine, the fae reopen the gate, and then they take their vengeance out on humanity."

His expression slackened. "And you were planning on telling me this when?"

Wincing at his accusatory tone, Rose reached out to place a soothing hand on his abs. "If you didn't choose me of your own accord, I was going to tell you and hope it would be enough to stop you." She grinned sheepishly. "Forgive me, yes? Okay, good. Let's go have epic sex."

Despite the anger flickering in his gorgeous eyes, his lips twitched with amusement. "Rose," he huffed, exasperated.

"Oh, come on! Surely, there's stuff you still haven't told me." The guy had lived for centuries!

The anger disappeared from his expression, leaving behind something like uncertainty.

"Ah-ha." Rose wagged a finger at him. "Let it out. Once it's done, we're even-steven, right?"

He shook his head, affection brightening his expression. A pleasurable ache spread through her, one only he inspired. Fionn covered her hand resting on his stomach with his own. "There is something."

"Yeah?"

"Rose."

"Yeah?"

He bent his head toward her. "Rose ... fertility amongst the fae doesn't work the same way as it does in humans. It can take time. Years. Centuries, even. But two mated fae can have children together."

Shock reverberated through Rose. She stumbled back from her mate, gaping, as she processed what this new, astounding, fantastic, life-changing information meant.

Fionn pressed a quick, hungry kiss to her mouth, a kiss she was too shocked to return, and said, "Forgive me for not telling you sooner, yes? Okay, good. Let's go have epic sex."

FIONN & ROSE CONTINUED...

If you enjoyed Fionn and Rose's story, you can read more about them in their bonus short story included in this upcoming anthology.

TEMPTED BY FAE: A MIDNIGHT COVEN ANTHOLOGY
Fourteen worlds. Fourteen women. One fate they can't escape.

From bestselling authors of fantasy and paranormal romance comes a breathtaking set of all new stories, available for a limited time only. Whether kick ass, shy, or vulnerable, the women in Tempted by Fae get more than they bargain for when mysterious and sexy immortals cross their paths.
Give in.
It's only forever.

Available May 5, 2020
Preorder:
Amazon
Apple
Kobo
Nook

WAR OF HEARTS

A True Immortality Novel
By S. Young

A standalone adult paranormal romance from *New York Times*
Bestselling author Samantha Young, writing as S. Young.

Thea Quinn has no idea what she is. All she knows is that her
abilities have been a plague upon her life since she was a child. After
years of suffering at the hands of a megalomaniac, Thea escaped and
has been on the run ever since.
The leadership and protection of his pack are of the utmost
importance to Conall MacLennan, Alpha and Chief of Clan
MacLennan, the last werewolf pack in Scotland. Which is why
watching his sister slowly die of a lycanthropic disease is emotional
torture. When Conall is approached by a businessman who offers a
cure for his sister in exchange for the use of Conall's rare tracking
ability, Conall forges an unbreakable contract with him. He has to
find and retrieve the key to the cure: dangerous murderer, Thea
Quinn.
Thea's attempts to evade the ruthless werewolf are not only thwarted

by the Alpha, but by outside dangers. With no choice but to rely on one another for survival, truths are revealed, intensifying a passionate connection they both fight to resist. At war with themselves and each other, Conall and Thea's journey to Scotland forces them to face a heartrending choice between love and betrayal.

Out Now in ebook, paperback & hardback edition.

Apple Books US

Apple Books UK

Amazon WorldWide

Kobo US

Barnes & Noble

Kobo UK

EXTRAS

<u>Kiss of Vengeance</u>

Conversations in Translation
Chapter Thirteen - Rose's First Dream-Walk

Light flooded into the gargantuan hall from the impressive arched windows that lined either wall. There was a cathedral-like quality to the room.

Rose blinked against the light, her vision focusing as she took in her surroundings.

School desks sat in rows, students at them bent over papers, scribbling furiously. Several older people strolled up and down and in between the desks. A huge clock hung suspended from the ceiling at the north end of the hall.

It's ticktock was distracting.

"Stop ticking," a voice hissed.

Rose glanced down and realized she was standing over the desk of a young woman whose face was scrunched up with frustration. She looked vaguely familiar as she glared at the ticking clock.

So consumed with the girl's mounting panic, it took Rose a

minute to realize she had no fucking idea where she was. Her own anxiety began to mount.

"Where am I?" she whispered.

The clock fell from the ceiling and smashed into pieces.

"Time is up!" a female proctor shouted from the other end of the hall. "Submit your papers, please!"

"No, no, I'm not done," the familiar girl murmured frantically as she stood, blank paper crumpled in her hand.

What the hell was going on? And why was everyone speaking Spanish? Rose glanced around, trying to piece this weirdness together. Hadn't she just been on the train to Barcelona with Fionn?

The stressed girl hurried toward the front of the room, and that's when Rose realized the girl had a glow of light around her that no one else did. It was like a full-body halo. Instincts told her to follow the girl. Perhaps she knew why Rose was here ... wherever here was.

However, as she took a step to follow the girl who was talking to the proctor, the room shifted.

It grew smaller, and Rose braced herself against the swift, strange change as it shrunk around her. Her heart pounded with fear; sweat coated her skin. What the hell was going on?

Attention fixed on the girl, Rose watched as the woman she was talking to disappeared and in her place was a handsome young man with dark hair and stubbled cheeks.

Rose spun around, taking in the dorm room they now stood in.

What the ever-loving fuck?

"You'll be fine," the young man said, patting the girl's shoulder.

"He's right." Another young woman appeared in the room, as if from thin air. She sat up from a sprawl. Her blond hair fell over her shoulders as she swung long, slender legs off a bed. "You'll be fine."

Rose frowned. The new addition was American.

The girl with the glow scowled, and Rose instinctually knew she hated the American. "I won't get into the program now," the girl said in accented English. "You don't understand. You have no ambition."

The American seemed affronted as she stood from the bed and

put her arm around the young man. "Are you going to let her speak to me like that?"

"No," he replied emotionlessly. "You should leave, Alejandra."

Hurt pierced Rose as the girl, Alejandra, stepped away from him and immediately collided into a guy who had appeared out of nowhere too.

What. The. Fuck.

Rose swayed as the room changed again and Alejandra turned to face the man. His features were slightly blurred. The room they were in was pitch-black, except for the three of them. The boy and his American had disappeared.

"What are you doing here?" Alejandra asked the man with the blurry face.

"You need me," his deep voice rumbled into the dark.

"No."

"Yes." His hand slipped under Alejandra's dress and she moaned, swaying into him.

Arousal instantly flooded Rose. What the— "Okay, get me out of here."

Her discomfort grew as the sounds of sex filled the room, her pulse escalating as her body reacted to the desire pulsating between the two strangers. It was unsettling to say the very least. "Uh, someone get me out of here!" she yelled into the dark.

Then she heard a gasp and spun back toward the couple.

She froze when her eyes connected with Alejandra's as she clung to her blurry-faced man. "Who are you?"

Rose shook her head at the accusatory question. "What? I don't understand. Why am I here?"

"Who are you?" The blurry faced man vanished and Rose faced Alejandra alone in the dark. "Who are you?" she repeated in her accented English. "How did you get here?"

"I don't know."

Fear suffused Alejandra, and Rose felt that keenly too. "How did you get here?" she demanded.

Rose shook her head, stumbling away from the girl.

"How did you get here? HOW DID YOU GET HERE!"
Rose jerked awake in her seat.

Chapter Twenty-One - Rose Dream-Walks Fionn

He reached into the bed of furs, giving her an amazing view of that muscular ass of his, and pulled on rough trousers. With a yawn, Fionn crossed the room and picked up something that looked like bread from a plate on the table. The wolf followed, and Fionn reached out to scratch behind his ears. "Good morning, Cónán."

Chewing on the bread, Fionn strode toward the entrance, the wolf shadowing him.

Rose followed.

It had taken her slumberous mind to catch up, but as she dashed out of the roundhouse, her consciousness realized she was dream-walking again, this time in Fionn's dreamworld. And he seemed to be dreaming about the past.

Rose marveled at the view as she skidded to a stop outside the house. She was on a hill. Sprawled below her was a village, a collection of roundhouses of varying sizes, all with land that was being tended. A great stone wall surrounded the village border. A pale blue sky hung above them as Fionn took in the view of people working and talking in the small town below.

She followed his gaze to what looked like the entrance to the fortified town where men with weapons sat outside what might have been a guardhouse.

"My king shows too much of himself to his people."

The foreign words brought both Fionn, Cónán, and Rose's heads to the left, where a striking redhead appeared, walking up the slope toward the entrance to the roundhouse.

Fionn strode toward the woman, turning her in his arms, and shocking the shit out of Rose as he broke into a wide smile.

She'd never seen him smile like that.

"Jealous, my love?" Fionn asked.

The redhead shook her head, laughing as Fionn pressed his lips to hers.

Jealousy seared through Rose as they held each other tight, their kisses passionate, their embrace loving.

Who was this?

"Aoibhinn," Fionn murmured as he broke the kiss. "I missed my queen."

"Your war is important."

Rose had no idea what they were saying, but the woman seemed to be reassuring him.

"Where are the children?"

The redhead grinned and turned her curvy body toward the entrance.

Fionn shook his head. "They're not in there."

The woman chuckled, tipped her head toward the entrance and yelled, "Caoimhe, Diarmuid!"

Two seconds later, a young girl, perhaps seven or eight, hurried out of the roundhouse followed by a tall, lanky young man who could have been anywhere between the ages of eleven and eighteen. His physique said he was older but his baby face said he was very young.

Rose frowned. Where had they come from?

Oh. Right. *Dream*.

But who were they? Taking a step closer, she peered at the kids as the girl wrapped her arms around Fionn's waist and he grinned down at her. He then turned to converse with the boy. Rose was stunned.

The boy had his smile. The girl had his hair.

Were these ... Fionn's children?

What?

Cónán moved toward the boy who curled his fist in the wolf's ruff as he grinned up at Fionn.

"You should not have gone to her." The woman's words, whatever they meant, caused a massive shift in Fionn's dreamscape.

The children vanished and the village faded to a forest lit only with flame from a massive fire behind the woman. And Fionn ... he was now beardless and wore leather trousers.

A gold circlet rested low around his neck. His torso was bare.

Without his beard, he looked more like the Fionn she knew, except his green eyes blazed with the light of another world.

Cloaked figures appeared out of the trees behind him, advancing menacingly as the redheaded woman watched on, chin raised in defiance.

"My love?" Fionn reached for the redhead.

Revulsion crossed her face, making her look hard and cold where only moments ago she'd been soft and loving. "I am not your love!"

ACKNOWLEDGMENTS

Diving back into the world of adult paranormal romance with Rose and Fionn by my side has been an absolute adventure. For them literally, as they ran across Europe to Ireland. Moreover, it was fun to venture into Iron Age Ireland to revisit Fionn's past. I've taken some liberties with historical accuracy regarding Fionn's life in Iron Age Ireland to fit with my reimagining of a fae invaded world. I also used modern Irish (of the Connacht dialect) for Fionn. But, of course, I don't know Irish and that's why my wonderful reader, Sally McDonagh, stepped in to help. Thank you so much, Sally, for all of your translations and help with pronunciation. It is so appreciated! Any errors are my own.

There are many reasons to thank my Facebook Group *Sam's Clan McBookish*, number one being their never-ending support and encouragement. I'm grateful to have members from all over the world in my group, and I have to thank a few of those ladies by name for helping me with translations for this book. For the Croatian translations, a huge thank you to Natasha Tomic, Iva Piva, Josipa Mateša, Jelena Grujic, Suanita Mesic, Ivana D'Storm, Kristina Hanicar, Teodora Bibic, Melinda Žvan, Dubravka Tarcal-Grabovac. You are wonderful! And for the Castilian Spanish translations Sarai Ruiz, Viridiana Jauregui, Raquel Duarte, Josefina Sanchez de Bath, Elna Nin, Merchy Lires, Susana Martinez, Maria Jose Ryan, María WieBitte Navalón-Castillo, Babel Td, Wilmari Carrasquillo-Delgado, Kayleigh Woods, and Charo Guismo. Thank you all so much for helping me with the translations in Alejandra's dream sequence!

For the French translation, a big thank you to Françoise Giang, Ave Line, Alecs Contreras, Jennifer Spinninger, and Aurélie Dee.

How lucky am I to have such amazing readers to turn to with research questions? You're all phenomenal! Again, any errors are my own.

For the most part writing is a solitary endeavor, but publishing is not. A massive thank you to my editor Jennifer Sommersby Young for taking a process than can sometimes be excruciating for a writer and making it pretty painless. I love working with you!

A big thank you to Kristen Callihan for reading an early version of Fionn and Rose's story and giving me much appreciated feedback that helped make their romance stronger.

And thank you to my bestie and PA extraordinaire, Ashleen Walker, for handling all the little things and supporting me through everything. I love you lots.

The life of a writer doesn't stop with the book. Our job expands beyond the written word to marketing, advertising, graphic design, social media management and more. Help from those in the know goes a long way. Thank you to every single blogger, instagrammer and book lover who has helped spread the word about my books. You all are appreciated so much!

To my family and friends, for always encouraging me to follow my gut.

Moreover, to Wander Aguiar for the beautiful cover image photography that encapsulates Fionn and Rose perfectly.

To Hang Le, thank you, thank you for creating yet another stunning cover that I cannot stop staring at! You're mega, my friend.

As always, thank you to my agent Lauren Abramo for making it possible for readers all over the world to find my words, and for always having my back. I'm so grateful for you.

And finally, the biggest thank you of all, to you my reader. Thank you for coming on this new adventure with me. I couldn't do it without you.

ABOUT THE AUTHOR

S. Young is the pen name for Samantha Young, a *New York Times*, *USA Today* and *Wall Street Journal* bestselling author from Stirlingshire, Scotland. She's been nominated for the Goodreads Choice Award for Best Author and Best Romance for her international bestseller *On Dublin Street*. *On Dublin Street* was Samantha's first adult contemporary romance series and has sold in twenty-eight languages in thirty countries. *True Immortality* is Samantha's first adult paranormal series written under the name S. Young.

Visit Samantha Young online at
www.authorsamanthayoung.com
BookBub
Instagram @AuthorSamanthaYoung
Twitter @AuthorSamYoung
Facebook @AuthorSamanthaYoung
Facebook Reader Group
Goodreads

CPSIA information can be obtained
at www.ICGtesting.com
Printed in the USA
LVHW091749210520
656195LV00004B/761